Emma,

You are a good kid
take care of yourself

CONVICT GRADE

CONVICT GRADE

AZRAEL PAUL DAMIEN

COVER ART BY SARAH JACKSON
USED BY PERMISSION

COPYRIGHT © 2009 BY SNAKE CREEK CREATIVE WORKS LLC.

LIBRARY OF CONGRESS CONTROL NUMBER: 2009902917
ISBN: HARDCOVER   978-1-4415-2346-4

This is a work of fiction. Names, characters, places and incidents either are the product of the author's imagination or are used fictitiously, and any resemblance to any actual persons, living or dead, events, or locales is entirely coincidental.

This book was printed in the United States of America.

To order additional copies of this book, contact:
www.convictgrade.com
or
Xlibris Corporation
1-888-795-4274
www.Xlibris.com
Orders@Xlibris.com
60451

For Lord Nibbler and Harold Chappell

CONTENTS

Acknowledgements

I would like to thank the following:

- My mom, Raye Ann Davis, for helping me when I needed it.
- My Dad, Jeff Davis, for always being there for me, even when we didn't agree.
- My sister, Angie Hiser, for pushing me by unconventional means.
- Casandra, for her unwavering faith, and Raiden, for just being himself.
- Brandon Lee Powers, for keeping me motivated when it seemed all but impossible.
- Ryan "Tigger" Nead, for inspiring one of the book's most notable characters.
- Katrina, his wife, for helping me get this thing going. And yes, Katie, I really did love that radio.
- Tyson Nead, for being supportive and always having my back.
- Kathy and Claude Nead, for treating me like family.

- Dawn Jensen, for going above and beyond the call of duty.
- Leslie Anne Tan Batac, for always taking the time to listen to me when I was stressed out and needed a friendly ear.
- Trent Silver, for all of his help in marketing. Keep the faith, Trent—you have a friend in me.
- The Dushane family, especially Chrissy, for helping me every step of the way in promotion.
- Craig Cervantes, for being the only teacher who never gave up on me.
- K&K Printing, for doing such a wonderful job on the Convict Grade T-shirts.

A special thank you to Sarah Jackson for providing all the artwork for the book, and David Humphries for his amazing website design. These two worked very hard for me, with no thought of return. Thank you, guys, so very much.

A very special shout out to my street crew who spread the word:

Matt Luvera, Glen Thompson, Mark Turner (www.rivergumpress. com), Nadine Harris, Jed Maxwell, Brett Daily, Lucky Singlestone, Briana Klien Pantoja, Gemma Cunningham, Mike Bogatyr, Dixon Stapleton, Sandy Kinsel, Lauren Stockman, Kerrynn Kraft, and Toni Lynne Mcleese (who has waited two years to read this book).

A very special thank you to Jeremy, my friend in horror. It's nice to know you're not alone.

And last, but certainly not least, I would like to thank "The Fat Old Guy" for his amazing editing skills. Without him, none of this would have been possible.

Thank you all, for everything!

Az

Chapter 1

THE FESTIVAL

A blinding sun beat down on the town of Convict Grade. Normally a sleepy little village with quiet streets and blooming flowers, today the place was bustling with the activities of a community that thrived on tourism. The trees swayed in their quiet way as citizens prepared for the beginning of their annual summer festival. The celebration treated tourists to the fascinating history of a village formed during the gold rush. Convict Grade was snuggled into the rugged Montana Mountains and, according to the town elders, had many deep secrets and disturbing legends. The town itself had a sedate and comfortable ambiance about it.

A young man trudged through the small town. He wasn't a heroic or intelligent sort of guy, but a simple one. He spent most of his time daydreaming, imagining a life less ordinary. His name was Ryan Curtis, but everyone except his mother called him Tigger, or Tigg, for short. Tigg was kind of a big, awkward sort: six feet tall, with a full red beard despite his youthful eighteen years of age. Quiet and shy, he was not very good socially. His only friend was Hammond, a tall, longhaired kid with a medium build and a wild imagination that rivaled Tigg's. Unlike Tigg, Hammond was a legend in his own mind.

This morning, Tigg was immersed in an intense fantasy about Sara Rikker, his dream girl who did not even know he was alive. With his mind wrapped around Sara, he didn't notice when his friend Hammond popped out from behind a tree.

"So kiss a little longer, hold tight a little longer, longer with Big Red . . ." Hammond belted out as Tigg walked headlong into him.

"Whoa, Tigger—ease up on the stick there buddy!" exclaimed Hammond as he regained his balance.

"Sorry, dude. Guess I was just a little out of it" Tigg said rather sheepishly.

"Dreaming of Sara again—huh, princess?" Hammond sneered.

"I . . . 'er . . . well . . . uh . . . yeah, I guess I was. Anyway, what are you doing here, other than scaring the crap out of me?" Tigg was slightly agitated by the fact that Hammond had so easily guessed his thoughts.

"I was just on my way to the festival to see if any hot tourist chicks have hit town. A man has to have his priorities."

"Well, that's where I was headed, too. Not much else to do around here". Tigg shifted uneasily, rocking on the edges of his feet.

"You just want to catch a glimpse of the lovely Miss Rikker, don't you!" His voice went sugary with a bad southern drawl, and he batted his long eyelashes.

"You're such a jackass, Hammond!" As Tigg said it, he watched the smile grow on Hammond's face. It was a fact that Hammond was good at needling people and he prided himself in it—after all, a man had to be good at something.

The two friends were easy together. They walked in silence toward the center of town. Hammond moved in his usual over-charismatic

14

way. His steps were quick and jerky, arms swinging erratically. Tigg was the antithesis—trudging slowly behind, arms hanging at his side, his scuffed boots dragging with every step.

In the town square, people were already beginning to gather. A group formed around the small monument dedicated to the hundred and fifty settlers that had mysteriously disappeared back in the summer of 1856. A small flame burned eternal at the base of a marble slab, topped by a plaque with the settlers' names. The town fathers would soon start the celebration with the telling of the most colorful of the local legends.

The mayor stood up and positioned himself behind the podium. He was a heavy man, balding, with a wide, pompous grin, looking a bit stiff and overly formal in his three-piece suit. He cleared his throat with almost comic sincerity. "Today, we celebrate the city that almost never was. It was almost one hundred and fifty years ago that the entire populace of Convict Grade disappeared without leaving any sign or warning." The mayor cleared his throat again and took a sip of water, preparing for the speech that he had worked on all winter.

"The town, as we all know, was founded during the gold rush. Settlers came here by the wagonload in search of fortune and prosperity. They threw together ramshackle houses and lived off the land. Things were going well for the first year or two, but then strange things began to happen. People back east reported receiving letters telling of missing animals and livestock found mutilated, dead, and rotting, but untouched by the many predators that plagued local ranchers. Then the letters stopped coming, and families began to worry. Most of our early settlers came form eastern Missouri, and public outcry from families left behind convinced the government to send a small company of men to investigate. When they arrived, they found the town desolate and abandoned. Food was left half-eaten on the table, and the personal belongings of the town folk were left undisturbed, as though they all just disappeared in the middle of their daily affairs. No door was closed or locked, yet nothing was ransacked or vandalized." The mayor took a breath as the stunned tourists listened eagerly. His beady eyes scanned the crowd as he thought of how this little tale would help souvenir sales down at the gift shop.

"To this very day, no trace of the one hundred and fifty missing souls has ever been discovered. The current town was rebuilt on the very same location as the original Convict Grade, and the second wave of settlers forged this new settlement into a safe and profitable little town, rising above the tragedy that happened before."

The tourists enthusiastically applauded as the mayor finished his speech. Tigg and Hammond just sat there and listened as they had every year since childhood. The details never changed much, but it was delivered with a little more flare every year.

"I wonder what really happened to all those people?" Hammond said in a soft voice. He wasn't a reflective person, and it caught Tigg by surprise. His friend sounded so sad and alone.

"Probably died of boredom", offered Tigg, trying to lighten his friend's mood. He knew that the odds were, it wouldn't work.

Edgar Earl Hammond, Jr. had always had trouble relating to other people. Tigg was the exception. They had been friends since childhood—or the beginning of time—they couldn't remember which. Hammond was somewhat eccentric and quick-tempered. He had spent most of his life in the tiny burg of Convict Grade living with his father, a violent alcoholic whose favorite pastime was handing out mental and physical abuse, and as a result, Hammond was very withdrawn. Though his acting skills were top notch, he could never convince Tigg that everything was fine.

"Hey Tigg," said Hammond inquiringly, "why do you think that God lets people suffer like this?"

"Like what?" Tigg asked as if he did not already know the answer. This was a conversation they'd had more than once. He knew perfectly well where it was going.

"Well you know . . . like I do." Hammond whispered as though the shame was more than he could bear. Even thinking about his life hurt. He tried to hide it with over-confidence and humor, and most everyone believed it. Not Tigger.

"Ham, you are the strongest person I know, and God must feel the same way." Tigg said, straining not to show the pain he felt for Hammond's very unfortunate situation. Tigg was a sensitive soul, and his friend's pain hurt him.

"Me thinks God greatly overestimates my abilities," said Hammond as an awkward smile curled in the corner of his mouth. All those years of fear and worry had prematurely etched lines into his thin face. He had a haggard and boiled down look about him, as if time was not on his side.

"Don't look now, Casanova . . ." Hammond said, trying to recover the fun, pointing down the street. There, on the fringes of the crowd stood Sara Rikker, a tall blond with a beautiful face, piercing green eyes, and a radiant smile. Sara was a lovely young girl, and as sweet as she was beautiful—the kind you would take home to your mother. Her body was slender, with curves like a Corvette—the wet dream of every American teenage boy, and Tigg's personal fantasy.

Sara stood solemnly, listening to the mayor unravel his tale. She was so lost either in his words or herself that when her friend arrived she didn't even see her until Bailey touched her arm.

She jumped, but quickly recovered. "Hey, Bailey—what's up?"

"Not much. My parents are running the pie booth and they drug me down here to show the town we belong or something", Bailey said indignantly.

Bailey was a gorgeous young woman with black hair, hazel eyes, a tight stomach, and a very cute Australian accent. Her family was from Melbourne, originally, but they moved to Los Angeles for her father's work when she was twelve. Bailey had adapted quickly to the big city—a true valley girl. Her parents, however, felt differently. They wanted to live in a small town and "get away from it all", so they packed up and moved again. Bailey was less than thrilled—she didn't want to get away from anything. She just wanted to be with her friends. She hated being in this small town where nothing ever happened, especially interesting things like romance. She had always dreamed of having a tall, dark, handsome man sweep her off her feet, but she knew that would never happen in this dirt hole of a town. Now she dreamed of being back in LA or Melbourne, anywhere but Montana.

Tigg and Hammond stared at the two women, dumbfounded. Hammond had never really noticed this new addition to his little burg. Maybe, just maybe, it was worth checking out . . .

"Yo, Tigg, check out the body on that chick!" Hammond chirped excitedly. "She has the face of an angel, the body of a goddess, and curves that just won't quit."

"Yeah, Sara is great, isn't she?" Tigg proclaimed softly, as if awoken from a dream. His eyes were dreamy and he was all but drooling.

"I wasn't talking about her, you twit. I meant her way-hot friend. I've never seen her before. Who is she?" asked Hammond, still overcome by the ethereal beauty of the woman who would now occupy his dreams.

"That's Bailey Stryker. She's kind of a snob. I've never talked to her myself, but that's what I hear." Then Tigg sat quietly for a second as if pondering the mysteries of the universe. "If that's true, then she's perfect for you."

"Screw you!" Hammond said bluntly as he continued to scan Bailey. He was never one to mince words.

"So, you like Bailey, huh?" Tigg said, jabbing an elbow into Hammond's stomach.

"If you mean, is she hot, then, yeah. That don't mean nothin', though, 'cause to her, I'm probably no more than the dung that gets stuck on the heel of her three hundred dollar boots." Hammond said, calculating his chances of making it with Bailey as slim-to-none, and sinking into the realization that he was only a pawn in a sadistic play that his drunken father forced upon him.

"Ham, you are the strangest, most out-there person I know. If anyone could make her turn her head, it would have to be you. How do you know how much those boots cost, anyway?"

Before Hammond could make up his mind on this, or come up with a pithy remark, Bailey and Sara were walking toward them. The girls had noticed them staring and decided to come over and talk to them. Hammond, seeing the two advancing, began to turn tail and run, but he couldn't leave Tigg standing there alone. He lived by the rule, "never leave a man behind."

"Pretend that we are just watching the mayor." Hammond said quickly.

"He quit talking like fifteen minutes ago, dude." Tigg was still focused on Sara.

"Dude, she sees you staring like a 'tard. Look away, man, look away! They're coming . . . 'er . . . *run!*" This was Hammond's big plan?

Before it could be executed, he heard a soft Australian accent and the words, "No, wait a minute." Hammond spun and stood face to face with Bailey for the first time.

"We just wanted to talk to you guys." Sara interjected in a soft, sweet voice. Tigg dropped his eyes quickly searching his empty head for the right words to say. He was struck deaf and dumb every time she came within twenty feet of him.

"Ummmmmmmmm . . . 'er . . . nice shoes. How much did they cost?" Tigg asked stupidly, unable to meet the gaze of the awe-inspiring Sara. She looked confused and decided the best approach was to simply smile. Unfortunately this only killed more of Tigger's brain cells. He tried to think of something clever, but was unable to. He was useless under pressure, like whenever a pretty girl looked at him.

At this point, Hammond was still at a complete loss for words as he and Bailey sized each other up. Hammond was wearing his hair down with Celtic braids coming off his temples. The rest of his jet-black mane flowed freely down his back. He was wearing a black fishnet shirt and black suede pants with at thin red stripe down the seam, a Guns and Roses bandanna tied around his thigh. A black leather and chrome belt completed the ensemble. Hammond stared at her through his whiteout contacts. He couldn't find words. She struck him dumb. Now he knew how Tigg felt.

"Hi-I'm-Hammond." He fumbled the words so poorly it sounded to Bailey like he said, "I like salmon."

Bailey laughed a sweet sound. "Yeah, salmon is good."

Embarrassed, all Hammond could say was, "Salmon, yeah."

He stood as though waiting for lightning to strike him down and end his misery, when Bailey took his hand. "Why don't you guys take us out for a soda or something?"

Hammond was so thankful for the reprieve, he simply nodded his head.

"So, Tigg, where should we go?" Sara asked with an intentional flip of her long blonde hair.

"Uh, with them." Tigg replied, dumbstruck by the events currently in motion.

"Duh, Tigg. I meant where should we all go, silly?" She giggled.

Tigg thought for a moment. Still flustered, he blurted out, "The Truck Stop."

Immediately, he realized he'd once again said something stupid. That was the traditional place for Tigg and Hammond to go to relax when life got out of control, usually when Hammond's dad became unbearable. While it was a place for calm thoughts, relaxation, small talk, and smoking, it was not the ideal place to impress a first date.

Before Tigg could correct his answer Bailey chimed in "Perfect. Let's go."

Chapter 2

THE LONGEST MILE

The teenagers made their way down the long, winding path through the park that would eventually take them to Tigg and Hammond's usual haunt: the Truck Stop. The way was very uneasy for the young men, as they weren't exactly used to the company of females, let alone the objects of their greatest desires. Time seemed to slow down, and the minutes stretched into an hour as the two boys drifted slowly behind the young women. Hammond drug his feet as much as he could to distance himself away from Bailey. When he finally felt comfortable that the two were out of earshot, he finally spoke to Tigg.

"Hey, bro-ha, why do you think that the girls were so willing to go out with us?" Hammond asked in an almost inaudible whisper.

"Go out with us? What did you say?" Tigg blurted it out loud enough for both girls to stop, turn, and stare at the two.

Hammond turned several shades of red motioning between himself and Tigg, trying desperately to think of a good explanation. Luckily for Hammond, Bailey and Sara didn't seem to mind. They just laughed, then turned back and continued walking. Tigg, realizing that Hammond had intended the conversation to be low key and private, now stared at the ground, knowing that he had let his friend down yet again.

"Don't worry about it, bro-ha, these things happen." Hammond said with a smile, knowing how bad Tigg must have felt. The two always seemed to have a sixth sense about each other's feelings. "So, anyway, like I was saying, why do you think they joined us so easily? Doesn't that seem a little strange to you?"

"Nah, man, why would it?" Tigg asked, managing a whisper this time, grabbing a leaf off a nearby tree and fumbling with it nervously. "I mean we aren't like trolls or anything—why shouldn't they wanna join us for a soda?"

"We may not be trolls, Tigg, ole buddy, but we ain't exactly their type, either!"

"Maybe not, man, but I have wanted a chance to go out with Sara ever since grade school and even if it is some kind of trick it's a risk that I'm willing to take!" Tigg said in a harsh whisper, trying not to get angry at Hammond's valid point. "I mean, yeah, maybe we weren't the most popular, or smartest kids in school but we are good people and that should count for something, right?"

Hammond was silent for a moment reflecting on all the things that Tigg had said. Tigg was a good person, of that he had no doubt; it was the dubious nature of his own character that he questioned. Hammond was not quite what anyone one would call a model student. The time that he didn't spend in detention was spent being lectured in the principal's office for his many fights. Hammond didn't have a very long list of friends due to having quite a short fuse. He took a lot of abuse at home and was in no way willing to put up with it from kids his own age. He was, in fact, a powder keg waiting to blow, and the slightest sign of hostility toward him was enough to set him off.

Tigg was quite the opposite. He was shy and very even-tempered. He always thought that everyone was his friend. He never knew that they were nice to him because they feared the retribution of his best friend. Tigger was clueless about the way that Hammond protected him everyday and Hammond wasn't about to tell him. Tigg's grades were far below average, but unlike Hammond, his lack of intelligence was genuine. Neither of the two boys ever had a girlfriend, so both of them were definitely on what would be considered "dangerous ground".

"People call us freaks and make fun of us all the time. In what way does a situation where two very beautiful girls wanting to hang out with us make any sense to you?" Hammond asked after a few moments of thought.

"Well, honestly, it doesn't, but, unlike you, it doesn't matter to me if it makes sense or not! 'Just as long as it is happening!"

"Fair enough . . . but could you really handle it if it's some sort of joke and they are leading us into a trap? I mean, the Truck Stop isn't exactly close. Suspicious choice, don't you think?"

"Well, I suppose it would be if we hadn't 've picked the place! Honestly, sometimes I wonder why people think you're the smart one." Tigg said with a snicker.

"Um . . . well, I just don't want to see you get hurt man . . . Remember that girl last year?" Hammond asked cautiously, not wanting to reopen an old wound.

"Yeah, I know—the girl who asked me to the prom just to have her boyfriend and his friends jump me in the parking lot. If you hadn't 've shown up just in the nick of time, they might 've killed me." For the first time Tigg thought about how oddly convenient it was that Hammond just happened to be there. "What exactly were you doing there, anyway?"

24

"I was, well, that is . . . just leave it alone, man. It really doesn't matter."

"No, tell me. I want to know. It's almost like you knew something bad was going to happen to me. You didn't know about it, did you?" Tigg started to fear the worst from his best friend. "Or did you really think that I am such a loser that I could never get a date, so it must be a trick?"

"No. Look, I don't have to explain myself to you, and if you're going to try and make me, I will just go back to the festival."

Although Tigg was not satisfied with the answer, he accepted it nonetheless. Tigg shuffled his feet along the narrow dirt path that he had taken to school several times before. It amazed him that there was no wind and that the birds weren't singing. That was really odd for this time of year. Normally the birds in the park were so loud with their summer song that he could barely hear himself think. The absolute calm bothered him greatly and Hammond's silence only added to his uneasiness. In an attempt to shake the eerie feeling, Tigg changed the subject.

"So, did you see the way that Bailey girl was staring at you?" Tigg asked almost loud enough for the girls to hear him.

"Yeah, I did. What do you think she was up to?"

"Why does everyone always have to have some dastardly plot against you? Why can't a look ever just be a look?"

"Because, my dear Tigg, everyone has a motive. Maybe she just thought I looked funny or maybe I had a booger hangin' out of my nose. D'ya ever considered that?"

"So you're saying that it's not even remotely possible that she might actually like you or think you're cute?"

"You know, bro-ha, there's just something about her I don't trust." Hammond said seriously.

"You know what, Ham? You could meet Jesus himself and all you would say to me is, 'you know, bro-ha, there's just something about him I don't trust."

"Point taken." Hammond said. They both fell silent for a moment, then burst into laughter.

The laughter of the two friends was so loud and full of good humor it made the two girls turn to look at them. Every time she heard the sound of someone laughing behind her, Bailey always got nervous. Cynicism was a trait that she had in common with Hammond. Bailey was very beautiful, but she never really thought of herself that way.

"What do you suppose they are laughing about?" Bailey whispered to Sara, feeling rather self-conscious.

"Who knows, with those two it could be anything. They don't exactly strike me as the type that possess sophisticated humor. So, my first guess would be a fart joke." Sara said, looking back. "But they are both pretty cute, so it can be overlooked."

"Well, I don't know what to make of it, but I'm positive that's him." Bailey said softly.

"The one from your dream . . . are you sure?" Sara asked incredulously. "Hammond is, um, not exactly what I would call the hero type, if you know what I mean."

"No, actually, I don't know what you mean. From the moment I met him, I felt a sort of connection. I really think that if push came to shove, he would rise to the occasion."

"Ha! You don't know him very well!" Sara said shaking her head.

"Well, duh! I just met him—I obviously don't know him very well. But I just have this feeling about him and it's a good one. Besides, I'm positive it was him in that awful dream."

Sara knew exactly how Bailey felt, but could not bring herself to tell her that she felt exactly the same way about Tigg. Sara had always liked him, but her social standing in the high school hierarchy would never allow her to express her feelings toward him. Sara worked very hard to get popular and was afraid of losing it all—even for something as important as love. Bailey, on the other hand, never had any use for popularity and always just went with her gut when it came to choosing her friends.

"So, what is it you know about him, exactly?" Bailey asked, letting her curiosity get the best of her.

"Well he's one of those weird kids that don't really talk to anyone. He just sits there in class, leaning back in his chair, staring at the wall like at any minute it's gonna pick a fight with him. He doesn't have any friends except Tigg, and he's in trouble like, constantly."

"So, he's a little different. Since when is that such a bad thing?"

"Well, since he beat up the English teacher for criticizing his essay about his mother."

"Now this I have got to hear!" Bailey said eagerly.

"Well, it started when Hammond got his essay back. The teacher had written something about how his mother was an inappropriate subject for his essay on people he most admires since she killed herself and all."

"Whoa, wait a minute! His mother killed herself?" Bailey blurted out loudly stopping the whole group dead in their tracks. Bailey looked back at Hammond sadly. Hammond just brushed past her. He lit a cigarette and acted as though he hadn't heard her but the tear in his eye was a dead give-away that he had. Tigg rushed up to join his friend.

"Way to go, Bailey! I bet that really helps your cause." Sara grumbled to her.

Bailey started to quicken her pace to catch up, but was met by Tigg standing like a stone wall between her and Hammond.

"Don't. In situations like this, its best just to leave it alone."

"But I don't want him to be mad at me."

"Trust me, I know him better than anyone. Just leave it alone and he will forget about it before we get there. But I guarantee you, if you push the subject, you will only make it worse. Just let it go and never, and I mean never, mention it to him again!"

Bailey knew that Tigg was probably right, but it still made her feel horrible that she had blurted something like that out. She would have given just about anything in that moment to turn back time and change things so she had never said it. She was truly afraid that in one moment of shock that she had possibly pushed away the man that she so desperately wanted to talk to. She waited for Sara to catch back up with her before she resumed her march up the old path.

"Wow, he looks 'kinda pissed, doesn't he?" Sara pointed out in a master of the obvious type of tone.

"Well, since I already got in trouble, you might as well finish the story!" Bailey whispered in a huff.

"Look, the story really doesn't matter. The point I was making is still valid. Hammond is the type of person that would just as soon kill you as look at you. I don't know what your obsession with him is, but if I were you, I would just get over it."

"Well then, I guess I'm glad that I'm not you . . ."

With a sudden and determined stride Bailey moved forward to make her peace with Hammond. She knew about his temper, more over, she knew that at that moment it was pointed at her. Hammond continued his cocky stride as Bailey slowly caught up to him. Hammond thought the girl was beautiful and though he never thought it was possible, just standing next to her abated his anger. He tried desperately not to show her, and succeeded brilliantly.

"Are you lost? Your friend is back there." Hammond said nodding back in the direction of Sara. As much as he wanted to be nice to her, he just still didn't trust her. He was always convinced that when a beautiful woman wanted anything to do with Tigg or himself, it must be some kind of trick.

"No, I'm not lost. I just wanted to apologize." Bailey said passing a glance at the clearly disappointed Tigg.

"Well, you did. Anything else you want?" Hammond's hard glance was almost too much for her, but she would not be pushed away. Not when she was so convinced that he was the one—the one that rescued her every night in a nightmare that haunted her even when she was awake.

"Just leave him alone already, can't you see that he doesn't want to talk right now?" Tigg interjected, hoping to give his friend the peace that he deserved.

"I can talk for myself, squirrel nuts." Hammond said with a sideways glance. He really didn't want her to leave him alone and couldn't figure out how Tigg could miss that. "Why don't you go back there and bother Sara? I'm sure she would appreciate your input more than I would at the moment."

Hammond shot Bailey a slight smile as Tigg dropped his head and stood silently waiting to match Sara's stride. Tigg's heart always skipped a beat when she even came close to him. He had no idea how he would ever carry on a conversation with her. Fear overcame him every time she flashed that scarlet smile—it made his heart jump right out of his chest. As much as it frightened her to admit it, Sara didn't think he was too bad, either.

"Yeah, I kinda got kicked out of the cool group." Tigg said as Sara caught up with him.

"Its okay. Sometimes being the kid in the back of the class has its advantages." Sara softly returned, reaching her arm out for Tigg to lace his arm through. With only a moment's hesitation, Tigg complied and the two walked arm in arm in silence.

Bailey wasn't faring quite as well with the apprehensive Hammond. She made every attempt to tell him about her dream but the words always seemed to stop in her throat. It was not that he was that intimidating—it was more that she couldn't build up the nerve to sound crazy in front of him. They walked silently in the midday sun, both wanting to do and say more, but neither took the initiative for their own reasons. The Truck Stop now appeared in the distance. Feeling that her time was quickly running out, Bailey made a move that neither she nor Hammond had expected. She reached out and gently took his hand into hers. Hammond winced in pain slightly as she touched him. Seeing the look on Hammond's face, she pulled her hand away, but he didn't let go.

"Are you ok?" Bailey asked nervously.

"Bad hand." Hammond replied dryly. "But I don't mind you holding it, if that's what you mean".

Bailey just smiled, content with his explanation, and was just happy that he didn't pull away from her. Although she had no idea whether or not she would be able to tell him what was on her mind, she had the feeling that he just might understand. As they reached the door to the Truck Stop she was almost sad that this moment was ending. In what was almost an alien action for him, Hammond reached out and opened the door for the young woman. Bailey was stunned at his chivalry, and just stood there dumbstruck.

"As much as I would love to, I am not going to hold this thing open all day." Hammond said rolling his eyes. He began to wonder if all those things his mother had taught him about how to treat a lady were just bunk.

"Sorry, I'm just not used to being treated . . . well, like a lady." Bailey said blushing slightly.

When Tigg and Sara caught up he was just as stunned by the courteous actions of his usually rude friend. After Bailey entered, Hammond continued to hold the door for the other two. Sara walked passed him and placed a grateful palm on his chest, he simply returned a scowl. When Tigg passed he gave Hammond his best curtsy in mock gratitude. When Tigg returned to his upright position, Hammond hit him in the back of the head so hard, you could probably hear it in the next county. The sound of the slap was like sweet music to Hammond's ears. A smile spread across his face as if he had just won the lottery.

When they finally got inside and were shown to their seats, Sara immediately decided that both she and Bailey had to use the bathroom (miraculously at the same time, of course). Hammond just nodded in understanding as Tigg sat looking confused. Bailey also had a bazaar look on her face, but went along with Sara nonetheless. The two ladies took their leave of the boys and headed for the women's restroom.

The Truck Stop was a shabby place with broken tiles on the walls, floors, and ceiling. The room was a bit stuffy, but well maintained. Sara walked over to the cracked mirror and in the dim, flickering light began touching up her makeup.

"I thought you had to use the bathroom." Bailey said, scanning her rustic surroundings.

"Of coarse I don't—I just wanted to know what the deal was with you and Hammond. So, come on and spill it, already!" Sara said as she worked on her lips with a lipstick brush.

"What do you mean?" Bailey asked apprehensively as she, too, set to the task of touching up her makeup. After all, she couldn't go out there with Sara looking better than she did.

"You were holding his hand . . . what was happening? Did you tell him?" Sara stopped looking in the mirror and turned toward Bailey eagerly awaiting her answer.

"Well, no . . . it was just like . . . it felt . . . I don't know." Bailey dropped her head trying to hide her ridiculous smile and the rush of blood that was threatening her cheeks. "It just seemed right."

"I know what you mean . . . there is just something about those two, isn't there?" Sara dropped her cool act and turned a deep shade of red ignoring Bailey's grin. "I really do think he's kind of cute . . . but we have to tell them about the dream. I think this whole situation would be totally messed up if we didn't."

"But, what do I say? 'Hey, Hammond, I had this dream about you and even though I don't know you, I think you're my hero, and I find myself falling in love with you!' That sounds even more stupid when I hear myself saying it." Bailey fidgeted awkwardly with the contents of her purse.

"I see what you mean . . . that does sound kind of stupid. Maybe you should just go out there and explain it from the beginning. Then it might not sound quite so bazaar." Sara said returning her makeup back into its case.

"Well, you had a dream, too—why don't you do it?"

"Look, Bailey—you're the one who saw them in the town square first and you're the one who thought that we should talk to them. This was your plan, so you can go first!" Sara said indignantly.

After a short debate the two girls decided to leave it up to fate. If the guys asked they would tell. Knowing that the likelihood of that happening was slim, they both breathed a sigh of relief and left the bathroom to rejoin their dates.

Chapter 3

SHARED NIGHTMARES

Hammond stared out the grimy window of the Truck Stop. The once-beautiful day had slipped away: the sky had clouded over and it was beginning to rain. He took one last drag and crushed out his cigarette. The restaurant was housed in an old, dirty building and was the classic greasy spoon. The place smelled of cooking grease, old leather benches, and cigarette smoke. The seats were old and ratty and so was the staff, but it was the only place Tigg and Hammond could smoke in peace. The air in the room loomed heavily as the elderly waitress brought them their sodas. The all-encompassing silence was almost too much to handle as Tigg and Hammond waited for their new companions to return from the restroom.

"Why do girls go to the bathroom in groups?" Tigg asked finally, getting antsy from the wait.

"So they can talk about us, numb nuts!" explained Hammond as he lit another cigarette.

"D'ya think they like us?" Tigg asked with a fearful expression, intensified by the poor lighting of the room.

"No," said Hammond at length "They probably want something or they wouldn't be here with the two of us." Hammond winced a little and looked at his right hand, feeling the tight pain that suddenly shot through it. It came on at the most unexpected times.

"It still hurts you, doesn't it?" Tigg asked as Hammond absently rubbed at the pain. He always felt certain sadness for Hammond when his hand hurt. It was a story that Tigger knew well. He always felt guilt for the injury.

The boys were hanging out in Tigger's basement one night, playing video games. Ham knew he needed to be home, but Tigg had talked him into just one more game. One more turned into ten more and Hammond finally snuck back into his house past two. His father, in a drunken rage, had waited up for the boy. An argument escalated into a fistfight, and Hammond's hand was broken as it plowed into his father's face. He was fifteen at the time, and on the small side. He had paid dearly for that, but had the satisfaction of seeing the blood gush from his father's broken nose. His father refused to pay for the surgery to fix the hand and the bones hadn't mended well with the cast alone.

"Not as much anymore. Just when it rains . . ." With that, they both fell silent in quiet contemplation of how at nineteen, Hammond could have experienced so much pain without giving up.

When Sara and Bailey returned, the mood had become somber. They sat down silently, not sure of what to say.

"What's on your mind?" Bailey finally asked Hammond with a look of genuine concern.

"Nothing, just an old ghost. They always have a way of darkening your happiest moments." Through the pain of his memories and his hand, Hammond no longer had the apprehension of a teenage boy.

"Okay, Bailey, what possessed you to come and talk to us? Sara never talks to Tigger on her own, so it must've been you." Hammond asked bluntly. His tone was dark.

"You wouldn't believe me if I told you." Bailey replied.

"Try me," Hammond said as he crushed out another cigarette.

"Well, there's this dream, Ok—nightmare, I've had since I was child. I don't know how many times I've woken up sweaty and scared. It's awful, and black, and there are these awful creatures. They look like people, but they're something else. Just when I feel like they have overcome me, and I'm falling into some kind of Hell, there's always a man that saves me. Then I wake up. I've never seen his face, really, but I remember this image of a man with white eyes and black hair, and he grabs my hand as I'm falling. When I saw you today, I couldn't believe it . . . you're the one!" She brushed her hair away from her face. "I don't know what it means, but there it is. I think you're the one in my dream. Ever since we moved to Convict Grade, I've felt this kind of evil growing, and the dreams have come more often. I would feel hopeless, but in the end, I'm rescued, and you're the one who makes it better."

Hammond was taken aback by this revelation. He had never really felt wanted before, let alone needed. He felt a kind of pleasure surge through him. It made him slightly uncomfortable. He wasn't used to warm, happy feelings.

"Must be nice," muttered Tigg. "You meet a girl for the first time ever and *bam*! Instant hero. Instant love! But oh no, not me! Not Tigger! They want nothing to do with Hammond's sidekick." Tigg was so busy creating a scene that he did not even notice that everyone was staring at him in silent amusement. He went back to playing with his straw and grumping into his soda.

35

"I like ya, Tigg." Sara said, smiling at him.

"Whoa. Hold the phone, Princess! No one said anything about love!" Now Hammond was embarrassed. Outside, he was denying it, but inside he was wanting it—terribly. As he said it, he gave Tigg a look that, well, if looks could kill, Tigg would have suffered a tortured and miserable death—one that involved drawing and quartering, or something like that.

"Ok, so this is going to sound crazy." Hammond started, "I swear, Bailey, I'm not trying to play with your head or anything, but—I've seen you before, too. Somehow I knew your face even before we met." Hammond trailed off. What he was trying to say was eluding him. "It was no dream or nightmare. It was more a . . . thought, a premonition maybe?" The rest of the group faded away in his mind as he tried to grasp the memory. "There was a long hallway and it was dark . . . That's all I really remember."

"It wasn't just dark, it was darkness . . . more of an 'it' than a thing, you know?" Tigg interjected with an almost agitated excitement.

"Wait, did we all have the same dream?" Sara said trembling. "The darkness was alive." A cold chill filled the room. It was a feeling Sara would equate to reading her own headstone. Cold and wrong, but distant and detached.

"The world suddenly feels like a much smaller place," whispered Hammond, breathing uneasily. "This," he emphasized, laying his palms on the table, "was all meant to happen. To tell you the truth, this is starting to scare the crap out of me. This stuff only happens in movies . . . bad, campy, B-raters."

Hammond tried to light another cigarette, finding his hands were shaking too much to flick the Bic. "I mean, do you understand what this means?"

"No, not really," Tigg said honestly.

"Well, neither do I," replied Hammond "It just can't be a good thing, though."

An ominous silence filled the room. Suddenly, the waitress looked older, the windows looked dirtier, and everything had taken on a gray pallor. The teens looked around, staring with new eyes. It looked to all of them as if an unknown force had suddenly and mysteriously aged the whole world.

"My dream always has the town square in it." Sara whispered. "I never really recognized it before, but it just came to me."

"I see myself. It's the only thing in the dream that I actually see. The rest is just . . . dark. So dark." Tigg spoke quietly, staring into the depths of his Pepsi.

"Okay," Hammond said slowly. "Is the town the link then?"

"There has to be a reason we all came together during the festival", Sara said quietly, looking around suspiciously.

"The day we celebrate the disappearance of almost two hundred people." Hammond scratched his head. "So, do the two have something to do with each other?"

"How's that possible?" Tigg glared at Hammond. "That's just ridiculous. This town has been occupied since then and nothing bad has happened."

Hammond glared back at his buddy. "Nothing bad?"

"You know what I mean, man—nothing evil, or whatever. Nobody has disappeared and no animals have been mutilated that I have seen."

Bailey laid her hand on Hammond's arm. "Maybe it's worth looking into."

Hammond stared at the link, wondering at how good human contact could feel. "I think it is. Somebody in this place knows something . . . but who?"

Chapter 4

THE FACE IN THE MIRROR

N ight had fallen on Convict Grade as Tigg, Hammond, Bailey and Sara parted ways for the evening. With feelings of unrest, they set off for their respective homes. Tigg walked silently as a cold wind now blew through the rain soaked town and brushed eerily across his cheeks. Time seemed to stand still. There was no sign of life anywhere. Tigg began to walk faster, uneasiness building in his mind. "Where are all the animals?" he thought to himself as he crossed the street. In the six years he had been walking home this way, he had never felt such a deafening silence. All Tigg could think was 'the darkness was alive.'

As he walked, he thought about how different Sara and he were. She was from a wealthy family, homecoming princess and head cheerleader, an only child, doted on by her parents. He was the youngest of four. His father worked at the mill and his mother stayed home and kept the house. There was never enough money to go around, especially when Tigger's older sisters had still lived at home. The three girls had shared a bedroom, he remembered, and they hated it. All of them were gone, now: through college and leading productive lives. He had never been close to them. He came along when Katie, the youngest girl, was twelve. He'd always felt like an outsider with his family. They all loved each other, though, and that was what counted.

Tigg stared at his feet as he made the slow trek home. He was not a proud man; in fact, Hammond was about the only one he could look in the eye. The rest of the time he spent staring at his boots. As he thought about the three hundred dollar boots that Bailey probably wore, a small smile threatened his lips. Suddenly, he realized that the pavement should have ended about a block ago. Tigg looked up to see a very familiar scene; he was right back where he started. "What the . . . ?" Tigg shouted out loud in surprise. He began to saunter back in the direction that he had believed he had already gone. Looking carefully where he was going, Tigg once again turned in the direction of home. He kept his eyes on the road ahead of him this time, trying to concentrate. One by one, the streetlights that stretched alongside the street flickered out.

As if Tigg wasn't nervous enough, he began to feel an ill-omened presence stalking him in the darkness. "I wish Hammond were here," Tigg thought as he deliberately hastened his footsteps. The darkness enveloped Tigg and he was forced to slow down due to his inability to make sense of direction. He heard footsteps closing in behind him in the darkness. Fear began to tear at Tigg's already strained sanity as he realized, with cold sweat beading on his brow, that someone was standing next to him. Tigg turned with a start and he realized that his fear was unfounded, as he found himself staring at his own reflection. A laugh began to trickle from his throat. Tigg made faces at his reflection, mocking his utterly ridiculous fear. Something caught his eye. The reflection was not laughing back. Suddenly, he stopped. What was staring back at him was wrong. There was something missing. The reflection had no eyes. Where the eyes should have been there was a bleeding emptiness, a midnight sky devoid of stars. With a scream stuck in his throat, Tigg turned away, and came face to face with this thing . . . this demon.

Tigg stood, petrified, as he looked at the sallow, gray, rotting skin. "Wh . . . who are you?" Tigg stuttered. The absolute horror of what he was taking in engulfed his senses.

"We are the embodiment of your insecurities, and fears, and hatred of your fellow man. We are the one composed of many. We are Legion. We are you."

"What do y-you want?" Tigg stammered, still trying to back away from this thing. Its rotten fingers scraped away the flesh of its face, exposing a horrific skull. As soon as it took its hands away from its head, the skin would close. Over and over it tore itself asunder, just to reform itself in the very image of Tigg.

"We want to give you all the things you desire to make you whole . . . to make you one of us." Tigg began to seriously consider this proposal and what it would mean. What did he desire?

The answer was simple. He wanted Sara. He wanted to hold her, to love her. He wanted to be more like Hammond, fearless under pressure, likable, and fun. The thoughts had barely made it across Tigg's mind when the thing spoke again.

"You would be like Hammond. You would have the girl love you?" The thing spoke clearly. "What are the deepest desires of you heart? All of these and more we can provide you."

The demon then stuck out a forked tongue. One half wrapped itself around a gigantic cockroach crawling from the empty eye socket sucking it into its mouth. The other side slid down its exposed jawbone and wriggled through a hole in the hanging lower lip, pulling it back into place. "All you must do is join with us. Become a part of us. You will belong with us."

Slowly, as if in a dream, Tigger reached a hand out to the creature. He could feel the cold radiating off its skin. Then it all became clear. "No" he screamed, then turned and ran.

He tore down the street in the direction he thought was home. At his back, an ice-cold wind howled. Bony fingers slid down his spine, causing him to break into a sprint. The breath tore from his pained chest, and he cursed every Marlboro he'd ever met. A sharp pain stabbed his side, but he didn't stop to see if it was internal or if the creature was stabbing him. He didn't want to know.

Finally, after what seemed like six eternities, his house was in sight. He leapt onto the porch and fumbled in his pocket for his house keys. He could feel the darkness closing in as the keys slipped out of his sweaty hands, clattering down the steps. He bent to retrieve them as the echoes of a thousand screaming souls pierced his brain and the darkness consumed his consciousness. He tried to shake it loose, but he couldn't. It became deafening and paralyzing. In some dim corner of his mind, he could hear Sara's voice. He couldn't make out her words, but they were frantic. With a new determination, he forced the darkness out and shoved the key in the lock. The door seemed to fight him, his hands were sweaty on the handle and it refused to turn. He swore and tried again, forcing it open. Tigg fell forward into the entryway, and slammed the door behind him.

Tigg panted heavily as he took the first few steps forward, immediately feeling the familiar and comfortable warmth of his home. He looked around uneasily as his thoughts came boiling to the surface. "What just happened?" After a moment, to regain his sense of self, he staggered through the wide, bright hallway to the oaken stairs, then climbed slowly to his private bathroom. He walked in, turned on the bath water and his radio, just as he had always done, then turned to the sink, which was now a safe haven for his watering eyes.

He opened the faucet full blast, letting the icy water wash over his hands. The chrome on the faucet glistened and the sink sparkled white. Dimly, he realized his mother must have cleaned today. Suddenly, he caught a glimpse of something in the mirror and realized someone was standing behind him. He instinctively jumped as he focused on the mirror to see the would-be attacker.

Tigg's mother stood in the doorway holding his Jack Russell Terrier, Deeogee. The dog had come to the family as a puppy when Tigger was a toddler, but was now getting on in age, and was half-crippled. "Mom, you scared the crap out of me!" Tigg said as he shut off the water and turned around.

"We're glad you're home, Ryan." It was his mother's soothing voice, but with a strange echo that sounded as though she said it twice. Tigg watched in absolute astonishment, then horror as his mother's bottom jaw dropped out of its socket, forming a hole nearly twice its normal size and filled with razor-sharp fangs. This ugly, deformed mouth suddenly tore through the dog's tender flesh. The dog yelped in pain as its skin was torn off by its mistress.

Tigg closed his eyes, shutting out the vision, willing it to go away, praying that it would. He forced them open again only to see his beloved dog half-mutilated—a retching lump of blood and fur, one eye dangling from its now empty socket. As if in some kind of horrible dream, Tigg stood paralyzed in fear and amazement as the miniature beast bared its teeth in a punished maw and lunged hungrily towards him—the pet he'd grown up with! As the dog latched onto his forearm, the pain brought Tigger back to full consciousness. Blood splattered everywhere as he tried repeatedly to shake off the attacking creature, whipping the dog about so violently that the precariously dangling eye fell from its socket and rolled across the floor. Still fighting fiercely with his estranged pet, Tigg slipped on the blood and the defunct eyeball, fell, and slammed his elbow into the mirror. It shattered into large splinters, filling the sink and crashing to the floor. Tigg hastily grasped for one of the shards, thinking it might help him escape from his desperate situation. His hand closed around a splinter of glass, slicing his palm. The thick blood made it impossible to get a good grip on the shard, and it clattered uselessly to the floor. The scent of blood doubled the little dog's efforts, as his sharp little teeth gnawed viscously at the arm of the boy that he once loved.

In a final fit of terror, Tigger swung his arm wildly, slamming the dog into the radio perched on the back of the toilet. Human, dog and radio crashed into the bathtub, now half-filled with hot water. The radio shorted out, sending a jolt through both the little dog and his master. Tigg was thrown across the room, his body hitting the wall and sliding limply to the floor. There he lay, covered in blood and broken glass, only vaguely aware of the smell of burning fur and the pain surging through his body. His last conscious thought was, "Sara!"

Chapter 5

A WALK IN THE PARK

As Sara parted ways with the group, she gave Tigg one last look goodbye. She always had kind of a thing for the big dumb lug, though she would be too embarrassed to come out and say anything. He was so different from the guys she usually dated; she knew her friends would only ridicule her if she mentioned her crush. Today's events had brought her feelings for him to the surface and she was thrilled to find that he had feelings for her, too.

Sara strode along a gloomy patch of dead grass as she made her way towards the town square. She began to sing 'I'm So Lonely' as she made her way forward through the gathering darkness. She smiled as she thought about Tigg's obsession with her shoes, watching them as she walked along the path that had been beaten down by so many teenage feet, hers among them. Suddenly, she noticed that her footfalls made no sound on the hard-beaten ground.

"Hello?" She tried to yell out into the odd blackness of the night. A cold shiver of terror filled her as she realized that no sound came from her vocal cords. It was as if the night had stolen her words before she could form them. For a terrifying moment, she started to believe that she might have been stricken deaf. Lightning streaked across the sky, but was swallowed by the darkness before it could reach its destination. Sara felt the darkness encumber her every movement as she tried to escape its smothering grip. She kept her eyes forward, focused on the town square. Had she dared a glance, she would have seen the encroaching darkness rushing up behind her, swallowing everything in its path. Somehow she knew that she had to reach the town square before the darkness swallowed her, too. She began to pant frantically as she ran down the narrow path, trying not to trip on the many small obstacles that littered the way. The darkness trailed behind her as she scrambled for the monument in front of her.

"Tigg, I need you!" she screamed into the darkness as she felt her tired legs giving out beneath her. She tripped and rolled head over heels into the bright lights of the town square. As the darkness ebbed away behind her she reached into her pocket for her cell phone, thinking it might be her salvation from this nightmarish situation. A sliver of plastic stuck into her finger as she tried to extract the device. Tears broke through as she ripped the remains of the phone from her jeans. A pink jeweled case lay in splinters at her feet, with little bits of metal, plastic, and wire surrounding it.

"Tigg . . . please, I need you . . . please!" she pleaded into the night air through her heaving sobs. One by one the lights flamed out, each with a bright flash, as if they were making one last brave attempt to fend off the encroaching darkness. Sara scrambled to the small monument that honored the missing settlers. For some reason, she felt she would be safe next to the eternal flame that had been placed by the elders in memory of the lost souls of Convict Grade.

The darkness was still growing around her as she reached the small statue. She could hear the outcries of thousands of tortured voices saying in unity, "Do not run child. We only wish to help you, to make you see."

Sara felt a warm sensation running down her back as the darkness flowed ever closer to her in the cold night air. It was just her, the flame, the blackness, and the words. She felt for a fleeting moment that she might be going crazy, that her mind was shattering.

"Don't you see, Sara? You don't have to live like this. We can help you! We can free you from yourself. Why be one when you can be many?" The darkness twisted itself into a grinning face in front of her as it danced fancifully around the edges of the flickering light. "Join us Sara, and all shall be forgiven."

Forgiveness—what a dream that was. Sara had death on her conscience. When she had been a freshman, a boy named Eddie had been foolishly and madly in love with her. She returned his affection with disdain, and found his attentions embarrassing. In a cruel joke, she had asked him to the school dance, where her friends were waiting. They attacked him, stripped him, and tied him to the flagpole, where he hung crying for almost two hours before the janitor cut him down. Eddie went home that night so shamed and embarrassed that he felt he never wanted to be seen again—by anyone. Deeply hurt and depressed, he sat down at his desk and wrote a long note, professing his undying love for Sara and recounting her betrayal. He then went to the gun cabinet, broke the glass, selected a handgun, and retuned to his room. He put the barrel to his mouth and ended his agony.

Sara blamed herself for Eddie's death. As she thought of this, a very familiar face formed in the darkness. It was the face of Eddie, and he looked very . . . dead. "Sara, we don't hate you. We love you, and we just want to be with you . . . we forgive you." Eddie said. Sara, both frightened and confused, was unable to speak. All she could do was shake her head at Eddie. Suddenly, he dissolved into a million tiny bugs that swarmed up the legs of her jeans. A scream ripped from her as she batted at them. They swarmed up her slender body until they covered her legs and belly and chest. She slapped and screamed and jumped and slapped some more, but couldn't free herself from the invasion.

Sara clawed fiercely at her skin. Some of the larger bugs began to burrow into her legs. The pain was swift and intense, made even more real as the night air cooled her seeping blood. Sara fought the onslaught by tearing off her shirt and using the monument to set it afire. She wielded the flaming material as a torch, trying to burn the swarming insects off her body. Desperately, she began to pray, then remembered the Bible. The eighth plague of Egypt—the locusts. She almost laughed, but choked out a sob instead. Her hands burned as the shirt was reduced to ashes, but she still swatted vigorously in hopes of some reprieve from the horrible torture.

A voice whispered into her fractured mind. "Go to the giver of life, Sara. Run to the water." Sara jumped to her feet. A block away was the city park where a small duck pond occupied one corner and a tiny creek trickled away from town.

As she ran, the attack intensified, gnawing at her as she made her way to water. When she reached it, she dove headfirst into the murky pool. As the muddy, icy water hit her skin, the insects seemed to melt away. Fully submerged she held herself under water, trying to hold her breath. Her chest felt ready to explode. Finally she could take no more and broke the surface, greedily sucking in air.

Cautiously, she looked around. The streetlights burned brightly, squirrels chattered in the trees. For a brief moment, she thought that she had imagined the whole thing. But then how did she end up in the duck pond? She shook her head, shoving her tangled mass of hair out of her eyes. Her hands felt huge and raw, the burns stung as if they were still on fire. She struggled out of the pond, the mud sucking at her feet as she made her way to the edge. Sara collapsed onto the bank. The breeze caressed her skin, and she became aware for the first time that she was nearly naked. Too tired for modesty, she forced her aching legs to stand.

She was more than a mile from home, half-naked, and she was cold. Blood dripped from her wounds. Briefly, she pondered her options. Her house was a mile past the courthouse, which would be a long and unbearable walk from here. Tigg's house, on the other hand, was two blocks from here. The decision was made easily, and she started for sanctuary, for Tigger.

She jumped at every sound during her short journey, her heart pounding as if it would explode. She wished she had something to cover herself as she knocked on Tigg's door. As she tapped lightly on the door, it swung open.

The house was tidy and well lit, and so very quiet. There was a faint smell of something burning in the air.

"Tigger?" Her voiced cracked as she called his name. "You in here?"

She stopped for a moment, waiting for him to respond. She was met with nothing but silence. "Tigg? Come on this isn't funny. Where are you?"

She figured if he were here, he would have helped her, so she decided to go ahead and help herself, surely one of his shirts would cover her. Sara started up the stairs. She'd never been in the house but assumed his room would be up there.

She stopped at the top of the stairs and glanced to her left. What she saw caused a scream to stick in her throat. A stream of blood red water was flowing down the hall. Sneaker treads imprinted with blood tracked up the hallway.

"No! Tigger!" She didn't know if she whispered the words or if she screamed them. Panic surged through her. She knew she had to look, but didn't want to. She wanted to go home and curl up in bed and have this all just be over.

She slowly approached the bathroom, gingerly stepping through the water. Through the bathroom door, she could hear water running and see a denim clad leg and a scuffed work boot. The terror refreshed itself. "Tigg?"

Sara stamped down her fear and ran in to where Tigg lay on the floor like a broken mannequin. His body was soaking wet and covered in blood. She quickly turned off the water and pulled the plug, all the time pleading for him to wake up. She knelt down next to him and shook him, but got no reaction. Was he dead? How could he be dead?

She laid her head on his chest, ignoring the blood. This was all just too much—she couldn't take it anymore. Tears began to fall. She lay there, half-naked, in the ruined bathroom amongst the shards of glass, the blood, the water, and the destruction, sobbing into Tigg's bloody body. Suddenly, she felt a hand on her back.

The scream shot through the room, echoing down the hall. Panicked, she spun around to fight this new enemy, but seeing no one, she looked back to Tigg's body.

"I thought you'd be happy I was alive." A soothing voice said.

Chapter 6

JUST ANOTHER DAY

Hammond bid everyone good night and started toward home. From the Truck Stop, he only had a block to go. Everyone watched Hammond as he lit a Marlboro and started off without fear into the dark night. Why would he fear a silent entity like the dark? The father that was waiting for him at home was the real enemy—one he feared more than anything else in the world. He walked down the sidewalk, up his driveway, and into his dilapidated house. The door to Hammond's house was never locked because they never really had anything worth stealing. As he walked in the front door, his father greeted him with the usual drunken sermon: the boy was a plague on this earth; his father should have taken Hammond out of this world when he was born; Ham's mother had committed suicide and it was all his fault. Hammond ignored this, just as he had always done.

"Where were you?" his father bellowed through his drunken stupor.

"I was out with Tigg, Sara and the most beautiful woman I have ever seen" Hammond said off-handedly as he searched through the fridge. He didn't know why he said it. He knew the old man wouldn't leave it alone.

"Beautiful? Do you really think that any woman with a pulse could ever love a boy like you? You're nothing more than a waste of skin." his father sneered as he moved closer to Hammond.

"Could be worse, Dad—I could be you!" Hammond closed his fist as he readied himself for what was sure to be the fight of the century.

Hammond's father decided to ignore the statement. The boy made his way through the dirty, uninviting house to his bedroom, if that is what you would call the laundry room that he crashed in. Banners from heavy metal bands blacked out all the windows, leaving the room dark even in the middle of the day. He slammed the door, crossed to the unmade bed, and pulled a bottle of Vodka out from under it. He sat down heavily and took a long pull. Sins of the fathers, he thought, as he let the alcohol dull the pain.

This day had been too weird. It was as good of an excuse as any to get drunk. He took another drink form the bottle, sucking the powerful stuff down like it was water. He was a fool. What good would it do to try and get close to Bailey, anyway? She would never go for the son of a drunk. She had a stable life and a good family.

Ham wondered again how much different his life would've been if his mother hadn't killed herself. He was only eight years old when he walked in and found her. She was hanging from the rafters in the garage, wearing her favorite dress. The image was permanently burned into his brain.

He drained the bottle and threw it on his bed. Hammond heaved a big sigh as he buried his head in his hands. From the top of his dresser, his little hamster started to run on his wheel. Ham decided he needed contact with something living and crossed the room to where the cage sat.

"What if he's right, Peyote?" Hammond let the hamster run from one scarred hand to the other. "Maybe Mom *was* my fault. Maybe I *am* nothing but a screw up. Why would Bailey be attracted to me, anyway? I'm not sexy or rich—I'm nothing but a freak," he whispered to his furry companion.

The Vodka was kicking in, giving him a pleasant buzz. He knew he should be startled at what came next, but somehow he wasn't. Peyote looked into his eyes and said, "We can help you, old friend." His voice was multitudinous and squeaky. "We will help you with your problem as a gesture of our good faith."

"Um, dude, you said we. What we? You're the only one here besides me. You're not pregnant are you? 'Cause I can't afford to buy any more food than I already do." Hammond knew he sounded stupid, but what could be expected when having a conversation with a rodent?

"Just let us work, human" Peyote said. He stood on his tiny back legs and cleared his throat. The voice that came from Peyote's throat was Hammond's. "Dad, I need you in here right now."

"What do you want now?" The old man hollered belligerently.

"I found a bottle of Vodka I think you lost," the tiny hamster shot back.

"Why didn't you say so?" his father said as he made his way through the filth to Hammond's room.

"What are you doing, Peyote? He can't come in here—he will kill you! I'm not supposed to have you in here." Hammond whispered to the hamster.

Edgar Hammond stumbled into the room, the eyes of his son and Peyote glued to him. The little animal glared at him with beady black eyes that were set in a cold stare. The hamster started to writhe and twist in Hammond's hands as it began to grow and mutate. The hamster's skin peeled back, revealing a bloody skull with muscle and sinew laid bare, the hamster jumped up and into the open mouth of the shocked Edgar Hammond. Hammond watched as the hamster burrowed down Edgar's throat, biting and clawing all the way. Edgar grasped at his own throat, trying helplessly to stop the invasion. A small bulge pinpointed the hamster's location as it moved deeper and deeper. His agonizing screams were quickly squelched as he choked on his own blood. Eventually, a mass appeared in Edgar's stomach. Hammond watched in fascinated horror as his father's gut twisted and distended. His father's shirt hung open, giving an all-too-clear view. Blood began to dot the man's skin as the hamster chewed its way out. Hammond stood paralyzed, helplessly watching. A furry head emerged, followed by bloody front paws as Edgar's now lifeless body collapsed to the ground.

The animal wriggled out of Edgar, glistening with blood and tissue. In an instant, it darted under Hammond's makeshift bed, which was composed of a grungy mattress on a two-by-four frame, which rose only a few inches above the soiled carpet. After a moment of silence, a bony, decomposing hand shot out from under the bed. The fingers wrapped around the blood-drenched leg of Edgar and jerked it back towards the bed. Edgar's body hit the wooden bed frame with enough force to peel the skin from its bones. Skeleton and skin were both sucked violently under the mattress. A torrent of blood came flooding out of the empty space, then was suddenly sucked back in. Hammond simply stood there, stunned by the chaos and horror he had just witness. His pleasant buzz had left him high and dry.

A voice sounded from beneath Hammond's bed. "That was our gift to you, young friend." The voice resonated deeper and stronger than when Peyote had spoken. "Become one with us and we will give you back your mother." Although that was the one thing Hammond had always wished for, he found himself unable to accept.

"I must say that sounds very tempting, but I'll have to go with, 'thanks, but no thanks'." With that, Hammond bolted out of the room, catching his arm on a nail. He ran through the greasy, foul-smelling kitchen and grabbed his father's car keys from the ring as he headed for the garage. With a thump-drag thump-drag following closely behind him, he threw open the door, leaped into his dad's cherished 1968 Pontiac Le Mans, and drove it clean through the garage door. He had a sudden and profound need to find the only person he felt would understand him—Bailey. Hammond made his way around the block as he realized that his arm was dripping blood. He glanced at it, discovered a wide gash, and laughed as the blood pooled on the seat of the car. "Now to find Bailey", he said to himself.

Chapter 7

CHICKEN FEED

When Bailey returned home she headed straight for her room. As she changed her clothes, she recounted the events of the day. Hammond seemed to be a really great guy—everything she had ever dreamed of. How could someone like that be hiding in a small, nowhere place like this? She sprawled out on her Hello Kitty blanket and glanced around her room. The walls were a soft shade of lavender with white trim; the carpet a soft tan. Bailey lay there, dreamily petting her stuffed cat as thoughts of Hammond filled her head. She rolled gently onto her stomach and began to wonder, could he really be as great as he seemed? Was he really the one she had dreamed of, time after time? She let her mind race, filling with fantasies of her newfound love. Bailey had often dreamed of being in love like this—and now she was beginning to feel that for Hammond. His character seemed a bit rough at times, but she detected a softer emotional side hidden behind those white eyes.

The night breeze began to intensify as Bailey drifted in and out of sleep, her thoughts still lingering in a fantasy of Hammond and herself. The glass in the frame of her window mysteriously began to frost over as the warm summer waft gave way to a cold current of air. Bailey felt a cold chill as she pulled her blanket up over her scantily clad body. The air in the room slowly grew colder and colder until the steam from her breath began to show. Bailey shivered as she arose to turn up the thermostat. The temperature continued to drop as she donned her robe and headed down the hall to get her father to check on the heater. She wondered how a winter storm could just move in any old time.

Bailey made her way slowly through the well maintained home searching for her father. He was an even-tempered, sophisticated man who loved his daughter more than life itself. He doted over her and would do anything to make his little girl happy, which included giving in even if he told her "no". He happily granted her every request. Bailey loved her father and mother, too, but at times her mother would get jealous. She loved her daughter, but knew that she could never have the connection Bailey shared with her father.

The whole house was empty and dark, with no sign of her parents anywhere. Bailey found that odd, considering the late hour. Gloominess stalked her as she made her way through the silent house. The absence of her sister and her niece made for an even more disturbing atmosphere. There had not been a quiet moment in the house since her older sister and her five-year-old niece arrived. Her sister had just gotten out of a bad relationship and moved back in with them, bringing her daughter, Emily, along. Bailey loved little Emily like she was her own little sister. The little girl was very rambunctious and full of life—there was never a dull moment with her around.

Bailey tugged nervously at the strings of her nightgown as she slowly and carefully made the descent into the living room. A chill began to follow her as she looked around the empty house for any sign of life. She found none. She saw what appeared to be lightning with no particular destination fill the outside sky. As she glanced outside through the window, a peculiar sight caught her eye: half of the sky was filled with stars, while the other half was filled with nothing but a deep, dreary blackness.

An eerie absence of light began to fill the house as Bailey tried to discover the whereabouts of her missing family. Echoes of far-off voices began to resonate through the halls as she fruitlessly called for her father.

"Auntie Bailey, it's so cold out here! We need you, Aunt Bailey! Please, come help us!" her niece's voice sounded from outside the sliding glass patio door.

Bailey ran for the door to answer her little niece's plea. When she arrived at the door and looked through the frost-caked glass, she saw little Emily feeding the chickens out in the dark. Bailey trotted outside with the mission of bringing the little girl back into a warm safe place, but to her surprise, when she went outside the weather was warm like any other summer night.

"This is impossible," she muttered as she felt her body warming in the balmy night air. "How could it be so warm out here and so freezing in there?"

She picked her way across the dew-dampened lawn, sending a smile to the little girl. Emily just stood there with a bucket of feed humming softly as she doled out portions of feed to the hungry chickens. The birds pecked excitedly at what they had been given. Emily continued humming with her back to Bailey as she spoke in a strange tone while somehow still humming. It sounded as if there were many voices coming from the little girl all at once.

"Hello, Auntie. We are happy you could come," the strange voices said as she continued to toss the feed. "Mommy didn't want to play with us. Now Mommy is part of us", the little girl's borrowed voice stated while still humming the disturbing song.

For the first time Bailey realized that it was not chicken feed the child was feeding the birds. It was a bloody mixture that appeared to be some sort of chum. The smell hit Bailey's nose like a freight train, confirming her observation. She grabbed Emily's shoulder and whipped her around to face her. With a sudden start, her mind went absolutely blank, as what she was taking in made no sense. Her cherished niece had no eyes! It was as though they had been chewed out, leaving a hideous vestige of her once adorable little face.

Bailey screamed as her voice finally came back to her. Seeing the feed bucket once again, she came to the horrifying realization that the stuff in it was, or used to be, her sister. She could see a beautiful silver crucifix protruding from the gore. It had been a gift from their grandmother—her sister never took it off. Emily cocked her head at a ninety-degree angle as the hollow eye sockets stared at her.

"Do you want to play with us, love?" The odd little creature that now occupied her niece's body taunted her as she made her first attempt at escape. "We let the others go, but we must keep you." Bailey wondered, "What others? Hammond? Her father? Who?"

As Bailey turned to run, a piece of the wire fence surrounding the chickens broke free and wrapped itself tightly around her bare ankle. It bit into her soft skin deeper and deeper as she struggled in vain to flea her young captor.

"Don't try to escape us, love! We need you!" The voices grew louder as she noticed a presence beginning to form around her mutilated niece. "We will sacrifice this one to you. Her blood shall belong to you," the voices echoed.

"Leave her alone." She heard many, but saw only little Emily standing before a black mass. Emily giggled as she emptied the bloody contents of the feed bucket over her own head. The chickens quickly enveloped the blood-soaked child and began to tear at her flesh. Little by little, Emily was eaten away by the hoard of ravenous birds, while Bailey could do nothing but watch in horror, disgust, and grief. The little girl she had grown to love so dearly was now reduced to nothing more than a puddle of gore filled with chunks of flesh and bone.

"Please don't kill me, please!" Bailey cried as the black mass behind her began to take the shape of her loving father.

"Come on, darling, I'm here, and we can be together forever, if you will just let us in." Bailey cringed as the eyeless form of her father came toward her. "Come on, Sweetheart. We won't hurt you. Just come and embrace us, love us, and be one with us!"

While the demon that appeared to be her father moved ever closer, Bailey managed to free herself from the entangling wire, turned toward the gate, and dashed madly in a bid for freedom. She almost made it to the wooden gate when a hand reached up from out of the grass and grabbed her still-bleeding ankle.

"We will not let you go, Bailey. We need you! Join with us or we will destroy you!" The tone of the beast became more sinister as it approached her. "You will like it here, honey. Your mother and father do, as will your friends . . . we will consume you all, for we must feed." Bailey could feel the blood drain from her face as the hope of surviving this encounter faded away, leaving her to imagine a ghastly, dismal fate. With renewed conviction, she drew herself up.

"I will never join you! I would rather die!" Bailey screamed at the demon as it began to descend on her.

"We can arrange that! Yes, we can!" it said as it drew her into a deadly embrace, its forked tongue lashing at Bailey's lovely face.

Bailey drove both of her fists into the face of the creature and jerked as hard as she could in a last-ditch effort to save her own life.

To her astonishment, she felt herself break free of the creature's grip and tumble to the ground. She scrambled to her feet and charged through the gate, slamming it shut behind her as she fled into the empty street.

The streets were wet, dark, and foreboding. Bailey ran toward the restaurant that earlier had been a refuge for her and her friends. This was her only chance of escape—to reach some sanctuary, to find help in whatever form it may be. She could feel the evil presence closing in behind her as she tried desperately to escape with her life and her very soul intact.

The ground began to shake beneath her feet as Bailey raced desperately to the Truck Stop. A huge fissure opened up beneath her and swallowed her down into the darkness. Screaming and clawing at the broken ground, she slipped further and further into the abyss. "So this is how I go", she thought to herself as her hands slowly slipped from the crumbling asphalt. "No hero to come and rescue me; no one to say goodbye to". With that thought she started to let go, hoping to end it quickly and on her own terms.

Out of nowhere a hand grabbed Bailey by the wrist and pulled her up out of the hole. Standing before her like an angel was Hammond, his countenance fixed, and his hair flowing in the breeze. Hammond turned to face the demon, his white eyes piercing the shadow as he spoke.

"You will not take her! I will stand in your way! She is the light that brightens my darkness, and I will not let you!" Hammond yelled as he stood between the demon and its intended prey.

"You cannot stop us, mortal! We will gladly take you as well!" The demon declared.

Hammond wasn't listening to what the demon had to say. He produced a bottle of vodka from one pocket, and his cigarette lighter from another. He had torn off a piece of his shirt and stuffed it into the neck of the bottle, which he quickly set afire. He heaved the Molotov cocktail at their attacker and grabbed Bailey. As fire burst from the broken bottle and engulfed the demon, Hammond forced Bailey into the Le Mans and climbed in behind her. Without looking back, he stomped on the gas pedal and they peeled out, fish-tailing around the corner and up the block.

Chapter 8

THE REUNION

Hammond slowly pulled his car into Tigg's garage and brought it to a stop. He finally relaxed and slumped into his seat, sitting motionless for a minute, engine still running, as he contemplated the possibility that he might once again have to face the demon. He silenced the drone of the engine and searched for a cigarette, slowly and deliberately extracting it from the pack as he mentally prepared himself for what the night might yet bring. He stared straight ahead as he lit up and took the first long drag. Bailey also sat in silence, but she was watching Hammond—this new friend who had just saved her life. She was still trying to understand what had just happened, still trying to understand what it all meant. The one thing she did understand was that Hammond was the one she wanted to be with. Hammond took another drag on his cigarette, then pulled it out of his mouth, gave it a disappointed look, and snuffed it out. He then took a deep breath, looked at Bailey, and fumbled for the door.

"You had better come with me," he said quietly. "I don't want to leave you here alone. You know—just in case."

Bailey nodded as they both exited the vehicle. She quickly ran to the front of the car to meet up with Hammond, taking his hand. Hammond seemed a little older, somehow, as though this evening had added years to his age. She could see so many things in him that she hadn't noticed before: strength, confidence, passion, love? What she did not see was fear. He had become a hero in her eyes.

And it was true—Hammond was a different sort of man, now. What was important a few hours ago was now meaningless. His own problems seemed petty—his weaknesses unacceptable. The whole awful experience with Peyote had stripped away any sense of childhood he had left. His concerns now reached beyond himself, as he realized his friends were counting on him, and he on them.

"There is no telling what we may find in here, hon, so just stay behind me and keep an eye out. I'll watch in front—you watch behind." Hammond issued the orders so confidently that Bailey felt compelled to obey.

The two entered the house through the open front door and made their way through the bloodstained hallway. 'I think we're too late,' Hammond whispered as they surveyed the damage. The pair crept to the stairway and then ascended toward Tigg's room. Bailey was shaking nervously as she followed along, clenching Hammond's arm and scanning what lay behind her.

Hammond heard the sound of someone's voice as he reached the top of the stairs and signaled Bailey to be quiet as he slowly approached the open bathroom door. He was horror stricken as he took in the scene. Half naked and sobbing, Sara was sprawled over a broken and bleeding Tigger. A smoldering dog lay lifeless in the bathtub next to a melted radio. At first glance, Hammond had assumed the worst and figured his best friend was dead—the one person he could count on was gone! Hammond just stood there, overcome by grief and not knowing what to say or do, when he suddenly regained hope: Tigger's hand was moving up and down, slowly caressing Sara's back.

"Damn," Hammond said with a sigh of relief, as his eyes met Tigg's. "I sure did like that radio."

The four of them looked at each other in silence for a second, then burst out laughing. Bailey found a towel to wrap around Sara and helped her up, as Hammond pulled Tigg to his feet. Hammond leaned against the porcelain sink and pulled out a cigarette and lit it up, trying to think of what to do next. But his thoughts were interrupted when he noticed a flash of movement behind Bailey.

What started as a formless shadow took on a recognizable shape as it moved closer. Instinctively, Hammond yanked the cigarette from his mouth and greeted Mrs. Curtis as she entered the room.

"Hello, Mrs. Curtis. How . . . how are you?" Hammond said, holding the cigarette behind him. He knew she didn't approve of his smoking habit. Tigg began to shake as he looked at his mother—she stood there, examining them like a monument to motherhood.

"Ryan, love, you should tell your little friends to go home, now. Look at the mess you've made. It won't clean itself, you know."

Tigg just stood there, speechless, eyes fixed, mouth gaping open. He looked like a mechanical figure someone had just pulled the plug on. Then, all of a sudden it hit Hammond—Mrs. Curtis had not answered him, nor had she asked him to put out his cigarette. She hadn't noticed the half-naked girl standing next to her son, and even more so, the dead, stinking dog lying in the bathtub. Hammond quickly pushed past Sara, Bailey and the still shaking Tigg, to stand face to face with Barbara Curtis. Hammond liked her a lot, and had come to think of her as his own mother, but despite his affections, he knew what had to be done. He quickly grabbed the strange woman, whose eyes were now as dark as velvet, and shoved her into the hallway.

They wrestled briefly, bouncing back and forth down the hall until Hammond gave one last big shove, impaling her on a coat hook as he fell to the floor.

"We will tear your flesh from your wretched bones! We will destroy you, you pathetic humans!" The demon screamed as it writhed on the hook, struggling to free itself.

"Some have tried, but all have failed," Hammond said as picked himself up and staggered to his feet. He turned to face his awe-struck friends "Don't be fooled—she's no longer the person you knew. These demons want only to destroy us, one way or another—this is about survival!"

The group watched in astonishment as he pulled the cord out of the base of a lamp and shoved it into the mouth of the screaming demon. It twitched and twisted, shaking violently from the shock until its head exploded into a thousand slithering leaches that covered the floor.

Sara held Tigg close in a consoling embrace for a moment, realizing he had just watched his best friend kill his mother, or at least what used to be his mother . . . Hammond walked over to Tigg and held out his pack of cigarettes for Tigg to take one. It was poor compensation for his loss, but between the two boys, this was the ultimate show of respect. Tigg took the cigarette from Hammond and lit it, then broke down into quiet sobs.

"It's late now and we all need some rest. We'll make a stand here tonight and try to find some answers tomorrow." Hammond said as though he were the general of some great army. "We'll take turns sleeping—I'll take the first watch."

"No" Sara interrupted, just as Hammond thought the plan was accepted. "Tigg needs to go to the hospital. He's lost a lot of blood and he's not looking so good." She paused for a moment, giving Hammond a determined look. "Besides—you're bleeding, too—pretty badly."

"I'm fine—I'll be alright. Don't worry about me." Hammond said as he looked around the room. When his eyes met Bailey he could see how frightened she was. He knew he had to get her to a safer place. "Okay . . . okay. We'll go to the hospital. Somebody there should be able to help. Daybreak is in and hour, we'll wait for first light. If nothing else, we can get Tigger fixed up."

With that, Hammond walked down the hall and into Tigg's parent's room. Tigg's father had a collection of souvenirs from World War II. He had some Nazi memorabilia and other interesting artifacts, but most importantly, Japanese war swords. Hammond looked carefully at the contents of the glass case and chose two katanas, one for Tigg and one for himself. Hammond tried to break the glass, but it was amazingly sturdy. He walked back into the bathroom, retrieved Tigg's melted radio, and hurled it through the glass doors, giving him full access to the treasure inside. "Yep", he muttered. "Love that radio".

Carefully moving the large shards of glass out of the way, he retrieved the two Samurai swords, then headed for Tigg's sisters' room. He knew they were away at college, but surely they would have left some clothes behind that the girls could wear. After rummaging through the closet he grabbed two pairs of pants and two shirts, then went to Tigg's room. He grabbed some dry clothes for Tigg and the knapsack that he always had hanging on his bedpost. Tigg always kept useful things in the knapsack, and Hammond thought they might come in handy later.

"My dad is really not gonna like this, Ham." Tigger said, looking at the sword in Hammond's outstretched hand.

"Somehow, I don't think he will care, my friend." Hammond said as he passed out the clothes. "Besides, I find necessity to be the mother of grand larceny, don't you?" this was clearly not the first time Hammond had taken something that didn't belong to him out of 'necessity'.

Hammond went down stairs and waited in the living room while the others got dressed. He was standing next to the window keeping watch when they finally joined him. Bailey curled up on the recliner near Hammond and Sara sat on the couch with Tigg's head in her lap. Tigg was very weak and kept fading in and out of consciousness. Hammond continued his vigil, keeping watch for any sign of danger. The mood was somber as they each related what had happened to them. The hour passed slowly as they waited for sunrise, all wondering what to expect next. Finally, Hammond turned from the window.

"It's time to go." Hammond said as he headed for the door. The others clamored to their feet and followed behind. Night was giving way to the approaching dawn—the stars were fading from the slowly brightening sky behind the mountains in the east. The group was about to climb into the Le Mans when Tigg motioned for them to stop.

"Remember your comment about the B-rated campy movies?" Tigg asked Hammond as he produced a flashlight from his knapsack. "Well, in those movies, there is always someone or something hiding in the back seat, and I just think it would be best if we checked it out before we climb into a car with some psychotic demon from Hell, don't you?" For the first time since Hammond had known him, Tigg had made a more intelligent decision than he himself was about to.

"Smart thinking, there, Tigg," Hammond said as he backed up the brave Tigger with sword drawn.

"Oh, crap!" Tigg said, eyes widening like dinner plates. "The front seat is covered in blood!"

"Yeah, that would be my blood, Tigg. I seem to have nipped a blood vessel or something. Is there anything in the back seat?" Hammond queried.

"Nope—we're good to go." Tigg learned military terms from his father when he was young, so in stressful situations he found himself using them to feel as brave as his father had been in Vietnam, or his grandfather, when he stormed the beaches of Normandy. They were only a few years older than Tigg was now when they had gone to war. Now, in a strange way, it was Tigg's turn.

Tigg and Sara piled into the back seat. Hammond and Bailey took the front. The engine roared to life and the headlights pierced the fading night as they pulled out of the driveway and headed for the hospital.

Chapter 9

HELL'S HOSPITAL

awn was breaking over Convict Grade. The cloudy sky turned bright red as the sun broke over the horizon. The quartet made their way to Our Lady of Mercy Hospital, the car slipping quietly through empty streets. No one spoke as they rode along—each one was still trying to make sense of the last evening's events. Hammond sat watchfully in the driver's seat, still on edge, scanning the streets in all directions. Tigg was sprawled out in the back seat with Sara tending his wounds. His arm had been sliced rather brutally by the mirror and bruises covered his battered body. Bailey shifted uneasily in her seat, still shaken from her ordeal and distraught over what had happened to her family.

As the car pulled into the hospital parking lot, Hammond spoke softly. "What are we going to tell them? Maybe that someone tried to beat us up? What d'ya think we should say?"

"We tell them the truth," Bailey spoke as though the thought of anything else was ludicrous.

"So you want me to go in there and say, "Hi I'm Hammond. This is my friend Tigger who was attacked by a demon dog after his mother ate it?"

"Ooh . . . I would have to go with Hammond on this one." Sara broke in. "They would just think we were crazy or something and try to lock us up."

"We need help—we've gotta tell someone. Tigg, back me up here," Bailey said, still determined.

"I'd have to go with Sara and Hammond." Tigg mumbled weakly. "If we tell the truth, the only help they'll give us is a free trip to the mental ward."

In the end, they decided the best recourse was to take things a step at a time. First, they had to establish whether or not anyone else had seen the "living darkness" or if they were alone in this. Hammond just leaned on the red and black hood of the Le Mans, not wanting to be the first to go inside. Hospitals were a place that Hammond just didn't like very much. Every time he had gone there for help, his complaints were dismissed and he was turned back to face his abusive father and receive more punishment. He had come to associate them with a repeated pattern of abuse—a place where he went for relief, but never received it.

Bailey got out and helped Sara pull Tigg from the car. He stood up straight for a second, then collapsed onto the two girls who struggled to hold up his limp body. Hammond ran over and grabbed Tigg, hoisted him over his shoulder, and carried him through the sliding glass door of the old hospital entrance.

Once inside, they found the place unusually quiet. Some things were strangely out of place. Yellow and red leaves blew around the corridor. This wouldn't be unusual in the fall, but in mid-summer it was simply eerie. Quietly, the four walked down the deserted hallway. Bailey wrapped her arms around her stomach as if in need of comfort or support. In the background they could hear the creak of the swinging doors to the emergency room, but other than that, silence prevailed as they made their way to the main floor nurse's station, which was usually always manned. Today, however, the desk was empty.

Hammond unloaded Tigg into an empty chair, and then stuck his head in the window to see if there was anyone sitting back behind the counter. Hammond had spent a lot of time in this facility and the stillness made the hair on the back up his neck stand on end. Fear began to set in—something was definitely wrong here.

"Hello? Anybody here?" he yelled. "We've got somebody hurt out here!" Hammond banged on the counter—gently, at first, then harder and harder. It was a toss up as to which would break first—his fist or the Formica.

"Hello?" Bailey yelled through the glass. "Please . . . we need some help out here!" Bailey hoped that niceness would open the door for them. Her mother had always said, "you catch more flies with honey". Hammond stopped yelling and looked at her. She craned her neck, trying to see through the glass. There were three empty chairs and a computer station that had been left on.

"Ok," Hammond said, "I guess we'll have to go find a doctor or nurse or somebody that knows something." The girls both nodded silently and Sara helped Tigg to his feet. She shreaked and almost dropped him when she heard the footsteps.

An old man stumbled down the empty hall scattering leaves as he walked. He wore a dirty, stained hospital gown and one grungy slipper. One leg drug uselessly behind him and he clung to the rail that ran along the wall. His lined face was covered with cuts and scratches, but there was no blood. As he approached the group, they were treated to a view of crooked yellow teeth set in a twisted grin. Hammond looked at him and saw pure insanity.

"If you have come here, you have come looking for death!" the old man growled as he slowly moved past them. "They will find you here, just as they will find me! We are marked, you and I." The old man was now looking directly at Hammond. "You and me—we're marked, you see! Marked by the sins of our fathers." The old man kept hobbling along as he let out a high-pitched giggle that ended in a hacking cough.

"That dude was a freak." Tigg mumbled out of nowhere, startling Sara so badly she let out a small scream. "I think I can walk on my own now, sweetie." He said quietly to Sara. Then he looked at Ham. "I think I'm okay now . . . how about you?"

"You had me scared there, buddy. I thought we were gonna lose you for a while." Hammond said with a genuine smile crossing his face.

"Eh—why walk when I can take the Hammond express and lean on a beautiful girl?" Tigg said, making everyone laugh.

The laughter was cut short as a man in blue scrubs and wrap-around sunglasses appeared out of nowhere. He spoke in a slow southern drawl. "Are y'all here because of the strange animal attacks?" The man asked, surveying the group. "We're treating everyone down in the E.R. Y'all come on with me."

Sara giggled a little at the man's accent as the group followed him. She put her hands in her belt loops and faked a slow cowboy swagger. Tigg followed, trying to hide his smile as he watched her. Hammond was not amused, however. He walked like a sentinel, as though he were Bailey's lone protector in this new chaotic world. Bailey followed close behind. The man with the southern accent made her uneasy.

He led them to a small trauma room where four people already waited. Bailey thought that seemed to be too many, but didn't want to say anything. The man in scrubs left without saying another word.

One of the people in the room was badly injured. Blood seeped slowly from the side of his head. Tigg took a seat in a chair in the corner. Hammond took Tigg's knapsack and started to rummage through it. He found a Mountain Dew and his old butterfly knife which he thought he had lost. He was going to say something about it, but this was neither the time nor the place. He was glad he'd found it, though, and worried he might have to use it. Hammond stuck the knife in his pocket and opened the warm soda.

The group in the room was quiet. Four sets of hollow eyes focused on the newcomers. They seemed to be drawn to Hammond and Tigg. Hammond stared at the pop can and the others turned their attention to invisible spots on the floor. They were all uncomfortable.

One of the patients was a young woman, around twenty. Her cheeks were slightly plump and covered with dirt. Black hair hung in a tangled mess past her shoulders. Her eyes were red from crying. Mascara had run down her face, leaving a black trail from the tears. She looked exhausted—spent, like there was nothing left.

Hammond began to rummage though the cabinets hoping to find something useful. Judging by the condition of the rest of the people, it looked like they had been there a while, and wouldn't be receiving any medical attention any time soon. Hammond was a survivor, trained by experience, and had learned the basic first aid skills needed to patch himself up after a severe beating. After a couple of minutes searching the cabinets, he found a bottle of rubbing alcohol and a suture kit. He laid out the kit, got out his knife, and dumped the alcohol over the wound in his arm. As he began to suture it, Bailey came over to lend a hand. She helped him cut the thread after each stitch—and it took about a dozen. Hammond winced a little each time he pulled the needle through his skin, but having Bailey so close, leaning over him like that was definitely making it better. He studied his arm closely as he took each stitch, then studied Bailey as she did the cutting—her hair . . . her eyes . . . her cheeks . . . her mouth . . . her neck . . .

"Thanks", he said softly as they finished the job. Hammond got up and took a new kit from the cupboard, then walked over to Tigg.

"Now I ain't no doctor, Tigg. And I ain't gonna lie to you, either—this is gonna hurt like hell", Hammond said as he started to pour the alcohol over his friend's wounds. Tigger screamed as the liquid hit his flesh. The burning sensation was intense. "If you thought that hurt, Tigg old buddy, wait 'till I find the ones that need stitching." Hammond knew his medical skills were lacking and his bedside manor left more than a little something to be desired.

Hammond probed at Tigg's cuts as gently as he could. He knew some of them needed to be stitched, but wasn't sure which ones. He didn't mind doing it, but hated causing his friend pain. He knew pain—Tigger didn't. Hammond found at least seven cuts that probably needed to be sewn up. He needed more suture kits.

Hammond walked down the deserted hallway looking for another medicine cabinet. He wasn't sure how he was going to patch up Tigg. It was going to hurt, and he had nothing to give him for the pain.

He slipped silently down the corridor. He heard low, distant voices, but saw no one. "Our Lady" looked like it hadn't been used in years. It was still pretty clean when they'd arrived but now it was dusty and grimy. He made a mental note of this fact, but was too focused on other things to process it. He was a man on a mission.

The creepy doctor with the southern drawl was nowhere to be found. Hammond made his way to the hospital pharmacy, navigating the maze of halls without a missed step. He knew this building like the back of his hand.

Footsteps echoed behind him, sending shivers up his spine. He ordered himself not to look back and picked up his pace. He passed room after room, and every single one of them was empty. Why did the doctor put them in the same room with the other four? He and his friends could've had their own space.

Hammond swung down the last hall before the pharmacy. The door was open, which saved him from another breaking and entering charge. He scanned the shelves for something to give Tigg for the pain. He recognized one of the meds that he had taken, and grabbed a bottle, moving the remaining bottles to the front. He didn't want anybody to know he'd been here. He scanned the labels and found Demerol, Lidocaine and Novocain, which he stuffed into the knapsack that Tigg had brought, and turned out of the room.

As he ran back to the trauma room where he had left the others, he heard the footsteps behind him again. They seemed to be getting closer, even though he was nearly sprinting. Just as he was reaching for the door, he heard a hissing voice. He couldn't make out the words, and didn't care anyway.

In the trauma room, Sara was bent over Tigg, putting pressure on the worst of his bleeding wounds. Tigg was staring down her shirt. Earlier, when she was half-naked, he may have been too out of it to care, but now he seemed to be feeling better . . . he had a clear view, and was taking advantage of it. Bailey glanced up at Ham and smiled. She knew right where Tigger was looking. Hammond returned the glance with a sheepish grin . . . hadn't he just done the same to her?

Hammond didn't want to interrupt, but he wanted to get this done before that doctor came back and busted him with the liberated medications. He gently pushed Sara aside and drew a syringe of

Lidocaine. He jabbed it into Tigg's arm, hoping he put it in the right spot. Soon, Tigg reported numbness, and Ham began stitching. Sara looked sick at the first needle puncture. She wanted to tell Tigg how she felt—that it was going to be okay—but she couldn't. Instead, she held his hand and looked away.

When Hammond finished stitching, Bailey wrapped both the boys' wounds with gauze. The four strangers stared at them. One of the men was growing increasingly agitated. He finally jumped up and began yelling at Hammond.

"What's going on here?" He shouted. "Who the hell do you think you are? Doogie Friggin' Howser? You're as crazy as a . . ." The man stopped short as Hammond rose, turned, and flipped out the butterfly knife.

The man stood silently as Hammond spoke softly and calmly. "I do not appreciate your getting up in my face, and if you continue to do so, I will use this knife, which is surprisingly dull, to slit your throat. I think you'll find it difficult to speak when your tongue is hanging out of your second smile."

The man easily had fifty pounds on Hammond, but when he spoke, his voice was quaking. "I don't want any trouble. I'll just go sit down now."

Hammond snapped the knife closed and stuck it back in his pocket. He went over and leaned against the wall, took up the Mountain Dew and nursed it slowly. After a while, he forced himself to look at Bailey, who gave him a reassuring smile. Everything was cool with her, but everybody else looked at him like he was some kind of psychotic maniac.

"Okay, I'm a little on edge." Hammond explained. "We've been chased by these demonic pets and creepy zombie things all night. Then we came here, only to find an empty hospital with no staff and eight people crammed into one room while all the others are empty." It sounded ridiculous to him, even as he said it. Maybe he *was* going crazy!

Three of the strangers nodded slowly. The woman who was sitting motionless earlier was now crying again. She seemed to understand completely what he was saying. She kept saying something under her breath, but no one could hear her.

"You okay, honey?" Bailey asked as she walked over to her. "What's your name, sweetie?"

"Stephie. It's sh-short for Stephanie," the woman heaved a sob as she spoke.

"Sh-she's dead. I watched. It killed her and I just watched. I am going to Hell . . ." Her tears were renewed as she began to tell her story. "Shelby and I were driving home last night. We were both kind of drunk and she shouldn't have been driving. She was just goofing off when she turned off the headlights to scare me. She turned them back on and there was this kid! He couldn't have been more than eight years old. He was standing in the middle of the road! Before she could stop, she hit him! She hit him! I felt the tires roll over him . . ." She paused her story as the next series of heaving sobs came through. "Shelby stopped the car and got out to see if her eyes had been playing tricks on her. I waited for what must have been ten minutes before I heard Shelby scream. I got out to try and help her—it was awful! We didn't hit a boy—it was a deer, the only problem was, it seemed to have been half eaten already . . . Then I saw him—there was the boy . . . standing over Shelby . . . eating her!" A blank look came over the young woman's eyes as she continued. "He turned and looked at me and smiled . . . Shelby started moving like she had a stream of electricity flowing through her dead body. Then, like, all at once, the deer and Shelby got up and all three of them started to come after me!

I did the only thing I could think of . . . I got in the car and drove as fast as I could out of there. I got all the way to town and ran into the stop sign on Briar Street. I hit my head on the steering wheel, and the next thing I knew I was here." She stopped and looked at Hammond. "Am I crazy?" She asked him as she pulled her knees up to her chest, and started rocking back and fourth.

"Well, first of all, lady, I think Hell is already here, so you won't have to go far to get there. Second," Hammond took a deep breath, "If you're crazy, then we all are, and that is something I'm just not willing to accept." Hammond pulled a cigarette out and went to light it, then thought about where he was. He stuffed it back in the pack and just listened to the group groan. "What does it matter—we're all dead, anyway."

Hammond stood against the wall and started to think out loud. "When I was a kid there was this place I used to go where I could feel safe. It was a church over on King Street." Hammond's mind trailed off as he slipped into memories of the past. "There was this preacher—Bachman, I think his name was. He used to stand at the pulpit and preach fire and brimstone. Well, when I was young, I used to hide from my dad in that church. I would hide between the pews and listen to that preacher work up these amazing sermons to teach his congregation about the dangers of the Devil and all those that may walk his path."

"The day my mother killed herself I went to that church and old Bachman saw me hiding there. He continued to work up his sermon and I listened closely, searching for anything that might take away the painful thoughts of my dead mother. I will never forget the bible scripture that I heard that day. I believe it was Mark 5:9 that said, 'And Jesus asked him, what is your name? He replied. My name is Legion, for we are many.' I think that it is what these creatures are. I think they are part of that Legion."

Hammond looked up to find everyone in the room staring at him, listening to his monologue. His account had offered at least some explanation for the horrors that everyone had been through, and his hypothesis seemed to provide answers that the nervous crowd sought. Hammond had unwittingly become the leader of the pack.

Bailey came over, hugged Hammond and kissed his cheek. He reveled in the moment. Somehow all the weird, horrifying stuff that had happened to them made the few good things all the sweeter. But the moment was cut short again when the doctor with the southern accent returned to check on the patients. The doctor ignored a barrage of questions as he entered the room and made his way straight through the crowd to a man who was stretched out on a gurney. Sara sat down next to Tigg and he put his arm around her. The Doctor reached into his scrubs and pulled out a bloody scalpel.

The already nervous crowd was now stupefied as, right there in front of them, the doctor carved out the man's eyes with the scalpel. The man screamed and jerked as the scalpel penetrated. The doctor held the man down with one hand as he worked. Screaming and sobbing, the man begged the doctor to stop, but was ignored. Then the doctor leaned down to the man and whispered in his ear. The onlookers heard a hissing sound, but couldn't make out anything else. The man nodded and the doctor bent down, as if to kiss him, when a black, dry mist came out of the doctor's mouth and entered the mouth of the man on the table.

The patient shook and convulsed horribly as a seizure took hold of him. The doctor simply held him down, as something seemed to work its way through his body. Then suddenly, the man fell calm. He sat up straight and a strange smile crossed his face as he arose from his bed and walked over to the man who had yelled at Hammond. His gate was uneven and jerky as he approached, and when he reached him, without warning, he shoved him against the wall, and whispered into his ear.

"Are you crazy?" came the man's angry response. "There is no way in hell!" He took a swing at the thing that used to be a man. It just took the hit, cocked its head to the side and stared at him. "Get away from me, I'm warning you!" The threat was empty, however, and the man was powerless against the demon. Its long tongue shot from its mouth and impaled the angry man's head against the wall.

The woman sitting next to him jumped up in surprise, but didn't run away. She just stood there, mouth wide open, screaming as loud as she could. The demon cringed at the ear-splitting display for a moment, then stepped up face to face with her and opened his mouth. Along with an equally loud scream came a stream of greenish black beetles that sprang from his mouth into hers. Her scream was cut short as she choked on the invading bugs, grabbing her throat, eyes wide open. The beetles exited her throat and her scream returned, but faded quickly into a gurgling sound when the flesh disappeared from her face as the beetles ate her from the inside out. She fell to the floor as the hungry, blood-drenched invaders sprang from her eye sockets, ears, and mouth, devouring what flesh remained on her skull.

At this, pandemonium broke out in the room as people screamed and ran in all directions trying to escape. Tigg stood clutching Sara as the doctor approached them. Bailey screamed as Hammond forced her out the door. He then jumped between the doctor and his two friends in an attempt to give them time to run. Tigg pushed Sara through the open door, then turned and stood his ground next to Hammond. Both young men fought to keep the attacking doctor at bay, but Tigg was knocked to the floor as the doctor grabbed Hammond by the throat and lifted him off the ground. Hammond struggled, legs flailing, in a vain attempt to work himself free. Stephie hit the doctor from behind but to no avail, as he continued to stand holding Hammond in the air.

"Get her out of here!" Hammond choked to Tigg

Tigg wasted no time in following his friend's order. He grabbed Stephie and made for the door. The doctor took off his sunglasses and stared at Hammond with large empty eye sockets. As Hammond stared back into the blackness, images began to penetrate his mind, and he seemed to hear one word echoing over and over . . . Enoch. He couldn't figure out what that meant, but it didn't matter right now. He fought unsuccessfully to free himself, for the strength of this thing far surpassed his own and he was trapped, hanging helplessly as the life drained out of him and he faded from consciousness.

The last thing Hammond saw as he hit the floor was a flash of silver light. The room spun around him as he faded from reality into a vision of a wholly different world.

Chapter 10

AN INTERVIEW WITH THE PRINCE

H ammond found himself walking down a path in the midst of fire and darkness as angels flew in the air above. Some wielded swords of light, others, swords of flames. Chaos and destruction surrounded him as he tried to make sense of the situation. Had he died? Was he just dreaming? Was this a vision of some kind? The path descended into a dark void, where dead bodies were piled in a great pit which was spanned by an ancient stone bridge. Hammond looked down on them on both sides as he crossed. At the center of the bridge he met a man—no, an angel—the most beautiful angel imaginable: tall, with a slender, yet muscular build; handsome countenance; and long, flowing, white hair. On the top of his head was a crown of fire. He turned to greet Hammond as he reached him.

"My name is Satanel. I am the prince of Legion. Welcome to your future." Satanel held his hand out, holding a scroll, and said, "This is the book of Enoch. Take it and understand your fate."

Hammond hesitantly took the scroll and tucked it away in the pocket of his jacket, never taking his eyes off of Satanel "What does this have to do with me?" He hesitated before continuing. "Are you the Devil?"

Satanel stood looking at Hammond with his head cocked slightly. A smile spread across his lovely face, and then he chuckled. "Everything is black and white with you mortals, isn't it?" His perfect teeth gleamed, even in the failing light. "Only one devil, you believe . . . No, I am merely the servant, not the master . . . the prince, not the king."

It was hard for Hammond to not like Satanel. He was so appealing, both physically and mentally. His smile was oddly comforting and his demeanor that of someone who could understand you better than any friend you ever had. As Hammond surveyed him he found he was, at least in appearance, everything he wished he could be, yet there was something about him—something that made Hammond very uneasy.

Flames danced in the darkness, lighting the stone bridge as Satanel turned to walk away. He signaled for Hammond to follow him as he headed further into the void. Hammond found himself mesmerized just watching him walk—there seemed to be meaning in every graceful step. Hammond felt compelled to go with him, as if he would have followed him anywhere. As they walked on, Hammond began to realize the horror of the scene that surrounded him. There was death and suffering all around. Angelic beings came into his view, impaled on long spears. They wretched in agony as blood trickled down their faces, which were twisted into a horrible death scowl.

The crumbling stones of the bridge were wet with blood and Hammond slipped repeatedly as he made his way across. "So what's in this scroll, Satanel?" he asked as he tried to keep up with the beautiful angel.

"History, my feeble little friend! It is the story of my brethren and I—the watchers . . . and how we were cast down from heaven." Satanel

83

stopped for a moment as he thought. At length he spoke again. "Do you know of the nephlim? Have you heard the stories of the children of angels and man?"

"Eh, there was a little something about it in church, but I really don't remember", Hammond said off-handedly as he made his way through the corpses that littered the ground. "So, you have some sort of plan for me, since you haven't killed me yet."

Satanel laughed at the absurdity of Hammond's comment—at his total lack of understanding. "Mortal trash! You never stop amusing me. Do you not see that this is only a vision? There is nothing I can do to hurt you . . . yet." Satanel smiled, as he thought of the ignorance of this human. How could God love these things more than he?

"Your pathetic little town is nothing more than a stepping stone in our path to victory! The world as you know it will soon come to an end! And, despite what you may have heard in your misguided Bible stories, no one is coming to save you! Read the scroll and find the man hidden in the courthouse. He will have the answers you seek, although I can't see how he will tell you anything—his light was extinguished long ago! Where once there was light, there now is darkness. Where once there was life, there now is dust."

"So, if you are against us, why are you telling me all of this?" Hammond asked. He grew more wary with each new revelation.

"Simpering fool, there is nothing you can do to stop us! The sins of your fathers have already condemned you. You, yourselves sin, even in the things you claim to have done to survive! I am sorry, my doomed, helpless friend, but you will have to suffer the judgments which are upon you—I can not, and will not, give you reprieve."

Hammond thought about the lying and liberating he had done just to get by. Now, in this awkward moment, he was beginning to find meaning in the phrase 'sins of the fathers'. It was a term he'd heard his entire life, but he never really got it until now. Did he ever really have a chance, or was he damned from the day he was born? If his father hadn't been a drunk, if his mother hadn't died, how different would his life have been? He wondered if there was a way to go back and fix it. He thought about asking the angel. Could Satanel change it? Surely there must be power there. He pondered it for a moment, then scoffed at the idea. While it was tempting to try to deal with Satanel, Hammond didn't trust him. And besides, deep down inside, he felt a growing determination to work things out for himself. Somehow he felt a strength and justification building within him. He answered quietly, but defiantly.

"I did what I had to, and I'd do it again. I won't go down without a fight, you know".

Satanel stopped and studied him for a moment. Hammond felt it coming, and braced for the retaliation. All of a sudden, Satanel appeared as his father, ready to strike him down. But instead, he smiled, dismissing the argument, and turned to continue down the path. Hammond, still feeling compelled, followed.

The two walked into what looked like a medieval castle. Walls of stone rose high, making the rooms feel cold and dark. An eerie breeze slipped through empty windows cased with iron fittings. Wet, rusty chains hung from the ceiling above their heads. Torches dimly lit the room and a blanket of soft green moss covered the walls and floor, thriving in the dark and the damp. Creatures in the darkness started to howl as the man and the angel passed them. In the flickering light, Hammond saw them gnawing on the broken body of one of the fallen angels. Satanel turned to face Hammond and sat down on a throne made of human bones. As Hammond stood there before him, the fear began to set in. The creatures began to gather in. Hammond could feel them closing in around him, lingering in the shadows, just out of the light.

"I have a surprise for you, my misguided pilgrim. Something to send you off, back to your pathetic little group of friends." Satanel waved as he spoke. Off to one side, a door swung wide open. As Hammond turned toward it, what he saw took his breath away.

The beast was ominous, huge in both stature and girth, with skin that looked slimy and scaly like that of a gigantic serpent. In the dim light, Hammond couldn't tell what color it was, but he knew it was dark. He could make out powerful legs and arms, blade-like wings, and what looked like snakes, writhing and hissing in every direction. As the demon drew near, he counted six pair of wings and seven snakeheads, which protruded from where the neck should have been. Each head had two faces, set with different snarling expressions.

"What is that?" Hammond almost screamed as he stumbled backwards. His feet tangled and he fell, hitting the stone floor solidly. As he lay there, panicked, still trying to pull himself away, he felt something dripping on his face. He ran a hand across his cheek and drew it back it to find it covered in blood. Blood and gore dripped everywhere from the chains in the ceiling, covering his hair, face, and arms. The foul, sticky ooze got in his mouth and ran down his throat. He choked out a scream as he tried to retreat from before the beast. It was to no avail, however, for in two quick lunges the monster was upon him, pinning and smothering him, heads snapping at him, grabbing and pulling at him on every side.

As warm fluid filled his throat it made him gag. Pain shot through his head, mouth, and down his back. He felt a death grip around his neck, the life being drained out of him as he was being drug downward and downward . . .

Chapter 11

ZERO

Hammond woke up fighting. He was being drug along the faded linoleum floor of the hospital corridor. He couldn't see. He jerked himself away from the hands of his captors and found himself face to face with . . . Bailey? She was standing there shaking, holding a bloody sword in her hand. As the world came back into focus, he realized the hands that were dragging him belonged to none other than his best friend, Tigg. He staggered to his feet, still choking and spitting blood from his mouth. The blood was his own—he must have hit his head and bit his tongue when he hit the floor, as he was still bleeding freely from his mouth and his tongue was starting to swell.

"Come on, Ham . . . that doctor thing is still coming!" Tigg yelled as he pushed him forward. Hammond was still dazed, and stopped in a moment of confusion.

"What's going on? How did I get here?" Then it all came rushing back. The trauma room, the man in scrubs, a flash of steel, and blood spewing everywhere. As Hammond looked around, he caught sight of the doctor approaching. The doc was covered in blood, and a ragged stump hung where his left arm used to be. Ham surmised that the flash of steel must have been the sword, and all the blood from the freshly severed limb. Could Bailey have really done that?

Stephie and Sara ran behind Tigg. Hammond took the sword carefully from Bailey and started covering the rear. He saw the one-armed doctor walking slowly behind them, yet with every step he seemed to be closing in on them.

Hammond's grandfather once told him that a man must choose his battles. He knew there would be a time to stand his ground, but it was not here or now. With his heart pounding in his bleeding ears, Hammond followed Tigg and the girls as they blew through the glass doors of the hospital. All of a sudden, Tigg stopped dead in his tracks and the others slammed into him.

A young police officer stood before them, his gun drawn. The nametag on his shirt read "Officer Jim Lerue". "Down on the ground! Now!" Tigg and the girls hit the ground. Hammond stood dumbfounded, staring at the cop. The officer leveled his weapon at Ham's heart. "Get down on the ground! Now . . . before I blow a hole in your chest!"

Hammond dropped, catching a rock in the gut.

"What is going on here?" The policeman demanded, as he studied the rag-tag group that lay on the ground in front of him. They looked as though they had just come from the battlefront of a major war.

"We gotta get out of here! They're gonna kill us!" Tigg shouted as he tried to look back to see if the demonic doctor had caught up.

"Who? There's no one behind you!" the officer said as he took the swords from Hammond and Tigg. "I want to know what is going on here, and you're going to tell me, so sit up, here, right now!" he commanded as he holstered his gun.

The officer was young and still new to both the force and the town. He was the only one on patrol at the moment—none of the other cops had shown up for work that morning. He figured they had just taken ill. There seemed to be something going around. As he drove around on his morning rounds he had noticed that the town seemed vacant. Stores were empty and locked, and the streets seemed oddly deserted. He had only seen a handful of people all morning, which was pretty unusual for this time of year.

Jim was a handsome young man with a decent build, generally friendly personality, but a fairly low IQ. His friends called him "Zero" because, they said, there was nothing going on in that brain of his. He was teased ruthlessly, but it didn't seem to faze him, and despite what most people thought about his intelligence, he was a good cop.

"They're coming! Just look at the hospital!" Hammond shouted impatiently. As he said this, Hammond himself turned to face the hospital and was greeted by an amazing sight.

He stared, dumbfounded, finding there was nothing wrong with the hospital. In fact, it looked almost new, as though it were finished only yesterday and no patients had ever passed through its doors.

"What the . . ." Before Hammond could finish his sentence the doctor with the southern drawl came out into the sunlight. He was wearing sunglasses and both arms were intact.

"Good afternoon, officer. 'Glad you're here. These kids just caused quite a stir in the hospital, there—broke some stuff, and disturbed a lot of people." The doctor waved his arm off-handedly to the hospital. "I'd press charges, but apparently there has been an outbreak of something like rabies infecting many of the animals around here, and these kids seem to have picked it up . . . at least they're acting that way."

"Look at his eyes! He is one of them." Bailey accused, interrupting the doctor as he spoke.

Zero thought for a moment, then turned to the doctor. "Let's see those eyes." Zero didn't really expect to see anything out of the ordinary, but he was more interested in making an impression on the pretty young lady in front of him. He had seen her around town many times before and secretly was quite attracted to her. This was his chance to get in good with her.

The doctor took off his sunglasses slowly. Stephanie yelped in shock as they all saw something that simply could not be—the doctor had eyes! They were extremely blood shot, but they were there! The teenagers stared, awestruck, as they began to question their own sanity. The doctor turned and looked at them, his eyes lolling in their sockets as he put the sunglasses back on. Now what were they supposed to do? There was no proof of their story and this stupid cop would never believe them, nor would he show any mercy to the two beat-up young men. The situation was becoming desperate.

Zero was wondering what to do with these hoodlums when a car pulled up. Hammond's father got out—he was surprisingly sober. For the first time in years, Edgar's clothes were clean and pressed, and his clean-shaven face smelled of Old Spice. He stood proud and tall, looking like he had before his wife had killed herself. Hammond hadn't seen him that way for many years.

"Hey officer, how are you?" Edgar asked in a friendly voice. "I'm Edgar Hammond. The boy with the long hair is my son, and I'd like to take him home if it's all the same to you."

"Well, have you got some ID, sir? I'd just like to confirm you're his parent." Zero said, trying to sound both intelligent and authoritative.

"I sure do there, buddy." Edgar said as he pulled his wallet out of his pocket. "And I'm sorry if the boys have been any trouble to you, officer, or the good doctor here. These kids just got a bit of a wild streak in 'em, I'm afraid." Edgar waved at Hammond to come with him, but Hammond just stood there, stunned.

"Well come on, sport. Your Mom's probably worried sick with you running off like that."

"My mother is dead! She killed herself!" Hammond shouted at Edgar as tears started to come.

"What the heck are you talking about, son?" Edgar asked incredulously as he looked at his crying son. "What's wrong with Eddie?" Edgar looked to the doctor for an answer.

"Well, Mister Hammond, he may have a disease that is going around, here—it seems to be carried mostly by animals. There is nothing we can do for them right now, so you might as well take him home. He should be fine in a few days. Just keep a close eye on him and make sure he doesn't do anything to hurt himself." The doctor said, looking at Edgar.

"I'm not going anywhere with you, you . . . monster!" Hammond yelled at Edgar. He held his ground, being driven by pure hatred for his father. "You're dead! And so is Mom! You won't get me without a fight!"

Edgar just looked at his son with a bemused look. "Why don't you call your mother? Would that make you feel better, Eddie?" Edgar produced a cell phone from his front pocket and handed it slowly to Hammond. "Just call home. She'll be wanting to know you're okay, anyway."

Hammond clicked on the button that said home, wondering if he truly had gone insane. Since when could his father afford a cell phone? The phone rang as Hammond nervously waited for the person on the other end to pick up, wondering if anyone would be there to pick it up at all. The wait was short, as a familiar, somewhat frantic voice answered—it was his mother!

"Edgar, did you find Eddie?" The voice asked in a worried tone. "Edgar, answer me!"

Hammond was so stunned at hearing his mother's voice that he couldn't say anything at first. At length he finally responded. "M-mom? It's me, Hammond." He thought for a moment about when his mother was alive and everybody called him Eddie. He hated it, but they called him that, anyway. "I mean, it's me—Eddie", he said in a quivering voice.

Hammond's eyes welled up with tears as her voice filled his ears, his mind, and every empty place in his heart. He was so happy to hear his mother's voice that all thoughts of the evil presence vanished. As he talked to her, years of suffering seemed to melt away and he felt a love he had not felt for many years. As he returned the phone to his father, Hammond turned and looked at Tigg, choking back a sob.

"It was all a bad dream Tigger!" Hammond shouted in joy. "She didn't die! We are just sick, like the doctor said. It was all a hallucination."

Before Tigg could say anything, Edgar handed the phone to him and told him that the rest of them had better let their parents know that they were okay. Tigg was the first to call and, much to his surprise, his mother answered and told him she would pick him up at the police station. Next was Sara—her parents said pretty much the same thing. And so it went with the others, too.

Hammond was elated, but before they left, he turned to Edgar and asked, "Can Bailey come too, Dad?" A broad smile spread across his face.

"She needs to call her folks and make sure it's okay." Edgar said, once again pulling the cell phone from his pocket and handing it to Bailey.

Bailey called her parents with some uncertainty. The explanation of the whole thing had not seemed adequate to her. Something seemed odd and out of place, but the second her father answered, she felt at ease.

"Daddy, is that you?" Bailey asked.

"Yes, honey. What's wrong? You sound upset. Are you okay, sweetie?" Her dad asked in concerned tone of voice.

"I'm fine, Daddy. I just had a bad night, I guess". Bailey still did not understand, but it must have all been some strange hallucination, because everything seemed normal now, if not better. "Can I go to my friend Hammond's house for a little while?" She asked a little sheepishly.

"Are his parents going to be there?"

"Yes, Daddy. His dad is taking us".

With that, her father gave his permission and she walked with Hammond and Edgar to the LeMans. The car seemed almost new as they approached it. On the inside, however, Hammond's blood still covered the front seat. Hammond felt his arm—the rough ridges of the stitches were still there. At least he wasn't totally crazy. He helped Bailey into the back seat and then got in the front passenger seat.

Edgar talked to everyone before leaving, expressing his concern for the other teens. The officer and the doctor both assured him that the children would be fine. With that, he opened the door and started to get inside. Hammond flinched as Edgar got into the car. He knew as soon as his father saw the blood on the seat, he was as good as dead. But instead, Edgar just looked at Hammond for a moment, and then sat down.

"First of all, are you alright, son?" He asked, looking intensely at Hammond through his sunglasses. Hammond just nodded in fear of what might be next. "Second, I would appreciate it if you fueled up the car when you're done using it."

Without another word, Edgar started the car with a rumble and they were on their way. Hammond kept looking back at Bailey, smiling as they made their way through the almost deserted town. Bailey smiled back at him. She was happy with the fact that Hammond, for the first time, seemed like he was her own age. Edgar just drove, looking straight ahead, whistling. Had Hammond thought about it, he would have recognized the song, but that didn't matter. All he knew was that his father was happy, and so was he.

The car made its way to the street that Hammond had walked along every day of his life. Today, things seemed different. The street didn't seem so . . . well, poor. Every house on the block was clean and well kept, like some upper-class suburban neighborhood. No tires or engine blocks littering the streets—somehow, even Jeff Davis' beat-up old Ford looked new. It was as though the neighborhood had never degenerated into a slum and the mine that was this town's livelihood had never closed. But the most shocking thing to Hammond was when he saw his own house. It was well taken-care-of and everything looked alive and pristine. As they pulled into the driveway, something struck him as odd—the garage door he had crashed through last night, or at least thought he had crashed through, was in perfect order, with fresh white paint and no broken windows.

For a mid-summer's day, the air was oddly cold as Hammond got out of the car and then helped Bailey out. A small amount of premature aging seemed to have returned to his face, but he still smiled at her with a look of love and relief. Even if last night was all in his head, it didn't change the way he felt about her. He was glad she was with him.

He casually took her hand as they made their way up the walk and to the stairs, then onto the porch—the porch he was sure his father had never finished. He took a deep breath and pulled Bailey close to him. She put up no resistance as she closed into his embrace. The doubts were growing inside of him, and he had some serious reservation about the situation he was about to face inside, but the one thing he knew for sure was that he felt better when she was close to him.

Hammond started to pull away as he reached for the door, but Bailey stopped him and pulled him back. "I love you, Hammond." She said softly, as she put her hand on his face. "No matter what happens, I want you to know that I love you, and I hope you feel the same way about me".

A moment of uncertainty lingered as Hammond looked at her in silence, then looked away. All doubt about the subject quickly disappeared, however, as Hammond turned back to her, leaned forward, and gently kissed her on the lips.

"I love you too . . . I think I've felt it since the moment I first saw you in the town square", Hammond confessed in an unusual moment of openness. He hadn't shared his deeper feelings with anyone in a long, long time. "I'm glad you came with me".

They both turned to go inside. Hammond's mind raced as he stood there, staring at the new glass windows with gold etching. The view was strange to him. Was this the dream, or had his whole life before this been the dream? The thought consumed him as he gripped the new brass door handle. This was the moment of truth. He pushed the handle down and he and Bailey made their way across the threshold into the Hammond home.

Chapter 12

A Mother's Love

T he carpet in the living room was clean and fresh, marked only by the telltale patterns of a recent vacuuming. The smell of bacon and eggs filled the house as Edgar Hammond sat in his easy chair reading the morning paper while his wife, Patricia, fixed breakfast in the kitchen. Everything seemed right and perfect, which was very uncharacteristic of the Hammond household.

Ham made his way through the house slowly; the gentle hum of the ceiling fan threw him off slightly. Bailey stayed close behind him, still clutching his hand tightly. Mrs. Hammond came in with a tray of drinks to greet her son and his new girl.

"Hey, Eddie—who's your friend?" She asked in that sweet, familiar voice that Hammond had missed so badly. "Would you kids like some chocolate milk?" She asked with a smile.

Hammond hadn't drunk milk since he was a child and had no real urge to drink it now. So he waved his hand in a dismissive gesture and instead hugged his mother so hard that she almost dropped the tray. His mother had an incredible look of sorrow in her eyes as her only son held her tight. She was hiding something, but Hammond dismissed it as merely the shadow of worry left over from her son disappearing the night before. The moment could not have been more perfect, considering the bazaar events of the last few hours and the fact that it had somehow all ended in the loving embrace of his mother. The only thing dampening the moment were the words of Reverend Bachman repeating in his head: "Suicides go to Hell."

Patricia led the two teenagers into the kitchen where a hot plate of bacon and eggs was placed in front of them. Bailey looked sweetly into Hammond's eyes, as she picked at the food in front of her. She was hungry, but still feeling a little uneasy about the whole situation and found it hard to eat. She was about to say something to Hammond when his father walked in.

Still wearing his sunglasses, Edgar came into the kitchen and kissed Patricia before sitting down at the wood-skirted glass table where the two teens were seated.

"So, how are you feeling, sport? You haven't properly introduced us to your lovely friend here." He gestured to Bailey.

"Oh yeah." Hammond said coming out of the daze he was falling into. "Mom, Dad, this is Bailey. Bailey, this is my mom and dad."

Hammond's mother stood quietly in the corner as she barely acknowledged Bailey with an offhanded wave. Her stare was still focused on her son. She still had a distraught look on her face and it was beginning to concern Hammond. The last time he saw that look in his mother's face was the day he thought she had killed herself. Patricia moved nervously back and forth in the kitchen as though she wanted to say something, but couldn't. Every time Hammond thought she was going to, she just busied herself with another meaningless task. Edgar, noticing this, told her to get the kids some desert.

"Patricia, these kids don't want breakfast—they want sweets. Why don't you be a dear and get them something more appetizing?" Edgar's words were kind, but his voice seemed a bit more hollow than it had earlier.

"Yes, honey. I have some cake and brownies. I'll get them right away." Patricia's voice also seemed a little cold, but sounded more fearful than anything.

The strangeness of the whole scene was finally starting to get to Hammond as he started to awaken from his euphoric state. The quiet calm and perfect cleanliness of the house was so uncharacteristic of what Hammond had known his whole life. His mother now seemed to be more of a presence than a person, and Edgar was more of a thing than a man. Hammond looked to Bailey for some form of confirmation that things were not as they seemed, but was unable to make eye contact. It was as if a strange fog was trying to once again cover Hammond's thoughts, but he shook it off as he started to focus on the subtle pain in his hand. The illusions were melting away from before him. He looked at his mother for hope when his own was failing, but she just stood there. For the first time he noticed a horrible sadness creeping across her face, as once again, echoing over and over in his mind were the words "Suicides go to Hell".

Edgar shifted uneasily as he watched the look on his son's face turn from bliss to skepticism. The table started to shake as Hammond's mother made her way across the room. Then the scene turned grisly as Edgar stood and turned, only to find a kitchen knife plunged into his chest. Patricia stood there with him, shaking and looking horrified as Edgar's face contorted into a vicious scowl. Bailey screamed as the white walls faded into the tattered, stained look they normally had, and the clean carpet and linoleum gave way to the rotting, dirty decay of the old wooden floor. As the illusion faded, the two kids were left to face the gruesome reality of the scene.

It was far worse than anything Bailey or Hammond could have imagined. They now stood face to face with true terror and it was like nothing they had ever seen before. Darkness filled the room as if the sun had been simply snuffed out; the only light that remained was the blood-red hue of a dying moon. Hammond realized this nightmare was only the beginning, and he wondered if he would be strong enough to survive it. For the first time, they caught a glimpse of what they were truly up against.

The creature formerly known as Edgar Hammond now stood towering over Patricia. The stalking darkness had taken on a form that was both amazing and hideous. It stood skulking in the dim light, its contorted legs bent so as not to reveal its full height. At the end of each of these wet, deformed legs were three large talons. Horn-like bones protruded from its back and neck, all the way up its slender, distorted body, which joined to a head that could only be described as half-human, half-reptilian. Its scaly gray skin was covered in slimy wetness, the putrid smell of which now filled the room. Its torn lips were stretched over three rows of jagged, razor sharp teeth. Instead of eyes, two sets of fangs protruded from its sockets, both with forked tongues wafting in and out, testing the air like a snake would. Atop its head were two long, black horns that curled down to Hell, as if to mock Heaven itself.

The beast let out a guttural scream as one of its long, bony-fingered hands wrapped around Patricia's neck. As it tightened its grip on her throat, she screamed for her only son to run, but Hammond was unable to move, as if his feet were embedded in concrete. The beast's head turned all the way around to face Hammond, its teeth chattering and tongues whipping about wildly. Bailey pulled at Hammond's arm as she shrieked in terror, but to no avail. Hammond stayed planted where he was.

With a grotesque cracking sound, the creature distended his jaw, first one side and then the other, as its maw grew to three times its original size. Its head spun back around as it bent Patricia in half, then swallowed her whole.

"She should have listened! We offered to restore her life, and she just threw it back at us. She will now suffer eternal punishment!" The thing hissed as it turned its attention to the two frightened teenagers, still frozen in place. "We offered you everything as well—every desire of your heart, yet you spurned our generous gift. We know you intend to stand in our way, and if we cannot seduce you, we will destroy you!"

The house shook wildly as the walls cracked and separated, leaving huge, gaping holes. Skinless, muscular arms reached out of the wall trying to grab them. Bailey gripped Hammond tighter as she tried to stay out of their reach. As the cracks widened, they revealed the bodies of men and women in various stages of evisceration, groaning in agony as they tried to reach the frightened teens.

Hammond was shaken from his trance as the floor beneath his feet split, shooting a lightning bolt-like crack between his legs, across the floor, and up the wall. The fiery light emanating from the cracks in the floor and the wall was all that defied the darkness of the room. Bailey and Hammond negotiated their way through the gauntlet of cracks as they tried to make their escape. Surprisingly, the beast did not pursue them—it just stood and watched in arrogant amusement as the two teens struggled towards the door.

"You will not escape us! You will die tonight!" The thing howled, taunting and laughing.

The tortured souls now surrounded them as they tried in desperation to find a way out. The floor beneath them continued to collapse and each path they tried turned into a dead end. Hammond shoved one of the approaching ghouls away, but as he did, his hands sank deep into its soft flesh. As he pulled them out, they burned from the acid-like blood of the creature. He wiped them madly on his shirt to rid himself of the burning slime. Hammond looked around in desperation but could find no way out. All he could see was a splash of red through the grime-covered window. Then it came to him . . . the window!

"Grab on to me, hon, and don't let go. This could hurt—a lot!"

"What are you doing, Ham?"

"I'm getting us out of here!" Hammond yelled as he threw Bailey and himself backward through the window.

Hammond grimaced in pain as he hit the deck, driving shards of glass into his back and shoulders. He lay there with Bailey on top of him for a moment, but the deck was already starting to split, and Hammond felt it giving way. He quickly threw Bailey off of him as the deck collapsed in the middle and he slid down towards the void. His fingernails gouged into the planking, ripping and breaking as he clawed and scratched, desperately trying to save himself.

"Bailey! Help!" He shouted.

Bailey, having been knocked almost unconscious by the fall through the window, sat up in a daze, unaware of Hammond's plea for help. Hammond continued to flail and struggle, but without anything to grab on to, he continued to slide. Then, in desperation, he produced the butterfly knife from his back pocket and stabbed it through his slipping hand, pinning it to the wooden planking of the deck. He dangled there for what seemed like an eternity, out of strength, exhausted from the struggle, and ready to give up. Pinning his hand to the plank seemed like a good idea at the time, but now he could feel the skin and muscle in his hand begin to tear. He was ready to accept defeat, just to end the pain and suffering, when he saw a beautiful dark-haired angel reaching toward him.

Bailey grabbed Hammond by the wrist and pulled. The blood and sweat covering his hand made it impossible to get a good grip, and she repeatedly lost hold. Then she tried to pull on his dangling body, but he was too heavy for her to lift. All of a sudden, she heard whistling behind her. She turned her head slightly to see Tigg standing there. Without warning, Hammond reached up and grabbed her shoulder, scaring her half to death. She wrenched beneath his weight, yelling for Tigg to help, but he just stood there, whistling. Hammond got a knee up onto the deck as he pulled the knife from his pinned hand, and without a second's hesitation, threw it, hitting Tigg squarely between the eyes. Tigg fell backward, hitting the ground, dead. Hammond pulled himself up to a stand, and rolling his head in pain, stumbled over to the lifeless body of his best friend.

"What did you do?" Bailey screamed as she pounded on Hammond's back. "He was your best friend! What is wrong with you?" Bailey was now sobbing as she continued to hit him.

Hammond bent over the corpse of Tigg, reached down and removed the knife from his head. Then he turned around and lifted the head slightly so that Bailey could see his face.

"We have a problem . . ."

Chapter 13

STRANGE THINGS AFOOT

Tigger sat restlessly in the back of the police car as Zero finished questioning Sara. He was worried about his friend because the whole rabid animal story was not holding water for him. Tigg didn't believe for one moment that they were all seeing the same thing like some sort of mass hysteria. He still remembered the attack of his dog quite vividly, and that animal was not rabid. It was something else . . . something not of this world . . . something that should not be. All these thoughts raced through his mind as he anxiously awaited Sara and Stephie, wanting to know if either of them felt the same way.

He sat there, stewing, becoming more and more frustrated with the situation. He didn't trust Zero, and he didn't like being held captive by the village idiot, but what he hated most was the fact that he could do nothing to defend himself or the girls while he was locked up in the back seat of this old, worn-out police car.

It wasn't long before Zero returned with the girls and started loading them into the back seat with Tigg.

"No funny business, now, you kids" Zero said in his most authoritative tone.

"I ain't a kid, you retard!" As the words came out of his mouth, all Tigg could think was, "Oh no, I've become Hammond"!

"What did you just say to me, pal?"

"And I ain't your pal, either, butch."

Sara was shocked by the way Tigg had confronted the officer. She was appalled, but impressed at the same time. This toughness was a side of him she had never seen before. Tigg had always been so quiet and reserved—she sort of liked his stronger side. Stephie just sat quietly, not wanting to make an already volatile situation worse.

Zero felt bad for the teens, but he didn't let on. He felt that if they were going to respect him as an authority figure, they shouldn't see him as weak. He climbed into the patrol car wondering exactly what he was going to say to them. There was definitely something wrong in this quiet little town, and he didn't buy into the doctor's story, either. He was also sure these kids knew more than they were telling.

Zero liked to do things "by the book", and his car, although the oldest on the force, was very clean and well kept. It smelled like one of those air fresheners from the car wash—vanilla, or mint, or maybe both. He sat in the driver's seat trying to bring up dispatch on the radio, but all he got was a bunch of static. It didn't bode well for him.

Tigg shifted uneasily in his seat—he was tired and in pain. He looked over at Sara who now had her hand on his leg. She was so beautiful that it seemed unfair. He finally gets to spend time with the girl of his dreams, and it has to be in this nightmare . . . did it take the end of the world for him to finally have his dreams fulfilled?

Stephie just sat watching the two in quiet contemplation, as she had no one of her own to comfort her through these dark and terrible events. Feelings of loneliness set in as she watched the two love-struck teenagers next to her. She wanted that, too, but there was no one in her life other than her parents who ever really loved her. She realized that whether it was sickness or something truly evil, she was different now and her life had been changed forever. The events of the last 24 hours had shown her just how bad, how evil things could be. Her notion of an innocent world had been ripped away, and she didn't think she could ever go back to the way she had been before: partying with her college friends, idly chatting, gossiping, chasing guys, and drinking beer. Her cares from then seemed so trivial now, and life seemed so much more serious—so much more desperate.

Zero started the car. The tension built inside him as he thought about the empty town he would have to navigate on the way to the police station. He was a brave enough man, but he lacked self-confidence. His fear wasn't in facing something evil, but in not having someone to lead him. Zero was the follower type, and if no one was answering his radio calls it meant only one thing: he would have to make some tough decisions on his own. The world seemed a lot bigger and scarier with no one to guide him.

The car pulled out of the hospital parking lot and started through the empty streets. No one seemed to be around, yet it felt like the buildings themselves were staring at them, mockingly, as if they knew some dirty little secret they intended use against them. The town was swallowed up in an eerie silence, permeating even the trees and grass. The breeze that constantly blew through Convict Grade was dead still. Trees no longer swayed; plants were dying. Even the Sun seemed to be fading—growing dimmer by the minute—its normal bright yellow hue turning a deep, brilliant orange. Huge black spots blocked the light and every now and then a meteor could be seen streaking across the darkened sky.

As Tigg looked around the empty town, the few people he saw seemed as if they came from another planet. He couldn't help but smile as he thought of the song "People are Strange" by The Doors.

"I bet even Jim Morrison himself hasn't seen stuff as weird as this" he thought out loud, which brought on quiet laughter from the two girls and even a chuckle from Zero. The thought was so random that Tigg himself started to laugh.

Though the comment eased the tension a little, everyone was still uneasy. The Sun, looking like a dying star, was casting only a dim light on the streets of Convict Grade, which were now filling with fog. As they got closer to the center of town, they started to see wrecked cars littering the streets on both sides. Small fires burned here and there where grass and garbage cans had been ignited. The sidewalks were littered with empty clothing and discarded personal items. Whatever had happened to them the previous night must have happened to the whole town. The extent of the damage was now becoming evident—the signs of chaos and destruction were everywhere. "This couldn't have happened all in one night" thought Tigg. "It would take an army to create this much havoc".

As they made their way through the maze of garbage, fires, and abandoned cars, they moved slower and slower—it was becoming nearly impossible to get through. A man and a woman were making out on top of a car as they passed. To Tigg it was like a train wreck—he didn't want to stare, but he couldn't look away. They were caught up in passion, oblivious to the situation around them. Tigg looked at Sara and smiled deviously. She looked out the window and saw what he was smiling at and coyly slapped his arm.

"Don't get any ideas, mister!" she said, playing hard-to-get. As he looked back through the window to see more of the act being played out on the car hood, the scene suddenly turned from passion to horror. He watched in disbelief as the man's jaw dropped down, exposing several rows of jagged teeth and a long, serpent-like tongue. In an instant, he savagely mauled his surprised and horrified victim, tearing the flesh from her neck and snuffing out her life, like a lion would its prey. The thing then snapped its mouth shut, turned slowly, and smiled darkly at Tigg.

Tigg turned and looked at Sara for confirmation of what he had just seen, but she had not been watching. She was staring out the front through the windshield. Watching the gruesome scene behind, he hadn't noticed that they had stopped. In front of the car stood a little girl, holding what looked like a dead cat. It was skinned, so positive identification of the species was impossible. She stood with her head cocked to one side, staring at them, if that were possible, with empty eye sockets. It looked as though she was trying to speak to them, but they couldn't hear what she was saying. Zero opened his door and started to get out to check on the child. The scene was all too familiar to Stephie, as she tried to scream at Zero to stop. But the return of the nightmarish spectacle upset and terrified her so much that all that came out was an inaudible squeak.

Stephie's silent warning went unheeded as Zero stepped out, fastening his nightstick to his belt. He walked towards the little girl who stood rocking with the dead cat in her arms. She continued whispering something, which the officer still couldn't make out. Zero cautiously approached the little girl, who backed away, somewhat playfully. He put both of his hands up where she could see them in a sign that he meant her no harm. The little girl giggled and stepped back again as if it were a game.

"Come on, honey, I'm not going to hurt you." Zero said in a calm voice, "It isn't safe here, sweetie—you'll have to come with us."

As the child looked up at him, Zero got a clear view of the empty orbital sockets, and he stumbled back as the child giggled and stepped toward him. He tripped on something in the street, falling backward. As he clamored to his knees, trying to get up, he found himself face to face with the little girl. She giggled again, then spoke, but the voice was not hers.

"When the light of man is extinguished, only darkness will remain. And in the darkness, he has found his true domain."

The girl giggled again and put her hand on Zero's face. It was deathly cold. She giggled again, and then exploded into a dry, black mist. Zero fumbled to his feet, ran back to the patrol car, and dove in. Without saying a word to the frightened teens, he threw the car into gear and jammed down the gas pedal, making the tires spin wildly. From the back seat, they pleaded for information and begged him to slow down, but the officer was too scared to listen. The car whipped around the corner where Zero lost control, tires squealing as they spun around to face the same direction they had just come from. The driver's side of the vehicle hit the wall of Carl's Laundry, situated only three blocks from the police station. Tigg was thrown into the two girls as the window next to him shattered, sending a spray of glass onto the disheveled teens. Sara seemed to be knocked senseless, and Stephie's head went through the passenger window before they finally came to a stop. Stephie sat holding her bloody head, shaking Sara, looking for any sign of life, but getting no response.

Zero just sat there frozen in the driver's seat, still shaking from the accident. Tigg screamed at him to let them out, which brought Zero back to reality. He climbed out the passenger door and let Tigg and Stephie out of the twisted metal coffin he had unwittingly created for them.

"I'm so sorry guys, I just, well . . . look, you didn't see or hear what I did, so you wouldn't understand" Zero snapped at the shook-up kids, knowing it was all his fault. "Old Zero messes things up yet again—God, I am so stupid!" he yelled at himself.

"I think he already knows that—you don't have to tell him." Sara said out of nowhere. She had finally come to and was stumbling out of the car.

"Um, guys—we have bigger problems to worry about!" Tigg pointed up at the sky, which was growing darker with every passing moment. The sun was almost completely blotted out by dark spots; the strange effect made the sun appear to be several times its normal size and seemed to fill the sky above them. A cloudless rain formed out of nowhere, soaking the small town, and a meteor shower filled the darkened sky. With the skies darkening, people started to come out from the shadows of the small town. Shadows moved around them in the failing light, as the group gathered in closer to each other.

"I strongly suggest that we get out of here!" Stephie whispered excitedly.

"Um, yeah, definitely." Tigg said as he shook Zero. "Take us to the cop shop, man. At least we can lock that place down".

Zero hesitated as he made his way forward. "Alright, follow me and stay close."

He pulled the Glock from his belt and took the safety off. Tigg stopped and ran back to the battered police car. He hesitated for a minute, then reached in through the passenger door and grabbed the shotgun from in-between the seats. He searched the glove box for ammunition and ran back to the others. The gun had a trigger lock on it so he hoped that Zero had the keys or the gun would be useless. Without a word Zero grabbed the keys from the hook on his belt and tossed them to Tigg.

"It's the short fat one. Make sure I get those back. Strictly speaking, you're not supposed to touch that."

Tigg took off the trigger lock and tossed the keys back to Zero with a nod of respect. Zero nodded back and placed the keys back onto his key ring as they started toward the police station. The rain was pouring down pretty hard, forcing them to slow their pace to a brisk walk. Tigg loaded the shotgun carefully as he tried to keep pace with the others. He couldn't afford to drop even one of the precious shells. The number of shadowy figures gathering around them grew as they tried to stay in the few places still lit by the dying sun.

The ground shook as an earthquake tore through the already besieged neighborhood. Buildings shook and pieces came crashing down around them as they pressed forward, dodging the fallen debris as they went. Sara screamed as a power line fell and whipped around on the wet ground in front of her. Sparks danced across the ground with flashes of white light that lit up the dark shadows of the sidewalks. In one of the flashes Stephie caught sight of a man crawling toward them with his legs twisted up like a disgusting human pretzel. With every flash of the power line, she saw the thing advancing toward them. In a flash of brilliance, which was uncommon for him, Zero yelled out to Sara.

"Jump over it—your shoes are rubber so you won't get electrocuted, I promise! Just move quickly and don't let it touch you anywhere above your shoes."

"What would you know about this sort of thing? I am surprised you can even tie your shoes in the morning."

"Trust me, my dad was an electrician, just do it—now!"

Sara gathered her strength, waited for the right instant, and then leaped over the slithering line. She barley made it over as the line flew up just behind her.

"Man, I'm glad your daddy was an electrician, Zero, or my goose would have been cooked for sure!"

"He wasn't—I just had to get you to jump."

Sara looked at Zero incredulously as he turned and continued forward. He was proving to be smarter than she thought. Stephie was also looking at Zero with some newfound admiration for his clever treachery.

They could see the lights of the police station in the distance. It had a backup generator, so they knew it should be a safe, well-lit place. A shot rang out from somewhere out in front of them and they heard screaming, then silence. Tigg instinctively cocked the shotgun as he became aware that someone was alive, or at least had been . . . He figured he had the upper hand, seeing as these things didn't seem to use guns. The sunlight had now faded to darkness and the rain was taking on a strange thick feel to it. The creatures lurking in the shadows continued to close in around them, and the fleeting streaks of the meteor shower were becoming the only thing lighting their way.

"Run—it's an ambush! Get out of there!" a familiar voice broke the silence. "They're surrounding you—I can see them! Go, go, go!" The voice shouted with such urgency that Zero pushed the girls forward and dropped his head, running towards the voice. Tigg brought up the rear, running as fast as he could, feeling a number of hands scratching at his back as they seemed to break through some invisible boundary. In front of him, Sara started to slow down. Tigg scooped her up in a fireman's carry and pumped his legs as hard as he could. The rain now clouded his vision, becoming a strange sort of red mist. He continued to run as his heart pounded in his ears . . . He ran for his life, and for Sara's—in a desperate race to escape the demons that had swallowed up his once-happy town.

Chapter 14

TOM'S HARDWARE

Hammond stood over the lifeless body of Tigg, holding the head up for Bailey to see.

"Tigg's eyes are brown, not blue. I have no idea who or what this is, but it's not Tigg."

Bailey sat down and began to sob, partly as a release from the grueling experience she had just been through, and partly because she felt bad for wrongfully beating on the already bruised and battered Hammond. She started to say something—to apologize, but Hammond just raised his hand and limped away toward the driveway. She followed him nervously, not knowing whether or not he wanted her to follow him, but she really had no choice. He was her only chance for survival. As she looked at his bleeding, exposed back, she felt a pain in her soul that she hadn't ever really felt before—a feeling of guilt and responsibility for someone else's pain.

Hammond mustered a smile for Bailey. She had not meant to hurt him and he understood that. He grabbed the knapsack out of the car and rummaged through it, pulling out a single bullet. Bailey watched curiously as he bit down on the bullet end and pulled it from the casing. He then dumped the contents of the shell into the bloody hole in his hand. He pulled his cigarettes and lighter out of his pocket and ignited the powder on his hand. As it flashed, Hammond howled in pain. Once the pain subsided, he lit a cigarette and sat back to rest for a minute.

"Those things will kill you, Ham—you know that, don't you?"

"Sorry hon, but right now I think lung cancer and low birth-weight are the least of my problems."

They both laughed as Hammond removed the tattered remains of his shirt. He then reached back into the knapsack, pulling out a needle and the Demerol he had taken from the hospital, and shot it into his shaking arm. He also pocketed a bottle of pills that Bailey didn't recognize, but she wasn't going to ask him about them given his current situation. When Hammond set down his jacket, something fell out of the pocket. It looked like a rolled up treasure map. Bailey bent down and picked it up.

"What's this?" she asked Hammond who was leaning over the car.

"That's not important right now. I need you to do something for me. I know you won't want to, but you have to."

"Just tell me what you want, hon—I'll do it."

"I need you to pick the glass out of my back."

Hammond reached under the seat and pulled out the bottle of Jack Daniels that the real Edgar Hammond had always kept there for "emergencies".

"First, wash my back with this, then pull out the glass and wash it again."

Bailey did as he asked, fighting off the urge to cry as she saw the bruises and bloody tears in his flesh. It was all she could do to hold herself together as she operated on him. Luckily, most of the pieces were large and came out easily; the ones that were small were harder to remove. She had to dig her fingers into the wounds to remove these. Hammond pushed in the car lighter as Bailey performed her slow and delicate work. When the lighter popped out, he handed it back to her.

"Now, I need you to burn the wounds closed—any big ones that are bleeding a lot. You need to do it fast, before the lighter cools down."

Bailey took the lighter and scorched the open wounds as fast as she could, but Hammond had to reheat the lighter three more times before she was finished.

With the crude surgery completed, Hammond took Bailey by the hand as he looked up at the sky. Day was quickly turning into night as the sun seemed to die from the inside out. "So it comes to this", he thought as he watched the meteors streak across the darkening sky.

"What do we do now?" She quietly asked Hammond, not really expecting him to answer her.

"Well, we should probably get to the police station. It's four blocks that way." He pointed in the direction he meant for them to go, and started off, limping in pain with every step.

"Why don't we take the car?"

"Well, the keys are in the house. If you want to go and get them, be my guest . . . I'll wait out here."

"Funny." She said as she gave him a dirty look.

"We need to stop at Tom's Hardware on the way—stock up on supplies. I have a feeling this nightmare is only beginning."

"What is happening here? What do you know that you're not telling me?"

"I will tell you once I figure it out. I have an idea, but there is no sense in getting you all worked up over it if I'm wrong."

"What's that supposed to mean? If you are implying that women overreact, I will kick your butt!"

Hammond grinned. "You already did that, remember?"

With a pang of guilt Bailey fell silent. Hammond threw her the knapsack and beckoned her to follow him. The two headed out, walking fast but cautiously, watching the shadows as they made their way down the street towards Tom's Hardware. Everything was deathly quiet, which disturbed Hammond greatly. Why wasn't the thing inside the house following them? What was happening to the sun? These questions would have to wait for now, as they had to focus on getting to the police station alive and without attracting too much attention.

The streets were empty except for the occasional rustle and movements in the dark places along the way. The scene was one of chaos—the town had gone through some immense changes from the illusion that was presented to them earlier. Jeff Davis' old Ford, that only an hour ago seemed brand new, sat ablaze in his driveway with the front end buried deep into the garage door. Blood stains randomly blotted the sidewalk along the way as they moved to the next block. Bailey looked into the window of a house as they passed and a pair of glowing red eyes stared back at her, making her jump closer to Hammond. The town lost all of its former charm and was now little more than a hand away from hell.

Bailey nervously fumbled with the roll of paper that had fallen from Hammond's jacket pocket as they crossed the street to Tom's Hardware Store. There were shadows crossing back and forth in front of the building. They seemed to be sniffing the air like dogs looking for food. The sky continued to darken and suddenly rain poured down on them from out of nowhere, it seemed, for there was not a cloud in the sky. Hammond looked nervously at the sky as if the rain and sun were confirming something he had already expected.

"We'll have to find another way in—we don't want those things to know we are in there. If my suspicions are correct, we don't have much time to get supplies and get to the police station, that is, if it's still standing when we get there."

"What is going on, Hammond? I'm scared and you know something that you're not telling me. I want to know what it is right now!"

"I don't really know, but if it is what I think it is, we will have to get what we need and make it to the police station quick, or we probably won't live to see another sunrise—that is, if there ever is another one to see . . ."

The cryptic way that Hammond kept talking was really bothering her, but Bailey knew he was right, and she could get the answers from him later. They made a wide circle into the ally that led behind Tom's. Creatures were moving all around them in the shadows, but they would not come into the areas of sunlight that still remained. Bailey heard a horrible crunching sound beneath her feet but she dared not look down. It felt like the ground was moving. A terrible stench came from the shadows as they drew closer to the hardware store. It did not take long before they found the source of the foul odor. Sitting on the stairs of one of the buildings was the maggot-infested corpse of a young girl holding a lifeless cat. Bailey felt so bad for the little girl. The cat was probably what killed her and she clearly loved it. As they passed the corpse Bailey took off her jacket and gently placed it over the head of the child.

"May the Lord take you into his loving arms."

"I don't think he'll be visiting this town any time soon, love. This is it—we're here."

Hammond stopped at the door and studied it to see if there was any way to get in without drawing too much attention to them.

"Try the handle, honey." Bailey said, trying to be helpful.

Hammond looked at her as though she was retarded. He made a big show of placing his hand on the door handle and turning it. With no effort the door swung open giving them access to the store.

"What kind of idiot leaves the back door to their business open?" Hammond said as Bailey smiled triumphantly at him.

"Oh shut up—let's go."

Bailey followed Hammond into the store. Hammond raised his hand for her to stop as he peeked quickly around the corner to see if anyone was there. He didn't see anyone, but he had learned from experience that just because you can't see something doesn't mean it's not there. He pulled the last can of Mountain Dew from Tigg's knapsack and tossed it into the opposite side of the room. There was a loud pop and fizzing sound as the can broke open and sprayed everywhere. He waited to see if anyone or anything would come and investigate. After a few moments with no more sound or sign of movement, he decided it was safe and motioned Bailey forward.

The outside windows had reflective glass so Hammond wasn't too concerned about being seen from the street; however, he was concerned about locking the doors. He pointed to the door behind them and motioned for Bailey to lock it while he cautiously made his way to the front door to do the same. As he reached the door he expected to see the things that were stalking around in front of the store through the one way glass, but all he saw were shadows moving back and forth with nothing there to cast them. He slowly turned the lock so as not to alert anything outside. He jumped as something touched his shoulder. He turned swinging his fist and almost plowed it into Bailey's beautiful face. She was barely able to duck out of the way as his fist came within inches of hitting her in the nose.

"I'm sorry, hon—you scared me. I thought you were one of them."

"It's alright. Even if you had hit me, I figure you owed me one."

Hammond smiled and moved past her, surveying the store. In a small town the hardware store was more of an all-purpose outlet than just a hardware store, and it served his purposes just fine. He grabbed a shirt off of the rack that had a picture of two bears picking their teeth saying; "Send more tourists—the last ones were delicious!" It wasn't Hammond's first choice for clothing, but it would have to suffice. Then he pulled a long duster off of one of the racks and put it on. The jacket looked quite good on him, but the real reason he chose it was that it would both hold and conceal items he needed.

"I'll hit the gun cabinet, and you find me a Bible and some food and water. Fill up the knapsack, and get another if you need it."

"What's the Bible for?"

"I'll explain later. Just do it, please!"

Hammond walked over to the gun case and tried to break the glass but it wouldn't give.

"Try the cash register." Bailey said from the section where Tom had kept the freeze-dried food.

"I'm on it." Hammond smiled at her "You're so smart, hon."

He picked up the cash register and threw it at the cabinet, shattering the glass doors.

"You're obviously not as smart as I thought you were."

"What's that supposed to mean?" Hammond asked looking rather offended by her comment.

Bailey walked over to the smashed gun cabinet in front of him, reached in and pushed the "No Sale" button on the register. The drawer popped opened, revealing the key to the gun case sitting in the extra change slot. She grabbed it and dangled it in front of Hammond, smiling.

He couldn't think of anything to say, so he just huffed, turned around, and started sifting through the broken glass and handguns. He found the ones he was after—two nickel-plated Desert Eagles. He had been in the store more than once admiring them, and now they were his.

"Sorry Tom—I told you they would be mine."

Hammond turned around and grabbed all of the bullets he could find that fit the two pistols, along with a 12-gauge shotgun and a .22 rifle from the rack next to the shelf. Hammond handed Bailey the .22 and she immediately set it down, then reached into the glass case and pulled out a 9mm Beretta.

"You want me to use a .22? I want to kill them, not piss them off."

"I just thought . . . you know . . . err, never mind."

Bailey had once again succeeded in leaving him speechless—something that he hoped she wouldn't make a habit of. All the same, they were good surprises, and his admiration for the girl grew and grew. Bailey filled the knapsack and a hiking pack with food and drinks while Hammond filled a large hiking pack with ammunition, a couple of knives, and a crank-powered flashlight with a radio. Bailey grabbed a pocket bible off the shelf and they were ready to go. Hammond walked around the room looking for the best possible exit when suddenly something dawned on him.

"Move slowly toward the back door and watch your back."

"What's going on, now?"

"Think about it. We walked in here and none of the doors were locked. Someone else is in here with us."

"But we checked the place out—wouldn't they have come out when you smashed the register?"

"Just move to the door and shut up."

Hammond cocked both of his guns and made his way for the back door, not taking his eyes off the dark corner of the room where the gardening supplies were displayed. The room was getting dark; Hammond put his fingers in his eyes and pulled something out of them. He looked back into the dark corner that was suspect to him. Something moved in the dark and Hammond opened fire into the corner. A terrifying scream emanated from the shadow as a human form launched out toward him. Hammond jumped out of the way and disappeared into the shadow himself. The thing stood up and made its way over to Bailey who was cowering by the door. It raised its arms toward her, ready to strike. She raised her gun up and pulled the trigger, nothing happened. She tried again, and again nothing happened. It was then she realized that, unlike Hammond, she had forgotten to load the gun. The being from the shadows advanced on her, quickly coming closer and closer, and was mere inches from her when she saw a glint of metal in the dimly lit room. She screamed as there was a bright flash, a loud crack, and then the thing slumped to the ground.

Hammond stepped out of the shadows with a smoking pistol in his hand. He reached down and took the sunglasses off of what was left of Tom's head and put them on. He turned around and surveyed the ceiling, locating a hatch that led to the roof. He climbed up onto the counter and pulled a dangling cord, which released and lowered a ladder. Without saying a word he went up and out.

Bailey grabbed a flashlight from the shelf nearby and searched the area where Hammond had been standing when he noticed Tom in the corner. It had become completely dark in just the short time they had been there. As she searched around, something white on the ground caught her eye. She bent down and picked it up to examine it closer—it was one of Hammond's contacts.

When Hammond returned he was covered in what seemed to be blood and looked very shook up.

"Time is running out—I saw the others and they're in a lot of trouble. We have to get to them before it's too late. It looks like those things are preparing to ambush them. We're not just dealing with the people from town, anymore—I saw a couple of them dressed in some kind of military clothing, and I also saw some strange creatures that look like they're not of this world."

"How can you see anything at all out there, and why are you wearing those sunglasses? As dark as it is, I'm surprised you can see anything at all."

"First of all, I wasn't wearing them when I looked outside. Second, mind your own business! Now, let's get going before it's too late."

Bailey shined the flashlight into Hammond's face. "I'm not going anywhere with you until you take off those sunglasses."

"We don't have time for this, our friends are in trouble!"

"Not until you take off the sunglasses. Those things cover their missing eyes with sunglasses . . . you disappear into the darkness, and when you come back you refuse to show me your eyes . . . what am I supposed to think?"

"Can't you just trust me? Besides, if I wanted to kill you, I would have done it by now."

Bailey slid a fresh clip into her gun and pointed it at Hammond's face. She didn't know if she had the courage to pull the trigger . . . could she kill this man that she felt such a connection with? The man she thought she loved? She didn't have much of a choice.

"Hammond, I love you, but I have to be sure."

"Bring that light down a little and I'll show you."

Confused, Bailey lowered the flashlight and gun down to Hammond's chest. He slowly pulled the sunglasses off of his face. His eyes were bright pink with huge pupils.

"I'm some kind of albino, and my eyes are hyper-sensitive. The contacts are opaque to keep the light from hurting them. Direct sunlight would burn my retinas and blind me. I dye my hair and wear contacts because my dad thought I was some sort of freak, so he made me hide what I am. I used to wear normal contacts until one day one of them fell out at school. The other kids, of course, called me a freak and made fun of me. When I saw the whiteout ones on T.V. one day, I thought they would be perfect because if one fell out it would just look like I was wearing two different freaky contacts or something.

Hammond put the sunglasses back on and moved past Bailey. She looked as though she wanted to say something, but didn't quite know what to say.

"Does Tigg know?"

"No. I hid it from him too, and that wasn't easy, hangin' around with him all the time. He just thinks I'm nearsighted."

"Can you see in the dark?"

"Yes—almost as good as most people can see in the daylight."

Bailey hesitated for a minute, then turned so she was face to face with Hammond. She put her hand on his face and kissed him sweetly.

"You're not a freak—you are someone very special—at least I think you are. And considering the crappy situation we're in right now, I'd say that makes you a pretty handy guy to have around. So, let's go save our friends, eh?"

"Alright, the quickest way to the cop shop is through the back door and to the right. If we can get there I can warn them before they walk into that ambush. Grab the stuff and let's kick rocks."

Hammond took the lead as the two of them prepared to exit the building. He checked his clip to make sure he still had plenty of rounds remaining, and Bailey checked to make sure her pistol was loaded and the safety was off. Hammond had Bailey open the door so he could be first to face whatever was waiting for them outside. Bailey swung the door open wide as Hammond made his way out, checking every angle, leading with his guns. Bailey followed closely behind him, covering backward to make sure nothing could come up from behind. The coast seemed to be clear—there was nothing but darkness on either side of them. Though still afternoon, only spotty light flecked down from the dying sun. A fog had crept in, covering what the darkness could not.

As they turned down the quiet alley toward the police station, Hammond grabbed Bailey by the arm and motioned for her to be quiet. Shadows slipped in and out of the dim light as Hammond once again disappeared into the darkness. Bailey stood alone and scared, hearing things scuttle about in the unseen places around her. In the near-silence, every little sound, even the slightest movement, caused her to jump. Hammond was nowhere to be seen, and for the first time since meeting him, she felt truly alone—truly vulnerable. Until now, she hadn't realized just how important he had become to her—how comfortable she felt when he was around. And now, without him, how empty and alone she was feeling. Her family was gone, but he seemed to be filling that need . . . the one who protected her, looked after her, and was willing to accept her and forgive her every trespass—even the ones that caused him pain.

A noise behind her shook her from her thoughts. The sound of a little girl giggling and singing echoed all around her. The sound of little feet hitting the ground surrounded her as she tried to find the source. The unseen child was singing something that she recognized but couldn't place. From the tiny voice somewhere near her, she heard the lyrics. "Please allow me to introduce myself. I'm a man of wealth and taste . . ." Giggles periodically broke up the song as a chill went down Bailey's spine. She turned around, hoping to find Hammond, but instead found herself face to face with the little girl she had draped her jacket over just a few minutes earlier.

"Pleased to meet you. Hope you guessed my name!" The little girl said, as she giggled and curtseyed.

"Who are you, and what do you want with us?"

"We are whoever you wish us to be, we are Legion!"

Bailey reached for her gun but the child simply vanished into a puff of black smoke.

"What was that?" Bailey said, shaken up.

"'Sympathy for the Devil', by the Rolling Stones." Hammond seemed to have popped back up from out of nowhere, still covered in blood.

"What is all over you?"

"The same thing that is all over you."

For the first time, Bailey looked down at her rain-soaked shirt, and found that it, too, was covered in blood. It was the rain—the sky was bleeding down on them through the dark blanket of fog that now covered the earth. But before she could ask any questions, Hammond grabbed her by the arm and led her skillfully through the darkness. She could feel things brush past her as they moved from one side to the other, avoiding the horrors that she could not see, and did not want to.

When they finally made it to the end of the alley, Hammond stopped and turned to Bailey. Things looked pretty rough around the corner, and if something were to happen to him, he wanted her to know how he honestly felt. He wanted to say something—he loved her, but couldn't think of anything to say that adequately conveyed the depth of his emotions.

"Bailey, I love you—not the kind of love you feel for a brother or sister, and not even the kind of love you feel in a crush. I truly and infinitely love you. I would gladly live and die for you, and that's about the only thing I can offer you right now—my undying love."

Hammond turned away embarrassed at what he had just said, but he was glad he had done it. Bailey stood in shock. To her, that was the most important thing anyone had ever said to her—he loved her! She wanted to tell him how she felt, too, but just as she started to reply, Hammond drew his pistols and ran around the corner, screaming.

"Run—it's an ambush! Get out of there! They're surrounding you—I can see them! Go, go, *go!*"

Chapter 15

UNWILLING MESSENGER

S ara screamed for Tigg to run faster as the creatures in the darkness moved in on them. She dug her fingernails into his shoulders as they plunged forward, just barely out of reach of their pursuers. The dark mist closed in around them, swallowing up the last bit of light.

Ahead of them, the figure that had warned them of the impending doom was coming into view. He stood like a proud statue and appeared to be holding something in his hand. Two shots rang out, shattering the creeping silence, and a terrifying howl sounded behind them. Sara felt the air separate as the bullets whizzed by her head. From behind, a foul stench was filling the air—the putrid smell of a thousand decaying bodies. It was enough to make her sick, but she had to keep it together—they were almost there.

Having put a little space between themselves and their pursuers, Tigg set Sara down, turned, and fired the shotgun blindly into the encroaching night. Pained screams filled the air as his shots tore through the blackness. Several more shots came from the man behind him. His aim seemed to be more accurate as Tigg saw shadows fall with every shot. He didn't know who the man was, but he did know he owed him a debt of gratitude. When the shotgun was empty, he turned and continued his escape.

Everything around them was turning to chaos. From the shadows now came laughter—incredibly loud, insane laughter. It was like a scene from a terrible nightmare, but worse, for there was no awakening to escape it. Tigg covered his ears, trying to stop the sound from getting in, but it penetrated his whole being in a symphony of ranting and raving madness that seemed to have no end.

Tigg looked ahead and saw Zero standing at the front door of the police station with his gun drawn. Tigg closed his eyes and ran towards him as the laughter became unbearable. He wanted to put the shotgun to his head and pull the trigger—perhaps in death he could escape the madness and the pain—but to his chagrin (and good fortune) the shells were all gone. No more than a few steps from the front door, the pain overcame him, and he collapsed, falling to the ground. He tried crawling but the insanity was burrowing through his mind like an insect looking for a place to lay its eggs. All Tigg could do was curl up like a baby and prepare to die.

Out of the darkness a man came running up behind him, scooped up Tigg, and dragged him through the door. Once inside, the laughter faded almost as suddenly as it had started, leaving Tigg feeling exhausted, but relieved. He now got a good look at his savior—it was none other than Hammond himself. Standing larger than life, he slipped on his sunglasses and looked over the group. With one gun in his hand and the other in his belt, he pointed to the door and Zero quickly locked it. Hammond seemed different to him—somehow older and more like a man than the boy he had always known. He took a moment to catch his breath, then began to shout orders like an old war general.

"You, cop, make sure this place is locked down. Stephie, find all the guns and turn on every light you can find. Tigger, you load that shotgun and look for any stragglers. Sara, you look for food—any kind will do. I want everyone to shout every thirty seconds so we know where everyone is. Any sign of trouble—scream like crazy". Hammond took the pills from his pocket and covertly popped a couple of them into his mouth. He was still in an immense amount of pain, but he didn't want anyone else to know it. If a man were nothing more than the sum of his experiences, Hammond would be "pain elemental". He didn't know how he would be able to keep up this fight, but he knew he had to—for the sake of his true love and for the sake of his friends.

Bailey came back with a first aid kit and some ace bandages and began dressing the wounds on Hammond's back and hand. Though she had already cauterized the wounds, she thought proper cleaning and dressing couldn't hurt, and might ease the pain. She had heard stories of pain making people die or go insane, but Hammond seemed to be taking it extremely well.

"How are you holding up, love?"

"I'm fine. When your whole life is pain, you actually start to like it—it lets you know you're still on the top side of the ground."

Hammond smiled wanly, trying not to show his pain as she put the finishing touches on his bandages. He looked at her sorrowfully, realizing that in a single night, she had lost almost everything dear to her—her family, her home, her life as she knew it. It was all changed now.

Every thirty seconds, as Hammond had commanded, a series of shouts were heard echoing through the hallways of the otherwise deserted police station. Everything seemed pretty normal, as though the evil had not yet been able to penetrate the walls. Though it may not have changed the building, the outbreak of evil had certainly changed the people inside. This rag-tag group of survivors was becoming a team. The two young men who were considered the community's most undesirable youths now found themselves leading a battle to save the whole town, and possibly the whole world? They didn't even want to consider it, but they seemed to step up to the task with ease. And Zero, once the laughing stock of the Convict Grade Police Department, was now the only one left.

Tigg walked down the empty hallways searching every corner for stragglers and the sinister presence that had been stalking them since early the night before. Zero followed close behind him, locking every door as they went, trying to avoid any unwanted surprises that could come from an unused room. All seemed quiet as they passed from room to room, until they came to the interrogation room. The two of them stopped at the same time as a thumping sound came from inside the room. Zero drew his sidearm and Tigg cocked the shotgun as they slipped in behind the one-way mirror of the viewing room.

The room on the other side was dimly lit by a bad florescent bulb that constantly flickered in a most annoying fashion. In the middle of the room was an old metal table with two chairs bolted to the floor. The walls were an unnerving shade of pink and the ceiling tiles were brown from some ancient, neglected leak. As they watched, a man stumbled back an fourth across the room, wandering aimlessly, running into the walls over and over again. He was about 5'11", with blond hair that hung down past his shoulders. His glasses were misshapen from hitting the walls, but he clearly had eyes.

"I'm going to find out who this joker is," Zero said at length.

"That's really not a good idea. We should go back and get Hammond and see what he says."

"I am still the ranking officer around here, and I say we investigate this."

"Look, dude, Hammond has somehow managed to keep us all alive through this, while you have almost gotten me killed twice today. So I'll have to go with him as the leader, OK?"

"Fine. What should we do, then, just leave that poor guy here? If he's had a night like we've had, he's probably already halfway to insanity. If we leave him here alone, who knows what might happen to him".

Tigg understood what Zero was saying. If it were him, he wouldn't want to be left in there, but then, the surgeon had eyes, too. At length, Tigg finally nodded back at Zero and motioned to the door. He kept the shotgun raised and ready to fire as Zero opened the door to the interrogation room. Once they were in, the man immediately approached them. He stumbled around for a second, then ran right at Tigg. Before Tigg could react, the man was upon him, and they both tumbled to the ground. Tigg lost his grip on the shotgun and it slid out into the hallway, leaving him defenseless. Blood was oozing from the man's open mouth as he hopelessly tried to talk. Zero drew his gun and leveled it to the man's temple. The man just turned to him, wide-eyed, shaking his head. He slowly got off of Tigg and looked at Zero, frantically pointing at his open mouth.

"What is he doing?" Tigg asked Zero, hoping for the answer that he, himself, did not posses.

"Oo, look at that—there is something stuck in his mouth!"

The man continued to point hysterically into his gaping, bleeding mouth, trying in vain to pull the object out. Zero tried to calm him down while Tigg ran through the halls, yelling for Hammond. He didn't know what Hammond could do, but he knew that Hammond's idea would be better than his own.

As he made his way around the corner, Tigg was greeted by the sight of Hammond and Bailey locked in a loving embrace. Tigg stood for a moment, watching in curious astonishment as the two kissed. He certainly didn't want to interrupt the moment—after all, he would kill for a little quiet time with Sara; however, there were pressing things at hand that required Hammond's immediate attention.

"Hammond, we need you in the interrogation room—right now. I think this is something you're going to want to see."

Hammond broke lock with Bailey and turned, aggravated, towards the intruder. But seeing the fear in Tigg's eyes, he realized the seriousness of the situation, grabbed his guns, and followed him out the door.

"Bring a set of pliers if you have one, man—you'll need it."

Hammond quickly grabbed one of the sacks that he and Bailey had loaded up in the hardware store and jogged after Tigg. His curiosity was at an all-time high. The two of them ran through the halls of the police station as fast as they could. As they rounded the corner where the interrogation room was located, Hammond lost his footing and slid completely past it. Tigg waited at the door while he picked himself up, and they entered together.

The sight that greeted them was one of nightmarish surrealism. The man with long blond hair lay dead at their feet, while the officer who was supposed to be watching him was sitting in a corner, hiding his face and crying. Hammond looked to Tigg to see if this was the situation he had been summoned for, or if it had escalated to what now lay before them. Tigg just stared gape-mouthed at the scene, indicating to Hammond that it was the latter.

"Get over there and talk to Zero, man. I'll take care of the whole corpse issue. And, oh yeah—what did I bring the pliers for?"

"There's something lodged in his mouth and you need to pull it out. I guess it's too late to save him, but I would really like to know what that thing is."

"Curiosity killed the cat, Tigger, old buddy."

"Yeah, well satisfaction brought it back. Just pull whatever it is out of his mouth, and let's get a look at it".

Hammond hoisted the corpse onto the table in the center of the room. The body was surprisingly light, considering the size of the man. When he got him up, the head of the corpse rolled back, and Hammond saw for himself that the man had indeed had something forced into his mouth. The object was long and slender and too big to fit, so half of it was driven through the roof of his mouth. Hammond reached in with the Leatherman and pulled at the object, but it didn't want to come loose. It was firmly anchored in the bone of the man's upper jaw and he couldn't get a good enough angle on it to pull it out.

"No matter what you hear, I don't want you to look over here, Tigger. You just keep wet willy over there distracted."

"No problem, dude. I've seen enough gore and crap in the last couple of days to last me a lifetime. So, just do what you gotta do."

Hammond took the already-cocked shotgun from Tigg and put it in the dead man's mouth. He took a deep breath and pulled the trigger, blasting away his lower jaw. Now there was nothing standing between Hammond and his objective. "The ends justify the means", Hammond thought to himself as he freed the object from the tattered remains of the poor man's face. Under closer examination, the object turned out to be a key with a piece of paper wrapped tightly around it. Amazingly, the paper had not sustained any serious damage, nor was it covered in blood, as one would have expected. To his surprise, it had the name, Hammond written on it in beautiful script.

"We need to get everyone together. I don't know what kind of sick game is being played here, but I think we should stick together and not get separated unless absolutely necessary. This is turning into some kind of strange treasure hunt, and I think it's time we tried to figure out the clues."

Tracking down the other members of the crew turned out to be an easy task. By the time they arrived back in the lobby, the others were already there, taking stock of the things they had gathered. Sara had pillaged every vending machine in the building and was unloading armfuls of junk food and soda onto the ground. Stephie had found seven pistols, four shotguns, and a few hundred rounds of ammo, which she had set on the counter for inspection. Bailey had used one of the couches in the office to set up a little nurse's station to tend to the minor cuts and bruises the other girls had sustained throughout the previous evening. Hammond was proud of the girls, although he didn't know how effective any of this would be if even one of those things were to get inside the station.

Hammond produced the paper-wrapped key from his pocket, which attracted everyone's stare as he held it in his open hand. "I pulled this from the mouth of a dead man about five minutes ago." Hammond said as he cleared his throat, preparing to tell the group everything he knew.

"While I was out cold in the hospital, I had sort of a vision, or dream, in which I met a man named Satanel. He handed me a rolled-up parchment and told me that our time as a race is at an end. I didn't think much of the dream until Bailey and I were leaving my house and the parchment fell out of my jacket pocket—it was real! I don't know how, but there it was".

"You didn't tell us about this? What did the parchment say?" Zero asked, glaring at Hammond as though he had been left out of a very important loop.

"I don't know—I haven't exactly had the time to read it, what with all the screaming and running around in the last few hours." Hammond seemed more annoyed with the interruption than its lack of thought. "Anyway, now we have this key with a note wrapped around it, and the note appears to be addressed to me".

"So, get to it—what does the note say?" Zero interrupted again.

"Look, you moron, I haven't even unwrapped it yet, so I couldn't possibly know what it says. If you are going to be stupid, could you please go do it somewhere else? Thank you very much."

Zero stood quietly wondering if this was a battle he should engage in, or if he should just let this one go, and listen. In the end, he chose silence and motioned for the haggard teen to finish what he was saying.

"Now, it is obvious to me that we are all part of some sick little game Satanel has set up for us. But the question I'm asking all of you is, should we play?"

Everyone looked to each other, but no one seemed to want to answer. Hammond took the parchment and the note-wrapped key and laid them on the little table in the center of the room. After much debate and argument, they finally decided that they had no real choice in the matter—they had to get out of there, somehow, and that meant they should accept any help or clue, no matter what the source. Hammond stood up, picked up the object he had taken from the mouth of the dead man, and unwrapped it. The key was old and rusty and the head was shaped like a skeleton. He sat the key on the table and began to read the note out loud.

Chapter 16

UNDERGROUND PASSAGE

T he room fell silent as Hammond cleared his throat, preparing to read the note that had been delivered in such a gruesome manner. The handwriting on the note was very stylized, and at the same time very cryptic. Who had the time to write a note in calligraphy and leave it in a man's mouth for him to find when he himself didn't even know he was going to be at the police station? All of a sudden, Hammond's life felt much too predictable. After a moment he cleared his throat again and read the letter aloud:

Hammond,

I am glad to see that my letter made it to you; after all, mortals can be so unreliable. If you are reading this, then you must be alive and in fairly good health. You may wonder why I am helping you in your futile efforts. The answer is quite simple. You intrigue me and I want to see just how far you can make it before my minions destroy you

135

and your pathetic little band of warriors. So, I have provided you with all the answers to who we are, and given you the key to the answers you seek. Just find your path and do your best—we look forward to whatever challenges you can provide, for we have not had a worthy opponent in ages.

Satanel

After Hammond had finished reading, the group sat silently, letting the words of the letter sink in. No one knew how to even begin to respond to the challenge posed in the letter. Tigg stood up and walked over and sat next to Sara holding her tightly as if he knew what was coming next. Hammond provided the next clue as to what was going on in the form of the bible that Bailey had found in the hardware store. It was a pocket bible, about four inches by three inches with a green plastic cover. Ham always thought it odd that they sold them at the register, but then again, if somebody wanted to find salvation at the hardware store, more power to them.

He opened the little book up to Joel. These had always been Reverend Bachman's favorite passages, so Hammond knew them all too well. He began to read, feeling that once they heard what he read, there would be little more to explain.

"Joel, chapter two, verse 28." he began to read. "I will show wonders in Heaven and on Earth, blood and fires and billows of smoke. The sun will be turned to darkness and the moon to blood." Hammond closed the book and looked at them somberly. "I would say that pretty well covers what's going on outside, wouldn't you?"

"So what are you saying, Ham?" Bailey asked with fear. She already knew the answer and she had no desire to hear it.

"Basically, love, we are living through some of the worst stuff the Bible describes, and so far, it looks like we are in it pretty deep, with no help from the good guys."

"Well, what do we do now?" Stephie asked calmly, as if she had already lost the fight.

"Well, just to be thorough—Bailey, you read the parchment and sum it up for us. I think that there is a clue missing somewhere, and I have to find out what it is." Hammond said, rolling the key through his fingers.

Hammond thought back to the dream he had back in the hospital, hoping for any clue that might help explain the purpose of the key he now had in his possession. Before he could come up with the answer, however, there was a loud crash at the front door. The team jumped, startled by the intensity of the sound as it hit the metal lock-down doors. The doors were quite heavy—installed back in the 1950's when everyone was worried about a nuclear attack.

Hammond motioned for them to follow him as he went to investigate. Stephie tucked the scroll and letter away into her jacket and followed. Windows crashed behind the doors that Zero had locked as they made their way down the corridor to the front entrance. Once they got there, they saw the doors still standing, but badly damaged. Cracks and crevices were present in the door and the surrounding wall, and hands were skinning themselves as creatures outside were trying to reach in.

"You have a sweet little town here, don't you, guys?" Zero shouted as he saw the first of the hands reaching in.

"Oh, man, that's right! Hey, Hammond, that's it! All this happened before, and they found a way to stop it then, right?"

"Sure Tigg, if you call 'everyone dying' stopping it, then yeah, they did."

"Well there has to be some sort of record of that, right? I mean like some sort of history book or something?"

"That's the stupidest thing I've ever heard."

"We could go to the courthouse—that's where they store all the old records and stuff from back then" Sara said, trying to make some sort of contribution. The doors bulged inward from the force of the creatures trying to get in.

"Okay, Tigg. I take it back—yours was the *second* stupidest thing I've ever heard—*that* was the first. In the first place, the courthouse is two buildings away, and in the second, assuming we could get there, exactly where would we look for these little mystery books of yours?"

"Um, what about the tunnels that run under the town? Couldn't we take those to the courthouse?" Stephie chimed in, seemingly out of nowhere.

"You don't really believe that, do you? Those tunnels are just a local legend. They don't really exist, and if they did, don't you think someone would have found them by now?"

"Actually, someone did, and we use them all the time. This town likes to keep its undesirables out of the public eye—we use them to transport prisoners from the jail to the courthouse."

"Zero, you are a genius." Hammond was delighted with this new development.

"I could kiss you right now, you big stupid animal!" Stephie said as she threw her arms around the stunned Zero.

"Well, get us down there before these things break through and turn us all into human suits, man!" Tigg yelled. The pins in the doors were looking as though they could give way at any moment.

Zero led the way down into the basement with the three girls followed by Tigg. Hammond took up the rear to make sure they were not being followed. The basement of the building was dark and damp, made up of a cobblestone foundation and a dirt floor. Though the police traveled through there on a regular basis, it looked like no one had cleaned it in years. Cobwebs hung low from the ceiling and the support beams of the building were large old timbers that had not been replaced since the building was first erected in 1871. The passageway that Zero had mentioned was quite narrow, with sides that looked more like wooden barriers than walls and floors made up of old planking that looked like railroad ties.

Once they were in the passageway, they walked single file in the same order they had come down in. Hammond pulled a cigarette from his pocket. When he went to light it the flame flickered to the side like the floor was breathing. He pushed forward trying to hurry the team on. The fact that there was enough empty space underneath the floor to create an updraft bothered him deeply. If there was room for air to move back and fourth under the rotting floor, there was definitely room for something else.

When they got about halfway through the tunnel, Hammond realized that they had forgotten most of their supplies, but he was not about to go back and get them. He carried only the one knapsack that he had filled in Tom's and that was not much. He dug through the bag and produced a flashlight, which he handed forward up to Zero who was running out of light. The lights in the ceiling did not go all the way to the courthouse, so from here on out they had to provide their own.

The darkening hallway only added to Hammond's uneasiness as they moved further down the passageway. Only Zero knew the end. Their footsteps echoed as they made the slow journey to the courthouse. On both sides, Hammond could hear the echo of their footsteps resonating below. When Zero finally spoke, it scared Hammond half to death because his voice echoed like thunder.

"Alright, we're almost to the courthouse, and I don't know what we'll find on the other side of the door, so be careful."

"What is below us, Zero? I don't really like the feeling of these boards."

"To the best of my knowledge, there is nothing, except maybe some sort of drainage canal or something."

"Who built the passageways?"

"Do I look like a library to you, man? How should I know? I haven't lived here that long, you know."

Hammond backed off from the group a little, feeling stupid that he had just asked the newest addition to the town about its history. Hammond stood still for a moment, awkwardly trying to get his cigarette lit, when he heard a cracking sound. It was slight at first, but quickly grew loud enough for the others to hear it. They turned around just in time to see the startled look on Hammond's face.

"Help . . . !" Hammond yelled as the boards below his feet gave way.

He tried to leap to safety, but everything around him collapsed, and he fell headlong into the darkness of the open hole in the floor. The others watched helplessly as he disappeared into the abyss that had swallowed him whole.

Chapter 17

HIDDEN LIES

H ammond lay motionless at the bottom of his new dark hell. The others stood above looking down, unable to see him. He was just deep enough to be veiled in a shroud of blackness.

"Hammond? You alive?" Tigg yelled down.

"Yeah, Man."

"Hang tight, dude. We're gonna try to find a way to get you out of there, so just stay cool."

Hammond scanned the area around him looking for any sign of light or life, but found neither. The area smelled musty and wreaked of decaying matter. The darkness, however, seemed to be just that—an absence of light, unlike the living darkness from which he had just escaped. This brought him at least a small bit of comfort. The echoes of the others swam around in his dizzy head as he tried in vain to make sense of his new surroundings. He let out a small laugh. "Caged rat", he thought as he composed himself.

Time seemed to stand still in the empty void that he now occupied, eagerly awaiting the return of his friends. Strangely enough, he felt at ease—all the things he had been running from now seemed like some distant war taking place in a country far, far away. He didn't think he could ever feel at home in the darkness again, but he did, now. And it was really, really dark. He could see only in shadows, which meant that there was virtually no light at all for his eyes to reflect. Absolute darkness was something he had not seen in a long time. It felt good to him, for if any evil lay in wait for him, he did not want to see it.

He sat, squinting into the blackness, trying to get a glimpse of something he could recognize. Then he felt it. Fear rushed back into him and a sinking feeling overcame him as he felt it—the feeling of eyes watching him. He felt something go by, then felt it again—they brushed up against him as they moved about in their preternatural way. Hammond crouched, hoping for some escape, hoping he might not be noticed, perhaps, and fearing what might next be in store for him. He could feel them all around him, circling like wolves stalking their prey. Hammond closed his eyes and began to pray out loud for help—the help that only the one who created all things could provide.

"Dear God, please help me through this. If you do I'll give you anything, anything at all, man, I swear." He scrubbed his hands across his face.

Hammond shuddered when a beautiful voice answered back, emanating from all sides in a sickly sweet tone. "The only gift *you* have to give me, my child, is the greatest gift our Lord has given you. And that is your free will."

"Well, I give it gladly. It has done nothing for me thus far." Hammond said, almost laughing in spite of himself.

"Then your gift is accepted," the voice echoed.

Upon hearing this, he felt something begin to crawl up his leg. A sense of panic gripped him as he felt it move up and around his right thigh and then climb up his lower back. He struggled to get the strange parasite off of him, scraping and clawing at it, but it was too late. It was out of his reach, and all he could do was scream as it imbedded itself deep into his spine, right between his shoulder blades.

Then, as suddenly as it had started, it was over. Hammond stood there calmly, the events of mere moments ago already faded into distant memories. The darkness around him was once again peaceful and comforting. It was the kind of darkness that made him feel like he was back in his room at home. He could hear the others in the distance, saying they would return shortly. To him, the world was drowning in nothingness and he found a sense of peace for the first time since the whole ordeal began. He sat down on what felt like cobblestone as he pondered his situation. The light from the hole above drifted slowly in and out of his vision as time and space lost all meaning to him. He felt the silence folding its dark arms around him, as he took comforted in the reprieve the calm had given him.

After what had to be only moments, but felt like hours, something hit him smack in the middle of the forehead. It startled him, terribly at first, and he scrambled to his feet, but he quickly realized it was only a length of rope that had been tossed down to him. The light had returned in the hole above and he was finally able to see his surroundings. It looked like an entire town.

"Tie the rope around you, man. We'll hoist you up," came Zero's voice, echoing through the emptiness.

"I think you guys should come down here. You have got to see this!" Hammond shouted back up to them. "Get the girls down here first, using the rope, then Zero and Tigg, you jump down and bring the rope with you. It's about fifteen feet, so be careful."

The group didn't know what to think of Hammond's request, but he had kept them alive so far, so it seemed like the thing to do. They climbed one by one into the hole and down the rope as Hammond had instructed: Bailey first, then Steph, then Sara, followed by Zero. After a moment, Tigg came crashing down, collapsing face first on the ground in front of Hammond. He just lay there groaning for a moment before he rolled over to face Hammond.

"I thought you were supposed to catch me, man!" Tigg said, still grunting at his loss of breath.

"I never said that, now, did I?" Hammond said as he looked innocently at Tigg.

Tigger felt Hammond was acting weird, but quickly dismissed the thought because, honestly, when wasn't he? Hammond stepped forward to Bailey, who was holding one of the knapsacks. He motioned for her to hand it over and riffled through its contents on a mission to help both himself and his sight challenged friends. After a few moments he produced a fluorescent camping light. Its design was a cheap imitation of the old kerosene lamps. He turned it on and handed it to Tigger, then walked forward so that he would not be exposed to the brightness of its beam. Hammond's mind was a sea of jumbled thoughts and emotions as he kicked gently at the strange cobblestone ground beneath him. "At least I won't fall through this stuff", he thought to himself as Bailey came up behind him.

Bailey's connection with Hammond had grown deep enough that she could sense when something was wrong with him. And right now, she could tell something was bothering him.

"What's the matter, Ham?" Bailey asked as she nuzzled up to him and wrapped her arm around his waist.

"Not that it really scores high on my weirdness meter, compared to all the other stuff that has happened lately, but there was this strange bug that crawled up my back and, like, bit me or something."

Bailey ran her hand up Hammond's back in an effort to feel whatever it was that was hurting him. She got up to between his shoulders and jumped back with a start, jerking her hand back as if it were on fire.

"There is something inside your back! I could feel it move when I touched it!" She tried to keep her voice calm and steady but she could not contain her disgust. "Eww, eww, eww!"

Hammond reached his hand down between his well-built shoulders and felt a strange growth that was moving inside of him. It was about the size of a golf ball and seemed to be alive. The thing had to have attached itself to his spinal cord, because when it moved it seemed to be telling his mind how it was moving or vice versa. He couldn't really tell which.

Bailey yelled at Tigg and the others to come and inspect the mass. They stood around in disgusted fascination, akin to a group of people who had witnessed a fatal car accident. They couldn't take their eyes off it—this thing that seemed to be alive and moving inside their friend. "We have to get that thing out of you, Ham—before it kills you or eats you from the inside out or some thing like that, man!" Tigger said.

"Will you guys get away from me? I'm not the local freak show! And besides, if you mess with it, without knowing what it is, you might just be signing my death warrant. I can feel it in there and I think it has connected itself to my brain or something."

Not wanting to question a clearly upset Hammond, Tigger decided not to push it, even though he thought Hammond was wrong this time. Instead, he focused for the first time on what now surrounded them. It was the strangest thing he had ever seen.

He looked around him, and then looked up. What he saw astounded him. They were standing where no one had been for more than a century. Then, a thought came to Tigger with a jolt. He suddenly knew what they had found—it was the original town of Convict Grade!

While the rest of them fussed about Hammond's back, Tigg stood, enthralled, trying to get Hammond's attention. "Dude, look around . . ." Tigg kind of trailed off in this statement as he took in the scene.

"What are you talking about, retard?" Hammond said with mock cruelty, thankful that the attention was no longer on him.

"Dude, look up!" Tigg was exasperated. "The ceiling is like metal or something."

"Dude, you need to get your brain replaced or . . ." Hammond stopped mid-sentence as he looked up above him.

The sight changed Hammond's perspective on everything he thought he knew about the world. Covering the expanse above him like an iron sky stretching as far as his eyes could see was a giant metal sheet that seemed to hold up his hometown. Large timber beams the size of redwoods joined with huge iron fittings made up the amazing structure. Rust streaks ran across the metal, leaving a creepy blood tone in the old shell above them. A cold shiver ran down their collective spines as they examined it for a few moments, but soon all were focused on Zero, looking for the official police answer as to what this thing was that they had fallen into.

"What *is* this, Zero?" Stephanie was the first to ask the obvious from the man who knew about the tunnels in the first place.

"How come everybody thinks that, just because I wear a badge, I'm supposed to know all the mysteries of the universe?"

"You're the one who led us down here, and I think you should explain to all of us just where, exactly, we are. I don't think you could possibly be as stupid as you look!" Sara yelled at Zero, frustrated. She knew it wasn't his fault, but she really needed someone to blame.

"Look, I don't know what's going on down here—it's not like I went around inspecting the floor, much less worrying about what was under it. We always thought it was just the sewer or something like that."

"The sewer. Why would there be hard wood flooring over the sewer, Officer Brain Dead?" Hammond snarled. He surveyed the area around them. "Wait, I guess that could make sense. There are pipes up there and I suppose the county guys could walk in them and not realize that they were suspended. Maybe you're not so dumb, after all."

With Hammond's recant, everyone eventually let go of the idea that Zero was trying to hide something from them, and went back to surveying their surroundings, trying to make sense of it all. Though Hammond had better longer-range night vision than the others, it was still limited by the availability of ambient light. He was shocked by what he could see, then mildly surprised by the fact that he could still be shocked. He saw buildings and streets and what appeared to be kerosene streetlights. The streets poured out before him, larger than life, as he was now taking in the full scope of the events that had transpired. The lines of reality were already blurred for Hammond the moment the darkness changed his life, but now they were totally blown away as he tried to comprehend the scene before him. He was starting to loose his grip on sanity.

Hammond was at a loss for words in trying to describe to the others what he was seeing, so he walked over to the nearest lamppost, climbed up its narrow base, and lit it with his Zippo. The sudden illumination put an end to the bickering and debate that the others were engaged in as the section of the street came to life. Steph walked forward with her mouth agape, intoxicated by the new scene in front of her. It was like they had traveled back in time and they were still above ground on a black night. From the streets, she could see it was like they were in a mirror of the town that they had left behind only an hour ago. If Hammond's sanity was stretched, then Steph's could only be described as shattered. She stared stupidly; gawking at the scene, then began to giggle, which soon turned to uncontrollable laughter. Tears streamed down her face as she fell to her knees, hitting the hard cobblestone road.

"None of this is real, don't you see? None of you are real, either! This is all just a hallucination brought on by too much partying. Any minute now, I will wake up and I will be in some frat house somewhere. At this point, Steph was going into uncontrolled fits of laughing and she kept shaking her head as though it would change what she was seeing. "Maybe if I click my heels together and say, "There's no place like home", I'll end up in some other fairy tale instead of this one". Steph's tone had turned from laughter to almost rage.

Sara held onto Tigg as Steph had begun to make everyone feel very awkward. They all just stared at her, horrified. None of them wanted to be there any more than she did, but they had no choice. Bailey wanted to help, but she knew getting close to this woman now would only put her at risk of some kind of psychotic attack by an extremely unstable woman. The last thing they needed was to turn on each other. Bailey turned and looked at Hammond, hoping that he had the answer, but he seemed preoccupied with something he had pulled out of the backpack. Zero just stood there biting his lower lip as though it would provide him with the nutrients necessary to come up with a plan.

Hammond composed himself the best he could. He smoothed out his ratted hair and walked toward the still freaked-out Steph, one hand behind his back.

"Hey, Stephie, you're right. This is all just a prank that me and my good buddy Ryan here put together, to see if you have what it takes to hang out with the Kappa-Rho-Gamma fraternity. Now all you have to do is kiss me and the initiation will be complete!" Hammond said half to Steph, and half to the on-lookers.

Bailey glared and clenched her fists, ready to deck Hammond. What was this all about? If he was trying to be funny, he wasn't doing a very good job. In a growing rage of jealousy, she slowly rose and started toward Hammond, but wheeled on Tigg as he grabbed her arm.

"Don't!" whispered Tigg. "He knows what he is doing. He has been in worse situations than this. I promise you, he's doing this because he has to, not because he likes her".

Hammond wrapped up Steph in a full-body embrace with one arm, kissed her on the lips, and produced a hypodermic needle in the other hand, which he plunged into her hip, administering the full dose and withdrawing it in just a second. Steph screamed and jumped, but Hammond had her locked in. She pushed Hammond away as hard as she could, staring down the man who had betrayed her. Her face turned to a grimace as a strange feeling began to cascade through her body. After a few moments, the grimace faded to a look of quiet calm and she slumped against the wall of the nearest building. The rage and fight drained from her, and she went limp and glassy, like a life-sized Raggedy Ann doll.

"What have you done to her?" Zero shouted harshly at Hammond, rushing to her side.

"I just gave her something to calm her down."

"You're no doctor! You can't just go around giving people shots!"

"Well, I'm not going to take her back to the hospital . . . How 'bout you?" Hammond retorted. Zero thought for a moment about the creepy doctor and the day's events.

"No, no, I guess you're right . . ." Zero admitted. Hammond went back to business as usual.

"Now, with that out of the way, maybe we could focus on the problems we are facing. If you think about it, man, we are in a town under a town, which is kind of crazy all by itself, but now we're faced with the question of what to do next. I don't know about you but I have no clue what that is."

"I have a suggestion: you should read that parchment thing, or is that just another stupid thought from the person you all seem to think is too stupid to tie his own shoes?" Zero stood staring and Hammond.

Bailey looked at Hammond and tears began to well up in her eyes. "We can't—I lost it in the police station."

"You stupid bi . . ." Before Zero could finish, he was smacked in the face and found himself on the ground with a mouth full of blood and two missing teeth. Hammond stood over him.

"Let that be a warning—I swear, if you ever say anything like that again, I will feed you to those things out there myself." Hammond said, gently rubbing his now throbbing knuckles. With all that he had been through in the last couple of days, his sore hand that had been broken, sliced and now bruised really didn't matter to him.

Suddenly the mental anguish and pain were not his main concerns. Staying alive was, and if he wanted his comrades to stay that way too, he had to keep them from self-destructing. All in all, this was a daunting prospect, considering that he himself wanted to do that very thing. He desperately wanted to fall apart. Hammond now had the undivided attention of everyone, with the exception of the drugged-up Steph, who was content at the moment just playing with her hair.

"Look, I know things are really whacked out right now, guys. We really have to stick together. If our little group falls apart then those things will pick us off one by one and you know that. So, I suggest we make our way to the courthouse down here. This place looks to be set up just like the new town, so that means we're on Gold Rush Street and that puts us about two blocks away. I'll take the lead and light the street lamps. You guys stay close together, got it?"

Everyone looked at Hammond and nodded in agreement as he pulled out his pistols and looked toward the courthouse. None of them knew what to expect from this trek. They only knew that they had to move before those things found them again.

Chapter 18

FATAL FRIENDS

The acrid smell of dirt and untouched ages filled the air as they moved slowly and deliberately through the desolate town. Their footsteps echoed ominously throughout the empty hollows of this strange shell. Real life seemed to give way to fantasy with every step they took into the long forgotten town, leaving the eerie glow of the streetlamps flickering behind them as they went. Hammond stalked through the darkness with guns drawn, lighting every streetlamp they came across. The ambiance of the place made for a somber trip.

There was a post office and a saddle maker. The scene before them looked like it came straight out of an old western movie. The difference was the metal sky and the lack of cowboys, or any other living thing, for that matter. They walked up to one of the buildings; above the door hung a sign that read "Frank's Mercantile". The windows were dusty and grimy. Bailey wiped it with her sleeve and peered in. The walls were lined with shelves full of groceries, clothes, and toys. Bottles full of candy were stacked along the checkout desk. The oh-so-familiar store was a place that they had all bought candy and soda from, or at least thought they had. Hammond led the way in, followed by Tigg, who still clung to the police shotgun like it was a barrel from a sinking ship.

Once inside, Hammond walked around the store checking every nook and cranny for any unwanted presence. There was no sign of life, or death, for that matter. It looked as if whoever used to be here just up and vanished. Hammond grabbed two hand-made quilts off of a shelf and proceeded to cover the storefront windows. As he grabbed the blankets, over a hundred years of dust wafted up into his face. He held back a sneeze, not wanting to catch any unwanted attention from things that might be lurking in the shadows. Hammond placed the blankets on the window, taking care not to leave even a single crack where light might shine through.

"What exactly are you doing?" Tigg asked in solemn wonder.

"I can only see about sixty feet in front of me, Tigg old buddy, and I am pretty sure those whatever-they-are's can see a lot further than that. I have no intention of putting up a 'Here We Are, Come Eat Us' sign. You dig?"

"Okay, then, why don't you put the dark side out?"

Hammond looked at his makeshift curtain and realized that Tigger was absolutely right. He had faced the side out that was emblazoned with bright colors, a "Come Eat Me" sign if ever there was one. Tigg helped Hammond take the blankets down and reverse them, and then they lit two more lamps inside the store. The light hurt Hammond's eyes, but there was nothing he could do to shield them. He just tried to stay in the shadows, away from the sting of the light.

"One problem you didn't think of, fearless leader—there's a trail of streetlamps leading right to us, so covering the windows is pretty pointless." Zero stated indignantly.

"I've already thought about that, actually. Once everyone is settled, I'll head out there and light more. I figured I'd hit the main street and all the side streets, lighting everything I see along the way. If you're not too big of a chicken, you're welcome to join me, although I have a feeling that it'll be good 'ole Ham out there alone on this expedition".

His friends looked at each other, then at the floor, shuffling their feet. This had the feel of a suicide mission. It was dark out there, and it was hard to tell what was in that darkness. They now knew what lived in the shadows of the world and they did not want to face it. Bailey burst into silent tears.

"I'll go with you," Tigg offered. Tigg not only wanted to do this for his friend but he also knew he wanted to keep those things away from Sara. He wanted her to be safe, and for that he was willing to risk his very life.

Zero stood scanning Bailey, enthralled in some strange daydream involving him and her. Having this man stare at her made Bailey sickly uncomfortable. Hammond noticed this and was not too terribly happy about it. The tension was building between the two men. Bailey did her best to cover herself from Zero's unnerving stare.

"Thanks dude, but I need you to stay with the girls. I don't trust him alone with them. Watch her and keep her safe, I'll be back as soon as I can."

"No problem, bro. I'll take care of her." With that promise, Tigg went and stood between Zero and Bailey like he was a wall of lead to the not-so-super-cop's X-ray vision. "What's your problem, man? Can't you see that she doesn't want you ogling over her?"

"Look, Tigg, I don't need your holier-than-thou attitude, alright? Here are the facts: I am the only real adult here, and if your little friend wants to play Johnny Rambo, then let him, because when he dies you will need me to survive. So cut the little tough guy act or I will kill you myself."

After this strange outburst from Zero, everyone just looked at each other in awe and disbelief. Sara moved closer to Bailey to comfort her while Hammond was gone. Zero stood sizing up the formidable Tigg as if he were contemplating how he would get around this particular obstacle as soon as Hammond left on his mission. The situation was becoming more unstable with each passing moment. Stephie, who was now coming out of her drug-induced haze, was realizing what was going on and didn't care for the fact that the only "unattached" male carried a torch for Bailey.

"Whaaas going on, here?" She asked Zero, her head still swimming from the drugs. Anger and narcotics slurred her words. "Why are you guys fighting? Don't we have enough trouble without having to swim through the testosterone from all you macho jerks?"

"I'm not being a macho jerk. All I'm saying is that I should stay here and protect you girls while Captain America, here, goes out there to lead those things away from where we are." Zero said indignantly. "Besides, we haven't seen any of them since we got down here."

This comment was about all Hammond could stomach. He stepped up face to face with the deputy. "If you're such a brave protector and you're so convinced that those things aren't down here, then why don't you just go out there and light the lights yourself?"

"Look, *bright-eyes*, you're the only one here who can see in the dark, so it makes more sense for *you* to go!" Zero growled in a standoffish manner.

"Yes, but you're the self-proclaimed authority figure in this outfit. By all means, lead!" Hammond and Zero were nose to nose.

"Look, *Edgar*, if you're scared, I will be more than happy to go out there with you to show you that there is nothing out there, and we are perfectly safe right here with the street lights just the way they are."

"If you thought that, then why did you tell me that it was stupid to leave a trail directly to us?" Ham's voice was cool, his words controlled. Zero could tell that Hammond was beginning to lose his temper. Since his jaw still ached from the last time he pissed Hammond off, he decided to back down. He dropped his eyes and backed up a pace. The situation seemed to be defusing itself for the moment, but Hammond now knew that Zero couldn't be trusted. Rather than an ally, he now considered him a risk, and a bad one at that.

Everyone else in the group seemed to catch on, and after a few moments of discussion, it was decided that Zero would be joining Hammond in lighting the streetlamps. Though Zero thought the idea was ridiculous, he had to go along with it, since it was his idea in the first place. The fact that everyone was against him didn't help, either. Bailey would have felt safer with Hammond there, but she also felt that Tigg could do a more than adequate job. And at this point, she thought that she would be safer sitting on one of those things' lap than being left alone with Zero. Although Hammond had comforted her and assured her everything would be fine, she still worried about what Zero might do to him when he had his back turned.

The light from the kerosene lamps danced wildly on the wooden walls of the old store. Tigg helped Hammond rummage through the items in the store looking for anything that might be of use to him on his short excursion. Tigger's mother had taught him that it is better to be over-prepared than to be under-prepared. Stephie also searched through the store looking for anything of interest. The place was very old and stocked with things that were common, everyday articles in the 1800's, but some of them were now antique treasures.

On a shelf behind the counter, Stephie saw something that caught her eye. It was an old china doll with a beautiful porcelain face. Ever since she was a young girl she had wanted one of those—she had seen china dolls like this in a museum, before, but they were no longer made, and couldn't be bought at any price. She reached out and grabbed the doll, admiring the carefully painted face. It had lovely curly red hair and a beautiful green dress. It was perfect and in that moment she felt almost normal again.

Hammond started for the door, but Bailey stopped him. In a great big "screw you" gesture aimed at Zero, she pressed herself up against Ham and kissed him passionately. It was so intense that Hammond almost lost his balance. Zero just turned away in an attempt to ignore the blatant show of partnership, but he turned only to see Sara and Tigg also embracing. Tigg held his girl, but his eyes were locked in a stare-down with Zero.

"Look, can we just get this over with?" The deputy spit out the words.

"Yeah, deputy dog, we certainly can, now!" Hammond smiled, purely satisfied that he had managed to make Zero jealous.

The two men readied themselves, then made a quick exit from Frank's Mercantile. The animosity between them was like electricity running through the stale air. Hammond kept his distance from Zero, who kept toying with his police-issue Glock. This made Hammond uneasy and he palmed his own weapon. He stepped cautiously forward as Zero lazily followed behind him, swinging the fluorescent light back and forth as he walked. Hammond found it increasingly irritating that Zero did not even seem to consider the fact that, at any given moment, one or all of those things could attack them.

"What's your problem? You've seemed kind of off since you guys left to get the rope." Hammond asked, trying to smooth over the wrinkles that had formed between them.

"I don't know, man. I feel like we could be getting more out of this situation than we are. We're the survivors! The chosen few!"

"Don't you think it's a bit early to be calling ourselves survivors?"

"Wake up, man—if this Satanel guy wanted us dead, he could have killed us a hundred times over by now. We were chosen to live, I think. We are the future of mankind! When all is said and done we will be gods!"

Hammond didn't like where this was going and instead, decided it was best to focus on what they were doing. They couldn't continue straight to the courthouse, as that was their intended destination. Instead, he worked his way down a side street. A cold shudder ran down Hammond's back as he felt Zero's hand touch him.

"Let's go that way. I think it would be the best." Zero said, using the same ridiculous tone of authority he had used when they first met.

"Sure, Zero. Your call—you point, we go." Hammond hated to follow a man who seemed so outwardly traitorous, but he placated him so he wouldn't set him off again. Another explosion was the last thing that he needed to deal with at the moment.

They traveled along the street Zero had chosen, feet clunking on the old board sidewalk, lighting lamps along the way. The streetlamps got fewer and farther between as they went. Hammond had a very uneasy feeling as they continued down the street. It just felt wrong to him. He thought about the lengths that people had gone to in order to hide this town.

"Why do you think they hid the town instead of just burying it or demolishing it?" Hammond asked more to himself than to Zero.

"They probably were afraid to. I mean, would you put something in a jar, then smash the jar, or would you put a lid on the jar and just let it suffocate?" Zero said, kicking at the dirt they were now walking in.

"That has got to be the smartest thing I have heard anyone say since this whole mess began, bro. I suppose that makes total sense, but why didn't they just bury this place?"

"How should I know? Do I look like a history professor to you?" Zero huffed rather rudely, not wanting to follow his moment of genius with a stupid return.

Hammond stood quietly in the artificial night of the town. He did not know what to do or what to think of the strange situation he found himself in. Was Zero just having a moment like Steph did, or had he truly lost his mind? These questions and many others filled Hammond's thoughts as he lit another cigarette. He glared at the crumpled pack, now almost empty. Without them, he wondered how long his own sanity would hold out. Hammond leaned against one of the old buildings, then slid to the ground. He picked up a stick and began to doodle in the dust as he smoked. Zero stood by, staring at him.

Out of the darkness they heard a scream. It wasn't the sound that one usually makes when they're frightened, it was more like the kind a child would make on a Christmas morning after receiving the gift that they had hoped for all year long. In any other time or place, it may have coaxed a smile, but here and now it sent a shiver down their spine. The echoing scream was followed by howling laughter that changed in tone several times as it echoed back to them.

Zero jumped up immediately, pointing his gun in every possible direction. The sound seemed to be coming from everywhere and nowhere at the same time. Scattered giggles filled the street like a fire that was blazing out of control. Hammond just stood still, listening closely, trying to judge the distance to the source of the creepy laughter. He couldn't pinpoint it, and he felt his grip on sanity starting to slip, but he couldn't fall apart—not like Steph or Zero.

A strange, dark colored ball bounced toward Hammond and stopped suddenly at his feet. He watched it for a few moments, then hesitantly decided to pick it up. The ball felt cold in his hands as he held it awkwardly, fearing the surprises it might hold. It felt like it was . . . sweating. The sound of children playing could be heard echoing through the streets as Hammond stood and waited. He volleyed the ball back and forth in his hands and looked at Zero to see what he made of the situation.

After a moment, a small child dressed like an old-time newsie stepped out from behind the wall. He seemed pretty normal, with the exception of his sallow skin and slightly jagged teeth. The child stood staring at the two men as Zero leveled the Glock at his head. Hammond quickly grabbed Zero's hand and forced the gun down.

"What do you think you're doing?

"We have him dead to rights." Zero whispered hoarsely with a mixture of shock and agitation.

"First off, we don't know how many of them there are, and second, you may just piss him off." Hammond whispered back.

"Hey mister, enjoy the ball. It belongs to you. It has always belonged to you," the child almost hissed at Hammond.

In that instant, Hammond felt the ball shift in his hands. He held it tighter as he heard a muffled voice coming from beneath his hand. He also felt a strange wet sensation on his palm. Was the ball licking him? He spun the ball in his hand in morbid curiosity. He was startled to see that he was once again face to face with his father. The bizarre-feeling material was actually stretched human flesh, stitched and filled with air much like the old cowhide balls.

"Daddy's home." The ball hissed and laughed mockingly at him.

"Why don't you just leave me alone!" Hammond shouted at the image of his father.

"Daddy just wants to take care of you, Eddie—to love you, to nurture you, to teach you the ropes here in Hell. Make no mistake, son. Children that kill their mothers end up in Hell. That's the way the world works."

After it finished its proclamation the thing bit off its own tongue and spit blood into Hammond's face. He quickly dropped the ball and turned to Zero, who was just standing there staring at the newsie.

"What are you doing? We have to get out of here, man!" Hammond yelled at Zero. But he just stood there, stupefied.

"Dude, move it! I don't think he's alone!"

"He's my big brother . . . he died when we were children."

Ham stared at Zero, dumbfounded. "Okay. Listen, I'm sorry. That's rough, but if we don't book it out of here, we're gonna end up as the main course in a freak-fest dinner." "You don't understand! I killed him. He used to make fun of me, always saying I was stupid. One day we were out playing by the pond and he called me a retard. I lost my temper and hit him in the mouth with a rock. I was so mad I couldn't stop, and the next thing I knew his face was covered in blood and his teeth were all broken and he just wouldn't stop screaming. I was scared he was going to tell Dad. You don't understand, Hammond. My dad was an angry man who loved my 'smart' brother more than me." He paused for a moment, and then began to laugh a hollow but meaningful laugh. "I couldn't let that happen, so I pulled him over to the shallow water of the pond and held him down until he stopped fighting."

Zero raised the gun once more and this time, without a moment's hesitation, pulled the trigger. The child's head split open revealing what looked like a newborn baby squirming around inside the child's damaged body. The child fell down and the baby crawled out. The twisted form of the newborn child grew and twisted, as it became an exact duplicate of the child that Zero had just shot. Zero just stood laughing as the child moved closer to him, exposing its jagged broken teeth. Zero once again shot the child in the head with the same result. This time, however, Zero walked up to the infant and smashed it with his boot.

"What is wrong with you, you freak!" Hammond almost screamed as he witnessed the atrocity that Zero had just committed. Even though it was an evil being, Hammond could not help but flinch at the killing of a baby.

"We are the gods, not them! Hammond, we are!" Zero shouted as he turned to Hammond with his gun still raised. "You are just like him! You think I am stupid, too, but I will show you! I will kill you, and then I will take Bailey. I'll probably have to force her at first, but she *will* come to love me. She will be the queen and I will be the king, and together we shall take our place among the gods!"

Before Hammond could respond to Zero's madness, he noticed that more and more children were appearing—coming from everywhere. They were slowly surrounding them. All of the children were dressed in clothing that dated back to the original Convict Grade era, and they were all in various stages of decomposition. They seemed to speak in one voice that echoed only in Hammond's mind. "We are his children . . . he took us, and he will take you, too!" Hammond did not know how they were getting into his head, but he sure wasn't going to stick around and find out.

"Look, dude, you can sit here and play 'happy time with Captain Psycho' if you want, but as for me, I'm getting out of here, now!" Hammond quickly told Zero, then turned and bolted down the street.

"Where are you going? They're just kids . . . we can take them . . ." Zero hadn't finished his sentence before taking off, too, running after Hammond.

Hammond was running as hard as he could. Every breath felt like an iron bar dropping into his smoke-beaten lungs. His whole body hurt, but he pushed himself to go faster and harder. Zero easily kept pace as they ran. Hammond ducked down side streets as much as possible trying to throw off their pursuers. But it didn't seem to matter—they just seemed to flash forward with every slow step they took.

"Don't run! We just want to play with you." The voices echoed as one from behind them.

Zero was still kind of laughing as he ran. Hammond, however, found no humor in the situation and became more disgusted with Zero with every step. Hammond was panting heavily now as he lost ground to the horde that was slowly overtaking him. He didn't know what to do, but he did know that they wouldn't stop until they had taken them. He could feel the panic setting in. And then, as if things weren't bad enough, Zero, once again, had another great idea . . .

"Why don't we just stand and fight? You will never outrun them. You're like, half dead already." Zero said, mocking Hammond who was struggling just to keep pace.

"You wanna fight?" Hammond was furious.

"Go ahead!" With that, Hammond shoved Zero, throwing him off balance. Zero hit the cobblestone street and rolled, then struggled to get back up. For a moment, Hammond thought about going back to help him, but he saw the hordes upon him and fear overtook him. Zero tried to get up, but found himself on his knees, face to face with his older brother. The young boy, whose eyes seemed to be an endless, empty void just stared at Zero with a bemused grin on his face. After a moment, all Hammond could hear were the pained screams of Zero and the gruesome sounds of flesh and sinew being torn from the bone. Hammond couldn't look back. He continued his gut-wrenching pace as he zigzagged through the streets, hoping not to lead them back to the others. He only prayed that they hadn't already been found.

Once he was sure that he had lost them, Hammond made his way back to the store. He was exhausted and guilt-ridden—he ached, both physically and emotionally. He didn't really mean to hurt Zero, or did he? Zero had clearly lost it—he was a threat. Hammond tried to justify his actions and his rage. The most pressing question was, how would Bailey react? Would she ever be able to forgive him? And what about Stephie? He didn't even know if he could forgive himself. As he made his way to Frank's Mercantile, he slowed down his pace and tried to steady his breathing. He was about to enter the store where his friends were hiding, just to tell them that he had sacrificed one of their own to save himself. He didn't know exactly how he was going to do that. The one thing he did know was, he wouldn't lie to them.

Chapter 19

SHOOTING STAR

Hammond steadied his nerves as he put his hand on the doorknob. What he had just done to Zero weighed heavily on his heart. He didn't know if he could even look his friends in the eye, especially Stephie, who he knew had feelings for the young police officer. Hammond breathed deep, pulled open the heavy door, and stepped into the dimly lit room. Every one breathed a sigh of relief when they saw him standing there, Bailey ran up to hug him, but in his shame, he couldn't return her affections.

"What's the matter, baby?" Bailey asked in that sweet Australian accent that Hammond had grown to love so much.

"I have to tell you all something." Hammond began slowly. "We ran into those things again while we were out there. They were in the form of children. Zero said that one of them was his older brother. He told me about how he had murdered him when they were kids". Tears began to fill his eyes as he continued with his story. "Anyway, Zero kind of went crazy and started shooting his brother over and over, and that is when I decided we had to get out of there".

"So you left him there?" Sara asked quietly.

"It's worse than that: Zero ran too, and caught up with me. He was like, totally nuts. He was saying there was no way we could out-run them so we should just stop and fight". Hammond's calm demeanor finally broke and he began to cry, heaving sad sobs as he explained. "I . . . I killed him!" Hammond fell to his knees with his head in his hands and he just sobbed. The rest of what he said was so muffled that the others could only make out part of it. "I'm sorry . . . I am so s-s-sorry . . .".

"You . . . murderer!" Stephie yelled. She made it over to Hammond in two quick strides and slapped him as hard as she could.

Hammond's head rocked back at the force of the blow. Although he was more than twice her size, he just sat there and took two more from the angry Steph. He felt like he deserved much more for letting his anger and fear get the best of him. Stephie struggled to compose herself for a moment, then stormed off to the other side of the room, and sunk down in the corner, glaring at Hammond. He was still beside himself when Tigg stepped up and put his arm around his friend's shoulder.

"What exactly did you do to him, man? No matter what you did, you know I'll stand behind you . . . all the way".

"He was acting so weird . . . talking about how he was going to be some kind of god. He even threatened to kill me! When we started to run, he kept wanting to turn and fight . . . I was so mad . . . I shoved him, and he fell. I would have gone back to help him, but they were already on him . . . it was horrible! I ran to save myself, and just let them kill him. I'm no better than those things out there—you don't see them killing each other!"

Tigg shifted his arm on Hammond's shoulder gently. His friend's body was sticky, smattered with dried blood, and didn't smell all that good. The disgusting growth between his shoulder blades was now the size of a soft ball. It had been a rough couple of days, and his friend looked like he had just been through a meat grinder.

"Dude, that doesn't sound like cold blooded murder to me. It's more like the time you kicked that guy at school in the nuts. You just call that self-preservation. That was pretty much what happened here . . . nothing more. You've got us all this far, and we need you, man . . . we need your strength".

Hammond looked up at Tigg bleary-eyed and just held his friend tight. Tigg had to fight off tears of his own as he held the one person he thought he would never have to hold up. Even Stephie softened a bit as she listened and watched the man who was once so strong, now down on his knees crying into his friend's chest like a hurt child. Bailey teared up at the sight of the man she loved in so much pain, but there was nothing she could do to take it away. Sara held Bailey as she, too, broke out crying. It was a first for the team: their first loss and the first real show of emotions, good and bad. It was a tough moment, but it brought them all closer together.

Hammond was going through a transformation of his own. Physical pain was always a part of his world, so it never really got the best of him. But this was different: this was a pain he felt in the deepest recesses of his heart. His sobs brought a release—a release from the remorse for his own weakness and failure, a release from the frustrations of a lifetime of being hated and abused, a release from feelings confusion and fear. And with this release came a new determination—a resolve to do better, to be braver, to protect his friends, to overcome this evil invasion, no matter what the cost. It took some time for Hammond to regain his composure, but when he did, he finally stood up and spoke.

"Alright, guys—I screwed up, and I know it. Lord knows I ain't perfect, and I never claimed to be. So what I gotta know is, are you still willing to stay with me, and follow me through what's ahead?"

Hammond looked around the room, getting looks of approval from everyone. Even Stephie gave a small nod, making the vote unanimous.

"Then it's time to get down to business." Hammond sounded even stronger than he had before. His new determination commanded respect and instilled confidence in the others. Except for Stephie, who stayed in the corner, everyone gathered around Hammond as he started to explain.

"Alright, let's look at the situation, here. There are about a gazillion of those things and only five of us. They seem to know exactly what hurts us and how to find us. They prey on our weaknesses and insecurities in an attempt to lure us into their sick little 'family of evil' thing, and if they succeed, we are dead. Did I miss anything?"

"Well, I didn't want to bring this up, man, but when I had my arm around you, bro, that thing in your back was like twice the size it used to be, and I might be crazy, but it moved." Tigg said quietly.

Hammond stared at Tigg with a sideways look for a moment. In his mind, the condition of a parasite that was probably nothing more than a bug under his skin was the least of his concerns. He dismissed it, and moved on.

"Okay, how about I word it like this. Are there any more *relevant* concerns?"

"How 'bout the fact that I lost that parchment thingy when we were trying to get out of the cop shop!" Bailey said, starting to tear up again. Her voice broke a little, giving away the fact that she was still upset over losing it.

"Well, missy, I don't think that's really a problem, since I grabbed the thing on the way out." Stephie got up and walked over to the group, pulling the missing scroll from her jacket pocket. "So don't go turning on the 'oh poor me' water works."

Tigger stared at Stephie with awe as she handed the scroll back to Bailey. Stephie just shrugged off the attention she was now receiving, picked up the china doll that had become her main source of comfort, and sat back down in the corner. Everyone went back to doing their own thing, and things calmed down.

Bailey sat quietly as she read the scroll to herself. She was taking it all in so that she could sum it up for the others. She was happy to have a job to do—something to keep her mind off of Hammond. She found herself watching him, thinking of him constantly, and wanted nothing more than to just hold him close and tell him how much she loved him, but this wasn't the time or place for it. She would have to put her mind into something productive, and keep all the emotional stuff under control.

Hammond stood in the shadows, away from the light, trying to figure out how to get everyone safely to the courthouse. He was starting to understand the old adage "burden of command", and he didn't like it one bit. As Tigger walked up beside him, Hammond found himself thinking of him more as his lieutenant than his friend. It almost seemed as if Tigger should have saluted him as he approached. The thought of this made Hammond chuckle as Tigger looked at him.

"Hey Ham, I was wondering . . . what's our next play gonna be?" He cleared his throat and continued. "I mean, with all those things out there, we can't just walk down the street to the courthouse—those things would tear us apart before we even got close. So, what do we do?"

"I'll tell you the truth, Tigger, ole buddy, I really have no idea. I don't know any more about this than any of you do, except for the stuff that Satanel told me, and trust me, mate, the stuff I didn't tell you wouldn't help. If anything, it would make it worse."

Tigg looked at Hammond with a respect that could not be questioned. Hammond seemed to always have the answers when it was most important, but when he didn't, he didn't try to hide it. It was a fact that Tigg truly appreciated, and he meant it when he said he would stay with him, no matter what. Tigg shuddered as he thought back to something Hammond had once told him, way back when they were kids. It was the first time Hammond had saved him from some schoolyard bullies. "Some day I won't be around to help you, Tigger, and when that day comes you will have to be like me for someone else". Those words had always stuck in Tigger's mind for two reasons: first, they were very prolific for a grade-schooler; and second, he dreaded the day when Hammond would no longer be there.

"Hey bro, I got an idea. It may sound wicked stupid, but it just might work". Tigger was afraid of the reaction he might get, but he continued anyway. "Dude, you still got those road flares, right?"

"Yeah, why?"

"Okay, here's my thought—you and I will take the straight shot and the girls will take the back way. If you can see in the dark and the lights severely mess with your eyes, then the flares should really put some sand in their motion lotion!"

"Great idea, but bad split-up option, bro. From now on, we stick together—win, lose or draw." Hammond thought for a moment. "What do you mean by, take the back way?"

"Um, go out the back door and follow the alleys", Tigg said, as if it were only obvious.

"What back door?" Hammond was a bit upset that no one had told him about the back door.

"Duh, dude, the one that is back over there. Which back door did you think I was talking about?"

"Tigger I don't know whether to kiss you, or strangle you, man. But that's a great idea!" Hammond couldn't believe he missed something as crucial as the back door.

"I suppose strangling me will have to do, because your breath would kill me long before I died of suffocation." Tigger's comment made them both crack up laughing.

Hammond was now thinking of how to use Tigger's plan effectively. He began to think of all of his weaknesses and how he could use them against his enemy. For the first time, Hammond began to realize the strange similarities that existed between his enemy and himself. Though he was human, he seemed to have strange attributes that resembled those things. His eyes were both his strength and his weakness, as they must also be to those demons. He also seemed to heal rather quickly, but that didn't seem to be of much use in this case. Then it dawned on him, black does not reflect light—it absorbs it. It was the only color he could not see in the dark . . .

"Everybody!" Hammond shouted enthusiastically. "Find all the black clothing, sheets, blankets, and stuff you can find. I have a plan!" Hammond started to do the same, but then quickly corrected himself. "Sorry—I meant to say, Tigg and I have a plan!"

Tigger looked at Hammond, smiling from ear to ear. No one ever gave him credit for anything, and it made him feel a sense of pride that he never felt before. Sara looked over at him and smiled a sweet smile, and just for a moment Tigg felt like the guy who scored the winning touchdown. When he walked past her, Sara grabbed him and gave him a quick kiss on the cheek. Tigg thought he'd died and gone to Heaven.

Bailey sat down, silently opened up the scroll, and began to read again. The papyrus felt strange in her hands: both ancient and new at the same time. As she read, the world around her dissolved and images of an old world took its place. What was once the mercantile was now a primeval place filled with people and beasts that she did not recognize.

Bailey closed her eyes in disbelief at what she was now witnessing. The scene was one of chaos and abominations, fornication and bestiality. Pounding music and chanting set the tone, men and women engaged in all manner of perversions. Animals were brutally slaughtered in barbaric rituals. Blood and horror were found on every side. The madness of the whole scene consumed Bailey as she tried to understand what she was seeing. A striking figure of a man sat before her on a throne made of human bones, overseeing the whole affair. He was a beautiful, yet very frightening figure. With a flick of the man's wrist all of the chaos froze and Bailey was left in deafening silence. The man stared at her with his cold eyes for several moments before he finally spoke.

"I had expected someone else. Where is my bloodline?" his words were stone cold and stern.

"Who are you?" Bailey questioned nervously.

"My name is Satanel, and never answer a question with a question. It is rude, my dear." His tone warmed up as he said this, but his impatience remained.

"I don't think I know who you're looking for", she said, cautiously.

"Stop playing stupid. Where is Edgar Hammond?" he demanded, standing up and raising his voice.

Satanel moved almost effortlessly as he approached the frightened young girl. She stood her ground fearing that she might regret having done so. Once he reached her, he raised his long-nailed hand to her trembling face. Satanel's touch had a cold, dead feeling to it, but she could not bring herself to move. His face went darker as her thoughts of Hammond flowed through him.

"So, you are Bailey . . . I wonder if you would still love him if you knew who and what he really was?" he asked as a sinister grin spread across his face. "You are probably wondering about the significance of the scroll that has brought you to me."

"Y-yes, I suppose I am." Bailey managed to get out, barely able to control her fear.

"Well, allow me to shed some light on the family history of your friend . . . who also happens to be my great, great, great grandson."

Satanel walked behind Bailey, whispering into her ear as his words began to spread like poison through her mind. After a moment that seemed like an eternity, the story unfolded to her like an old movie flickering on a silver screen. The images were both frightening and exciting. It felt like her head was going to burst as the images came in full color and sound, as if they were her own memories.

Bailey's mind focused and she saw seven angels that were assigned to protect man. They were strong and beautiful, the most beautiful of which she recognized as Satanel himself. There was another more terrifying angel at his side named Azazel that looked almost like a beast. Men and women alike gathered around them, drawn to them by their ethereal beauty. At first the angels were just and true, and kept their charge of watching over the children of Adam and Eve. As time passed, though, the daughters of Eve began to catch the eye of the watchers. Though it was a sin, the watchers lusted after them, growing ever more needful as they watched them grow.

Azazel contented himself more with teaching the humans his skills and magic. He taught them how to create great weapons of iron and use them against each other. He reveled in the chaos of watching them fight each other to a bloody end. Satanel reveled in the joys of the flesh that surrounded him. He could not stop himself—he had to sample them all, and as a result, many of them were with child.

Watching from above, the angels known as Michael and Gabriel could no longer stand to see this fornication and brought themselves before God himself to ask his permission to step in. God ordered that the watchers be thrown into darkness and Azazel be bound and thrown into a pit covered with jagged rocks. Michael was more than pleased to do so, for he did not much care for the watchers. Gabriel and Michael descended upon Earth with an army of angels and smote the children of angels and man known as the nephlim.

Bailey watched, awe-struck and horrified as the protectors of God tore through the wretched horde of the nephlim. When he realized what was happening, Satanel called upon Azazel to go to battle with these angels. Azazel fought, brutally killing many of the angels before being brought down and bound by Michael. The angel did as instructed and from a distance Satanel watched as they cast his most noble servant into the depths. He swore revenge on both angels and men as he disappeared, screaming, into the pit.

This vision faded and Bailey found herself face to face with Satanel. From the look of horror on her face, Satanel guessed that she had understood what he had shown her. The still frame of orgy and sacrifice that had once filled the room now gave way to cold emptiness that only she and Satanel occupied.

Hammond saw Bailey, walked over and sat down next to her on the old, dirty bench where she was sitting. Hammond's presence shook her from her vision. She looked at him with sad eyes and leaned on his shoulder, as if she had just received word that he was going to die.

"What's wrong, love?" Hammond asked as he put his arm around Bailey. This was the first time he had ever called her that, and she liked it.

"Well, honey, this scroll has stuff in it that I really think you need to know about. What do you know about things called nephlim?" Her tone implied that she already knew what they were, and it had something to do with him.

174

"Nothing, really. Satanel mentioned them, but nothing that I would call interesting or important", he said kind of off handedly. He was enjoying the feel of her body against his.

"Well, sweetie, the nephlim are the children of the fallen angels and women, they are the product of the ultimate sin. You are the product of that sin, Hammond." She fell silent waiting for his reaction.

"What? I am not. My dad was Edgar Earl Hammond, a drunken, unemployed truck driver, and Mom was Patricia St. John, housewife." The thought that he was anything more than the unwanted child of his parents was absolutely absurd to him. "So you're saying that I am some sort of crazy demon-boy? That stuff only happens in supermarket tabloids and ridiculous sci-fi shows."

Considering the topic closed, Hammond hugged and kissed Bailey and went to help the others in search of black cloth. He kind of chuckled inside as he thought about all the times his father had called him a demon child. Could he have been right? He quickly dismissed the thought and went on with the chore of fine-tuning his plan to get the group to the courthouse. His fingers fumbled with the key that was in his pocket while he paced, casually looking through the assortment of items on the shelf. How was it that all this stuff was still here when back up top everything was so trashed? Then the virtual rebuilding of the hospital reminded him that evil could hide its tracks even better than the good guys could.

Tigger had collected all of the quilts with black backing and placed them in the center of the room. The others were still looking through the stuff when Stephie started laughing.

"It talks!" she said, holding the little doll up like a woman would hold her child.

"What?" Sara asked as she looked oddly at Stephie. "What do you mean, it talks?"

"She said my name and told me she wanted to be my friend," Stephie said, grinning.

Sara was going to say something else but Hammond grabbed her arm and shook his head. "She's a few french fries short of a happy meal right now, but she's happy and quiet, so just let her think that a hundred and fifty year old doll can talk. We have bigger things to worry about."

Sara did not want to leave the subject alone, but she decided that Hammond was right. This was a lot better than her freaking out and giving away their location. She just didn't understand how Stephie could just check out of reality like that, leaving the rest of them to do everything. It was kind of irritating. "Crazy or not, she could at least pull her own weight." Sara mumbled under her breath. Doing her best to ignore Steph, she went about, busying herself with the chore Hammond had assigned her. Instead, she started singing in a whisper, 'Don't Worry, Be Happy'.

"You do know that that guy killed himself, right?" Hammond said offhandedly.

"Hammond, you are such a kill-joy, you know that?" Sara retorted, still humming the song.

"Actually, he's not dead, moron. That's just an urban legend created for morbid people like you who would like to think that even the happiest person is not really happy." Steph stepped in.

"Well, I hate to tell you this, but he's probably dead, now." Tigg shrugged as he fished some marshmallows out of Hammond's knapsack.

After a few moments the whole group was singing it. The moment of levity was much needed and for the first time it seemed less like they were fighting for their lives and more like they were on a camping trip. Tigger roasted marshmallows on the kerosene lamps while Bailey and Hammond danced to Sara's masterful rendition of 'Don't Worry, Be Happy'. Stephie sat quietly, still immersed in the china doll. All in all, they were enjoying themselves as though the nightmare that awaited them did not exist.

Hammond and Bailey decided they were going to explore the building a little more and left Sara, Tigg and Stephie to their own devices. They went up the short staircase into the loft. Once they were out of sight of the others, Hammond grabbed Bailey by the waist and started to dance with her as he serenaded her with his own particular rendition of 'Shooting Star' by Bad Company. Bailey just laughed and danced with him. The moment could not have been more perfect for the two of them. Hammond held Bailey close as she kissed him softly between verses. She was very happy. In that instant, the world could have stopped right where it was, and that would have been just fine by them.

Bailey started slowly pulling Hammond's shirt off as he sang to her. She kissed his lips, then trailed her warm mouth down his neck. Her lips traveled across his shoulder, then down his muscular chest. When she reached his well-defined abs, he choked in shock. Hammond tried to keep singing, afraid she would quit if he did, but he didn't have the breath to go on. Bailey slowly took her own shirt off, exposing her lovely breasts in a lacy black bra. She pressed her warm body against his, and kissed his fears away as the two of them melted together. He lowered her to the floor, kissing her softly and holding her tight. This time there were no interruptions as the two of them made love. Hammond could not contain himself as he heard her sweet voice call his name in the eternal night of this strange place. With the smell of love and sweat heavy in the air, the two of them fell asleep in a lover's embrace, both dreaming of a life together, without the end of the world looming just around the corner . . .

Chapter 20

INTO THE COURTHOUSE

Hammond awoke to see a snickering Tigg staring down at him as he lay there half-naked. Everyone else was already up and getting ready for the journey to the courthouse, which was now only a block away. Tigger threw Hammond a black shirt that he had found and Hammond buttoned it up slowly, trying to figure out exactly what to say to Tigg. Bailey came in and gave Hammond a kiss and told him they were ready when he was.

"Stop looking at me like that, fool—a couple hours ago, she was naked too!"

"Right, Ham—whatever gets you through, man . . ."

"Shut up, you boob. I'll be down in a minute and you can make fun of me all you want while I am feeding you to those things out there!" Hammond thought for a moment—that was what he had said to Zero. "Dude, you know I'm just joking, right?" Hammond said in a faint whisper.

"Well, all kidding aside . . . if you think you can run faster mad then I can scared, you're dead wrong."

Tigg always seemed to have some smart-alec comment to ease the tension, and Hammond appreciated it more with each new challenge. He got up slowly. The lump on his back seemed to have gotten bigger. He didn't want his friends to know, but he was worried about it. It was pretty hard not to be worried about that thing moving under his skin. He buttoned up the shirt Tigg had given him and went back down the stairs. Stephie looked at Hammond and giggled like she knew some dirty little secret. Hammond saw the excited little girl look on her face and had to smile. She looked so young and innocent.

They all seemed to be more prepared to deal with everything, now, after getting some much-needed sleep. It was like a whole new group of people, refreshed and ready to face the day. Hammond felt different, too—good or bad, he felt older. He looked at the equipment they had packed and was rather surprised to see an old six-gun and a cavalry sword that were among the things they had gathered.

"Hey, I don't suppose I could have the sword, eh?" Hammond asked as he viewed the sharp object. "Shi—ny . . .", he thought.

"I thought you might like that, knowing your fascination with blades 'n all." Tigg said, handing the sword to Hammond, who looked like a kid on his birthday.

"Alright, this is the plan, people. We all dress in black and form a chain. I will take the lead. There will be no lights except the ones in the street that Zero and I lit. I will guide us to the courthouse. Don't show any part of your skin or they might see you. The only color that I cannot see in the dark is black, so I am hoping that it is the same for them. As Tigg suggested, you will each be given a flare. Do not, and I repeat, do *not*, light them unless you absolutely have to."

Hammond took one last look at the black-clad crew and hoped this wouldn't be the last time they were all together and happy. He feared that the chances of making it might not be too great, but they had to try. All of their lives depended on the choices he made, and up until last night, he didn't know if he could make the ultimate choice of who lived and who died. Today would be another test of his courage and leadership.

The group lined up single file at the back door. Hammond was first, then Bailey, Stephie, Sara and finally, Tigg. Tigger had given the shotgun to Hammond in favor of Hammond's pistols. If one gun was good, two were better. Hammond sighed and cocked the shotgun as he put his hand to the old brass door handle that hung loosely on the dry, cracked door. He was afraid, but he wasn't going to let anyone else know that.

Before he could even turn the handle, the room started shaking violently. Things came crashing down off the store shelves and the old windows broke behind the quilted covers. Dust fell from every board as the building felt like it was going to rattle apart around them.

"They've found us!" Tigger yelled from behind them as he covered his head to shield it from the falling debris.

"No . . ." Bailey said with her voice shaking. "This is something else."

"Well, I for one am not gonna hang out here—lets beat it!" Hammond said, forcing the rickety old door open and moving quickly outside.

Hammond immediately realized that Bailey was right—this was something different. In slow, sucking motions the dome above them seemed to be moving as if someone were trying to pull it off. Everything around them was shaking as the metal sky above them started to split. Cars and other objects fell down from the giant crack, but they all turned to dust before they hit the ground. It was as if the town they had known all of their lives was just a fading illusion giving way to a much harsher reality. Hammond now knew what Chicken Little must have felt like when the sky started falling.

Hammond grabbed Bailey's hand and went into an all-out run for the courthouse, giving up on the plan in favor of just making it to solid shelter. Bailey grabbed Stephie as they formed the chain Hammond had originally suggested. Every so often as they ran, flaming rocks would come down out of nowhere, almost hitting the team as they bounced off the ground and rolled along the cobblestone streets. "It's impossible to win a game where the rules keep changing", Hammond thought to himself as he ran.

As the courthouse came into view, Hammond pumped his legs all the harder to get there before they were either crushed or burned by the falling debris. The scene was so chaotic that he didn't realize that he was practically dragging the others behind him. His legs began to burn as he thought to himself, "only a few more feet, and I've got them there". A strange light glowed from over by the hill next to the cemetery. Fear overruled his curiosity for the time being and he ignored it.

The courthouse door grew larger in Hammond's view as his sprint began to break. He got to the door and shot it open with the gun. He pushed Bailey in first and waited for the others as the light by the cemetery grew brighter. If there was anything that cheap sci-fi and horror movies had taught him, it was that a large, glowing red light was never a good thing. Tigger was the last one to reach the door and Hammond almost threw his friend inside before stepping in himself, closing the door behind.

Tigger fell to his knees to catch his breath as Hammond lit a kerosene lamp. The light provided a good view of the hallway. It looked very different from what Tigg had imagined: not dark, dank, or nasty, but a rather comfortable, formal-looking place. The paint on the walls was remarkably well preserved: not chipping or fading, and the floor tiling looked almost brand new. The whole building had almost a museum-like quality to it. The design was quite ornate, considering its remote location and period. Although constructed mostly of wood, like other buildings in the town, the builders had put a lot of effort into making it look like one of those fancy buildings made of marble or some other stone. It even had pillars and a domed ceiling. The walls were lined with gaslights that were controlled by a little key located on the wall next to the door.

Tigg walked over and turned the key, and the lights came to life. Some of them faded the second they came on, but others remained, flickering like Christmas lights in a storefront window. In most situations the flickering lights would have bothered Tigg, because of the way they cast eerie shadows, dancing around like ghosts on the old walls. But in this case, they were a welcome change from the ominous darkness the group had become accustomed to.

Bailey reached down and handed the squinting Hammond the sunglasses that he feared he would never need again. He was reminded how much the light hurt his eyes as he put them on. Sara stood looking from the door to the end of the hallway.

"Guys, I hate to interrupt, but don't you think we should find a safer place to stand?"

Hammond turned and looked at the splintered door that he had just blasted through to get them in. It was closed, but would not, in fact, keep anything out for very long. Outside, he could still hear the crashing and chaos that had befallen the underground city.

"We made quite a ruckus gettin' in here—that's for sure. With all the fireworks outside, though, we may have gotten in unnoticed—or maybe not. Either way, she's right—we ought to keep moving".

The only place to go, really, was down the hallway. They moved together, examining each room they passed to make sure nothing was inside. They didn't get far before they started to hear noises. Rustling sounds, like someone, or something was moving with them. It was almost as if they were waking sleeping residents as they moved through the place. The rustling noises seemed to be growing in number and frequency. They were faint, yet distinct—there was no doubt these sounds were real.

Suddenly, a curtain over to one side moved. There was a thud as a book fell from a shelf and hit the floor. Everyone jumped, and scampering sounds broke out all around them. Things started to move—the curtains rustled again. Bailey screamed, and in response, Sara screamed, too. Tigg yelled, "Over there!" as he thought he saw something move along the wall.

Hammond spun around and let loose with the shotgun. In the closed space, the sound was deafening. Dust, plaster, and bits of wood erupted into a cloud that filled the room. Everyone stopped screaming and yelling, and just stared at the destruction. Tigg, guns drawn, carefully approached to examine the scene.

"You got him, dude!" Tigg shoved one gun in his belt, reached down and picked something up, then turned around to show everyone the bloody carcass of . . . a rat.

"Yep, he's a big one!" Tigg was enjoying the moment way too much as everyone breathed a sigh of relief, and for some, disgust. Jeers started to rise from the group, when Tigg stopped them.

"Wait, wait, everybody—hold on, there! Hammond, I think you might want to take a look at what's behind door number one, here."

Hammond came over and looked at the hole he had just made—the plaster and lathing had fallen to reveal a door behind it.

"That's weird . . ." Hammond said, a little puzzled. "Why would someone hide a door like that?"

"What's weird is the fact that out of this whole hallway, you just happen to shoot a hole in the wall right here where this door is?" Steph said, breaking in. "Try the key that you got with that note. I think we were led here, somehow, and were supposed to find this door." Steph stood there petting the hair of the china doll as she spoke. That dumb doll was really beginning to annoy Hammond. He was starting to wonder if it really was telling her things.

Hammond reached into his pocket, pulled out the key, and walked forward to the big steel door. He pulled away more of the wall and slid the key gently into the lock and turned it. To his amazement the door swung open easily to reveal a staircase that twisted down into the abyss. The scene was almost surrealistic. There were torches on stands mounted snuggly against the walls, and looking down the staircase, it looked like it went on forever.

"Hurry, hurry, hurry! Be the first to step onto a one-way ride to Hell, folks! See the staircase that goes on forever, and watch the five stupid teenagers go down to seal their fate!" Hammond said, mocking an old time ringmaster.

"Oh that's funny, Hammond." Steph said, looking at him with a sideways glance, trying to hide the smile sliding across her face.

"Alright, already. I'm going." Hammond said at length, realizing his joke came at the wrong time.

Hammond cleared more of the debris away from the opening and started down the long staircase. One by one, the others followed step-by-step, down into the cavernous depths. The stairwell was so cold, they could almost see their breath as they made their way downward. The walls were wet with mildew and smelled oddly like stale bread.

Hammond breathed uneasily as he thought this seemed all too well planned, too coincidental. When he finally got to the bottom of the stairs, it wasn't the dungeon he had expected but more like the archives of the local library. This caught him unexpectedly, as he had anticipated a scary and gruesome scene. The walls were a pleasant painted plaster the same as they were upstairs, and these, too, had lights that worked on gas.

"What do you make of this, Tigg, ol' buddy?" Hammond asked, looking around.

"Well it's not really dank and dark enough for my taste, but it will do." Tigg said in false sincerity.

Hammond kept the girls on the stairs while the two of them checked the place a little more thoroughly. Tigg stopped suddenly as he brought one of the pistols up in a defensive gesture. There, curled up in the corner, was a corpse, remarkably well preserved, withered hands tightly clutching an old, tattered book. It was still, yet a look of horror was permanently emblazoned on his wrinkled and dusty face.

Hammond carefully approached it, fearing that it may be one of Satanel's tricks. When he got close enough, he poked at it with the barrel of the loaded shotgun. The man's head fell off and rolled along the floor to the foot of the stairs where Sara stood. She shrieked, horrified by the open-mouthed stare of the severed head in front of her.

The cold hand of death had clearly touched this place, but it was not the hand of Satanel. His hand never left a print, death's hand always leaves its mark for all to see and know that it is coming. Was this the fate that awaited them too? Would they survive the demons onslaught, just to die, shriveled and lonely? To have your only legacy be the book that you clutch in your dead fingers until someone finds you and knocks off your head? These things raced through Sara's mind as she stepped back into Bailey.

"Get that creepy thing away from me right now, Tigger!" the way Sara yelped this, Tigg didn't know whether it was a request or an order.

"Yes, my lady!" Tigg said as he walked over and casually kicked the head away.

Hammond stood looking at the poor soul that sat on the floor. A chill ran down his spine as he tried to pull the book from the poor man's hand. He could have easily been one of them, had the time been right. The brittle fingers snapped under the pressure of having the book pulled away from them. With one last quick jerk the book was free from the unfortunate fellow's hands and the rest of his body crumbled along with the fingers.

"God rest your vigilant soul, my friend." Hammond said as he made the symbol of the Father, Son, and Holy Ghost.

"I didn't know you were Catholic, Ham." Tigg whispered to Hammond.

"That's because I'm not. I just wanted to show our friend, here, some respect. And why are you whispering? 'Afraid you're going to wake him up?" Tigg thought about arguing for a moment, but instead simply made the same symbol and bowed his head. Everyone in the room observed the moment of silence. Though no one had announced it, they all respected it. After a few moments Hammond lifted his head and looked down at the worn out old book. In beautiful Italic letters the book title read, "*The Journal of an American Traveler*". Judging by the writing, it was a gimmick used to sell these books to prospecting families, to make their lives seem a little more important.

"It's his journal. We may find some answers about what's happening in this God forsaken place." Hammond spoke softly. He wasn't really comfortable reading the contents of this guy's private life, but to know the future he had to know the past. "Tigger, take this key and run upstairs and lock the door. Maybe this time we can get through something without being attacked."

Stephie took a place at the bottom of the stairs and continued stroking her china doll. She sat attentively as she waited for Hammond to read them the contents of the journal. The others also found places to sit as they prepared to hear about the life and times of an American traveler. The impact of this book would probably never be known to the people who made it, but Hammond was sure that the person who wrote in it and clutched it until he was found, did.

After Tigg returned and everyone was settled, Hammond took a seat on the reading bench at the far end of the room. The table was old and it creaked and wobbled as he slowly rested his weight upon it. All eyes were now on Hammond and the tension peaked as he turned the old book in his hands and gently cracked it open. Time had crisped the pages and he had to turn them delicately. The handwriting was barely legible, but it was clear a teenager had written it.

"So, he was one of us". Hammond thought as he cleared his throat to read.

Chapter 21

A Traveler's Journey

January 12, 1855,

    I think I shall start this journal with my name. I am Marcus St. John, and I am eighteen years old. My family is getting ready to leave from Jamestown, Missouri. We are heading west so my father can seek his fortune in the territories. I am not really sure about this trip, but strange things have been happening around here of late. My father does not seem quite right, and to be honest I am very worried about Mother.

    Mother gave me this journal; she says it will be extremely important to someone, some day, to know what we have gone through to get our fortune. I don't think that anyone will really be interested in reading it, but I think it will help ease the monotony of the trip. I will be leaving all of my relatives, other than my immediate family, and all of my friends. I'm not sure I want to go. Things are not right here, just now, but I don't really think I should talk about that, just yet. My mother says it's just my imagination. I disagree. Mother just called for evening prayer so I will write more later.

January 13, 1855,

Prayer was so odd last night. My father started singing the hymns in some weird language and he went around the house turning all the crucifixes upside down. No one said anything; we all just watched him do it. Father always said that that was sacrilegious. It was one more disturbing event in a long line of strange happenings. Lately, when he speaks to himself, he says "Us", even though there is just one of him. It frightens me. Ever since father got back from his mining trip to Africa with his employer, he has not been himself. All of a sudden, he is so quiet and withdrawn. Then he started speaking of the west, and of a town called Convict Grade.

February 16, 1855,

I have not had a chance to write in a while. We have been busy packing and preparing the house here. Mother's sister and her husband are moving with us. We pulled away from home three days ago. The trip has proven to be strange. The only time our wagons move is at night. This seems dangerous to me. I can barely see the path we're walking on, and I can hear wild animals all around us. Our wagon train is growing daily as we move across the plains. Mother has been out of sorts lately. She says that father is doing what is best for us and that we should trust his decisions. The people that have been added to our party keep looking at me queerly and I am beginning to worry that they may mean us harm. Father says it is just my imagination, but I swear I saw one of them eating a dog!

I just got back from gathering wood for the fire. I saw one of the other men and my father down by the creek talking in that bizarre language again. They seemed to be planning something but I have no idea what they were saying. I tried to hurry so they would not see me. I do not trust Father anymore, but I am afraid of what he will do if he finds that out. I am really frightened. I don't know what to do. Mother even seems to be afraid now, but she will not speak of it. She has changed somehow and I fear that she might be thinking unholy thoughts about a man who visited our camp last night. She was looking at him like she used to look at father.

July 23, 1855,

The man came back this morning, just as we were setting up camp. Father talked to him for a while and then the man retired with my mother into my father's tent. I questioned my father about this but he just said, "We know what we are doing, and I should not interfere". I looked around but my father was standing alone. I want to know why he keeps saying 'we'. I have started sleeping away from camp. I fear that what is happening to the others may happen to me if I stay there. I keep my watch from a distance. They keep trying to get me to go with this man they call Satanel. They say I should ride in his wagon with him. Every day, I get more frightened as we travel further into the mountains. Satanel has made himself the leader of the train. He is a very appealing man: charming and likeable. Everyone seems to have fallen for his charm but me.

October 28, 1855,

We arrived in Convict Grade this morning. I would just like to set up our new home and forget about all of the strange things that took place during the trip. Father and the rest of the men have started a new church. I have not been writing lately because I don't want them to find this book. It has become my only solace in the bizarre turns my life has taken over the last year. My father, who used to promote reading, will no longer let me read my Bible. He says books are the means of evil. Such a huge change!

My mother is with child now and I am somewhat worried about who the father really is. I know I should not think this way about my mother, but I have my suspicions that it was not my father. I will love my new brother or sister either way, but I still feel an inkling of doubt. My poor mother! I know this was not her doing.

October 31, 1855,

Good news! I have met a girl. She is incredibly beautiful and she seems to always know what I am thinking. Her name is Rachel. She is so amazing and she believes me about all of the strange things that are happening here in Convict Grade. Her father is a Christian preacher. I fear, though, that whatever strange magic is affecting this place was brought with us. Rachel and I hope to get married someday and move back to civilization. My parents hate her and that makes me love her all the more.

Rachel told me about the night terrors she has. My blood turned to ice and the hair on the back of my neck stood on end as I listened to her describe them. The dreams were so similar to mine. Well, I have to go now. It is almost time for the party. My father keeps calling it something like "Samhain". And they are planning to sacrifice two lambs, one for "God" and the other for Azazel. I believe our Lord in Heaven would never ask for sacrifice. I do not know who their God is, but he is not the same as mine. Their souls will pay.

November 8, 1855,

Today I made a new friend. He is not so bright, but he is a very nice man. He told me stories about the Freemasons and the Knights Templar. These stories are entertaining, even if they are not true. His girl, Rebecca, is very nice. She is a friend of Rachel's and the four of us now spend most of our time together. Last night we made a fire down by the river. I played my guitar for them and Gabriel told us stories of the great army of God and the Templar Knights. It was so exiting to hear about this army and how they defeated the sinners to restore peace to the world. Someday, I would like to be one of these knights. Gabriel says they still exist.

I kissed Rachel for the first time last night. It made coming here all worth it, and I hope someday to take her into my marriage bed. I cannot believe I just wrote that! I hope she never reads this, or I will have some explaining to do.

My mother is heavy with child now. She is only five or so months along, yet she looks like she is overdue! I don't know what form of witchcraft this is, but I do not like it at all. Gabriel keeps talking about the nephlim and how an angel can make a woman conceive a child. I don't know about that, but one thing I do know is that this is no angel that is inside my mother. She is sick all the time: almost completely bed-ridden. I fear for my new friends but I am not ready to tell them about my journey just yet. I am not sure how they will react.

November 18, 1855,

The Christmas season is quickly approaching and nobody seems to even care. It is almost as if it means nothing to them that the Son of God was born! Rachel says that it is very strange indeed, because her family practically lives for Christmas, and yet this year they have not even begun to sing their usual Christmas hymns. My family usually talks about the big Christmas celebration that we always have, and when I mentioned it to Father, he simply ignored me and went on with his daily tasks.

Another thing that strikes me as odd is that, although we have come here to make our fortune mining gold, my father does not seem to be working. We seem to be wealthy, but I have yet to see him work. He goes out to the mines, but he comes back clean as the new day! This is much different from back home. He used to come home completely covered in dirt, but not here.

Gabriel and I have a plan to follow our parents to find out where it is that they go when they are claiming to be working. Rachel and Rebecca think that it is a bad idea, but I have to know what is going on.

November 30, 1855,

There are very strange things going on around here. What started out as just my family and the strangers that joined us on our trip has become everyone in town. They all seem to be worshiping this Satanel. He has started coming around here a lot. I am very angry because he is turning everyone against the God that I have known all my life. Rachel, Gabriel, Rebecca, and I are planning on setting up a permanent camp up in a cave past the cemetery. We have to stay away from the people in town because they are getting more and more crazy. They are beginning to talk about human sacrifice!

We are also planning to take steps to ensure that Rebecca and Rachel don't get sacrificed to my father's angry god. Gabriel thinks that we should inform the Templar Knights about our situation and I do not have the heart to tell him that they don't exist. Today I will write and mail his letter for him, but I don't expect any real results.

December 14, 1855,

I received word that my baby brother was born today. Rachel and I have decided not to risk going into town to see him. I have not been to my father's home for over a week, now. Things are getting bad down there, from what I understand. We are now trying to find another exit from the cave, in hopes of leaving unnoticed. We are hoping it comes out in the hills on the south side of town, and we can head east unnoticed. Gabriel and I have been sneaking into town during the day to steal provisions for the trip. It is very strange but the people around here do not seem to go out during the day anymore, and we have been taking full advantage of that.

December 15, 1885,

I am very concerned for Rachel and Rebecca. When Gabriel and I went into town for provisions this morning, I was horrified to see the bodies of two girls that we had done our studies with. They were pulled inside out and looked to be half eaten! I don't know how to tell Rachel and Rebecca, but I fear that this may be the virgin sacrifice that I heard about. Apparently, people who worship the devil sacrifice virgins in some barbaric ritual designed to please the Lord of Sin.

Gabriel and I have come up with a plan to rescue our women from this horrible fate. We will marry them and take them into our beds. It is the only way that we can truly protect them from sacrifice. It may not fully protect any of us from what the future now seems to hold, but at least it will save them from this evil ritual. We plan to wed them on Christmas, the holiest of days, and we hope that the Lord will honor our union even though we do not have a priest to deliver our marriage into the waiting hands of our God.

December 25 1855,

Today I got married! Rachel and I are so happy together. We are planning an escape to Virginia where we will start our new family in the lap of luxury. We have found several storehouses of raw gold and have begun taking it with our usual supplies. Today we had a marvelous feast of turkey with all the fixings. It was absolutely wonderful. Gabriel married Rebecca as well and we are celebrating both unions and the birth of Christ! A better cause for celebration you could never ask for. I cannot wait for tonight, when we can make our marriage official!

January 1, 1856,

Things are not well around here. We have found our means of escape but it is still winter and we would not survive the trip. The animals in the area have started acting very peculiar and the sky is growing ever darker. The days should be getting longer, but they only seem to be getting shorter. The people in town have not yet discovered our hideout, but I am afraid that it is only a matter of time. The people that we once knew have either gone strange or disappeared altogether. These are dark days indeed, and I am not really sure how to lead the others. This morning I told them the whole story about the journey here, and of the strangers, and of the man Satanel. They did not seem to hold it against me, but I still feel badly for not telling them sooner.

Gabriel and I followed my father last night. He went to the mines on the south side of town. Everyone in town seemed to be there. We saw father and another stranger cutting out the eyes of the others. How horrifying! There is still no word from Gabriel's precious Knights as I had figured it would be. We are now utterly alone . . .

January 23, 1856,

We found Rachael's father today. He was barely recognizable. His head had been cut off and placed on a stick in the middle of Town Square. I cannot help but wonder what they will do to us if they did that to a preacher . . . Rachael is taking it pretty well, considering, and Rebecca has been a saint in taking care of her. I don't know how much longer we can stand this. I have to come up with a plan and fast. We need to get out of here before it is too late and we, too, are consumed by this evil. We just have to bide our time until about March or April and then we will be able to get out of here, hopefully undetected. I will not be writing for a while as I have very little ink. I hope to have good news the next time I write.

March 15, 1856,

They are all dead. Gabriel, Rebecca, and Rachael. All of them. He is coming for me next. I have locked myself in the courthouse and I intend to tell you how this all ends. Here I sit and here I shall stay for all eternity. I care not to leave because without the others, I am nothing. They called me leader and I let them down. I do not deserve to live.

When they find you, they give you a choice: join them or die horribly. Gabriel chose to die instead of joining them. They drug him behind a horse for almost a day before they tied him to the tree outside of town. He was still alive and I tried to free him but Rebecca, or what used to be Rebecca, attacked me and stabbed me in the shoulder. She then tried to eat me. I barely made it out of there with my life. That night they tore Gabriel into pieces, slowly. Somehow they kept him alive so that his screams could be heard through the whole valley. I could still hear him when I awoke this morning. I wish I could help him, but I cannot. I will be forced to hear his screams until I die, or go mad, whichever comes first.

Rachael came to me two days ago and told me she had some sickness that would not go away. She showed me her arms and a strange blackness was creeping up them. She felt as if she was being eaten from the inside. As the last couple of days passed, she got sicker and sicker. Then her skin began to rot and fall off. I did not know what to do. I could not stand to see my sweetheart suffer like that. She was in so much pain, but I dared not even touch her, as it hurt her so. Finally, I did the only thing I could think to do. I killed her this morning in the cave. I took up the Winchester and shot her in the back of the head as she lay there, half-sleeping, exhausted from pain and suffering. I did not want to hurt her, but I could not stand to see her suffer like that. I truly hope that God will forgive me for what I have done.

I am sure that it will not matter for very long, as I do not know how long the door will hold out. It may be steel but there is no telling how strong they really are, or if they even know that I am down here. I have little food and only one jug of water. I am not foolish enough to think I will survive this ordeal. I cannot help but think about Gabriel's great Knights. If they had shown up, maybe I would be living in Virginia with my wonderful wife and possibly some kids. But I have no hope, now. The sun has turned black, and I think I will never feel its warmth again. My dreams have faded, and my life, too, will soon be done. This book shall be my legacy: may it serve as a valuable warning to someone.

March 16, 1856,

I have heard some strange noises upstairs but I am too afraid to investigate. Every time I think I get the courage, I see Gabriel being dragged, screaming, behind the horse and I lose my nerve. Fear steals my every movement now and I don't even want to leave the little corner that I have occupied since yesterday. Every once in a while I hear someone upstairs. Just vague noises, but I hear them. Sometimes late at night I swear that I hear cannon fire. What is going on up there? Have Gabriel's knights actually shown up? I don't know. With every passing moment I feel hungrier and hungrier. I have rationed out my food and water. It all seems in vain, though. I feel an obligation to my dearly departed wife to make sure that our story gets told. And I am afraid of what might come when I meet God. Will he forgive me for killing her?

March 20, 1856,

I miss them all so much. Every time I close my eyes I see their shining faces. I remember the way that Rachael kissed me on that great night. She was my everything. Why has fate been so cruel to us? I guess I will find out soon enough. I am out of water and it does not seem that I will be alive much longer. I heard sounds upstairs again, and this time I was prepared to face them. I grabbed my Winchester and headed up the stairs but when I got up there the door was blocked! Something very peculiar was going on up there and now I am sure I will never know what that is. But it has been a while now, and I think that this is where my "Great American journey" will end. I cannot help but feel sad when I think of the things that the darkness did to my family and all of the ones I love. What would have happened had the darkness not followed us? Would we have our riches and would I be happily married to the lovely Rachel? I don't know but I do like to think about it. It occupies most of my time down here.

March 22, 1856,

I am so hungry and thirsty I don't know what to do. My stomach hurts so bad. I guess that I am paying for my sins now. I cannot help but to think that this is a cruel, cruel fate. I will now tell you what I know of my little brother. He was born prematurely after only six months in the womb. He had very strange eyes. They were red. I don't know what has happened to him, but I do know that he was not sacrificed as we had feared. I hope that God sees him safely through so the St. John name can live on well beyond this horrible year. I know now that I will not.

March 24, 1856,

I had a dream last night . . . five people found my body and they were going through the same things I did. If that is true and you are reading this, I have to tell you this: these people do not like direct light. They are led by a being known as Satanel, and you must not join him. He promises everlasting life, but all you will get is a tormented existence. Most importantly, in the cave to the west, by the graveyard, there is a way out of this place. The entrance is hidden by a large rock. Stay away from the mining tunnels on the other side of the graveyard, as that is where they worship him. I really hope that my dream was a prophecy and that my life was not a waste . . . oh yes, and if you find my wife's bones, please say a proper prayer for her as I was not in the right state of mind to do so myself.

March 25, 1856,

Goodbye, Hammond and Tigg. Take care of Bailey, Sara and Stephanie. They mean more than you will ever know. Save them from the fate that swallowed my family. Please do not forget, watch out for Z . . .

Chapter 22

THE CHINA DOLL

Hammond leaned against the wall and slid slowly down as he read the last passage in the journal. All of this seemed way too familiar, and he didn't know what to think of finding his name in the final paragraph. Tigg shifted awkwardly as he looked at Sara. He was more determined than ever to stick by her, to protect her from those things out there. The journal seemed to affect everyone except Stephie, who was still immersed in the china doll. The journal meant more to Hammond than it did to any of the others, but he didn't know if he should tell them why. He quickly decided that he had better not make the same mistakes as those in the past by keeping things from his friends.

"Guys, I have something I think you all should know. I'm not sure how important this is, but my mother's maiden name was St. John".

"I know that. I have known you forever, bro; I just didn't want to say nothin". Tigg said this with such authority in his voice that Hammond couldn't help but chuckle a little.

"That piece of information was more for the benefit of the others, Tigg, old buddy, but thanks, anyway."

Tigg shrugged sheepishly as he went and sat down by Sara. Bailey looked at Hammond, wondering what to say to him. She could tell he was disturbed by the writings in the journal, in need of someone to help him understand it all, but she didn't know how. The journal made it sound as if he were the enemy, even though she knew in her heart he was not. She had already figured he was a nephlim, but a direct descendent of Satanel himself was a little overwhelming. It didn't change the fact that she loved him. You can't control who your relatives are—she knew that, and she didn't want to dwell on what his lineage might mean. She shook off the thought and went over to comfort him. She was in it for better or worse—no matter what.

Tigger stood up suddenly, looking around the room. Something wasn't quite right, but he couldn't put his finger on it. It was like there was a piece of furniture out of place or something. It wasn't like an acute sense of fear or anything like that—just something deep down inside that was nagging him. The others began to focus their attention on the wandering Tigg, who was looking behind things for whatever had drawn his attention.

"Dude, I have a question for you." Tigg said, looking over to Hammond.

Hammond looked over at Tigg questioning, "What's up Tigg?"

"How are we breathing right now?"

"With our lungs . . . duh! What are you getting at?" Hammond's curiosity was building.

"No, dude. I mean, that steel door upstairs was sealed, and homeboy over there didn't die right away from lack of oxygen." Tigg said, still looking puzzled.

Hammond hadn't given it much thought before, but Tigg was right. There had to be air coming in from somewhere. He didn't dwell much on seemingly mundane things, but Tigger was like a factory for abstract thought. He wasn't necessarily a genius, but he did have amazing powers of observation. If there was air coming in, then maybe there was another way out. If that was true, then why had Marcus just stayed there and died? He seemed smart enough, yet he was still there. It didn't make any sense. Maybe the opening wasn't big enough to get out, or maybe the path had been blocked like the door. "Alright, let's see if we can find the source of the air. It might just give us a shot at getting out of here and past those things."

"Look, Ham, I don't want to be pessimistic, but I'm pretty sure it's just a vent. And it's probably not big enough to fit through, so I think we should spend our time on something a little more productive." Sara piped up from her corner.

Hammond didn't want to admit it, but she was probably right. They were just wasting time looking for the vent. They couldn't hide down here forever, and they weren't going to get out without being noticed. It was time to face the fact that they were in for a fight, and they had to get ready. The man before him had lost everything—his family, his dreams, and his love—and he died hiding in fear in this dark, dreary room. Hammond was determined not to make the same mistake. He began to realize that if Satanel had his way, that is just what they would do. Everything he had told Hammond was aimed at making him feel hopeless, discouraged, and that there was no point in even trying. But as he thought about their struggles over the last couple of days, they had, in fact, escaped these demons—perhaps Satanel was not as invincible as he wanted them to believe. Hammond had been a fighter his whole life, and he wasn't about to give up now.

"Alright, guys—I think its time we realized we're in for a fight—those things out there are everywhere, and we're not going to get past them without being seen. They probably know where we are, even now. I, for one, am tired of sneaking around, hiding all the time. I think Satanel and his minions might not be as all-powerful as they want us to believe, and I feel that if we do this right, we can make it out of here alive. We're going to give them a fight they never expected!" Hammond's speech did not fall on deaf ears. The others seemed to take heart in his resolve, especially Tigger.

"Yeah let's kick some demonic ass!" Tigg shouted proudly.

"You cowboys need to hold your horses." Bailey said firmly. "Yes, we need to be aggressive, but I don't think running out there with a death wish and guns blazing is the answer. We need to use our heads and think things through."

"But we need to get going, Bailey. If Satanel knows about the key, then he knows we are in here and that's pretty scary, so I think we really need to get out of here." Sara said in a shaking voice.

"Don't you think if he were going to kill us, he would have done it by now?" Stephie whispered. Her eyes never left the doll.

"Wait a minute", Hammond interrupted. "Something is definitely wrong, here. Tigg is right, but it's not where the air is coming from that's strange. Breathe in and tell me what you smell." Hammond spoke softly.

"I don't smell anything." Sara hesitated after she said it, like she just now understood what Hammond meant.

"Exactly. Remember how the air had sort of a stale smell to it? Well that smell is gone. The air smells fresh." Ham's eyes darted around the room.

"Do you think maybe they went away?" Tigg asked quietly.

"No, but I think that the deception of the people who hid this town has gone away. In no uncertain terms, if we stay here, we are going to get our heads handed to us."

"So what do we do now? I don't think we can just waltz up to the cave as nice as you please!" Tigg sneered back at Hammond. "With all those things waiting out there, we won't even make it halfway. We're all gonna die!"

Tigg could be right, and Hammond knew it. Some days Hammond felt like he could take on the world, and others he felt so small and insignificant that even leading them to the zoo would be a daunting task. This was one of those days, but he had to get over it. He had to prepare himself for a deadly journey and he had to face the fact that all of them might not make it to the end. He straightened himself up and looked Tigg straight in the eye.

"Look, maybe your courage has failed, man, but mine holds strong, and if I have to, I will walk straight up to the gates of Hell and face the Devil himself, if that's what it takes to get us out of here alive. I haven't even begun to fight, yet, so if you want to curl up and die like old Marcus over there, then have at it. I think its time we took the offensive—time for us to make a move, instead of always waiting for them to do something to us." Hammond stared menacingly at Tigg for a moment before speaking again. "Now listen, we have to go out there, right?"

"Yeah, I guess." Tigg stammered, thankful that Hammond had his head back in the game.

"So this is what we'll do. I'll take the front. You'll take the rear. We'll keep the girls in between us. I'll take the shotgun. You take the pistols. Make your shots count—there's only four clips left." He scanned faces to make sure everybody was listening.

Hammond loaded the shotgun and he raised his hand to silence Sara's protests before she could even make them. This was not the time for conversation and over-thinking. It was the time for action. They had to get to that cave and get out of Convict Grade, or they would end up just like the others. It was time to go out and face the world again. They didn't even know what it looked like anymore, but one thing that they did know was that things had changed forever for them. Life as they had once known it was gone, never to return. Getting back their normal lives wasn't even conceivable at this point—the only thing on the agenda was survival, and that was what Hammond was good at—it was all he had ever known.

"I don't have a plan beyond getting out of Convict Grade, so for now, that will just have to do. Keep the flares handy, and only use them if those things get in close. We only have six of them, and there's probably hundreds of those things out there."

"Are we ready to go?" Hammond asked as he looked around at everyone. He slung the shotgun over his shoulder turned to the staircase. The crew quickly gathered their gear and followed Hammond. They fell silent as they started a cautious ascent up the stairs, anticipating what waited at the top. The tension began to grow. They hadn't gone more than a few steps when a scream made everyone jump. It was Stephie. She was standing by the foot of the stairs, cradling a bleeding hand. Her precious doll lay at her feet. Sara, who was standing next to her, screamed in shock as the doll stood and careened across the floor, laughing madly. Tigg shot forward and attempted to flatten the crazy doll with his massive boot, but it was just too fast. Hammond shouted for everyone to stay close together as he bolted back down the stairs to help Tigger find and destroy the possessed toy. Stephie just kept crying as she grasped her hand tightly. Bailey tried to comfort her, but she herself was afraid of the doll. Something so little could hide anywhere and attack them out of nowhere.

Without warning, the gaslights began to fade, then went out one by one, leaving them in almost total darkness. Hammond could see by the small amount of light that was coming from a vent under the table. "Well, that's one mystery solved", he thought to himself as he scanned the room for movement. High, squealing giggles filled the room, echoing off the walls. It seemed to be coming from all around them.

Tigg inched slowly backward, trying to keep the predatory doll from sneaking up behind. Tigg felt something brush against the back of his leg. He panicked and fired one of the pistols down behind him. The sound was defining in the small room. Tigg had no time to think before he was shoved against the wall. All he could see was two glowing eyes floating in the darkness face to face with his own.

"Now listen, I am only going to say this once. Do not fire a gun or light a flare! This room is filling with gas. The lights are fueled by gas and even though they have been blown out, the gas is still flowing—I can smell it. So, unless you want to blow us all into Satanel's lap, I suggest you put that thing away, and turn off the gas!" Tigg felt a moment of relief as he realized the eyes were Hammond's. He lowered his gun and shoved it in his belt.

A ticker-tack sound was filling the air as the impish doll ran around the room. Tigg felt defenseless because he couldn't see and he couldn't use his guns. Being at such a disadvantage, he decided to let Hammond search for the china doll. He went over to the stairs, found the gas key and shut it off, then huddled up next to the girls.

With a loud shriek, something laid into Stephie's leg and she batted at the air, unable to see her attacker. She could feel tiny teeth ripping at the flesh of her shin. After a few seconds she jumped up and started running madly around the room, trying to shake off the tiny terror that, only moments ago, she counted as her dearest possession. She screamed as it took bite after bite out of her bleeding skin. Hammond caught her in his arms as she tried to run. She struggled in his grip as he tried to remove the doll from her leg.

Hammond couldn't hold on and she ripped free of his grasp. She ran face first into the wall, knocking herself out cold. The small doll was moving slowly up her motionless body. It clawed its the way up to her throat and Hammond swept the butt of the shotgun over her in an attempt to remove the vicious doll. It was squirming violently, not wanting to give up the ground it had made on the poor girl's body. Hammond finally reached down and grabbed the doll. It fought wildly to escape his grip, slashing at his already wounded hand with its sharp fingernails.

Pain shot through Hammond's arm as he felt the claws sink into the still fresh wound in his hand. He jerked it back violently, launching the wicked toy across the small room. It slid across the floor and disappeared under the table. Hammond hoped that the thing would just run away, but he knew that would not be the case. The five of them were like fish in a barrel, and he knew that monster knew it. It didn't take long before the eerie giggling started again.

Tigg held Sara as close as he could, covering her body with his own in hopes of protecting her. The china doll only seemed interested in Stephie, though, so his heroism was horribly misplaced. As it came in for another assault on the girl, Hammond jumped forward, pinning his now hapless prisoner under his foot. The doll howled in hate under his heavy boot, but Hammond was not about to let the thing get away again. He was about to bring the butt of the shotgun crashing down onto this foul thing's head when, to his surprise, it began to speak.

"We just want the girl. We have already killed her—she just doesn't know it yet!" the doll squeaked in a high-pitched voice. "She will join us or perish! You mortals are so weak!"

Hammond was fed up with this thing threatening him and his friends. If now was the time to start fighting back, he certainly wasn't going to put up with idle threats made by an insignificant toy. Humans have lived on this earth for thousands of years, and that was not going to change on his watch. The demon doll started to say something else but was quickly cut off as Hammond brought the shotgun crashing down on the little doll's head, shattering it into a million tiny pieces.

"Alright, guys, grab onto me and form a line. I am going to get us out of here before the gas kills us or those things find us." Hammond took a deep breath as he helped Bailey find his shirt. "I'll carry Stephie. Tigg, you watch our backs."

"Right, chief. I got it." Tigg replied. "Can't see anything, but I got it".

Hammond bent down and hoisted Stephie up as carefully as he could, not wanting to hurt her anymore than she already was. The pain in his back was becoming more and more intense. The thing under his skin felt like it had grown to twice its previous size. To tell the truth, he was afraid they had killed him, and he was the only one who hadn't caught on yet. He didn't want to worry the others, so he sucked up the pain and made his way up the stairs, carrying Stephie and leading the others. When he reached the top he took another breath and slowly opened the metal door, once again facing an ever-changing world that he knew very little about.

Chapter 23

NEW ENEMIES

The large steel door swung open, and they re-entered the hall of the courthouse. A blood red light poured in through the windows, filling the place with an eerie glow. The air was fresh and they suddenly felt less constricted than they did in depths of the courthouse's mysterious basement. The red light was almost worse than darkness as it cast a dead feeling over everything. Hammond's eyesight, however, seemed to be even more acute in this light than it had been in the dark. The red spectrum felt good to his sore eyes, although the others didn't share his appreciation for it.

The area around them was still and quiet. It seemed as if the whole world had stopped to watch the events that were about to unfold. Hammond checked both to the right and left, trying to figure out which would be the best course to take. They had entered through the rear of the building, but with the way things were changing, he wasn't sure what surprises lay in either direction. Both ways were probably dangerous, and he wasn't sure how he would make the right choice.

There was a strange clicking sound to the left side of him and he decided they had better investigate. Friend or foe, they should find out what it was if they didn't want to be surprised by it later. Hammond gently set Stephie down and pulled the slide on the shotgun back slowly, hoping not to make enough noise to attract any unwanted attention. He waved for the others to hold back as he made his way quietly toward the sound.

Tigg came up so silently behind him that Hammond almost jumped out of his shoes when he put his hand on his shoulder. "If you're goin' into a scary situation, you know that I'm right behind you, dude, whether you like it or not."

"I'm cool with that. Just stay quiet and watch our backs as best you can." Hammond whispered.

"What is with this funky light, man? It's really messing with my eyes. I can't see too well. How 'bout you?" Tigg asked quietly.

"I can see just fine, bro. You just have to make sure nothing sneaks up behind us, all right? I may have good eyes, but they aren't in the back of my head".

Hammond and Tigg walked slowly, keeping their backs to the wall as much as possible to avoid an attack from the rear. Bailey took Stephie and Sara back behind the door to the basement. It was, at least for now, the safest place to be. Hammond tried not to make any sudden movements as he motioned for Tigg to take the other side of the hall so they could see behind each other at the end of the long hallway. The light in the room faded to a dull red as if the light had all of the sudden been blocked, leaving only small traces for them to see by. This made it all the harder for Tigg.

The closer they got to the end of the hallway, the louder the sound in front of them became. It seemed to be moving around the foyer of the courthouse. It moved strangely—not slow like the other things did, but almost like it was making leaping movements. One moment it was behind the wall that Hammond was leaning against, and the next it was over on Tigg's side. Tigg pointed back to the way they had come, gesturing silently that they should just go back and hope that whatever was out there did not notice they were there. In Hammond's mind, it was far too late to turn back now. Even if it still had not noticed them, it would only be a matter of time before something else did. He decided that the best thing to do would be to find out what it was and if it was a threat, kill it before it killed them.

Hammond moved his head beyond the wall that Tigg was leaning against. He heard the sound but saw nothing. The noise still echoed behind Tigg, but he still couldn't seem to find its source.

"Psst! Yo, Tigg, do you see anything?" Hammond whispered as quietly as he could.

"No man. I can't see anything but I hear it behind me." Tigg whispered as he motioned behind himself.

Hammond wasn't sure what to do at this point. He looked past Tigg again, hoping that he might get a glimpse of what was behind him. The clicking sound got louder as the thing he could not see got closer. The sound was almost unbearable now and it almost seemed like it was standing right next to them. Hammond looked left and right but there was nothing to either side. Suddenly, it hit him like a ton of bricks—he darted to the other side of the hallway and jerked Tigg into the main room. Tigg yelled as he and Hammond both hit the floor. Hammond scurried to his feet, trying to bring the shotgun up.

A large black creature that seemed to be all teeth with long spindly legs dropped down from the ceiling to where they had just been standing. It stood at a full height of about eight feet. The mass of it was very bulky and had a large muscular almost human form at the center, but the head was composed almost solely of rows and rows of jagged, shark-like teeth. Saliva dripped down to the floor from its massive fangs.

After a few seconds of surveying its new prey, the thing charged them with swiftness unlike anything they had ever seen before. Hammond and Tigg barely escaped the creature's charge as they split and jumped to the sides opposite each other. The creature ran straight between them into one of the stylized pillars, bounced off, and fell to the floor, as if it had knocked itself out. Hammond quickly ran up to it and put the muzzle of the shotgun to what looked like its head and pulled the trigger. It exploded into a mist of blood and what could best be described as brain matter.

"That little guy wasn't so tough." Hammond boasted. He slung the shotgun over his shoulder like a hunter that had just taken down a great lion. "Now those things will know better than to try and mess with me!"

"You just got lucky, man. The dumb thing knocked itself out. Let's get out of here, eh?"

Hammond and Tigg turned around and started back down the hall the way they came. As they turned their back to the fallen creature and started down the hall, they missed what was happening behind. Without warning, the creature sprouted another head and got up, then lunged forward toward the two men. Tigg took the full force of the pounce and was unable to fire even a single shot before his head hit the floor. The old, rotting carpet didn't provide much padding and he was knocked senseless. Hammond spun on his heels, firing the shotgun into the mass of blood and teeth as he hit the floor. The thing exploded from the center, releasing thousands of small spider-like creatures into the hallway.

Hammond grabbed the dazed Tigg and quickly dragged him down the hallway as the fiendish little spiders gave chase. They were covering his back and legs, biting him all over as he tried to shake them off. Once he reached the hallway, he rubbed his back against the walls as he ran trying to peel off the spiders that were eating him alive. He almost dropped Tigg as he jerked his shoulders from side to side, trying to fling them off his body.

When he got to the door leading to the basement he kicked it hard and yelled for Bailey. She opened the door to find Hammond down on his knees with the spiders covering him, biting him relentlessly. Bailey screamed as she started swatting them off of him but there were so many of them. Sara came out and helped her pull the two men inside and throw the door shut. Batting, swatting, and stamping, they fought to get the ravenous creatures off of Hammond. Strangely enough, they hadn't shown any interest in Tigger.

Hammond lay there in a tormented state. His body was covered in sores, bleeding and swelling from the venom of the creatures' bites. He began to shiver and shake, so racked with pain that he was ready to give up and just let the evil consume him. Bailey knelt down next to him and took his hand, surveying his wounds, wiping away the blood here and there. She started to cry as feelings of desperation and helplessness set in . . . she wanted to help him, but didn't know what to do.

Sara helped Tigg sit up against the wall. He was still in a daze, and as he came out of it, he reached for his pistols and started waving them about, still in a fighting state of mind.

"Spider! Look out for the . . ."

Sara gently pushed the guns aside, trying to calm him.

"You don't need those now, Tigg—you're safe. It's okay".

Tigger jerked and sat straight up, looking around, realizing his surroundings. Then he saw Hammond sprawled on the floor with Bailey crying over him.

"What happened to Hammond? Is he dead?"

"He's alive, but he's in bad shape. Those spider things nearly ate him alive".

Tigger was already struggling to his feet, staggering over to Hammond and Bailey. He was panicked that he might lose his life-long friend. He was almost more panicked about what would happen to all of them without him.

"Hammond, I need you to be alright for me, man. I can't do this without you." Tigg sounded like he was talking to a man on his deathbed. Hammond suddenly convulsed in a new state of pain. His eyes opened wide, a look of terror crossed his face.

"What is happening to me? Something's happening to me!" Hammond started screaming in pain. The mass on his back erupted as worm-like bumps began to course through his body, just under his skin.

The others drew back in surprise, watching, horrified, as the bumps spread over his whole body with amazing speed. Hammond screamed in pain as his entire body was enveloped. Then, to their amazement, the bites and sores on his tortured body began to heal. In a matter of moments they were almost completely gone, leaving only scars that appeared as if they had healed many years before. Hammond fell quiet as the pain subsided, and his body finally relaxed. He seemed to be just fine, with the exception of the large mass still on his back. The lump only seemed to have gotten bigger—again.

Hammond sat up, then slowly stood up. The mass stopped him from standing completely straight, but didn't look much worse than a slouch. It was the only thing that still hurt. The rest of his body, however, felt as fresh as that of a young man. He looked himself over in amazement, running his hands over his arms and chest, down his hips and legs, feeling the flesh, the strength, and the absence of pain.

He felt his strength return, and more—like he had never felt before. The others just watched him, somewhat fearful, but mostly in awe.

"Sweetie, are you alright?" Bailey asked gently as she approached him cautiously. Every turn of events seemed to reveal some strange, new thing about Hammond. Yet she still felt comfortable with him, and her love for him was still growing.

"Yeah, I feel fine enough, I guess. As a matter of fact, I'm feeling better than ever. I don't really understand what just happened, though, and I don't think I really want to know." Hammond spoke calmly.

"Dude, I think that that thing in your back just saved you. I don't know what they were but they looked like worms digging around under your skin. There had to be like thousands of them, bro. Then they all went right back into your, um, hunch thingy." Tigg was a little hesitant towards the end, not knowing what he could call the growth on Hammond's back without making him upset.

"Whatever it was, I don't know, man, but one thing I know for sure is, we need to get moving. I think we're up against much more now than we were in the beginning. They seem to have spawned new creatures and they are even worse than the half-human ones we faced before." Hammond cautiously opened the door and went back out into the hallway, looking toward the back door, which seemed as daunting as going out the front.

As the others came out, something caught Tigger's attention. Lying on the floor by where they were standing was an odd, blood-soaked feather. The thing seemed so out of place there that he felt it could not be ignored. He reached down and picked it up—it was sticky with blood and felt strangely heavy. It must have come from a very large creature.

"Guys, I hate to say this, but I think one of those things out there can fly", Tigg said, holding up the heavy feather. Hammond looked at the feather for a moment and then nodded in agreement. Tigg passed the feather to each of the girls, who examined it in turn, but Hammond would not even touch it—he wanted nothing to do with it. There was something strangely familiar about it and he didn't like it. The more he thought about it, he realized that Satanel was an angel once and they had wings. Was it that, or something else that bothered him?

Hammond tried to clear his mind and focus on the problem at hand. How would he get them out of there and up to the cave safely, and once there, how would he get them to the exit? So much was changing so fast; he decided to just take things one-step at a time. The first was to choose which door to go out—the back was more familiar, so he headed that way.

Right behind him was Bailey, Stephie, Sara and Tigg. Bailey and Sara were doing Okay, and Tigg seemed back to normal, but Stephie was still hurting from the attack of the demonic china doll. She noticed that her foot was asleep. She tried to shake it and twist it to get it to wake up, but all she felt was a strange numbness.

Hammond stood at the doorway, getting ready to push it open and see how much things had changed while they had been down in the basement. He looked back at Bailey, who returned a look of encouragement. He wondered if the growth on his back was having any affect on the way she felt about him. He felt horrible about the fact that all his dreams were coming true in this horrible world, but he did not necessarily want things to go back to normal again, because here, he was needed. Here, he was loved. This world was better than anything the former world ever gave him.

As Hammond slowly pushed the door open, red light flooded into the courthouse. As he made his way outside, the source of the mysterious light became evident: the moon resembled a glowing sea of blood hanging ominously in the night sky. The strange light it cast down on the newly uncovered Convict Grade revealed for the first time the vastness of the town. It also reflected off the mountains, showing the absolute geographic isolation of the place. It seemed like Marcus was right: the only way out was through the mountain. All the roads that once led in and out of the town were now gone. The remnants could now be seen, perched precariously on the mountaintops.

The change in terrain made a straight shot to the cave all but impossible. Instead, they would have to make their way through the demon-infested city and then up to the graveyard, which seemed like a daunting task. Hammond could already see the shadows of people walking past in the main street. The back street that he had seen when he came in was now blocked by a huge boulder and was impassable. The town had taken on a strange mix of old and new. Cars still littered the streets, yet lining those streets were both modern and old west-style buildings. It was as if one time period had merged with another to form some otherworldly hybrid of the two.

Hammond stepped back into the courthouse. The others gathered around as he sat down and rested his arms on his knees. The moon outside was setting and the sun was beginning to rise. He didn't know whether the sun would still shine, but he had hopes that it would bring at least a little bit of light to keep the creatures at bay. Although his eyes were overly sensitive to light, he found himself missing the brightness and warmth the sun had once provided.

"Okay, guys, here's a new plan. Let's wait for the dawn to see if the sunlight will help our situation. With any luck, the sun will shine bright and be a help to us." Hammond looked out from the hole in the door. The red light outside was fading. "When the morning comes, which I guess will be in about an hour or so, we will go out and face them on the streets. If the sun doesn't bring light, we will use the flares." When Hammond finished he got up and started back towards the door to the basement.

"Where are you going, love?" Bailey asked as she followed close behind him.

"I'm going downstairs to try and get some sleep. It'll be good to get some rest before morning comes. We will need to be at our best in order to face what the day may bring." With that, Hammond went downstairs and quickly fell asleep. The others followed suit.

Chapter 24

A New Light

H ammond awoke to find that he could no longer lie on his back. Other than that, he felt pretty good, especially considering all he had suffered over the last couple of days. Bailey still lay sleeping in his arms and if he could have things his way, she would stay there forever. Stephie was sitting awake in the corner. He understood why she couldn't sleep—had it not been for shear exhaustion, he probably couldn't have slept, either. Tigg sat on the stairs sleeping with the shotgun in hand and Sara nuzzled gently on the other side of him. Hammond dug gently into Bailey's pocket and pulled out her cell phone. It was no surprise to him that it had no service but what did surprise him was that it was already almost noon. They had slept for a little over six hours.

Hammond nudged Bailey softly to wake her up. He hated to bring her out of whatever beautiful dream she was having back into the nightmare they were living in. She stirred slowly and when she finally awoke completely, she pulled her legs up to her chest and sat for a moment collecting her thoughts. Hammond decided Tigg would be the next one to wake up, but he was not as gentle about stirring his friend.

"Wake up, squirrel nuts! We're burning daylight! Now, move! Move! *Move!*" Hammond smiled on the inside as Tigg jumped up, startled, slid down the last few steps, and hit the ground, dragging Sara with him.

"Dude, how 'bout like a "rise and shine" or something. You didn't really need to scare me half to death! There's enough going on around here to do that without your help." Tigg stared wickedly at Hammond and then the two of them started laughing, like there was some joke that only the two of them understood.

"Alright, you two yay-hoo's, we've got a lot to do, so how 'bout you quit screwing around and lets get down to business, huh?" Sara said, sounding serious, but still shaking off the ride down the stairs with Tigg. She tried to stand up, but slipped and fell squarely on top of Tigg. That set everyone to laughing, especially Sara, who was now a little embarrassed, and brought Bailey to her feet, running over to Sara to help her off of "poor old Tigg".

Everyone was smiling with the exception of Steph. Her foot had still not recovered from falling asleep, and she was starting to worry about it. She figured it was swollen or infected or something, but she still wasn't willing to take off her shoe and check it out just yet.

The laughter was a welcome break, and after a pretty good night's rest, the team seemed less beleaguered; especially Hammond, who looked almost fully recovered. He was walking with more of a slouch than usual, but that was one thing no one wanted to mention, including himself. He grabbed his trusty knapsack and shotgun and started silently up the staircase. Stephie was having trouble walking, so Tigg carried her; the other two girls trailed close behind.

Hammond pushed the door at the top of the stairs open slowly with the shotgun, not sure what kind of strange beast may be lurking on the other side of it. He was flabbergasted by what he found. Instead of some gruesome monster preparing to eviscerate him in new and interesting ways, he found the courthouse looking like the one in his home version of Convict Grade. Light poured in, reflecting off of the soft white walls. The carpet looked brand new, as did the curtains, but when he looked to his right, he saw the door that they had originally come in, and the handle was still missing, so he knew this wasn't a dream. Hammond stepped out into the hallway and looked back the way he had come. The door was no longer hidden by torn and broken lathing but was now perfectly framed out. When the others came out into the hallway they had pretty much the same reaction that Hammond had. Tigg found a spot where the sunlight was coming in through one of the windows and just plopped down, basking in the light it cast onto the floor.

"Hammond, if you don't mind, I just want to enjoy this moment." Tigg preempted Hammond before he could say anything.

"Don't worry man, I feel the same way." Hammond said softly as he put his arm around Bailey's waist.

"You know what, honey?" Sara said to Tigg, who was sprawled out on the floor. "I never thought the sight of this old carpet would ever make me happy, but I think it has just become my favorite color!"

Tigg nodded in agreement with a smile beaming across his face. They all knew they still had to stay on their toes, but they were certainly not going to pass up this moment of reprieve from the horrible nightmare that had been consuming them for the last few days. The sunlight felt better to them than any man-made pleasure. It had a certain unmatched perfection that no one could really explain, so they just enjoyed it in silence.

After a few minutes Tigg got up and began to look around. He wandered down the hallway, looking in each room as he passed. A couple of minutes later, he came running back to find Hammond.

"Hammond! Follow me, dude—there is something that I definitely think you need to see, man!" Tigg yelled as he came back into the foyer.

Hammond followed Tigg into the main part of the courthouse, moving very cautiously, remembering the strange creature that had attacked him the last time he had gone that way. The hallway looked so different than it had just a day earlier: there were long fluorescent lights above them and the walls were covered with old pictures of people that were long since dead. It was like any other courthouse in the free world, but the things that were once normal now seemed different and out of place. The offices to the sides of them with their little help windows seemed like something more out of a distant memory than something that they might have seen only a couple of days ago.

When they reached the end of the hallway the carpet gave way to tile and their footsteps could be heard echoing throughout the building. The old oak front desk stood empty against the wall on the right side of the hallway. Hammond thought about the people who had once worked in this place and how they thought their jobs were so important. It all seemed so insignificant, now, and the emptiness of this place just seemed to drive that point home. But that wasn't why they were here—they were here because Tigg had something to show him.

"Alright bro, look up." Tigg said as they reached the front door. Hammond humored his friend and did what he asked.

"So, it's a stained glass window . . . I don't really think that's terribly impressive, Tigg." Hammond was pretty irritated that this had not been the revelation he was hoping for, and really didn't appreciate leaving the girls behind just to see this. He started looking through the windows at the scene outside, and noticed that the debris in the streets was gone—they were clear.

"Ham, it's not just the fact that it's stained glass, you twit—it's the sign of the Freemasons!" Tigg couldn't understand how Hammond had not caught on to this.

"And your point would be what, exactly?" Hammond asked, turning his attention back to the stained glass above him.

"Do I have to spell it out for you?" Tigg started raising his voice to Hammond. "The Freemasons and the Knights Templar are like the same thing, man. Gabriel's Knights did show up! And they are probably the ones who buried the town. Dude, this is important!"

Tigg was right—how could he have missed it? That would explain the secrecy of the underground city, but it still didn't explain why they had not just destroyed it. Everything was starting to come together, though, like a puzzle that you had to find the pieces to before you could even start work on it. The more they learned, the more they realized they understood very little about what had actually transpired in this unfortunate little community.

The two looked at each other for a moment, then passed each other an understanding nod and turned back toward the girls. The mystery of Convict Grade and what was happening to them seemed to get deeper with every new revelation. The answers seemed to be everywhere, but the more answers they got, the more questions came with them. They knew they had to escape, and they decided not to get hung up in the details, yet Hammond kept wondering if there was something in the history that would help them get out alive.

When they reached the girls, they were still basking in the sunlight. Even Stephie, though still in pain, was humming softly as the sunlight covered her aching body. Hammond and Tigg reported to the others what they had discovered with an emphasis on the empty streets. Bailey pointed out that maybe along the way they should see if they could find some food, as they had left most of their things in the police station. Nobody wanted to argue that, as they all felt pangs of hunger.

They all filed to the door in their own fashion. Hammond stayed next to Bailey as they walked, holding hands. He knew there were still more dangers lurking out there, but with the sunlight he was no more equipped to deal with them than the others were, so he felt no need to take the lead. He just slipped on his sunglasses and walked side by side with the others. It felt good to be walking with them instead of in front of them. When he had to take the lead, he couldn't help but feel separated from them and somewhat alone. In the sun, he was just another member of the group and he liked that.

As they reached the front door they stopped and looked at each other, making sure they all felt this was the best way to go. They nodded understandingly to one another as Tigg reached out and grabbed the door handle and pulled it open with authority. The warm light flooded over them as one by one they stepped out into the world. Hammond had to flinch at the brightness, even through his sunglasses. The streets were a peculiar mixture of cobblestone and asphalt. The buildings were a cacophony of old and new styles, and the world seemed to be frozen in a mock of two different eras.

Tigg stepped out onto the sidewalk and looked around at the strange scene. He could hear voices somewhere in the distance but couldn't make them out. The scene seemed almost surreal, like something you would see in an abstract painting. Sara stood next to him, equally amazed at the change. Bailey just leaned on Hammond, taking in the beautiful sun she thought she might never see again. It might be an illusion like the one she and Hammond had faced at his house, but it felt so good, she didn't care.

"What do you make of this, Ham?" Tigg asked in astonishment. "It's like the world we left and the world we found, all rolled up with a little Twighlight Zone!"

"Well, Tigg, old buddy, it sure looks like you hit the nail on the head with that one. I think we should get out of here, though, while the getting' is good!" Hammond made his point rather clear.

Although life had taken many bizarre turns in the last few days, Hammond had learned not to take anything for granted. If this was some evil trick to lure them into a false sense of security, Hammond was going to make the most of it. He knew all too well how quickly these seemingly good times could take a turn for the worse, and he was not willing to just stand around and wait for evil to find him.

"Okay, guys, let's stick to the original plan. But don't forget to keep an eye out for anywhere that might have food. If I get any hungrier, I'll have to just eat one of those things before they get a chance to eat me!" Hammond's comment, however gruesome, still struck the others as funny. And in the beautiful sunlight, they felt a lot freer to laugh.

They started down King Street, methodically checking in every direction as they went. The evil seemed to have dispersed for the moment, but they knew that it could be lurking around every corner. Tigg suggested that they head towards the Truck Stop, knowing that it would probably be well supplied. Lacking any better plan they all agreed: first to the Truck Stop, then on to the cave.

Chapter 25

LOST SOULS

Despite the change in appearance, it was a beautiful summer day in Convict Grade. They had traveled a few blocks so far and there was absolutely no sign of the evil presence or the darkness it inhabited. Nevertheless, as the quintet walked down the sunny street, they couldn't shake the feeling that something was amiss. They kept hearing distant voices or seeing curtains move here and there in the windows of the strange new houses that had appeared. All in all, it would have seemed normal except it usually required people to make these sounds and motions . . . they hadn't seen any normal people in days.

Hammond walked a little behind Bailey, checking her out as she went. He marveled at how a small amount of normality could heavily alter one's prospective on life. Things were pretty close to perfect right now, as far as he was concerned. He didn't care much for people anyway, so the quiet, empty town bathed in sunlight was all he needed. He was there with his friends, whom he cared deeply about, and that was all he ever wanted. The thought that a woman of

Bailey's caliber could actually love him had been nothing more than a distant dream. Here she was, though, right there in front of him and possibly even more in love with him than he was with her. Yes, it was perfect—yet he feared the moment was fleeting.

Tigg walked beside Hammond with Sara slightly ahead of him and to his right. He seemed to be thinking the same thing Hammond was, in unknown concert with his best friend's mind. For him, this was a perfect moment, too, but unlike Hammond, he didn't sense the end of it. Tigg, as usual, was blissfully unaware of the future—too caught up in the moment to even think about it. Tigg had always been the sort of person to take in a good feeling and hold on to it as long as he could, living life moment to moment, hanging on to the good ones, and letting the bad ones go. It was something about him that Hammond truly envied.

Sara and Bailey seemed to have taken the lead, which is the way things would have always been, had it not been for the nightmares. Tigg and Hammond, the two easy friends always seemed to lag slightly behind the rest of the world, while Sara and Bailey continually set the pace for it. Stephie was limping, but kept stride with the other two girls. While she didn't hold any false hopes that this sunny, happy day would be permanent, she was determined to make the most of it.

Hammond was a little concerned about her limp, but if she wasn't saying anything about it, then he figured it must simply look worse than it was. Stephie had a smile on her face, and life seemed to be falling right back into place for her. Even with the pain in her leg she seemed like just a normal college girl again. No matter how long it lasted, she was thankful for the chance to feel like a person again rather than some animal that was being hunted down.

The sun beat down on them as they walked along the asphalt and cobblestone street. The air around them filled with anticipation as they approached the town square. With the murmuring noise getting closer, Hammond thought it would be best if they kept a low profile by taking side streets to the Truck Stop. He led them, zigzagging through the side streets and alleyways in an attempt to stay out of sight, but still watch what was happening in the town square. Their curiosity was overwhelming. The voices seemed to be disturbed and panic-stricken. To Hammond that didn't sound the way he would expect demon-possessed people to sound, but then again, he had never actually stopped to talk with one.

Hammond leaned with his shoulder against the brick building. He was trying to catch a view of the people gathered in the Town Square, however, his vision was obscured by both cars and the bright sunlight. Tigg couldn't see any better because he was a little less willing to expose himself to the possible threat ahead. Sara knelt quietly behind a big green dumpster that kept her well hidden with Stephie right behind her. They all wanted to know what was going on, but no one was prepared to go out there, knowing the possibility of what might be awaiting them. Bailey looked at Hammond with absolute fear, as if she could read his mind.

"Don't even think about it, love!" She hissed at him through her teeth. "You had better not be thinking what I think you're thinking! I'm not about to let you leave me here alone while you go out there and get yourself killed".

"Look, one of us needs to get a closer look. Whether we go straight to the graveyard, or go to the Truck Stop, we've got to go that way, so we need to know what we're up against". Hammond seemed determined.

"I'll go . . ." Tigg offered, solemnly.

"Oh, no you won't!" Sara said, yanking him back to her.

The argument ended quickly when someone walked right in front of them. Hammond ducked down quickly so he wouldn't be noticed.

Before anyone could say anything, Tigg reached out and grabbed him around the neck and dragged him back into the ally. The others stood stunned as Tigg threw the man up against the wall and shoved a gun in his mouth.

"Who are you, and what are you doing here?" Tigg demanded of his new hostage.

"What do you think you're doing Tigger?" Sara yelped out in surprise.

"I'm getting answers. Now, just step back and let me do my thing!" He told Sara sternly. "You don't want to get any blood on you".

"Okay, Hammond—do your stuff, man, cause I'm really not sure how to help you".

Hammond was so stunned that he really didn't know what to do. He looked over at Bailey for the answer but she just shook her head. This was a situation that Hammond had not even considered. Every now and then, Tigg surprised him—and this was definitely one of those moments. He felt like he had to do something, so he cocked the shotgun and placed it firmly under the man's chin.

"Mister, there is some crazy stuff happening in this town, so we'd all like to hear what you've got to say about that. I want an explanation, and I want it right now!" Hammond demanded through clenched teeth. "If you're willing to cooperate, blink twice, and I will have my associate, here, pull the gun out of your mouth. If we get anything but two blinks, we're going to turn your head into some sort of new wall covering".

The man blinked twice, very carefully, and Tigg slowly pulled the gun out of his mouth. He appeared deeply panicked and scared even more than they were. He looked at them as if they were the monsters and he was the victim. He was so scared, in fact, that he had urinated on himself. Hammond pulled the shotgun away from his chin and stepped back in disgust, realizing he was no threat. The man just stood there, petrified, eyes wide open, trying not to blink.

"Uh, you can blink now, man. It doesn't look to me like you're one of those demon things. I'm sorry for the way we treated you, but you have to understand that we've been through a lot of really weird, scary stuff in the last day or two." Hammond spoke gently, not wanting to cause the poor guy any more discomfort than they already had. "I'm Hammond, and the gentleman that pounced on you and shoved the gun in your mouth is Tigger. This lovely young lady is my girlfriend, Bailey; the blond is Tigg's girl, Sara; and the pretty young woman sitting next to the dumpster over there is Stephie."

"I'm Myles . . . Myles Bennett. I live down on Oak Street. All I know is, I went to sleep, and when I woke up, the town looked like this. I saw people going to the town square and decided I should go with them to see if anybody knew what was happening. It's like the whole world changed overnight!" The gentleman surveyed the ragged band of teenagers as he spoke.

Hammond sat down and pulled out his pack of cigarettes—it was empty. He threw the empty pack down in a huff and started rummaging through the knapsack for another pack. He looked up at Myles crossly and said,

"We have been fighting demons for the last two days, and it ticks me off that all you did was sleep through it . . . and what's even worse is, I've run out of cigarettes!" Myles quickly reached into his pocket, and Hammond, still on edge, swept up the shotgun and jammed it firmly into the stranger's chest.

"Whoa there, what are you doing?" Hammond said nervously. "You had better just rethink that, man!"

"Easy . . . easy . . . I'm just trying to help!" Myles said softly as he produced a fresh pack of Marlboros, offering them to Hammond.

"Oh . . . well . . . thank you, man—I really needed one of these." Hammond seemed relieved at the prospect of having a few more smokes. He lit up and took a drag—the calming effect of nicotine soon began to sink in. Hammond decided he could believe his story—it seemed reasonable enough, and what was more—the man used the word "I" when he introduced himself. That was proof enough for Hammond that Myles was indeed what he said he was.

"So, Myles, have you talked to the others? Are they like you, or are they, uh, different?" Bailey inquired.

"I don't know. I was just heading there when Captain Caveman, here, pulled me into the ally." He replied. "I don't really know what's going on, yet, but I was about to find out. It can't be good, though, considering the way you kids are treating me."

Sara felt embarrassed as she realized what they had just done—basically, abducted a stranger at gunpoint and threatened to kill him! A few days ago, she would have never thought it possible that she could even be involved in such a thing. This whole thing was turning them into animals, she thought, and she felt ashamed at how it had changed them.

"We are truly sorry for the way we treated you, sir." Sara said quietly, with total sincerity. "You can't imagine what we've been through in the last few days—nothing has been what it seemed, and we've found that . . . well, we just can't trust anyone".

"I still don't trust you, but I don't think I really have a choice." Tigg said as he eyed Myles, pulling a cigarette out of the pack and lighting it.

"Think about it, junior . . ." Myles was starting to get his courage back. "If I wanted to kill you, don't you think I could have done something like poison the cigarettes?"

Tigg quickly spit out the cigarette and looked at Myles incredulously. Hammond just stood leaning against the wall and continued to smoke the one he had. A wry smile crept onto his face.

"If he were one of them, he wouldn't be trying to kill us with cigarettes, man. Besides, killing us straight out isn't really their way. They like to twist the knife, if you know what I mean." Hammond said, turning his back to Tigg exposing the watermelon-sized protrusion.

"Yeah, I guess you're right, man, but do you really trust this guy?" Tigg whispered to Hammond.

"I don't trust anyone but myself, Tigg, old buddy—that's how I've made it this far." Hammond quipped as he turned around and walked slowly past Tigg. "The question is, what do we do now? I think we should go out there with our new buddy, here, and just play dumb." He looked at Bailey. "All of us."

The decision was quickly made for them as eerie black clouds started spreading across the sky from one central point. Hammond had seen many storms in his life, but he had never seen one that spread from a pinprick in the sky outward. And it was quickly filling the whole sky. It wouldn't be long before they were once again shrouded in a cloak of darkness.

Hammond crushed out his cigarette and started walking toward the town square. Despite the large hump on his back, he still walked in his usual over-charismatic way. He just walked right out there like a man on a mission, shotgun slung over his shoulder. The others quickly fell in behind.

Caught up in Hammond's bold moment, they had sort of forgotten about poor Stephie. Bailey was the first to realize it and turned around to go back and get her, but she found Myles was already there, helping her along. Stephie seemed happy, so Bailey just smiled at them and kept walking toward Hammond. She was glad to see Stephie had made a new friend. Hopefully, Myles would turn out better than the late Zero.

When they arrived at the town square, there were about 50 people all standing around, talking about what had been happening. A man stood on the base of the statue bearing a cross with an "X" cut into his forehead and a hand made cardboard sign on his chest that said "The end is nigh!" Hammond slowly made his way through the group, listening to their conversations. After a couple of minutes, he walked over to the center of the square and climbed up onto the pedestal of a statue, roughly pushing the self-proclaimed holy man off of his pedestal, cutting off his sermon. He looked over the crowd, put his thumb and forefinger to his mouth, and gave a shrill whistle. Everyone turned and looked at him with a start. A ray of sunshine still penetrated the clouds, and shone down on him as he stood there, exuding confidence, posed like some mythical hero from the past. The rest of the world seemed to be cowering, fearful, and unsure.

"Now listen up, everyone, 'cause I've got a few questions for you all". Hammond said it boldly, with authority. "I want everyone here to listen up and raise your hand if you have noticed anything out of the ordinary in the last day or two."

Everyone in the crowd slowly raised their hand. Hammond motioned for Tigg to cover the rear of the crowd in case any of them tried anything. Individually, they all looked pretty timid, but Hammond wasn't sure what they would do as a group. The people murmured to each other about the events that had transpired, some slept while others experienced their own form of the nightmare. Some looked strong, but for the most part they appeared weak and afraid. Only a couple of them were armed, and they only had hunting rifles, which were not well suited for what they were up against. Others had hand weapons like lengths of pipe and gardening equipment. It almost looked as though they were the proverbial angry mob.

Hammond once again cleared his throat and began to speak. "Over the last couple of days, a lot of strange and terrible things have happened in this town, and you people all seemed to have missed it. What I need to know right now is if any of you have come into contact with any strange creatures".

Everyone in the crowd stood looking at Hammond like he was the only one who knew anything. As he surveyed the crowd, he noticed a pair of young men with hunting rifles. They were two boys that had given Tigg and himself a hard time when they were in high school. Of all the people who had lived through the first part of this nightmare, he wished Barry and Bart Ridgeway had not been among them. It seemed the natural thing for Satanel's army to do—take out the strong first and then strangle the weak at their leisure, although Hammond had his suspicions that Barry and Bart were alive just because Satanel truly hated him.

The crowd grew nervous as the clouds now started choking out the light. A bright flash of black lightning struck down on them causing the statue where Hammond was standing to erupt in sparks, showering both he and the crowd with burning debris. Hammond jumped quickly from his pedestal as, one after another, the bolts came down with a deafening crash following each. The wind picked up to a howl, nearly knocking some of the people to the ground.

"Run! We have to get out of here before we run out of light!" Hammond yelled to his friends as he broke through the crowd.

"Just who the hell put you in charge, boy?" The grating voice came from none other than Bart Ridgeway.

"I don't really care if you stay here or not!" Hammond yelled back at him. "Let those things feast on your dead carcass for all I care!"

236

The two boys had tormented him and Tigg for so long, there was no sarcasm in his voice at all—he meant every word.

The scene was getting more dangerous with every second as the familiar sight of the living darkness began to grow out of the clouds. Hammond did the best he could to gather up his small group to try and get them headed to the safety of the Truck Stop. The noise of the storm and the crowd were driving him insane as he tried desperately to find Baily, Sara and Tigg.

Just when he thought that the noise would drive him mad it stopped all of a sudden, leaving everyone and everything silent. Hammond looked nervously behind him with the sound of his own heartbeat echoing through his worried mind.

The man with the cross pointed it to the sky. He seemed to be laughing, but no sound came from his wildly moving lips. Time seemed to slow down for a second as the darkness hit the ground with explosive force. Everyone nearby was knocked off their feet as it tore through the holy man, bursting him like a bubble, sending a fine mist of his blood onto the faces of the stunned crowd. Hammond stood for a moment in shock as he tasted the poor man's blood that was now trickling off his nose into his open mouth.

A hand grabbed Hammond from behind, spinning him around. He was greeted by the terror stricken face of Tigg, who was now dragging him toward his friends. Tigg was also covered in blood. Tigg was screaming something at Hammond but he couldn't seem to hear any of it as he followed his friend. Bailey and Sara stood at the edge of the group motioning for Tigg and Hammond to hurry toward them.

Slowly, the hearing returned to Hammond's ears and he began to sense the crowd screaming and trying to follow him. The panicked people combined with the sound of the darkness eating everything behind him fueled him to run faster. He wasn't sure how close it was, but he wasn't about to turn back and find out. When they reached the girls, the whole group started running in the direction of the Truck Stop.

Myles watched the painful grimace on Stephie's face as she struggle along. He jumped up quickly and put her arm around him and helped her walk. He seemed to be different from the rest of the group. While most of the others seemed sheepish and weak, he was strong and proud. Undaunted by the approaching darkness, he stayed back to help her. Then, as the darkness reached them, he grabbed the helpless woman, threw her over his shoulder, and ran. Myles could feel the cold touch of the darkness as he ran, but he would not leave the poor woman there to die.

Myles pumped his legs as hard and as fast as he could, trying to keep up with Hammond and the others. About a dozen or so survivors were also in hot pursuit. The crunching sound of the darkness began to fade behind them as they ran. His lungs burned with every step as he tried to outrun the devil with Stephie on his back. They had gone about two blocks before Hammond and the others stopped to catch their breath. Once he caught up to them, Myles collapsed under the weight of the wounded Stephie. The sound of the darkness was now only a faint echo, but it still gave them only a moment to rest as it continued to spread.

"We're in some pretty heavy shit now, man! We're gonna die! What the hell did you bring with you, freak?" Barry yelled at Hammond.

"First of all, just watch your mouth around my girl. And second, you retard, This is what I was trying to warn you about!"

"You know what, man? You can just get . . ."

Before he could finish the sentence, Myles jumped up and stood between the two men, remembering how quick Hammond could be with the shotgun he carried. He was still trying desperately to pull breath into his encumbered lungs as he held his hands up between the two.

"Look, I don't know what the history is between you two, but you need to just check your baggage at the door! You're right—whatever is in that thick shadow is going to kill us if we don't get a move on. The only chance we have for survival is to quit bickering and get out of here!"

Hammond turned away from Barry with a look of disgust. He wanted nothing more than to beat some sense into him, but he knew Myles was right. The darkness would soon catch up to them if they didn't get moving. Bailey put her arm around Hammond but it did little to quell his hatred for the Ridgeway brothers. He struggled to regain his composure.

The day was passing quickly; the sun was already more than halfway to the horizon and the darkness was creeping up on them. Clouds almost completely covered the sky, now, choking out the sun. It would be getting dark early. Hammond took a deep breath and started forward again, focusing on his goal of reaching the relative safety of the Truck Stop. Tigg was just a few steps behind with Sara and Bailey nearby. A young man named Matt helped Myles carry Stephie. One by one they ran, almost in single file, as they made their way through the town. They were getting strung out—some of the group were having trouble keeping up with the more nimble youths who were leading the way.

It should have been easy to get to the Truck Stop. Hammond had gone there almost every day of his life since he was ten or so. But this new version of the town was like a maze. It seemed like every turn revealed a new obstacle blocking their path. The normal route to the Truck Stop seemed all but impassable. Water from the storm had collected in pools in the streets, already filled with debris and refuse. Shadows were setting in, leaving only narrow passages that were well lit.

Hammond turned one more corner, and there it was! The Truck Stop was in sight, but something didn't seem right. Hammond paused in front of the bank building, eying the reflective pool of water that filled the street in front of him.

"Come on, you wuss! It's only a puddle!" Bart yelled from the middle of the crowd.

"There's something wrong, here. I don't know what it is, but I don't think we should cross." Hammond said in a low voice. He didn't know what was bothering him, but he really didn't want to step into the water.

"It's only a couple inches deep, man, why are you being such a pussy?" Barry insisted.

"Ok, tell you what—if you're so brave, why don't you take the lead? When you make it to the other side, I'll follow", Hammond said with an uneven tone.

With that, Barry pushed through the crowd and stood face to face with Hammond. Hammond had always hated the smell of the brothers. It reminded him of cat urine. Though the smell was as strong as ever, Hammond stood his ground. He was not willing to let Barry think he was afraid of him.

"Alright, everyone, I'm Barry, and I am now in charge. Follow me!" Barry said confidently as Bart followed him. Some of the others started to follow behind them as well, but Hammond held out the shotgun to block them.

"Just wait until they get across. I have a bad feeling about this, and as my friends will surely tell you, my feelings are usually pretty accurate." he said calmly with his eyes still fixed on the brothers.

Barry looked around confidently before taking the first step into the puddle. Everyone held their breath as he slowly stepped in with the other foot. He took a couple of steps more and turned around, holding out his arms in triumph. The whole group exhaled in unison as Barry stood there, completely unscathed. Confirming that a two-inch

240

deep puddle was nothing to fear, he turned to Hammond and started waving his middle finger at him as he laughed. As he started to walk back towards the crowd, the ripples in the water started to shiver. Barry stopped in his tracks and looked down.

"Get out of there!" Tigg yelled, as the memory of his own reflection came screaming back to him.

Barry looked up at Tigg with a look of disbelief. "What are you blathering about, Curtis, you idiot? I don't know what the hell is wrong with you guys—its just water!"

Ignoring Tigg's warning, Barry looked back down at his reflection. The water was smooth, now, and he could see himself clearly in the water. As he started to move again, the water around him erupted and in an instant, a creature emerged, grabbing Barry and pulling him down into the depths of nothingness. Hammond grabbed Bart and pulled him back, as everyone gasped and scrambled away from the puddle. The water fell calm again; only small ripples broke the surface of the water. Hammond cautiously moved to the edge, looking in for any sign of the missing Barry, but all he could see was the pavement below. The only sign of Barry that remained was a pair of vacant tennis shoes, half-floating in the water.

Hammond turned away and gave Bart a look of condolence before starting to move forward again. He didn't get far before he heard a splash behind him. Before he could turn around, something reached up and grabbed his ankle and started pulling at him. Hammond tried to pull away but the thing would not let go. He turned his body and pointed the shotgun down, but Bart pulled the shotgun away before Hammond had a chance to shoot. Was Bart one of them?

Tigg leaped forward planting his fist squarely in the face of the unsuspecting Bart, knocking him to the ground. Hammond turned his attention back to the thing that was pulling him, and was shocked to see Barry, holding on for dear life, looking up at him, blood flowing from his mouth and nose. Hammond reached down quickly to pull Barry out of the water. Whatever was holding Barry was very strong and fought Hammond as he tried desperately to free him. Barry screamed in agony as Hammond pulled on him—he was not about to let the creature win. Hammond took a deep breath and secured his hands under Barry's armpits, then yanked with all of his might.

The crowd screamed as Hammond stumbled back, hitting the ground hard. He screamed, too, as the fall crushed the thing inside his back. When his eyes cleared up he found himself face to face with the vacant stare and open mouth of Barry. Hammond threw him off of him and scrambled to his feet. He looked down to find that he hadn't really pulled him out—well, not all of him, anyway. Barry had been torn in half at the waist and what was left of him was now quivering on the ground like a dying fish. This was a sight beyond anything Hammond had seen. So gruesome was the spectacle that he was instantly overcome with nausea. He turned and vomited on the ground. Many others did the same.

"Can't I get a damn break?" Hammond yelled to the sky as he turned and dropped to the ground. "This is just too much . . . I'm done! No more! I'm just gonna sit here until the darkness comes and takes me!"

"It'll be okay, honey." Bailey said, trembling. "We have to go. We need you . . . I need you. Don't lose it on me now, please!" Bailey said, now crying.

"Yeah, man . . . I, uh . . . please . . . Hammond, don't give up." Bart sniffled through his tears over his brother. "I'm sorry . . . I know we were mean to you and your friend . . . but please . . . we can't stay here!"

Tigg walked over and put his hand on Hammond's shoulder as he helped him up.

"Come on, buddy, we gotta go".

The moment had gotten the best of him, again, but he knew he had to go on. Hammond quietly pulled himself together, wiping the tears and blood and dirt and mud from his face and clothes as he turned and studied every possible route. They were almost completely cut off by the darkness and shadows, now. There was only one path left to take, and Hammond didn't like it one bit. He turned to Tigg and beckoned him forward to whisper into his ear.

"Dude, I hate to say it, but it looks like your house is our only option. It sucks, I know, but we have no other choice. At least we'll have a roof to protect us from the storm of darkness. There's no way we will make it to the Graveyard before the darkness reaches us."

Tigg thought about this for a moment. His house was the last place in the world he wanted to go, but he knew that Hammond was right. "Alright, man. At least we can re-supply there . . . hey, you got any more of those smokes Myles gave ya?"

Hammond reached into his bloody, wet pocket and produced a soaked pack of cigarettes. They had become all but useless.

"Sorry, man, I don't. I sure could use one myself about now."

Tigg nodded in understanding, then turned toward the street he knew well, but now feared. "Alright then . . . lead on, Bro-ha."

"Listen up! Change of plans. We are going to head to a house on Gold Rush Street instead. There is no way we can make it through here. Time is running out and we need to get there fast, so I'm going to start running. If you want to live, you will follow and do your best to keep up!"

With that, Hammond began to run down Gold Rush Street with the others trailing not far behind. They had only gone about half a block when a scream came from the rear. Hammond turned and saw that in the reflective glass of the bank, demons were following them. The hideous things wafted their tongues out as they reached out through the glass, but were unable to reach the running group. The darkness was gathering behind them and Hammond knew that the minute the light disappeared those things would be free. He did not want to be around when that happened.

Tigg caught up to Hammond as his house came into view. Hammond slowed down to make sure that everyone caught up safely. Whether or not he liked it, he was now the shepherd of this lowly flock. He pushed them all past him as he stood sentry with Tigg taking the lead to his house.

Once Tigg got to his front door, all of the memories of his first encounter with the demons came flooding back. Fear consumed him as he put his hand on the brass handle. He didn't know exactly what to expect, but he did know that there were probably horrible things inside. With a deep breath he resigned himself to opening the door and leading everyone in. He hoped that he had made the right choice.

Chapter 26

DEATH OF A LOVED ONE

Tigg walked slowly into the house he had lived in since he was a little boy. It seemed that every step brought to mind another memory from his childhood. There were so many happy times here—his family, his friends, even the dog—they had all been such an important part of his life, but now they were all gone. It was as if he had lost everything he loved. And he did love his family, even though he was often overlooked. He always thought that one day he would do something that would make them proud, but now they were all dead. The place that had been his home was now nothing more than a tomb.

Tigg made his way up the stairs to where his nightmare had taken place. Hammond followed close behind to make sure his friend would be all right. Bailey and Sara went with the others into the kitchen to load up on food and water. They cared about Tigg, but their hunger had consumed them, and nothing could have gotten between them and the food. Tigg walked up to the top of the stairs and stopped just short of where he would be in full view of his mother. He wasn't sure how he was going to deal with it, so he turned to Hammond.

"Could you go up there and cover her up?" he asked Hammond solemnly. "I really don't want to see her like that."

"Of coarse, bro. No problem. I got it." Hammond replied with the same solemnity.

Hammond moved passed Tigg to the top of the stairs, but when he got there, he was surprised to find that Mrs. Curtis was no longer hanging from the hook he had impaled her on. He was greatly disturbed by this, as he hoped that he had finished the job. He stepped forward in the direction of the bathroom where the dog had died. He expected the dog to be gone as well, but when he got inside, the dog still lay motionless in the bathtub. The rest of its skin had been rent from its bones, and bite marks covered the dead animal's bones. The stench in the room was so bad it felt as though it was burning the hairs in Hammond's nose.

He had no idea what he was going to tell Tigg, but he had to do something quick because Tigg's mother could be anywhere. He figured it would be best to just give it to him straight and hope that he took it well. When he turned to walk out he could hear the sickening sound and feel of dried blood sticking to the bottom of his boot. He looked down at his feet and thought back to the first time he had met Bailey. He kind of smiled when he thought about the three hundred dollar boots.

He looked into the bloodstained sink, picked up a broken piece of the mirror, and looked at himself. His face was worn and old looking. Any remnant of youth he processed had been washed away by the events of the last couple of days. He found that his life was now measured less in the passage of years but more in a matter of moments. And for the first time he was acutely aware of the hump on his back. How could Bailey still love him, knowing that he was infected with this thing? What if it was contagious, or worse, contained a whole slew of those little bugs? He didn't even want to think of what that could mean. He just knew that a change of clothes might help him feel a little more like himself.

Hammond walked out of the bathroom to see the stunned face of Tigg staring at the coat hook where his mother had hung. Hammond didn't know exactly what to say to him so he just shook his head. Tigg nodded like he understood and started looking around, worried that she might be hiding in some corner.

"I'm sorry, man, but she's gone. I don't think she's still here, but we'd better be on guard. I need a change of clothes and some food real bad, so lets get this done and get out of here." Hammond's voice was shaking; he was not good at emotional moments, especially when it involved someone he cared about.

"I know you're right, man, but I can't help but miss them. I never got good grades, or was the captain of the football team, or anything even close to that. Truth be told, man, I never did anything to really make them proud of me."

"Tigg, if they could see you now, man, I bet they would be incredibly proud of you. I know I am, brother!"

"You know Ham, it seems like no matter what kind of mess we get ourselves into, we are still always together. I hope that never changes, cause I don't think I could ever do it without you, man."

Hammond raised his hand up so that they could do the secret handshake they had made up when they were kids. They clasped hands, went up to a high-five and followed through to hit the bottom of each other's boots. Tigg wasn't sure what to think of feeling his own sticky blood on the bottom of Hammond's shoe, but he took it in stride. The two of them then went into Tigg's bedroom where Hammond had left some of his own clothes. He grabbed a fishnet shirt and pulled it on over his head, then slowly slid it down over the large hump on his back. It was tender and he didn't like the feel of the fishnet covering it. He looked over at Tigg, wincing as he squirmed to rearrange light fabric on his back. Finally, he he pulled his hair forward, took out his butterfly knife, and handed it to Tigg.

"Will you cut the shirt to make room for my little friend, here?" Hammond asked in an attempt to make a joke of it.

"Sure thing, bro . . ." Tigg said. He really didn't want to go anywhere near that hideous growth on Hammond's back, but he did what his friend would have surely done for him.

Hammond looked around at the room that had once been the center of their universe. The two teens had spent most of their lives in that room playing with toys when they were young, or video games as they got older, and later graduating to talk about girls or cars. He longed for the return of those days, not really wanting to be young again, but rather feeling a need for the simplicity, the safety, and the comfort that at the time he took for granted. He missed the times he and Tigg spent daydreaming together about one day leaving this town. Well, the time had come for them to leave, and it was turning out to be a lot easier than he had thought it would be. Life was so complicated all of a sudden, and Hammond was feeling a lot of very grown-up things—the pressures of leadership, the frustration of his own failures, the worry over that thing on his back, the fear of what might happen to all of them, and so it went.

"Don't you have any cigarettes around here?" Hammond asked, fidgeting nervously.

"Yeah man, Dad always keeps a few packs of cigarettes in the top drawer of his desk. And if we're lucky, they might even be Marlboros!"

"Could you get those, man? I need a minute to myself, if you don't mind. I just got a lot on my mind right now." Hammond said, settling slowly onto Tigg's bed.

"No problem. You feeling ok, dude?" Tigg asked with genuine concern. He had never seen his friend look like this before, and it worried him.

"Yeah, I'll be fine. Just go get the smokes, man, I'm dying for one!"

The flickering light in Tigg's room was giving Hammond a horrible headache as he sat quietly on his friend's bed. He didn't want to tell Tigg how worried he was about the thing on his back. It seemed to be growing a lot faster now—so much so that he could almost feel it get larger with every passing moment. What was growing inside of him, and why did it heal him? The more he thought about it, the more he realized if the host body dies, so does the parasite. Coming to this realization was bittersweet for Hammond. He didn't like the idea of this thing living off him, but at least it would keep him alive long enough to get the others to safety. Eventually, he would have to consider what would happen to him when this thing reached its full size . . .

Tigg walked slowly into his father's office. The room was darkly lit and lacked any form of creative touch. It was empty, with the exception of the desk and chair at the far end. His footsteps echoed hollowly on the hardwood floor. Tigg thought that he heard breathing in the room, but when he looked around there was no one there. It sounded like someone had just ran a marathon; the sound was so heavy in his ears it was like the person was standing right behind him. He whipped around, expecting to catch sight of the heavy breather, but still no one was there. He just had to grab the cigarettes and run. He was getting nervous, and didn't want to be in the creepy, dark office any longer than he had to be.

He walked quickly over to the desk and rifled through the drawers in search of the cigarettes. He thought he heard something and stopped suddenly to survey the room one more time. There they were. Luckily, there were still two packs left. He scooped up the cigarettes, gave the room one last look around, and stepped out from behind the desk.

He started to make a mad dash for the door, but he had only taken a step or two when suddenly it closed. Tigg was now left in the darkness of this windowless room. He heard the breathing coming ever closer too him as he stood frozen in fear. The sound of footsteps echoed in the room. He couldn't tell from which direction they came. His heart was beating so hard and fast that he could almost hear it. His palms were sweating as he backed himself against the wall. He grabbed for his trusty guns, but they were gone—he must have left them back in his room. He just stood there hoping that the end would come quick for him. Dying didn't scare him as much as thinking about the pain. He closed his eyes and felt his whole body shaking.

In the darkness, he felt a hand touch his chest. He wanted to scream out but his voice failed him. It wasn't at all what he expected. The pressure of the hand was so soft and delicate that it almost felt good to him. The soft touch turned into a gentle caress, two hands were now on his body and they felt so good to him that his body started to quiver. What form of madness was this, and why was he still alive? He was scared, but more surprised . . .

"What's going on?"

Then he heard it—a familiar giggle.

"Sara! You scared me to . . ."

Before he could finish, she wrapped her arms around him and kissed him hard. He kissed her back, overcome with relief, and then passion. He had wanted her for so long that just the idea that she was there in the dark with him made him as savage as a wild animal. He tore at her clothes like a man possessed. For a moment he was afraid that she would find his actions too forceful, but instead she did the same to him—she wanted him as bad as he wanted her.

She pushed him back onto the desk and helped herself to his body. She was soon on top of him, then he on her as they wrestled, almost violently, in the dark. She scratched his back while he bit softly on her shoulder, trying not to moan. The two stayed in their embrace as long as they could until finally, Tigger could take no more. He collapsed under her as his body gave up. They lay together on the desk for a moment, Sara breathing quietly as she rested her head on his shoulder.

"I love you, Tigger!" She said as she kissed his heaving chest. "Promise me you'll never leave me, that you'll stay with me forever!"

"Sara, you don't know how long I've dreamed of holding you, of loving you! I will always be there for you . . . no matter what happens!"

She now understood what Bailey had felt when she told her about her experience with Hammond that night in the old store. She felt happier and more in love than she had ever felt before.

Tigg sat reveling in the feeling of the moment, and in amazement at having the woman he loved resting gently on him. He mused on how just a few minutes earlier, he couldn't get out of the room fast enough, and now, he never wanted to leave.

"We don't have a lot of time . . ." Sara whispered softly to Tigg. "We better get dressed and join the others."

"Yeah, Hammond is probably ready to send out a search party."

Sara giggled softly as she slowly got off of Tigg, kissing him as she pulled away. They felt around for their clothes and started to dress, when suddenly the door flew open and light flooded the room. A shadow stood in the doorway as Tigg now did a one-legged dance, trying to get his pants on, and Sara dove under the desk. The dark figure stood there without saying a word. Tigg didn't recognize the shape in the doorway—slightly shorter than Hammond; its head had an irregular shape and appeared to protrude from its shoulders without a neck.

Laughter suddenly filled the little room. The person in the doorway was now moving in on them. He was laughing rather hysterically as he drew closer to the half naked Tigg.

"I sent you in here to get me some smokes, and what are you doing?" Hammond continued to laugh as he sat down on the desk that Sara and Tigg had just made love on. He looked down to find a torn, pink bra lying on the desk next to him. "Whoa, Tigger, don't you think using old underwear is a little kinky?"

"Umm, that would be mine, actually." Sara said blushing as she reached up and grabbed her clothes.

"Whoa, now, this is awkward! Umm, hey, Tigg, why don't you just hand me those smokes over there and I'll let you and your little love bird finish up!"

"Like you and Bailey in Frank's Mercantile?" Sara said smugly. "Bailey told me about you two".

Hammond once again found himself without a pithy remark to fall back on, so he made a hasty retreat with the cigarettes.

As he walked out into the hallway by the stairs, Hammond could hear all of the people downstairs bickering. It seemed now that they had eaten, they were all in a hurry to get going. Hammond couldn't blame them one bit for their nervous anticipation, as he felt the same way himself. He knew they should get moving again as fast as they possibly could. The sun was hanging low in the sky, now, and the fear of what the night might bring was sinking in.

Hammond descended the stairs to where all the people were waiting in the Curtis' living room. Bailey stood in front of him with a slight blush, sensing that Hammond knew she had told Sara about their moment of indiscretion. Hammond just smiled at Bailey and held her close for a moment. A couple of teenagers sat on the couch; the girl seemed a bit on edge, sitting with her legs crossed, fidgeting nervously. Hammond recognized her from school. He didn't really know her very well. Her name was Chrissy Dushane. She was beautiful, yet unassuming. Hammond could understand why her friend, Matt Luvera, looked at her in that way. Hammond just laughed and made his way back to the top of the stairs.

Tigg and Sara came downstairs shortly after Hammond, more than ready to get a move on. The others grumbled quietly about having to wait for the over-sexed teens but they were too afraid to try and go out on their own. Myles was on the couch with Stephie, whose leg seemed to be covered in some sort of white stuff.

"What is happening to your leg?" Hammond asked.

"I don't know, but it really hurts. Do you have any more of those pain pills, Ham?" She asked, her voice confirming the pain.

"Yeah, let me grab you one. Are you alright . . . well, considering the situation, I mean?" It was strange for Hammond to have to make that distinction, but that happens when your whole world turns upside down.

"I don't know what is wrong, but I think it's spreading. I can't feel anything in my feet, but from my calf up the pain is excruciating."

Hammond nodded to her in understanding as he went back up the stairs for the knapsack he would have otherwise forgotten. He couldn't believe that he could be so careless and wondered if maybe the hump on his back was making him lose his edge.

The upstairs seemed a lot creepier when he was up there alone. He immediately started to fear whatever might be lurking around the next corner. All he had to do was run in, grab the bag, and run back downstairs—that shouldn't be too hard, he thought. The disappearance of Tigg's mother still bothered him greatly, though. She could be around there, anywhere, watching and waiting for an opportune moment to strike.

He took out his butterfly knife, almost instinctively, ready for any surprises, and moved along the wall, trying to defend as much as possible against any attack from behind. When he got to the bedroom door, he peeked cautiously inside, and there, sitting right on the edge of the bed was the knapsack. He darted into the room and grabbed it, but as he did he felt a hand grab his shoulder. He spun around quickly and sunk the knife into the soft flesh of his attacker's belly. Fear and adrenaline were the only things he could feel as the body went limp and collapsed into his arms. But then he saw the mass of curly black hair and realized it couldn't be Tigg's mother. The woman with the dark hair could be only one person, but he couldn't bring himself to pull the hair away from her face to confirm it.

Hammond fell to his knees, holding the poor woman in his arms. Blood began to soak the front of his barely clothed body. The warmth of it only fueled his pain as he cradled her, rocking back and fourth, weeping as he thought of the future they might have shared together. He loved her—how could he have done something so stupid? Accident or not, it didn't change the fact that she was going to die in his arms. He cried for her, and himself, and all the others. With her gone, he had no reason to continue—he would just sit there, holding her until they found him, and killed him, too. He began moaning in pain, the kind of pain that stays inside of you, eating at your very soul. He had killed her! He killed Bailey!

Chapter 27

FROM BAD TO WORSE

Tigg stood in the living room waiting for Hammond to bring the knapsack from his room. It had only been a couple minutes since he went up there, but Tigg had a bad feeling. He didn't like the idea of anyone going anywhere alone in the house. Even though his experience in the office was great there was always the chance that it might not have been Sara that was stalking him in the dark. He walked toward the stairs and looked up. He didn't see anything and became even more worried. Hammond should have been able to run up there, grab it, and run back down by now. He didn't understand what could take so long.

"Hey guys, I'm going to run upstairs and see what's taking Hammond so long. I'll be down in a second."

Before he could even get a few feet, Bailey grabbed his arm. "No, it's okay, Tigger. I'll go up and get him."

"Oh, come on, we don't have time for that." Tigg said with a giant grin spread wide across his face.

"Shut up, Tigg!" Bailey said blushing as she started up the stairs.

Tigg stopped her before she got too far up the stairs and threw her one of his guns. She didn't think it was really necessary, but took it anyway. She walked slowly up the stairs thinking about how she would grab Hammond by the shoulder, spin him around, and kiss him so passionately he would barely be able to stand afterward. She smiled just thinking of the reaction that would bring.

When she got to the door of Tigg's bedroom, she paused and thought about the best way to get his attention. She looked at the baby blue shirt she had found in Mrs. Curtis' closet, and unbuttoned a few of the top buttons. They may not have time for it, but that didn't mean she wasn't going to try. Their brief romantic escapade in the old store had been like a wonderful dream, and she was hungry for more.

She pushed the door open gently and started to walk inside. The sight that greeted her, however, left her standing in fear. Hammond was kneeling on the floor, cradling the body of a woman in his arms that she could have sworn was herself.

"What's going on here?" Her distinct accent gave away her identify, but did not hide the fear.

"Bailey?" Hammond asked in a mixture of excitement and astonishment.

Hammond finally had the courage to do what he was unable to do before. He brushed the hair away from the woman's face to see her looking up at him with cold, dead, staring eyes. It wasn't Bailey, but she was definitely human. Deep in his heart he had been hoping that it would turn out to be one of those things, but the blank stare of the girl was all too human. The tears in Hammond's eyes refreshed again as he realized he had still taken the life of an innocent human being. Even though it wasn't Bailey, he still felt a huge weight upon his heart. From the nose down she looked like the splitting image of Bailey, but this woman was older—probably forty-something, at least.

Bailey knelt down next to Hammond, examining the woman more closely. She thought that something didn't look quite right about the body, but couldn't figure out exactly what it was. She rolled the body slightly away from Hammond and pulled the dead woman's shirt down a little, looking for something around her neck. She didn't want to believe it, but it looked like her mother! That didn't seem possible, though—what would her mother be doing here? Something just didn't seem to fit. Slowly, her eyes started to well up with tears, and she pushed the body away. This woman may have looked like her mother, but she knew that there was no logical reason for her to be in Tigg's home.

"I killed her . . . I killed her." Hammond kept saying over and over again as Bailey held him. "They trusted me, and I have already killed one of them!"

"If it makes any difference, she wasn't one of the people you were trying to help . . ." Bailey didn't know how to tell him, but she figured the truth would have to do. "She's my mother."

"What?" Hammond felt worse than he had before. "Your mother?" The main question on his mind was, if this was her mother, why was she still holding him like she loved him? How could she ever forgive him?

"I understand if you hate me, now, honey." He said softly as tears rolled down his face.

"I can't hate you, Hammond. I've already cried my tears for her. I thought she was dead from the beginning . . . and besides; something just doesn't seem right about this. For one thing, her necklace is missing. It had a crucifix on it. She never went anywhere without it. I don't think she even took it off to shower. And for another thing, if it were my mother, she would have come down the second she heard voices—especially mine".

Hammond had already guessed what that meant. She had sold out to those things. But why wasn't she one of them? Even if she had, he didn't feel any better about taking her life. Why did this have to happen to him?

"It's all right, love. This was an accident, not that it really matters . . . I still think this is just some kind of trick. You need to pull yourself together so we can get moving."

Hammond still wasn't feeling any better about what had happened, but he knew she was right. He got up slowly and gently laid the body of Bailey's mother on the floor. He stood and held her as they both looked at her mother. It was sad they had no time to really even say goodbye, let alone have any kind of a proper burial for their loved ones. Hammond turned and looked at Bailey, but said nothing. He thought about how strong she was, how calm and collected she remained, even in this moment of great loss . . . and his love for her grew even stronger.

Hammond turned and walked over to the bed were the knapsack lay and picked it up sadly. They were just about to leave, when all of a sudden the shadows in the room started moving. Bailey hurried over to Hammond's side as the shadows slid across the floor and into the open mouth of Bailey's mother. Bailey screamed as her mother's body started to twitch and writhe on the floor. It jerked and moved like it was being electrocuted. Bailey watched in absolute horror as her mother slowly came back to life.

"*Run!*" Hammond screamed to Bailey as he pushed her forward to the door.

Bailey's mother stood up so fast that Hammond didn't have time to join her. Hammond reached forward and pulled the knife out of her stomach. He didn't know what good it would do against the possessed woman, but it was still better than nothing. The thing that was once a lovely middle-aged woman was now something else, something Hammond was hoping he would never see again. She stood up tall and a snake-like forked tongue lashed out to lick her wound. Blood flicked across Hammond's face as the tongue sucked back into its mouth.

"So, we could not turn the dark-haired one against you. She is stronger than we anticipated, but it matters not, for we will kill you both! Our victory shall still be complete!"

The demon lunged forward at Hammond before he could react, but a loud blast rocked the room as a mass of wet, sticky matter covered his face. The body of the demon fell on top of him with a dull thud, knocking him to the ground. He lay there in a daze, the room spinning, the world fading in and out. He heard voices around him and felt hands touching him. If it was the demons, he would just let them take him. If it was his friends, they were lucky he felt that way.

After a moment, Hammond came to his senses and realized that the nearly headless body of Bailey's mother had him pinned down. He struggled to throw it off and scrambled to his feet. He was really ready to leave, now. He grabbed the knapsack off the floor and walked past Tigg and Bailey like they weren't even there. When he got to the base of the stairs he threw the pain medication to Stephie.

"Alright, everyone, we are moving out right now!" He said rather harshly.

"I heard a gun shot—what's going on up there?" Myles said as he helped Stephie to her feet.

"Does it really matter? Just get your stuff together, and lets get out of here before anything else happens!" Hammond was clearly losing his grip on his humanity as he opened the door without even checking on the others.

Hammond stepped out the door without saying another word. This needed to end and he knew it would, the minute they made it to the other end of the cave. Even if this evil spread, there would be someone else to take the lead, someone more capable. He didn't like having all these people depending on him to save their lives, and didn't want them following him anymore.

The others filed out of Tigg's house, all of them watching him, wondering if it was okay to follow. Sara looked at him from behind several of the onlookers, not knowing what to think of his behavior. She turned around to find Bailey and Tigg, but they hadn't come out yet. It was strange to her that Hammond didn't even seem to care that they weren't with him. For a split second, Sara thought that Hammond might have shot them, but moments later they came out and joined the group.

The sun was setting and Hammond knew they were running out of time. His mind was a jumbled mess, but he knew that he had to get this one thing done. After he got them to the cave, all bets were off. The cemetery by the cave was only ten blocks away, but by his calculations they only had about fifteen minutes of daylight left, if even that. The world already seemed darker and the light was fading fast. He cocked the shotgun that had become a part of him and waved at them to follow him. It would have to be a fast flight to the cemetery—he just hoped for their sakes that they would be able to keep up.

Bailey, Sara and Tigg tried to catch up to Hammond as he broke into a slow jog. He didn't know if he was running to get there in time, or running to get away from all of them. The buildings started to blur together as his jog became an all-out run. Myles had to take Stephie on his back, trying to keep up. He and the others were getting strung out behind. Hammond just kept running like the devil himself were chasing him, and he just may well have been.

Hammond ran until he was exhausted. Finally, his body refused to take another step and he was forced to stop. He was at least a block ahead of the others. He was spent, physically and emotionally, and stood there, hunched over, hands on his knees, secretly praying for the return of his sanity. He was haunted by all the mistakes he had made, both in his former life and in the one he was now thrust into. At first, he had to admit he kind of liked the adventure, but as more terrible things happened and more people died, he came to hate both the situation and himself. He needed something to bring his senses straight again, or he would never be able to face any of them, good or bad. He tried to think of the things that kept him going in the first place, but nothing came to him. His mind was filled with confusion, sorrow, and despair.

After a few moments, Bailey and Tigg caught up to him, and Bailey waived at Tigg to hold back a little so she could talk to Hammond alone. She walked up to him carefully and put her arm around him. He resisted a little at first, but soon relaxed and just fell into it. No matter how bad things got, her touch would always be welcome. He tried not to show the pain he was feeling inside, but as she held him, it all boiled over. He buried his head in her chest and sobbed.

"All I do is screw things up—and all these people—I don't know if I can do this". He fell silent for a moment. "Do you think we really even have a chance?" he asked her in earnest.

Bailey just held him tight for a moment, then pulled back to look him in the eye.

"Yes I do. And I think you will get us there just fine. I have faith in you, sweetheart. No matter what, I always will." She pulled him in again and embraced him even tighter then before.

Hammond slowly relaxed. In her arms, there seemed to be hope. He felt his strength returning, his determination growing. He thought about how wonderful it would be when this was over, and they could start a new life together.

"Well, let's get this over with".

Hammond straightened up as much as he could. The hump on his back was now like carrying a small child. He was hunched down further than he had been before, but just shook it off like it was no big deal. He took Bailey's hand as they started walking again.

The group rejoined them as they continued on, still at a hurried pace. As they made their way past the local Pump-and-Go gas station, Chrissy decided that she had to go to the bathroom and couldn't wait any longer. She motioned for Matt to go with her, as she was afraid to go alone. Matt wasn't thrilled with the idea, but couldn't turn down the request of his friend. They walked carefully toward the gas station, carefully avoiding the puddles along the way, and staying in the well-lit areas.

When they reached the door, Chrissy was relieved to find it unlocked. She peeked inside before carefully entering. Matt started to follow her in but was quickly met by Chrissy's disapproving glance.

"I just want to make sure you're safe." Matt said sheepishly.

"I'll be just fine!" She retorted in a huff as she spun around, closing the door behind her.

Though she didn't often return his affections, Matt really did care for Chrissy. He really wasn't trying to take advantage of the situation—he just wanted her to be safe. He contented himself with the thought that not much could happen in such a confined space, especially with him standing guard just outside the door. The twilight was setting in, and taking on an eerie tone. Various movements in the shadows began to unnerve him, and skittering sounds in the dark places surrounding him gave him the creeps, but he held firm, not willing to leave his post at the door.

Chrissy was somewhat grossed out by the sight of the bathroom. The light flickered annoyingly and the room looked like it hadn't been cleaned since the station was first built back in the 50's. She pulled off half of the roll of toilet paper to cover the seat before using the toilet. As she began to sit she thought about how those things attacked out of the puddle in the street, and quickly changed her mind. She pulled her pants back up, and stood there, torn between the need to go and the fear of what might happen if she did. Maybe she'd take a moment and touch up her make-up . . .

The light started to flicker more intensely as she looked into the mirror. It only took a moment before she caught sight of something behind her. It looked like Matt was standing behind her. She turned quickly to face him, but there simply wasn't anybody there. The light flickered one more time and then went out completely. Just enough light came in under the door for her to see. Fear set in as she tried to grab the doorknob and escape the darkened room. She grabbed on and pulled as hard as she could, but the door simply would not budge.

A splashing sound suddenly came from the toilet next to her as she backed into the sink. It took a moment for it to come out, but she screamed as loud as she could. Her scream, however, was cut short when her reflection sprang from the mirror and put its hands over her mouth, then pulled her in as she fought violently against it, kicking so hard that she lost one of her shoes. She fell completely silent once her head passed through. The thing continued to pull her until her feet disappeared into the rippling liquid of the mirror.

When Matt heard the short scream, he turned and pulled on the door. It was stuck for just a moment, but then opened easily. When he entered the room the light had flickered back to life. Chrissy had vanished. A sense of panic started to set in. He looked franticly around the small room, trying to find where she could have gone, but found nothing. As he was about to leave, something on the floor caught his eye. He bent down and picked up the shoe, and realized it was hers. At that moment he knew she was gone.

Slowly he pulled himself up and looked around the room one more time. As he glanced in the mirror, a strange movement caught his eye. To his surprise, there was Chrissy, banging on the glass and screaming silently like a mime. She was pointing behind him but he didn't understand. He moved in closer to see if he could read her lips when he felt a sudden, sickening shock. Blood began to run from his mouth as he looked down and saw a hand sticking through his chest. He turned to see Chrissy standing behind him with an evil smile.

"Why?" was all Matt managed to get out before falling dead to the floor. Blood began to pool around his body as it lay there. The demon Chrissy looked up to see the screaming girl in the mirror. It casually watched her as it washed the blood from its hand before leaving the gas station to join the others.

The town's streets and sidewalks gave way to dirt paths as they came closer to the graveyard. Tigg and Sara had caught up with Hammond and Bailey, and they walked side by side. They paused at the bottom of the hill to let the others who had fallen behind catch up. It seemed all too easy, after everything they had been through, but they were now only a few hundred yards from the location of the cave described in the journal. Hammond intensified his watch as darkness was now settling in. The area around them was quiet and the haunting light of the strange new moon started to cover them with its eerie glow. Myles, who had been carrying Stephie, came up to Hammond panting.

"We need to stop for a minute, man. I can't go any further. It's strange, but I think she is actually getting heavier!"

"We don't have much time. The sun has already set, and it will be completely dark soon. Once that happens, all bets are off!" Hammond said, surveying the area.

Hammond considered the idea of carrying Stephie himself, but he realized that the hunch on his back made it almost impossible. He looked at Tigger and caught his eye, then looked down to Stephie. Tigg knew immediately what Hammond was trying to say. He didn't wish to bear her weight any more than anyone else did, but he would not question Hammond's unspoken order. After a deep breath, Tigg bent down and picked up Stephie in a fireman's carry. Myles was right—the girl seemed to be insanely heavy for her size.

"Whoa, hold up there!" Tigg said, exasperated. "Myles wasn't just being a wimp, man, she feels like she's wearing an iron suit."

"You're probably just tired, or she's wearing a chastity belt, but with her, I somehow doubt that." Hammond smiled wanly.

"Aren't you the funny one!" Stephie said as she was slung over Tigg's shoulder.

"Well, come on, Tigg, old buddy. You're a big guy, so lets get a move on, huh?" Hammond chuckled.

As they ascended the hill, the blood-red moon rose in front of them. The red light, which flooded the hillside, was comfortable for Hammond, and he no longer felt the need for his sunglasses. As they made their way up the long grassy path, he started to think about the journal. Deep in his heart he wondered if it was really all true. When they got to the cemetery, would the cave be there? And if it was, would it provide their escape as the journal had said?

Tigg struggled to carry Stephie as the incline of the hillside increased. Hammond felt bad for his friend, but there really wasn't much he could do to help. He needed someone else from the group to step up and lend a hand. Just then, Myles caught up and tucked himself under Tigg's arm, trying to help bear some of Stephie's weight. It was just a few feet now until they reached the crest of the hill and the entrance to the cemetery. The crew looked ragged and tired. They all needed a rest, but Hammond knew if they stopped to rest now it would be too dangerous. If they could make it to the other end of the cemetery, they would be safe, he hoped. The large wrought iron gates of the graveyard swung loosely on their hinges. The rust on the gates seemed decades old, yet Hammond remembered them being put up less than a year ago. Time seemed to have a different way with things while these evil forces were in control. And there was no doubt in Hammond's mind that they were the ones in control. He glanced back just in time to see Tigg and Myles collapse.

"Dude, hold up! We have to stop for a minute!" Tigg hollered.

He had no choice. They had to stop. "Alright, if you're too tired, you won't be any good to us, anyway" Hammond said after a moment's hesitation.

"Thanks man. I don't really know what the deal is but she feels really heavy!"

Hammond didn't like the idea of stopping one bit, but he felt like he had no choice. He looked down at Stephie as she lay there, helpless. It looked like the white substance on her legs had spread further up her body. And worse, it seemed to be hardening almost like . . . Porcelain. All at once, he realized what was happening to her. The doll was right—it had already killed her! Hammond reached down to the poor crippled Stephie, not knowing what to do. Tigg stood hunched over, catching his breath, as Sara came up and held onto him. They all thought about how easily it could have been any one of them. Bailey looked at her with tears in her eyes. For one shamed moment she actually thought they should just leave her there.

"What do we do, love?" She asked Hammond.

"I don't really know", he whispered. "If we leave her here, she will die. If we take her with us, she will still die. It's one of those no-win situations, you know."

"How 'bout we give her the choice. It's her life, after all". Hammond felt this was the only fair thing to do.

Hammond turned back to Stephie who was on the ground in front of them. The rest of the group was gathering around. He didn't really know what to say—how do you ask someone how they want to die? He knew that Myles would gladly carry her, but how long could he hold out before she became someone else's burden? He couldn't do it, Tigg had already tried, and none of the others were volunteering. There was no way. Hammond knelt down next to Stephie and spoke quietly. He struggled to find the right words to say.

"Now sweetie, you know you're very ill and, well, it's not likely you will live much longer. As the disease spreads through your body, it's getting harder and harder to carry you. There are men here who are willing to do that, but at great risk to themselves. I'm not telling you that you have to stay here, but I am giving you a choice. If you think about the others, if we leave you here, it is more likely they will survive." Hammond couldn't believe that he had just said that to this poor girl, but it was a harsh reality in a harsh world.

Stephie shook her head in obvious protest against the idea of leaving her there alone to die. "No . . . no don't leave me, please! I can try to walk, please!"

"I'm not making the choice for you. I just want you to think of everyone here. We will have to go slower to carry you, and if those creatures attack, we will not be able to out-run them."

Sara looked at Hammond with an evil look. She simply could not believe that he would even consider leaving her behind. Myles clearly did not approve, either. There they were at the gate of the cemetery—almost to their final goal—and he asks her if she wants to be left behind!

"Look, I can tell by the way that you guys are looking at me, you think that I'm some kind of monster. Let's get real, here. If those things are around, we are as good as dead if we can't out-run them. I know I'm not exactly in the greatest shape, right now, and if you guys needed to leave me behind, then I would expect you to do just that!" Hammond was getting angry with these people. How could they be so stupid that they didn't understand this? Myles stepped up and confronted him.

"Alright, Hammond, is it? I think you've heard her answer, and she doesn't want to stay, so let it go." Even though he was shaking, he still stood toe to toe with the hunched Hammond.

"I told her it was her choice. But I have to think of everyone else here, too—including you. I can't risk anyone else's life to save one that is already doomed."

"You don't know that for sure!"

The air was thick with tension as the two men stood staring at each other. Neither said a word. Both were standing by their own point of view. Neither of them wanted to give ground. Both felt they were right.

Without warning, a shot rang out in the night, shattering the silence. A young man standing behind Myles jerked suddenly. The look on his face went blank. He stood stone still; a small round hole on the right side of his forehead slowly began to bleed as he collapsed to the ground. Everyone in the group dove for cover, yet they all kept looking at the young man on the ground. The cold reality of the situation began to sink in: the battle was at hand, and some of them were going to die.

The unknown attacker never fired a second shot. It was as if they took out the man just to prove a point. The whole situation was unnerving. The demons had never used guns before, and this new development did not sit well with Tigg or Hammond. As the two men hid behind a rock, Hammond looked around at the rag-tag group of folks that were now his only soldiers in the most important of battles. Most of them looked like they couldn't hold their own in a schoolyard fight, let alone a battle against some demonic army. The situation was desperate.

Tigg looked at Sara, not wanting to think about what they were about to face on the other side of those gates. He didn't want her to have any part in the conflict, but he also knew they needed everyone to fight. He caught her attention, and threw her one of his pistols. Sara took the foreboding gift hesitantly. She had never thought she would ever have to fire a gun, especially in a life-or-death situation. Up to this point, she had relied on Hammond and Tigg to do the fighting. She realized now, she was going to have to stand on her own.

Bailey knelt near Hammond, taking stock of the situation. On the one hand, most of them were still alive, and they were almost to their destination. On the other hand, it seemed like this trial would never end; like there was no way they could make it to the cave. She looked at Hammond, afraid of what might happen to this man that she had come to love so much. Hammond met her gaze, contemplating his next move. It really bothered him that nothing had happened since the young man was killed. Why didn't they attack? What were they waiting for?

"Let's get everyone together".

Chapter 28

THE GRAVEYARD

The group gathered behind a small stand of trees, blocked from the view of anyone in the graveyard. Hammond stood and addressed the group of people who were now his soldiers. "Everyone, we've got a tough road ahead of us, and I need to know what we've got to work with, so what I'd like you to do is just quickly introduce yourselves and let us know if you've got any experience that might help us get through this fight. I'll start—I'm Hammond, and this is Bailey. Over here is Tigg, and next to him is Sara. We don't claim to be any kind of heroes or anything, but we've been fighting these demons for the last two days, now, and have managed to survive. Time is short, so a quick introduction is all that we need. Let's start with you." Hammond said, pointing at a squat man in front.

"Me?" The short bald man started. "I am Alexander Mayfield. I am, or rather, was the curator of the museum here in Convict Grade. Um, I once took a karate class at the YMCA, but that was only for a couple of weeks, so I don't know what good it will do." After Alex finished speaking he sat down nervously and the man next to him followed suit.

"Um, yeah, I guess that I should go next. I am Jared Berkley. Um, I don't know karate or nothing, but I do have a .22 that I brought with me, if that will help. I have never really been in a fight before, but I think I could do it if I had to." Berkley didn't seem too sure of himself, but at least he had a gun.

"I'm Jeff Davis. I served two tours in Vietnam, and then I was a cop until I got shot in the knee. I'm not as fast as I used to be, but I feel sorry for anyone or anything who thinks I'll go down easily. I've got my military-issue Colt and I am more than ready for action, sir." The man said, ceremoniously saluting Hammond as he took his seat.

About a dozen other men and women introduced themselves in the same manner. Other than Mr. Davis, there didn't seem to be a lick of talent between them. They all seemed to have varying degrees of ailments. Not exactly the Special Forces, but they would have to do. To Hammond's surprise, almost all of them had brought some sort of weapon, which was a definite plus. They all looked pretty scared, but then again, he thought, if they weren't scared that would mean that they didn't understand the situation. The thought that Satanel had played them like a fiddle weighed heavily on Hammond's mind. They were probably waiting for them, and would attack once they got into the graveyard. But delaying would just leave them open to be picked off one by one. Hammond figured if they were going to make their move, the sooner they did it, the better. The worst part was, they had no information on how many of them were out there, or where they really were. It was going to be a tough haul. Hammond stood back up to give his band of warriors a pep talk, like a high school basketball coach before the big game.

"Alright now, listen up, everyone." Hammond began slowly. "We can't really tell what's out there waiting for us, and there's a good chance that some us are not going to make it. I know that all of you are scared, and I'm just as scared as you are. Use that fear to your advantage. Don't be foolish—use any cover that's available, and watch each other's backs. Those things are tough, but they're not invincible—we've already seen that. That means we can beat them if we work together. So, get your things together, and let's go do this!"

"Yeah!" Tigg shouted, "Let's send those demonic sons of bitches back to hell where they belong! This is our world, and they can't have it!" Some of the others started to cheer. Hammond looked at Tigg and smiled. His friend had beat him to the punch line, and done a fine job, too. His enthusiasm was contagious—just what the group needed.

Hammond realized there was one more thing to take care of before they started. He went over to where Stephie lay to see how she was doing. He expected to find Myles with her, but didn't see him anywhere. Stephie was crying, barely able to move. Most of her body had turned to porcelain. He knelt down next to her and watched in amazement as her neck and face started to freeze in a look of absolute terror. She was barely able to speak, but managed to get out two words:

"Kill me!"

Hammond's heart sunk. He realized that if he were in her position, he would probably have asked for the same. Hammond looked down at her like one would look at a loyal family dog that had gone rabid. You knew it had to be done, but you loved that animal so much that you couldn't bring yourself to do it. He cocked the shotgun but couldn't bring himself to point it at her. His mind started to rationalize . . . If he shot her, that would be one less round for him to fire at the demons, and he knew he would need every last shot.

Tigg had been watching and listening from a distance, and now walked over to where Hammond and Stephie were. Tigg pulled out his pistol and put it to her head, ready to put her out of her misery. The dark and sinister evil was culminating in the ruination of every life form that inhabited Convict Grade. The evil had seeped into every pore and was now seeping through every fiber of this innocent girl's flesh. "It isn't fair", thought Tigg. Stephie had been a member of their company almost since the nightmare had begun. She had done nothing to deserve this. He withdrew his pistol, and sat back on the lawn. He couldn't bring himself to do it.

Hammond looked at Tigg, then back down at Stephie's face, now a beautiful shade of white that glistened in the moonlight. Only her eyes still moved. She was staring at Hammond, her glance still begging him. Guilt was gnawing at the two men, and it seemed to be feeding whatever was hiding out there in the graveyard. Excited howls floated in from far-off places as the tormented, inner screams of Hammond's guilt flowed like energy through the night. The howls from the graveyard were turning into moans of ecstasy as Hammond raised the shotgun above his head and brought it crashing down into the center of Stephie's face. Her head shattered into a thousand splinters of porcelain, splattering her innocent blood over both Tigg and Hammond.

"What is going on here, Ham?" Tigg asked in exited fear. "I mean, what the hell is going on?" Tears ran from Tigg's wide eyes as he looked down at the shattered head of Stephie.

"I had to do it . . . and I hope that when whatever is happening to me starts to take me, that you'll do the same for me." Hammond whispered somberly.

Their sorrow was interrupted by a scream that penetrated the night. The scream was not a quick shriek of someone surprised, but the slow and abiding wail of someone in terrible pain. Hammond and Tigg looked at each other, both trying to figure out what could be the source of the horrifying sound.

"Is everyone accounted for, Tigg?" Hammond asked, looking around at the group.

"Well, Yeah, Ham, 'er . . . everyone but Myles." Tigg answered.

As the scream rose again, Hammond and Tigg looked at each other in an awful awakening—they both recognized the voice. It was Myles. Hammond could easily guess what had happened. Myles had taken quite a liking to Stephie, and seeing her mortally wounded was probably more than he could handle. Hammond didn't know exactly what Myles had planned to do—maybe negotiate some relief for the girl. But it was perfectly clear that he went in there alone, and it had been a terrible mistake.

Hammond turned to Tigg and motioned for him to follow as he walked up to the gates of the cemetery. Tigg wasn't sure what Hammond was doing, exactly, but he thought that he must have a good reason for making them prime targets for the mysterious shooter. Hammond stood as still as a statue, only moving to light a cigarette, as he surveyed the poorly lit graveyard.

"Tigg, do you notice anything odd?" Hammond said, taking a long drag on his cigarette.

"Not really. Why? What do you mean?" Tigg asked vaguely.

"I mean, here we are standing in plain view, smoking, and nothing has happened to us. No shouted threats or gunshots, nothing! Don't you find it kind of strange that they would randomly kill someone, then leave us just standing here?"

Tigg thought for a moment, and then spoke hesitantly. "So what do we do, Ham? I don't know why we are standing here and not laying in a pool of our own blood. But I'm glad we aren't. The real question is, what now?"

"I don't really know the answer to that one, old buddy, but I will probably end up winging it like I always do", Hammond said with a grin.

Bailey walked up to the two men, but stopped short. Her eyes were wide and full of fear as she pointed down to the grass in front of them. Hammond looked down at the scene in front of him—it looked like something out of a slasher movie. There in the brown, withered grass was a trail of congealing blood. A steamy mist from the warm blood wafted up into the crisp mountain air. The trail led directly through the gates and off into the shadows of the old cemetery. Hammond had seen a lot of blood in his time, but not like this. He couldn't imagine how Myles could still be screaming after losing so much blood. Any hope that they could get him back alive quickly faded.

A cold breeze blew past them, making Hammond's hair flow back. The smell of blood was so thick in the air that they were nearly choking on it. The gates on the small hill swung wildly as the wind picked up. The weather was quickly turning against them as the thunder rolled off in the distance and streaks of blinding white light flashed in the night sky.

"So this is what Hell looks like, huh?" Jeff Davis said, as he limped up behind them. "Looks to me like we only have one direction to go, so why are we just standing around? Lets move!"

"Look, dude, we have no idea how many of them are out there, or where they are. Don't you think it would be stupid to just go charging in there like a pack of screaming morons?" Tigg retorted.

"Well, back in 'Nam we didn't know their numbers or where we would find them, but we still went in and won campaign after campaign." Jeff retaliated. This was war, and this man knew more about it than any ten people in that town. Everything this 'crazy old man' said should be treated as gospel, Hammond thought. He also felt a measure of guilt for the way that he had ruthlessly made fun of the somewhat eccentric Mr. Davis. When he was a kid, he used to throw rocks at his house and spray paint wicked things on the side of this poor man's beat up 1960 Ford pick-up.

"Ya know, man, I'm sorry about the things I did to you when I was a kid. I was young and stupid and didn't think about the people I hurt." Hammond apologized. "I didn't even know that you fought in the war, man. I should have treated you more like a hero and less like a freak. I was wrong, and I'm sorry."

"I'm sorry, too." Tigg said quickly, not even making eye contact. He was also ashamed.

"I'm not interested in your apologies", Jeff said. "What I am interested in is whether or not you are ready to stay with me in this battle."

"You bet we are" Hammond replied. "Win or lose, this thing will end tonight and we will show them what Hell really is!" Hammond then turned to face the others as he shoved his cavalry sword in his belt and checked his shotgun one last time. "Its show-time, guys! Lets go in there and show them this is our world, and they can't have it!"

Chapter 29

THE BATTLE BEGINS

Hammond, Bailey, Tigg, and Sara all stood close behind Jeff as they prepared for their push through the graveyard. The tension was thick in the air as Hammond took the lead. His acute sight made him the perfect point man, but it also made him an easy target. He didn't like taking the lead against an enemy with guns, but he was the best man for the job. Jeff took up a place next to Tigg and they kept Sara and Bailey close, in case they ran into trouble.

Their faces were whipped by the crisp mountain breezes that always came at night. But despite the breeze, it was oddly silent in the cemetery as they crept, step by step, through the rows of tombstones. The crickets and barn owls that usually frequented the area were nowhere to be found. Myles' screaming had ceased only moments before they had entered the gates. Tigg felt the same ill-omened presence he had felt on the first night of the demons' attack. The thought of once again facing his reflection haunted him as they reached the McPherson gravestone. It was close to the center of the graveyard and was well known in the town. That stone was always a favorite of visiting photographers. It had at one time been a beautiful angel, but through the course of time the wings had been broken off. Hammond always thought of himself as an angel with broken wings and he spent a lot of time sitting near the stone. The calm that the stone used to bring him was all but gone, now.

So far, it had been all too easy. Hammond had expected to see at least some hint of what was to come, but there was nothing. Even the usual shadows that stalked them from a distance were nowhere to be seen. They approached the mausoleum in the center of the graveyard. Anyone who visited it had called it "The House of God". A wealthy family built it back when Convict Grade was first re-settled. Hammond had never really known who was inside the building, nor had he ever really cared. Tigg had always posed his ridiculous theories, but Hammond just ignored them. It looked oddly like one of those old churches with the long spires that shot up toward Heaven; only it was about one third the size of a normal church.

Hammond could see one of the spires and knew that they were getting close. Bailey tripped on an old granite gravestone that had been broken off near the foot. She fell and tumbled down, almost knocking Hammond down with her. He fell to one knee and caught her head just before it hit Carl Wagner's headstone.

"Be careful, sweetheart." Hammond whispered gently into Bailey's ear. "If anything happened to you, I wouldn't know what to do!"

"I will, love." She said in that sweet Australian accent that Hammond loved so much.

"You need to stay on your toes, Hammond." Jeff said quietly. "You never know when you might run into Charlie".

Hammond couldn't help but to laugh at the thought of someone calling a bunch of demons "Charlie". It all seemed so surreal to him, like he was living some twisted fantasy that was inspired by the purest form of evil. Up until now, he had always thought that man was the worst being out there. But now he knew the true devil inside and the world was becoming a much scarier place.

Bart walked casually behind the rest of the group. He had no yearnings for the upcoming battle, and hoped that he could hang back and sit this one out. Chrissy stood, watching him menacingly, waiting for an opportunity to strike. Bart looked at the young lady with lust in his eyes. There were none of the telltale signs of demon on the young woman. She was just as beautiful as she was deadly. Bart let his fantasies run wild as he watched her turn and walk away. Her sweet body swayed in the soft evening glow and in his mind, he was casting her in his own private porn film.

The more he fanaticized about her, the slower he walked, until the others were all but out of sight. Chrissy seemed to keep pace with him as his mind continued to wander. His heart leapt as he walked almost head long into her. She turned to face him with a mischievous smile on her face.

"Hi there, um Bart, is it? We've been watching you and we think you're really cute." The demon said with a smile spreading across her face.

"Who's we?" Bart asked, still blinded by lust

"It's just a saying, silly. Lets sneak off somewhere and have some fun. What do you say? We're tired of all this talk about fighting."

"We are? Oh, yeah . . . I am too".

She grabbed his hand and led him quietly into the shadows below a withered old tree that Bart saw as a lovely blooming oak. She looked at him as he looked down at his feet. Bart had always liked Chrissy and was thrilled with her sudden attraction.

"Wait a minute . . . I thought you were with Matt". Bart almost detected something wasn't quite right.

"We broke up". Chrissy announced as she smiled deviously and started to unbutton her shirt. It was almost as though she had read his thoughts and was acting them out right before his eyes.

"Are you sure we should be doing this here?" Bart asked nervously. He tried to look around, but couldn't seem to take his eyes off of her. "I mean, I'm not saying I don't want too, but what if those things come?"

"Shut up and give us a kiss, lover". Chrissy pulled him close and kissed him, slipping her tongue into his mouth. Bart's eyes opened wide as he pulled back.

"Didn't you like it?" Chrissy teased. "That's only the beginning . . . we have a surprise for you, big boy!"

"Well, yeah, I liked it a lot!" Bart said as he closed his eyes and leaned toward her. This moment was something he had fanaticized about since he first laid eyes on her. His lips caressed hers as she put her tongue into his mouth again. Barts eyes started to widen as Chrissy's tongue left the inside of his mouth and started making its way down his throat. Bart tried pulling away from her as the deadly attack moved down his throat and into his chest. He started shaking, wide eyes fixed in a silent scream as blood began to leak from his mouth.

Bart tried desperately to pull himself away from the demon but it was no use. A lump appeared in his chest as an object the size of a soft ball was now being pulled up through his throat, his gargling, muted cries went unheard by the rest of the world. In a few moments his feeble struggle to escape subsided and his body went limp. Chrissy's tongue snapped back, tearing the sides of his mouth as it ripped his heart from his body.

Chrissy eyed the heart and was about to pull it into her mouth when a man stepped from behind the tree and put out his hand, motioning for her to surrender her prize. The demon seemed to be reproached as

Satanel took the heart and turned to the body of Bart. Chrissy slunk back away from him as he kneeled and set the heart down gently onto his chest. He then crossed Bart's arms so that his heart was in his hands. Satanel closed the dead man's eyes and whispered in his ear.

"Go kindly into the darkness with your brother. You have to understand that the choices were never truly mine, nor yours, to make."

Satanel then stood and faced Chrissy. "Get back to town and look for survivors . . . and try not to be such a monster." There was almost a tone of remorse in his voice as he gave the order, as if he was given a job he didn't really want, but felt duty-bound to complete. The demon skulked off like a beaten dog as Satanel turned his attention to the group. His keen eyes focused on Hammond as he smiled, turned, and disappeared into the night.

The grass waved in the cold, gentle breeze like the ghost of a reality they had all once inhabited. They were now within a few feet of the mausoleum; after they passed the halfway point Hammond figured that there wouldn't be much more to it. Sara had to fight the urge to push past the men up front that were walking so slowly. This place gave her the creeps, and she just wanted to get out of there as fast as she could.

What was to come next would haunt Sara for the rest of her life. Up ahead, the men had stopped and were looking at something. As she approached, she looked up and saw immediately what had made them stop and stare. Amidst the blood stained and decaying structure that was once the center of the graveyard, there stood a shrine to the evil that now inhabited their world. Hanging down from the center spire of the Mausoleum was a man, crucified upside-down on a cross. The man's face was so torn up it was almost unrecognizable, but despite the gruesome wounds, they all knew who it was. It was Myles, and he had been completely eviscerated. His chest cavity was splayed wide open; all that was left inside was his spine. The smell was so intense that Sara almost threw up before she even got close.

Those that saw it were all a-buzz with fear, but Hammond just stood there staring at it, the anger inside him growing and growing. Finally he turned and shouted into the darkness:

"Cowards! You say you will take the world, but you hide in the shadows! You can only defeat the unarmed and the weak! Not one of you has the courage to come out and meet me face to face!"

Hammond's challenge went unanswered at first, but after a few moments, a voice came out of the darkness.

"Well if it isn't my old buddy, Quasimoto!" The voice was very familiar. "So how are you and that little whore of yours?"

Hammond knew the voice—someone who he had almost mercifully forgotten. It was Zero. Somehow he had survived, or maybe he was just . . . back. He moved out from behind the top spire of the Mausoleum and looked down on Hammond as a king would look down on his subjects. This was something that made Hammond even angrier—the thought that an idiot like Zero could possibly think he was better than anyone else, was offensive.

"Why don't you drag your dead, stinking carcass down here so I can kill you again—I rather enjoyed it the first time!" Hammond shouted up to him.

"What makes you think you could ever beat me, you pathetic cripple! I'm not alone, now—they worship me, and they will happily kill you!"

Zero snapped his fingers and demons rose up from the ground like plants shooting up from fresh soil. There were about a hundred of them, and they all looked ready to kill, growling and waving various weapons in a menacing threat. Hammond and Jeff stood their ground and Tigg backed up slightly to protect the girls. Hammond was completely unmoved by the appearance of the demons. He stared Zero down like a man obsessed. All he could think about was tearing Zero's black heart out his chest and handing it to him.

"If you are their leader, then they must really be desperate . . . or stupid!" Hammond shouted back. "Are you too much of a coward to come down here and fight your own battle? You haven't changed one bit!"

"I am a god now, don't you get that? There is nothing you can do to me! Especially with that hideous growth on your back, you freak! Join me, and I'll make all of this go away." Zero retaliated.

"So, that means you're not coming down, then?"

Hammond didn't wait for Zero to respond. He simply raised the shotgun and fired. The rock arch that Zero had been standing on gave way as the blast from the shotgun broke it apart. He came crashing down onto the ground in a landslide of debris. Hammond brought the barrel to Zero's eye level. His lips curled into a wicked smile as he prepared to pull the trigger. He was only a moment away from splattering Zero's brains all over the mausoleum wall when the sound of stampeding hooves drew him off. He turned just in time to see a four-legged demon charging straight for him. He quickly pulled the shotgun around and fired twice. The demon hit the soft ground and slid to a stop at his feet. Hammond spun back around to get Zero, but he was gone.

"Kill 'em all!" Jeff shouted as he started shooting at the nearest demon.

The host of demons started their assault without hesitation and the battle was on. Bailey fired her pistol repeatedly into the approaching hoard, and was soon out of ammo. She was now defenseless as a demon bore down on her, and screamed for Hammond to help. Hammond saw what was happening, turned, and threw her the shotgun. Without hesitation she caught it and shot the approaching demon, blowing it nearly in half.

Demons were everywhere and the handful of townspeople defended themselves as best they could. The whole battle became a crazy mix of blood and confusion. Human bodies blurred together with demons as both fell to the ground. The coppery smell of blood filled the air. Though it seemed overwhelming, Jeff was able to hold his own against them. Demon after demon fell to his bullets as he fought courageously. Hammond used the cavalry sword to fight off the demons, working his way through the battle in search of Zero. Lightning flashed across the sky and rain began to fall, turning the soft dirt of the graveyard into sloppy mud.

Suddenly, Zero appeared out of nowhere, firing on Hammond several times as he moved in for the kill. Fortunately for Hammond, he was already moving, which forced Zero to miss. The shots at close range, however, deafened Hammond and shook him up. He turned about as he raised his sword, then brought it down, slashing half of Zero's face off. Zero howled in pain and Hammond screamed in hatred as he jumped forward for a second strike. Zero ducked under the second swing and fell to the ground. He skittered backward as fast as he could, almost melting right through the closed door of the mausoleum. Hammond stood there in shock for only a moment, then swung his sword wildly at the closed door.

Chapter 30

WAYWARD SOULS

Hammond pushed as hard as he could on the large oak door but it stood firm. Sweat poured down his rain beaten brow as he began kicking it furiously, wanting nothing more than to break through and tear Zero apart with his bare hands. The rain beat down heavily, lightning shot across the sky, and thunder crashed, seemingly with each blow he delivered to the door. The sounds of gunfire, yelling and moaning, and the roar of the storm filled his ears as the battle raged on, yet he ignored them all and continued his relentless assault on the door.

Lightning struck nearby, followed immediately by a huge crack of thunder as Hammond threw himself against the door. It finally gave way and he came crashing through, slamming down hard on the floor. His long wet hair slapped roughly on the carefully laid stones, leaving a large wet spot. The inside of the Mausoleum was bigger than it looked from the outside. In all the times he had visited the cemetery, Hammond had never realized that this building that looked like a church actually was one. There were several rows of old, black, wooden pews that were rotted to the point they were no longer able to bear the weight for which they were intended. A thick layer of fine dust covered the floor and cobwebs filled the corners of the pews, proving no one had been in there in years.

Hammond quickly scrambled back to his feet and looked around. The door had closed behind him, and the thick walls muffled the sounds from outside, leaving a morbid stillness within. Hammond's heavy breathing seemed thunderous as he slowly made his way down the aisle, expecting Zero to pop up at any second. Every step he took kicked up more dust, which soon enveloped him in an eerie cloud, illuminated by the moonlight that penetrated the gaps in the dilapidated roof above. Something flittered in the rafters, causing him to stumble back slightly and look up. The ceiling was ornately decorated, and though in disrepair, still reflected the grandeur of the original structure.

Hammond was startled by a skittering noise behind him and he spun around to kill whatever it was, but there was nothing there. When he turned back, however, he found himself face to face with a strange man standing mere inches in front of him. The man stood about three inches taller than Hammond. His hair was black and slicked back, and he was wearing the vestments of a catholic priest. They appeared very old, but well kept—no wear spots or tears, but still had quite an antique look to them. The man looked at Hammond, studying him.

"I am Father Claudius", the priest said at length. "I have been expecting you, young Master Hammond."

The middle-aged priest walked slowly to one side of the room and lit the paschal candle on a table against the wall. Hammond watched carefully as the priest performed the curious, yet common ritual. Hammond had spent some time in the local Catholic church and it was familiar to him, yet in this setting it seemed out of place. When the priest finished his prayer he turned to Hammond and motioned for him to join him. Hammond looked at the priest, hesitantly at first, but then decided there wasn't any harm in it.

Zero was still in the front of Hammond's mind as he knelt down slowly on the dusty floor and crossed his hands in front of him. The candlelight danced wildly across his face as he settled softly onto his knees. The scene was bizarre, yet Hammond felt an unexpected comfort and relief kneeling next to the priest. The weight of the world seemed to be lifted off his shoulders as he knelt in prayer.

"Just open your heart and tell the Lord what you need, my son." Claudius whispered softly as Hammond prayed. "The Lord works in his own way. Even though it may seem like you are fighting this alone, the Lord is beside you all the way. When you feel that your strength is giving out, just trust in him, and he will carry you onward."

"Well, he hasn't really been doing a whole lot of anything, if you ask me." Hammond retorted as he got to his feet. "We've been through hell, and so far we seem to have been doing it without any divine intervention, thank you very much."

Hammond was almost angry as he walked along the pews, running his hand over the old rough oak. The feel of the rough wood on his fingertips soothed him. There was something about churches that always made him feel comfortable. In his mind it was nothing more than an illusion of safety brought on by legends of a mysterious god, but now he started to wonder if it was something else. This strange priest looked a lot like the preacher that he had always known as Bachman. His head swam in these puzzles as he looked up toward the crucifix that hung ominously above the pulpit of the old church.

Hammond could hear the pounding of the rain on the roof and stared in awe as not one single drop fell through the obvious holes. He turned back and looked to Father Claudius for the answer. The priest simply kept his candle light vigil as he prayed to a god whose existence

Hammond still questioned. The priest's muttered prayers seemed to melt slowly into the steady beat of the rain. Was God to be found in this old run-down mausoleum, listening to the prayers of a dead priest?

Once Hammond's anger subsided he returned to his place next to the priest. "Are you a ghost or something?" Hammond asked cautiously, not wanting to invoke the anger of someone or something he knew so little about. "I don't mean any disrespect, Father, of course . . . it's just . . ."

"Don't worry, my son. It's a perfectly legitimate question, given both our location and the circumstances that you find yourself in." The priest paused for a moment, choosing his words carefully. "Well, I am not so much a ghost, as a spirit, my son. I have left my corporal form, that much is true, but unfortunately, I was not able to take my place at the side of my Lord. When Satanel prematurely released me from my earthly bonds, I refused to join his heresy, and for that I was sentenced to an eternity serving what was once my congregation. Now I just try to help wayward souls like yourself find their way back to the Lord."

"Forgive me father, but you seem to have made a mistake, sir. I am not dead!" Hammond said nervously. "What I mean is, I'm still breathing, if you know what I'm trying to say?"

"I know that, Hammond, my son, but is it not also true that you cannot find that which you seek?" The priest asked as he continued to stare at the candle.

"What I am looking for is hardly salvation." Hammond said, somewhat defiantly.

"Salvation can be found in the love of the Lord, or perhaps in finding the truths that have eluded you." The priest stated as he got slowly to his feet. "The war outside will always take second place to the war within, my son. To find what you seek, you need only look to the Lord Jesus for your answers. But if I were you, I would consider which is more important—saving your friends, or seeking revenge."

Hammond stood up in sudden shock as he realized that he had left the others to fend for themselves. He made for the door but was stopped short by the priest before he could charge out. Hammond tried to dodge Claudius but was entirely unsuccessful.

"That is not the way to save your friends, my son!" Claudius said, raising his hand in resistance to the forceful teen. "Your friends are not in any immediate danger, but they soon will be. You need to see what the Lord has to offer you!" He said pointing to the crucifix that was dangling precariously from the ceiling.

"Look, Casper, I really don't have time to sit here and mess around with you. I have to help the others!"

"And I told you, my son, this is not the door that will lead to salvation. The door to your salvation, and theirs, is over there." Claudius once again pointed at the crucifix. "You know, a long time ago a young man named Marcus found his way here, and I told him the same thing I told you. He was not one to listen, either. Had he just listened to me, he would not have spent most of the end of his life in that cave up there. That was back when I was still alive. I found the bones of the young lady in that cave."

"But they did find a way out, didn't they?" Hammond asked indignantly.

"No, that was the place where Satanel was bound before those people released him a few days ago. There is no way out up in that cave—only death, or worse. I tried to stop them, but not many people can see, well, beings such as myself."

"How do I know that you're not just trying to lead us to him? I mean, only a few moments ago one of his minions came in here and just disappeared, or did you miss that?"

"He did in fact come in here, yes, but he left just as quickly through the door back there", Claudius pointed to a door back behind the crucifix in irritation. "Now if you wish to find salvation for you and your friends I suggest you get acquainted with your Lord and Savior!"

Hammond at length resigned himself to going over to the crucifix to seek his 'salvation', even though he didn't feel like there was any salvation to be found. He walked silently up the center isle between the pews. He could still hear the sound of the rain beating against the roof, but it was not this sound that really disturbed him. A scream tore through his mind as he tried to ignore the obvious pain of the people that he had charged himself with protecting. Hammond had no idea if he could trust the strange Claudius or not, but he saw no other alternative. Ever since he found that journal he had thought of it as too convenient, which is why he was quick to listen to the mysterious priest. He had done it often enough in the past, and here he was again: trusting a complete stranger to give him the right answer. Only this time, that person was dead.

The air got noticeably colder as he approached the pulpit—a large pine podium that had clearly seen many years of the old preacher shouting brimstone and hellfire. There were places along the edge that had been clearly worn by his palms. A quiet discomfort settled on Hammond as he got closer to the crucifix that was hanging above it. As much as he tried to push the thought away, all he could picture in his mind was the image of Myles hanging there, tortured and torn wide open. His soul was wracked with regret for all the mistakes he had made. It seemed like everything that he had tried to do for the others only seemed to end in disaster.

The wood trim of the pulpit was originally decorated with an ornate design, carved with great care by skillful hands. Time had clearly taken its toll on this piece, but as he examined it, Hammond's mind was suddenly filled with images of when this church was new and fresh, and its patrons filed in to hear the great preacher teach of life after death and eternal hope, eagerly receiving every word and answering his hallelujah's with amen's. It was a better time for Claudius and the people, just as it had been only a few days ago for Hammond and his friends.

Hammond looked closely at the floor below the hanging crucifix. It was emblazoned with the mark that had become so familiar—the mark of the Knights Templar. A cold calm filled him as he started to realize what had happened. It was now clear to him that the message Gabriel had sent did, in fact, reach its destination and the great knights had come. He ran his fingers along the embossed mark and his mind was suddenly flooded with memories that were not his own.

Images came in droves as he struggled, at first, to maintain his sense of self and his consciousness. Finally, he closed his eyes and relaxed, slowly rocking back and forth as he relinquished control of his mind, opening it to the vision that presented itself. He made an attempt to stand up, but his head was spinning such that he fell to the ground. He experienced the sensation of having his soul ripped from his body as he was sent back through the ages that had passed since the original calamity struck the ill-fated town. The world he had inhabited only moments ago dissolved around him. The walls and pews seemed to age in reverse and the holes in the roof magically repaired themselves. The darkness suddenly turned to light.

Chapter 31

TRUTH REVEALED

Hammond found himself standing in a brand new church in the late 1800's. The stone walls were bright and fresh, glistening in the sunlight, which spilled softly through unbroken stained glass windows. Outside he could hear the pleasant chirp of a bird's quiet song. Several parishioners sat in the pews awaiting the arrival of the preacher. The mood was somber, and all of the people in the room looked like mourners at a funeral.

Hammond moved closer to try to get a better look at the veiled face of one of the women. She seemed to be crying but that was all he could get out of the view. Time was a mysterious whirlpool that seemed to have swallowed the young man. Hammond's body ached all over as he watched the scene unfold before him. The preacher walked into the room. His pace was slow and labored as he made his way to the pulpit. Almost immediately, Hammond recognized the preacher as Claudius himself. The preacher limped along slowly, resting his weight on a poorly fashioned cane. A small trail of blood left behind marked his path. The poor man's injury was still fresh, but his concerns were focused on his bereaved parishioners.

Hammond put his hand up in acknowledgement of Claudius, but the hobbled preacher acted as though Hammond did not even exist. Hammond found this rather rude so he stepped right in front of him. He felt a most bizarre feeling as the preacher walked right through him. In shock and amazement Hammond turned around and stared at the man who he had only known in ghost form, which bothered him enough. When the preacher reached the pulpit he sighed heavily before speaking to his sorrowful parishioners.

"As all of you know, the devil has made an appearance here in our small town. Many have fallen for his evil ways and in the last few days we have quickly gone from many souls to just a few. I have personally come face to face with this evil, but I could not subdue it, even when I tried with all my faith and might. Many of the children fell to his wicked promises, and their parents soon followed. This evil being is on his way here now. I cannot and will not lie to you. The demon plans to kill us all, just like the others. If we do not join him, we will truly feel hell before we meet the Lord. But if we do join him, we will never meet the Lord. The choice will be yours to make".

The preacher's head slumped down as he finished what he was saying. It was not long before the sun in the windows began to fade out, letting the darkness spread dangerously throughout the room. The parishioners screamed as the doors of the small church flew open wildly. Hammond ran outside to see what was coming. He was surprised to find that in this time period he was not standing in a graveyard at all, but on a small grassy knoll. The sun was fading out of the sky much like it had in modern times. A large black cloud was rolling in dangerously fast, heading right to where the small church stood.

The cloud was pure darkness and in it were small red flecks that Hammond presumed were eyes. The demons moved so fast that it almost looked like a storm cloud spreading across the sky, killing every ray of light and blotting out the beautiful sun. Hammond's jaw dropped as he stumbled back, slipping on the wet grass. The darkness was rolling in like a herd of wild horses. The demons in the darkness ran on all fours as they moved up the hill. The way Hammond figured it, they would be up that hill in only a matter of seconds. He got back to his feet as quickly as he could and ran into the church. He tried to slam the door behind him but he couldn't grasp it. Hammond suddenly realized that he was not a solid form at the moment—he was more like a ghost. He could move through walls and solid objects.

"Get out of here, people! Those things are coming! Run!" Hammond yelled as loud as he could. "Why are you just sitting there? Get out, you morons!"

The parishioners did not even seem to notice the young man who was yelling so furiously. Hammond looked at them incredulously. He wanted to yell louder, but realized that no matter what he did, he couldn't change the past. He was left there to watch the horrors unfold in front of him. The darkness continued to approach rapidly as the people just sat there, praying and waiting for someone to come and save them, but no one would ever come.

Hammond's eyes were turned suddenly to one of the parishioners who was holding an old leather-bound book. The cover read 'An American Traveler' on it and he immediately realized who it was. A young Marcus St. John sat quietly, praying, with his journal clutched firmly in his hand. Hammond stepped back and stopped trying to interfere, and just watched carefully as the events that would lead to the discovery of the journal began to unfold. His eyes were fixed on the young man that he had felt a strange kinship with to see what had actually happened to him. The young man had tears in his eyes as he scanned his fellow parishioners. He had a guilty look on his face and there was dried blood on his hands. Claudius moved toward him and put his hands on the boy's shoulder, trying to provide comfort to him in this, their darkest hour.

"You did what you had to do my son; the Lord will not hold it against you. It was not your brother—it was the spawn of that beast."

"I know, Father" Marcus said quietly. "He is coming for me, isn't he?"

"He is coming for all of us, Marcus. We are the only ones left who still oppose the dark prince and he intends to bring all of us into the darkness, one way or another."

Tears filled Marcus' eyes as he put his head into his blood stained hands. Marcus didn't appear to be the strong leader that Hammond had pictured him to be. Instead, he was nothing more than a frightened boy that couldn't hold himself up in this most dire situation. He shook in the arms of the priest and he cried as the doors of the church heaved violently in and out. The boy was clearly afraid of the things on the other side. Hammond was in shock that the man that he thought was a hero who tried to save his friends, didn't even try to fight the incoming disaster.

The doors flew open and broke apart as the first beast burst into the church. Its large clawed legs were the first part of the beast to make an appearance. One large talon at the end of its toe tapped on the floor as the other leg followed. A large mouth full of razor sharp teeth followed the legs and a brief moment later the thing stood to its full height, letting out a guttural growl that made Hammond stumble backwards. The creature moved closer in as others came up behind it. The frightened parishioners huddled close together as they continued to pray for deliverance from these evil beings. One lady stood up and raised her hands to the heavens and almost immediately the first beast was upon her, tearing the woman's flesh from her bones with its massive teeth.

Hammond tried to look away as the demons went about their gruesome business. One by one the parishioners were killed in a similar manner, until only Marcus and the preacher were left. The preacher raised his cane in defense against the onslaught but he was simply knocked to the ground with a single stroke of the monster's clawed hand. The preacher covered his face expecting the demon to eat him as it had the others; instead it stepped back and moved to the side so that a dark figure in a red cloak could move forward to him.

The man pulled the hood of the cloak away, revealing the beautiful face that Hammond had grown to both know and fear. Satanel looked down at the carnage that now covered the small church, his footsteps made sucking noises as he walked through the tacky blood that covered the stone floor. He looked down at the old priest and smiled as he slid his fingers into the bleeding gash on his forehead. The priest grimaced in pain as he screamed prayers at him with no effect.

"Now, now, let's not get all melodramatic, Claudius. You knew that I was coming for you and the boy. What did you think I would do—smile and wish you well?" Satanel laughed as he turned his fingers in the poor priests' wound. "I gave you the choice to join me, old man, and instead you chose to continue to worship a God who won't even come down to save you in your moment of need!"

The priest tried to pull Satanel's fingers out of his head, but Satanel would not budge. Instead he forced them further in and Hammond could see the bulges as they moved around inside the preacher's scalp. He wanted desperately to look away from this savage sight but could not bring himself to turn his head, having the impression that if he was going to save his friends in the future, he had to understand the past. Satanel turned his eyes up to Marcus who was standing there watching in horror as he tortured the preacher. A smile curled up on Satanel's face as he stood up and pulled the cross down off the wall.

Marcus just stood and stared as Satanel turned to one of his demons and pulled out three of its razor sharp fangs. The beast just stood still as its master took what he wanted. Each fang was about four or five inches long, starting at about an inch wide at the base and narrowing to a very sharp point. Satanel took his time to show these to Marcus before he started driving them through the priest's hands and feet, crucifying him on the old wooden cross. The priest fought him, tearing his hands with every movement. It wasn't long before Satanel finished his evil task and turned the cross upside-down, resting it against the wall. The priest had exhausted his energy and just hung there, waiting for the Lord to bring his tortured soul to rest.

Satanel then turned his attention to the terrified Marcus. He calmly walked over to him and sat with a creak on the wooden pew next to the trembling young man. Marcus turned and looked away, only to be greeted with the sight of one of the beasts defiling the corpse of a young woman. These things did not seem to have any remorse for the vile acts they committed and in fact, seemed to enjoy them. Not wanting to watch the thing violate the woman he turned his attention back to the beautiful man who was sitting next to him.

"Hey there, friend, it's been a while hasn't it?" Satanel said calmly to the frightened Marcus. "I gave your family eternal life and to show your appreciation, you killed my son. Now how do you suppose I feel about that?"

"I did what I was told. The child would have destroyed the world and everyone in it!" Marcus said with slightly renewed conviction. "You kill everything you touch. You killed my friends and my family. I just got even!"

"You are so cute, boy, if I were you, I would do everything I say or you will suffer the same fate as your precious Father Claudius, here."

"What do you want from me?"

"I want you and your fancy book there to do me a little favor. Someone will come looking for the truth of what has happened here one day, and you will tell them, but only what I want them to know. You will go to the cellar of the courthouse and wait for them to arrive and when they do, you will give them that book. In return, I will not kill you."

To Hammond's disgust Marcus nodded in agreement and ran out of the church. Satanel stood for a moment staring at the dying priest and before he left, he put the mark of the beast on the poor preacher's forehead and left him there to die.

The world started to spin around Hammond as the sensation of being ripped from his body took hold once again. The scene around him dissolved, giving way to a new view of a rock wall. The room he was now standing in was incredibly dark and it took a while for his eyes to adjust to what he was seeing. After a few moments his eyes regained their focus and he saw dimly lit torches lining the walls around him. The place was cold and dark, and had a strong sense of foreboding about it. Hammond had learned by now that, frightening as they may be, he was safe from harm in these visions . . . at least he had been so far.

Voices echoed from down a corridor and Hammond decided he would investigate. Deeper and deeper the tunnel went towards the center of the earth, and Hammond followed them all the way down. The passage was narrow and the torches became fewer and farther between. The men in front of him were adorned in silver shirts with black robes. They didn't seem anything like the men that Hammond had seen possessed by the demons.

The passageway opened up into a large cave. The men stopped just beyond the entrance and started to put something on the wall. Hammond was curious as to what the men were doing, so he walked through them into the large room in front of them. Men in hoods stood around a large throne, worshiping the man who was seated there. The man was Satanel, and the men were the eyeless minions that now plagued Convict Grade. Chains swung lazily from the ceiling with skulls and partially decayed heads hanging loosely from them. Some were hooked through the mouth and the others were hanging from their eye sockets.

Hammond watched as they raised the bodies up to Satanel, where he ripped out their still-beating hearts and consumed them. In the corner of the poorly lit room Hammond saw a pair of glowing green eyes that seemed to watch the scene hungrily. A long forked tongue shot out from the darkness and dragged one of the bodies back into the shadows. Hammond moved in for a closer look at the thing that was hiding in the shadows of that dark and sinister place. He moved slowly, still fearing that he might be seen.

Hammond followed the rocky wall, stepping softly into the shadows where the creature dwelt. The shadow felt cool on his goose-bumped flesh, leaving him to wonder if he were in more danger than he had presumed, but the feeling of impending danger wasn't about to deter him from finding out what, exactly, lurked there. As he made his way slowly to where he had seen the eyes, he was startled to see not one, but seven pairs of eyes. He stood stone still as the creature slinked towards where he was standing, then took a deep breath and held it while the massive beast stalked past him. Even after it passed, Hammond barely dared to breath as it stopped and rested on its hind legs.

It sat there cleaning its twelve wings with one of its seven long-necked heads. The creature appeared to be made up of the parts of several different animals. The heads and necks were like a serpent, although the faces had human qualities. The body seemed to be a combination of a goat and a bird, its wings arrayed along its back. It had a very distinct smell, so foul that it made Hammond almost vomit. After seeing this thing up close he realized that it was time to get out of there, before something went terribly wrong. Despite Hammond's bravery, there was something about this creature that had him nearly paralyzed with fear. It was almost as if this demon could sense his presence, but couldn't quite pinpoint where he was.

The brute sniffed around with its seven heads writhing wildly in all directions, making Hammond very nervous. He crept along the wall as silently as he could, trying not to touch it as he went. He stumbled on a rock and almost fell face first onto the floor. With a movement that rivaled a bullwhip, all seven of the thing's heads focused near Hammond, searching all around as he tried desperately not to attract any more attention to himself. This thing was different than anything else Hammond had faced in this dream. It seemed to know he was there and it wanted to kill him. He decided to make a run for it—just flat-out run for the exit and hope for the best. He took one more deep breath and took off for the opening of the cave.

Hammond darted past the hunting beast, half expecting it to give chase. To his relief, it didn't follow him past the shadows. But in his mind, the thing was snapping at his heels with every step and at any moment, he expected to feel one of its gigantic talons tearing into his back. He just closed his eyes and sprinted for the exit. All of the sudden, the ground shook and a blast of hot air and dirt hit Hammond squarely in the face. Hammond was turned around by the blast and lost all sense of direction in the confusion and the dust cloud that filled the chamber. He heard the hateful screams of the half-human demons that inhabited the cave and above everything else, the vengeful howl of Satanel as it pierced his eardrums.

When the dust settled and the situation calmed down, Hammond found he had been trapped inside the cave with Satanel and his angry minions. The darkness was broken only by three or four torches that were still burning in the devastated chamber. Satanel settled quietly into the chair that he had occupied during his dark service. If he was bothered by the situation, he certainly didn't show it. He just sat with his fingers interlaced at his mouth. The others wandered around, clawing desperately at the pile of rubble that had blocked the mouth of the cave. Satanel turned his attention to the demon that still lurked in the shadows.

"Azazel, if you would be so kind, knock down this pathetic attempt to hold us." Satanel said calmly to the beast.

Azazel charged from the darkness and threw the weight of his massive body against the blockage, but to no avail. He howled and once again made his charge at the wall of fallen rocks, but it was no more successful than his first attempt. With his final attempt, Azazel bounced against the wall and fell lazily to the floor. It didn't take much more than this for Satanel to realize that his attempts were futile and he once again brought his hands up to his mouth.

Hammond didn't get to find out what happened to Satanel, as the world once again began to spin and that increasingly familiar feeling of having his soul ripped from his body took hold again. Hammond found himself on the other side of the rock pile that entombed Satanel. The thought that it took all of that to pull him no more than a few feet was amusing to him. On the outside of the cave-in, a large wall had been built to cover it up. Hammond walked through the wall to see what it was and when he turned around he saw it had been inscribed with a giant cross and a bunch of strange writings that looked like Latin.

Hammond tried to walk down the hallway where he had followed the men, but it was no use—most of it had caved in and was now in a state of disrepair. It was then that he realized he had been pulled not just out of the cave, but into a completely different time. Hammond thought about all he had seen and how it had changed his understanding. Hammond knew that all of this was simply telling him the story of what had happened in the past, but it still took its toll on him, because it all seemed so real.

Hammond had just started to sit down, put his crippled back to the wall, and rest his head when he heard voices coming down the corridor. The men were laughing and carrying on like nothing had ever happened. Hammond found this relaxed conversation out of place, considering all that was happening. For a moment he allowed his mind to wander back to the days when he and Tigg had walked around town talking about trivial things and laughing at the way people thought their own lives were so important. He had always viewed other people like ants in an anthill and he definitely never thought he would actually miss any of them, but he did now. He even missed the way that people used to look at him like he was from another planet.

The voices moved closer and Hammond could almost hear what they were saying. It was mostly mindless chatter about women and who won the ball game. When the voices got close enough for Hammond to hear them clearly, he recognized one of them. It was Nathan Jones, one of the guys who had come in from the neighboring town of Rattlesnake Ridge to help them reopen the mine. Hammond didn't know him too well, but he had once offered Tigg and he a job at the mine. The two men he heard continued to move closer as the pounding sounds of moving rock and excavating equipment echoed behind them. The way he figured it, he only had a few more moments before they broke through to the little cubby that Hammond now rested in.

When the men broke through, they all seemed puzzled at the sight of the wall with the strange inscriptions on it. Nathan walked up to the wall and rubbed his hand over it, scanning it in wonder.

"What do you suppose we've got here, eh?" Nathan asked.

"I dunno, Nate, but I bet someone put that wall there for a reason. Don't ya think?" The dirty man said wryly.

"What do you think all this weird carving is?" Nathan asked pointing to the writing on the wall.

"I really don't think we should screw with this thing, Nate. It looks like some pretty serious stuff!"

"Well, Bob, I seem to remember reading something about hidden gold in these here mountains from old stagecoach robberies."

"I don't know about this, Nate. It looks more like some sort of warning to me. I mean, who would put religious symbols on the outside of a gold stash?"

"Look, Bob, if you want to be a wimp and call the museum and lose your chance at the treasure that might be behind this wall, then be my guest. As for me, I'm gonna grab my trusty sledge hammer, here, bust through it, and take whatever's behind!"

With that, Nathan went to work on the wall with his sledgehammer. The wall was so old that it crumbled easily with just a couple of swings of the hundred-pound sledge. He was disheartened, however, when he saw the rock slide on the other side of the wall. Nathan was convinced that there was some sort of treasure in there and he was not willing to just let it go.

"Bob, get some of the other guys to help me clear these rocks out!" Nathan was growing more and more exited as he started pulling away the fallen rocks.

"Nate, I think this mine was closed off for a reason. Remember those stories about how all those people disappeared? Tomorrow is like the anniversary of that . . . Its just bad juju!"

"What do you think is behind here? Freddy Kruger?" Nathan laughed at his own wit.

"Well, no, but what if it's like some radioactive waste that killed them. You know? They didn't know about that stuff back then, so maybe they thought that it was like evil ground or something."

"Stop being a chicken and get me some help, would ya?"

Nathan went back to trying to make his way through the debris. He made a small hole at the top and pushed forward in an attempt to get to the other side. Everything became clear to Hammond as he watched it unfold. It was these two morons that caused all the terrible things they had all been through. It was greed that let loose the greatest evil that the world had ever known. Hammond thought about what might have happened if he had accepted the job—he and Tigg could have ended up on this crew and been right there with them setting these demons free.

After what must have been a few hours, Nathan broke through to the other side. He started to yell back to Bob when his calls were suddenly cut short and his body was pulled forcibly through the little hole. Only the sound of crushing bones could be heard as it went. Hammond heard the man scream from behind the rocks but he wasn't willing to go to the other side to see what was happening to him. Moments later, Bob returned with the others. He had assumed that Nathan had made it through so he and the others climbed up to the place where Nathan had made the hole.

"Stop it! They killed him! Get out of here, and tell someone about this!" Hammond yelled in futility. "Don't go up there, you morons!"

Hammond put his head in his hands and just thought about the things that happened on the day before he met Bailey. He wished that he could do something to stop what he knew was next. Before he could see Satanel release himself, the nauseating feeling of spinning and the ripping of his soul took over.

The sparse contents of Hammond's stomach released onto the floor when he finally came to. He found himself back in the mausoleum like nothing had happened. Hammond half expected to see sunlight through the holes in the roof but there was none. The sounds of the battle outside filled his ears. The world slowly came back into focus as Hammond got to his feet. Claudius was still kneeling by the prayer candle that hadn't burned down at all since the vision had started.

Hammond walked over to the kneeling ghost and put his hand on his shoulder. Claudius didn't even move from his position. He just reached a boney hand up and placed it on Hammond's. When Claudius turned to face him Hammond stepped back as he saw the flesh falling from the old preacher's face. His first thought was that he was one of the demons, but that thought was washed away when the preacher smiled at him with the half of his face that had not rotted away.

"I see that your vision is no longer clouded, my son." Claudius said as he got to his feet. "I know how I must look to you, but you have to remember, I have been dead for over a hundred years."

"You look pretty messed up even for a hundred year old corpse, my friend." Hammond laughed. "So what was the point of all that stuff you showed me? Are you trying to say that no matter what, we're all screwed?"

"That wasn't the purpose, my son. Someone needs to tell the story of what happened here. There is a group of people called the Templar Knights. You need to get out and find them and tell them about what you were shown. Underneath the cross over there is their mark; under that mark is a way out. Use it and save as many as you can."

With that, the preacher faded away into a cloud of dust, leaving Hammond with more questions than he had answers. It was odd, but Hammond felt somehow alone after the disappearance of Claudius. There were not a lot of people that he trusted lately, but Claudius was one of them. He bent down on one knee, bowed his head, and made the sign of the holy trinity.

Hammond took a moment to collect his thoughts before plotting his next move. His main concern now rested on helping his friends and getting the information to the people who could do something about it. Hammond was thankful that he now had a direction, a sense of purpose. He walked over to where the crucifix hung and grabbed his sword. When he looked up to the cross, the images of both Myles and Claudius passed through his mind. He thought about what that must have been like and shuddered. In his mind he decided that if it came down to that, he would kill both himself and his friends before he let that happen to them.

Hammond made his way through the decaying church back to the door. It was now time to "do or die", and he had no plans of dying just yet. He took one last look around before pulling the door open, revealing the rain, the lightning, the thunder, and the battle.

Chapter 32

RETRIBUTION

J eff Davis watched Hammond kicking madly at the door of the mausoleum. He felt that the battle was now his responsibility while Hammond went after Zero. Jeff had a hard time with life since the war. The horrors and atrocities he had experienced in Vietnam had taken their toll on him, and it seemed the world no longer wanted him when he returned. He couldn't seem to find a decent job, and before long, even his wife left him. Fighting was all that he had ever been good at, and when it was over, his life was nothing more than a hollow shell. For a while, he thought things would be better if he could somehow get back into the military, but every time he tried, he got the same answer. Finally, he was just too old, and there was no hope of ever returning. So there he was—a second rate mechanic in a third rate town.

The rain poured down heavily on Jeff as he reloaded his army model Colt .45. This was familiar ground to him—down in the mud and muck, surrounded on all sides by a merciless enemy. Jeff looked around from the small trench that he had liberated from one of the demons. He jumped up and charged the group of demons that were closing in on him. The light was dim but the red moon clearly outlined the black shapes of the approaching horde. He opened fire, emptying an entire clip as he raked the nearest four or five demons. Jeff broke into song as he reloaded.

"It was an itsy bitsy teeny weenie yellow polka dot bikini . . ." He turned and fired another shot that hit its mark between the eyes of the next demon. ". . . that she wore for the first time today!"

Jeff seemed to have lost his mind as he pulled a knife from his boot and ran through the slippery mud toward one of the largest demons. The demon stood about four times his height, but this did not deter him. He figured this must be the leader, since it was the biggest. In his wayward thoughts, he believed that if he killed the leader, the rest would simply fall apart. He jumped with all the force that his once-wounded body would provide, and landed clumsily on the creature's back. With legs flailing, Jeff held on to its hair for dear life, stabbing furiously as it spun around. The demon reared back in pain, trying desperately to knock him off, when Jeff seized the opportunity to pull himself forward and slit the throat of the massive beast. It writhed and collapsed as a gush of greenish yellow blood spewed from the wound. Jeff fell to the ground hard, snapping his wrist as he landed.

The fight was far from over. They had killed so many of the demons, yet more just kept coming. Jeff's theory had been wrong: even though he killed the big one, the others still attacked, driven by an unseen force. One by one, the townspeople fell to the demonic onslaught. Jeff did his best to protect them, but he was just one man against many.

Jeff pulled himself to his feet using a large tree-shaped headstone. Pain shot through his arm but he simply ignored it—he had to go on. As he stood up, he found himself chest high to a humanoid-looking demon. It had long hair, wicked-looking horns, and its face was covered with a large bone mask. It carried an oversized sword that looked like it was made from the bone of some giant prehistoric animal. All told, the demon stood about nine feet tall, with a large muscular frame, and had to weigh close to 400 pounds.

Jeff quickly dropped back down behind the gravestone. Fortunately for him, the demon hadn't even noticed him, as it was busy pointing at things and shouting commands in some unintelligible language. This new form of demon surprised and frightened Jeff. It seemed more intelligent and powerful than the others, and looked like it would be much harder to kill. It trudged past him with heavy steps that sent small waves sloshing against his feet.

The ground was now so wet and sloppy that his mind wandered back to the rice paddies of Vietnam. He carefully moved along, ducking behind the tombstones, waiting for the perfect moment to strike at the big demon. His mind kept straying back to the war and he struggled just to stay in the here and now. He wondered in morbid amusement what effect this would have on his already damaged mind. Jeff had no expectations of surviving the battle, but he was determined to take as many of them with him as he possibly could.

While the others had been able to hold their own against the lesser demons, this one was something different. No one who faced it had lived. The monster wielded his sword with great skill as it cut down several of the townspeople that Jeff had traveled with. He couldn't stand to see it take even one more life, so he decided that it was now or never. As the demon raised the mighty sword one more time, he leaped from behind a gravestone, firing his gun into the powerful arm of his adversary. It swung back with such force that Jeff was thrown back against the wall of the mausoleum, some ten feet away. He was dazed from the impact, but once again willed himself back to his feet. His head was swimming in a sea of confusion, and his eyes could barely focus on the world around him. All he could see was a large black mass charging him at full speed. Jeff desperately felt around, searching for anything that could help him thwart this deadly attack.

He could only watch as the demon lowered its head to impale him with its long bull-like horns. He knew it was only a matter of seconds before the thing got to him and he would be nothing but a bloodstain on the wall. He straightened up, preparing for the moment he had expected since 1976. He was going to die, and he was willing to accept it. He closed his eyes and awaited the impact.

Jeff heard a loud crash and thought about how painless the whole thing really was. He slowly opened his eyes to examine the damage to his old body, but found that he had not been hit at all. The beast was lying on the ground at his feet, barely able to breathe and vainly attempting to get back on its massive clawed feet. Jeff looked at its side and saw that it was torn open by something—he didn't know what. Then he looked off to his right and there, through the pouring rain, he saw a young woman holding a shotgun, smoke and steam still rising faintly from it's barrel. Jeff realized what had happened—she had saved his life. He raised his hand in acknowledgement, picked up the bone sword that the thing had been carrying, and lopped off its head.

Four or five more demons came at Jeff but he made quick work of them with the oversized sword. The battle was taking its toll on him as he felt the exhaustion setting in. He was ready to back out and make camp for the night, but this was one war that couldn't be fought like that. There was no base camp, no air support. They were totally on their own. He surveyed the battlefield in front of him, looking for others that needed his help, and saw Alex off in the distance.

Alex Mayfield fought to the best of his ability, but he was being over-run by the horde of demons. For every one he killed, two or three took its place. Seeing his desperate situation, Jeff ran as fast as he could to where Alex was fighting. The thoughts of all of his friends dying around him in the last war filled his mind as he rushed to get to Alex before it was too late.

Jeff raised the sword above his head and swung with all of his might, taking off the heads of two of the demons in a single blow. Alex fell to the ground as Jeff continued to swing madly until all of the creatures around them were dead. Jeff finally relaxed and turned back to Alex, but Alex lay there motionless, his blood pooling beneath his chest. The pain and memories came flooding back as Jeff realized Alex was dead. He had lost another solider in battle.

On the other side of the mausoleum, Tigg was fighting off another onslaught of demons, trying to protect himself and Sara. The horrors of the battle had been too much for Sara. Overcome with fear, she cowered behind Tigg, unable to bring herself to do anything else. Tigg was being overwhelmed by the demons, but there was no one else close enough to help. One by one, he shot them down until his gun was empty, but there was still one big demon left bearing down on him.

He struck at the demon with his empty gun as it charged him. The demon raised one big claw and brought it crashing down into Tigg's chest, knocking him to the ground. Sara screamed and backed away as it grabbed Tigg and lifted him up, roaring and distending its jaw to swallow Tigg's head whole. The beast's saliva dripped down on him as it's hot breath warmed his face. He felt a sudden shudder as the thunder crashed, and in that moment he thought that his life had ended. The thing bent forward with its massive jaws wide open, and the red world turned black as it came down on top of him. This was the end and he knew it—he just waited for the pain to end when its jaw snapped shut.

The darkness surrounded Tigg for only a moment before he heard a pop and the beast suddenly went limp, releasing him as they both fell to the ground. As Tigg struggled to get out from under the fallen creature, he looked up and saw Sara standing there, watching him. Her eyes were still so beautiful, yet different—the fear was gone, and a look of cold determination filled them. As he scrambled back to his feet, he looked down and saw the thing lying on the ground, the back of its head had been blown off. Sara had finally swallowed her fear and killed the monster that was attacking the man she loved. Tigg pulled a clip out of his back pocket and reloaded his gun, all the time watching Sara.

"Thanks", he finally said. "Are you going to be okay?"

"I'm feeling much better, now, thank you", she said dryly as she tucked the pistol into her belt. Sara followed Tigg as they made their way back to the other side of the mausoleum. Hammond and Jeff were standing in front of the door.

"Hey Hammond, long time, no see. Where ya been?" Tigg asked with a smile.

"Well, you know I had to make a quick stop at the Seven-Eleven to grab a much-deserved Slurpee. And you?" Hammond responded in kind.

"Not to interrupt this touching moment, but we're kind of in the middle of something, here. So if you two girls want to kiss, get it over with so we can get back to work." Jeff said with authority.

Jeff stepped forward to survey the area, carrying the massive bone sword of the demon that Bailey had slain. It looked like there were a couple of dozen of the creatures left; some of them were the bipeds, and the others were the four-legged variety. Jeff stilled himself and looked to the sky, watching the red rain patter down onto the blood soaked ground, and it occurred to him that blood could never wash away blood. This thought was like a metaphor for his life. Through all that he had done, he longed for justification—for some solace in knowing that what he had done was right. Lord knows Vietnam didn't make him feel that way, but in this battle, the lines seemed clear. There was no doubt who the bad guys were, and Jeff was determined to stop them. There were good people out there fighting and dying, and he had to save them—save them all.

Lightning ripped across the sky as Jeff made his charge for the largest of the creatures. The rain poured down harder as Jeff raised the demon's sword high above his head and struck down the large beast with one massive blow. Jeff howled in hate as he made for the next one. He was a man possessed, striking down everything that crossed his path. Hammond watched Jeff in awe for a moment before charging out to join him in the fight.

As Hammond ran, he looked down at the fallen townspeople, and the feelings of hatred for Satanel and his evil horde grew within him. Hammond struck down demon after demon—his blade sliced almost effortlessly through their gray rotting flesh. The beings that had once frightened and intimidated him now fell one by one to his vicious blade. As the rage within him grew, Hammond's attacks became cold, merciless, almost mechanical, and precisely focused. He heartlessly slashed his demonic victims, bringing them to their knees before taking their heads with a vengeful scream, then watching cold-heartedly as the torrents of blood flowed from their empty necks.

Hammond stopped suddenly as a familiar form appeared out of the fog. The being approached but stopped just short of his reach—Hammond once again stood face to face with Edgar Hammond, Senior. This man had made his life a living hell, and every encounter with him had ended in a painful defeat for Hammond. This time, however, he vowed in his anger it would be different. Hammond was determined that his evil existence would come to an end—and he would wait no longer.

Hammond's heart beat furiously as they glared at each other. Hammond watched without expression as Edgar senior transformed into the horrible beast that he had faced back at his house. Tigg stepped forward in an attempt to help, but Hammond waved him back. The beast growled and smiled its uneven toothy grin as it crouched down onto its haunches, preparing to leap.

Hammond drew his sword and readied himself for the monster's attack. They stared at each other again for what seemed an eternity. As lightning struck and the crack of the thunder sounded, the beast, his father, leapt into the air. It all appeared to happen in slow motion: the rain beating down, Edgar flying through the air, Hammond screaming in rage, furiously thrusting his blade upward. Edgar came crashing down on top of Hammond, and they both fell to the ground. But Hammond's sword had found it's mark, and Edgar, impaled on the blade, writhed and moaned as he slowly transformed back into his human form. Hammond rolled and gently set his father down onto the blood-soaked grass.

As Edgar's eyes returned to their normal shape and size, Hammond was shocked at what he saw in them—tears. Edgar looked to be crying as Hammond knelt by him, pulling the blade slowly out of his body. Edgar reached out for his son and wrapped his arms around him as he cried gently. Hammond tolerated his father's grip on him as he listened to the gargling last words of the dying man who had once loved him so long ago. His mind drifted back to the days when his father treated him like a son, taking him for walks and playing baseball with him.

"I am sorry, son! I loved you ever so much, but somehow that love turned into hate and jealousy. You grew up to be a better man than I ever was, and I'm sorry I turned on you after your mother died. Don't end up like me, Eddy. Don't let your hate and self-pity consume you, or you, too, will be damned as I am . . ." Edgar said as his words trailed off into oblivion.

"I'm sorry, too, Dad. I loved you even when you hated me, but this is something that I regrettably must do" Hammond said coldly as he swung the sword, removing his father's head.

The survivors gathered around Hammond. The battle was now over and there were only six of them remaining. Besides Hammond, Bailey, Tigg, and Sara, only Jeff and Jared Berkley, the man who had nothing but his .22, remained. The battle was over, but Tigg was still very nervous about the fact that they had not seen Satanel or Zero. It made their victory somewhat hollow. It was a victory, nonetheless. Sara had a blank stare that would not subside. Tigg had the woman of his dreams, but wondered if the price had been too high.

Bailey got up off of the tombstone she was resting on and moved to the man she loved. To her, his heroism was what had got them through, and she felt that it was finally over. They had fought Legion and won, and that was something that, from the beginning, she hadn't dared to think of as being possible. They had made it, and they were now only a cave away from freedom . . . or so they thought. Only Hammond knew the truth. The truth was, the cave was nothing more than a cleaver trap that Satanel had laid for them. Were it not for the kindly priest and Zero's foolishness, they would have fallen right into it.

"Honey, don't you think that it's time we went to the cave and got out of here?" Bailey whispered into Hammond's ear.

Hammond pulled away from her and turned to the group. "I have seen the truth. The cave is not the way out. It is the lair of the beast.

There is nothing at the end of that place but our own demise, and if you still trust me and wish to live through this, you will follow me."

There were mixed reactions to Hammond's revelation. The general consensus of his friends was that he must be right, but the other two were not as sure of his decision or whether they should trust his source. Jeff had come to trust his new companions, but in his mind it was never about getting out. It was about making sure others did. And Jared—well, he just didn't trust anyone after what he had seen in the last day or two.

"The path that you choose does not concern me." Jeff said at length. "I have my own path that I must follow. I'm going back into town to look for more survivors. So, if you know the way out, tell me so I can take them there."

"The way out is below the crucifix in the mausoleum. It is the only way out. Look for the mark of the Templar Knights." Hammond said in a very stoic tone.

"I'm going with Jeff", Jared said. "I have family back there and I would like to think that at least some of them may have survived".

Jeff wished Hammond a fond farewell, then he and Jared made their way back down the path leading out of the graveyard. Hammond and the others headed for the mausoleum. There was a gentle, easy feeling as they walked through the mud and rain: a peaceful calm that they had not felt since the night at the Truck Stop was slowly returning, Tigg smiled and whistled as he held Sara around the waist. Hammond stopped and spun Bailey around and kissed her passionately. It was the perfect kiss: long, and heartfelt.

"I love you Bailey, I love you more than you could possibly ever understand. You make me feel like the man I always wished that I could be, and that is the most perfect feeling that anyone could have." Hammond said without stumbling on his words.

"I love you too, baby, more than life itself." Bailey replied.

"Wow dude, you sound like such a fag." Tigg said, laughing as Sara slapped him playfully.

"Hey Tigg, do you remember how your mother said you were a special young man?" Hammond asked Tigg.

"Yeah, dude, what about it?"

"She lied." Hammond smiled as he said this.

Tigg broke out laughing at the return of his old friend. Things were good: the friends were tired, but they were all together, safe, and could finally relax. Hammond was happy just to be in the company of his friends. Bailey smiled in that cute girlie way that she had when he first met her. Her face glowed with love as she opened the door to the mausoleum.

As the door opened, Bailey was greeted by a loud bang. She stumbled back before loosing her footing and falling back onto the muddy ground. Hammond felt his heart shatter as he looked down at his love who was now bleeding from her heaving chest. He fell to his knees to help her, frantically pulling her shirt open to assess the damage. He was relieved to see that the bullet had not hit her heart, but had deflected upward and lodged in her shoulder. Hammond thought his rage had peaked in the confrontation with his father, but now, it was blinding.

"Take care of her—I'll take care of him!" He shouted as he stood up and grabbed his sword, then ran into the church before Tigg could stop him.

He bolted through the door and into the shadows where he knew Zero couldn't see him. Laughter echoed around the room. He knew that arrogant laugh, and he hated it with every fiber of his being. Zero stood on top of one of the rotting rafters, mocking Hammond from an unreachable distance.

"So, it looks like I got that little bitch back for treating me like some sort of freak, didn't I?" Zero said, laughing and hopping from one rafter to another. "I watched you talking to yourself in here, earlier. You're quite the little psycho, aren't you?"

"Why don't you come down here and face me like a man, you worthless piece of trash!" Hammond yelled up to Zero, as he stepped out into the open. "I would be happy to free you from your pathetic existence."

Zero just laughed at Hammond and pointed his police issue Glock at various parts of his body. Hammond stood his ground, undaunted by this man who had no morals or sense of humanity.

"You can just go ahead and shoot me . . . I will come back from hell just to tear you apart and eat your dead heart!"

"Oh my, dear Hammond, I have you so scared that you're speaking in rhymes! How sweet is that!" Zero said, once again bursting into his annoying laugh.

He raised his gun and shot Hammond square in the chest. Hammond spun around and came to rest on the floor. His sword flew from his hand and lodged under a nearby pew. He tried to crawl over and grab it—he didn't know why. He thought of everything that had happened to him and would have been glad to have his life end were it not for Bailey, Tigg and Sara. As he reached for the sword, Zero fired again. Hammond felt a sharp pain in his back as his vision went smaller and smaller until it was gone, like turning off an old T.V. Hammond's life was being extinguished and all he could think was, "I'm sorry, Bailey". Within a few seconds Hammond faded from consciousness, feeling nothing but a sharp pain in his back.

Chapter 33

TRUST ME?

Hammond awoke to find himself standing over the shredded body of Zero. Blood and feathers littered the floor. He had no recollection of what had occurred. He was still dizzy and disoriented when Bailey came through the door with the help of Tigg and Sara. Sara took one look at the ravaged body of Zero and threw up violently. Even Tigg had to turn away from the sight. Zero was barely even recognizable as a human being.

Tigg sat Bailey down on one of the pews as he carefully approached Hammond. The hump on his back was no longer a lump nor did it make him bend over like it once had. His back was so full of blood that the back of his shirt was dripping. Hammond quickly turned to face Tigg as if he were hiding something behind his back. Upon looking at what Hammond had done to Zero without a weapon made Tigg eager not to push the point.

"Give me your Jacket." Hammond said darkly.

"What's wrong, man, are you okay?" Tigg asked in genuine concern for his dearest friend.

"Now, Tigg—give it to me. I don't have time to explain—just do it!"

Hammond's tone frightened Tigg and he did what he had been told. Hammond wouldn't look his friend in the eyes as he took the jacket and put it on. On a normal day, Tigg's jacket would never have fit him, but this was hardly a normal day. He didn't even look at Bailey as he passed. He seemed to want only to get out of there. Hammond was distant and far from the man that Tigg had known for most of his life. He was darker yet somehow more amazing than any human man should be. Hammond now walked taller and prouder than Tigg had ever seen him, yet he seemed sad and detached as if his mind were somewhere else.

Tigg walked up to Hammond and tried to put his hand on his friend's back to comfort him, but Hammond turned to face him in an expression of rejection. Hammond's eyes glinted bright silver as he stared down the man who thought he was his best friend. The air between the two of them had clearly changed from what it was before they entered the church. The once easy way that they had held together now gave way to an unsteady feeling of mistrust.

Bailey looked up at Hammond with tears in her eyes. Hammond had always had a strange knack for understanding the emotions of others, but now he actually felt her fear and could hear her thoughts. He knew she feared that whatever had inhabited Zero may now be controlling him. Hammond stopped to look deep into her eyes and mind. He knew she was hurting and somewhere beneath his slightly changed exterior he was still the man who loved her. He turned to her, held out his hand, and waited for her to take it.

"Sorry—I'm just not really myself right now. I'm not a demon—I'm something else." He then turned his attention back to Tigg. "As for you, squirrel nuts, you're still my friend. I just can't let you touch me right now. Keep your greasy paws to yourself . . . this is an expensive jacket, you know." The smile was returning to Tigg's face.

"Things are happening that I just can't explain. We still have to get out of here and when we do, I'll explain everything." Hammond said as he walked over to the hanging cross.

Hammond looked up at the cross and shuddered in remembrance of the indescribable torture that Claudius had endured at the hands of Satanel. He almost regretted the fact that he did not get the chance to face him and make him pay for what he had done to his little town. That thought was quickly washed away when he remembered the way that he had felt in Satanel's presence. He felt weak and insignificant and even with the changes that he was now going through, he would never match up to Satanel.

"It's down here, everyone. We have to go down here". As he said it, he pulled on the cover. With a flick of his wrist the panel that had been covering the exit hatch went flying into the air.

Although Hammond was shocked at his own strength, the others stared at him as if he had just turned into the incredible hulk. Tigg started to say something about it, but Sara tugged on his arm to quiet him. She didn't know what to think of this person who inhabited the body of her one-time friend, but she did know she didn't want to make him angry.

Her mind wandered back to when she was a child and she had met her father's 'friend'. The man was always a little dark and different. She had grown to trust him, which turned out to be a horrible mistake. One evening he came over to their house when her parents weren't home. He seemed distant and detached, a lot like Hammond was now.

Sara tried desperately not to remember the horrible images that came flooding into her mind. The man took off his shirt and then forced her to do the same. She knew in her mind what was about to happen to her and she was afraid. The man would have taken her virginity, and probably her life, had it not been for two kids breaking into the house. They set off the alarm when they tried to come in through a side window, and her attacker got scared and ran out the back door. She didn't know who they were, but she thanked God every day for their providential appearance that night.

"It was Tigg and I. We were just hoping to find enough money to go and see a movie. We weren't going to take anything valuable or anything like that. We were just looking for some loose change." Hammond said with his back still turned to the others.

"What . . . Can you read my mind?" Sara screamed, startled.

"Not so much read it, as hear it, but yes, I can. Tigg and I were just poking around when I heard you scream, so I picked up one of those little statues on your patio and through it right through the Brinks sign on the window. Please don't be afraid of me. Whatever was in my back has been released, and I'm changing, I know, but I am still the same guy—I'm still your friend".

Hammond turned to face her with tears flowing from his bright silver eyes. Sara felt terrible for the way she was treating him. She knew she was wrong. He had kept them alive all this time—why did she doubt him now? She lowered her head gently down onto Tigg's arm and he held her. Bailey stood up and walked over to Hammond and touched his arm gently, and he put his arm around her.

"If you really can read our minds then you know what I am thinking" she said with a tear in her eye.

"Yes, I love you, too, and I know that you trust me, baby."

Bailey kissed Hammond gently on the lips, then turned and started down the hole in a show of trust. She didn't know where it led, but he calmed her by humming the song that he had sung to her the first time they made love in the old town. The rhythm of 'shooting star' calmed her as she made her way down the rickety wooden ladder that led into the blackness that was below her. She was afraid, but she trusted Hammond more than she had ever trusted anyone in her life. She went step by step, nervous that at any moment the rotten rungs could give way. Her worst fear was realized about half way down the unsteady ladder. The wood broke with a sickening crack—the kind of sound that only seems loud when your life depends on it. As the rung gave way, she let out a terrified scream. The whole ladder beneath her disintegrated, leaving her hanging from a single scrap of wood, and with the wound in her shoulder, she couldn't hold on more than a second or two. She screamed again as she lost her grip.

In that brief moment, Bailey's life flashed before her eyes as she felt herself falling. The last thing she saw before she closed her eyes was a flash of white streaking past her. Then she landed. It wasn't the crushing impact she expected, but an abrupt stop into someone's arms! She opened her watering eyes only to be greeted by the smiling face of Hammond.

"'You all right, sweetheart? If I had known you were in such a rush, I would have gone first!" Hammond said with a slight chuckle.

"How did you get down here before me?" Bailey asked in astonishment.

"Eh, I just figured if I waited down here for you, I would be here to catch you when you fell."

Bailey gave Hammond a strange glance, then just laughed, a bit nervously, as he put her down. Hammond looked up to see Tigg's worried face looking down from above. The scene was kind of funny to Hammond and all he could think was "What Lassie, Timmy is trapped in a well?" Hammond let out a loud laugh and threw a small pebble up at Tigg, bouncing it off of his forehead. Tigg couldn't help but giggle knowing it was Hammond that threw it at him.

Tigg's heart had skipped a beat when he heard Bailey scream, but it totally stopped when he saw Hammond dive down the hole headfirst. He was afraid that he had lost them both in one brief moment. Sara turned her head and tears rolled down her battle-worn face as she thought that it was just she and Tigg, now. Tigg's first action was to run to the hole in hopes of grabbing his friend's feet, but he wasn't nearly fast enough. Trying to see what happened below led him to this moment of having the pebble bounced deftly off his forehead.

"What happened to you, man? I thought that you were total sidewalk paste!" Tigg yelled down to Hammond. "I thought I was going to have to come down there and collect your dead body".

"Well, first of all, there's no sidewalk down here, and second of all, you couldn't climb down here if you wanted too." Hammond responded. "The ladder is gone".

"Well then, what are Sara and I supposed to do?"

"The way I see it, Tigg old buddy, you can either jump down and trust me to catch you, or you can just sit up there and wait for Satanel to show up—your choice!"

Sara declined. She was still leery of the new Hammond. Tigg reached out his hand and looked at her with a look of authority. It took her only a moment of receiving that look from Tigg before she reached out and took his hand. Tigg kissed her softly then pushed her gently down the hole. Sara screamed like a maniac all the way down, but was surprised at how soft the landing in Hammond's arms was. He smiled as he set her down softly on her feet.

"Still don't trust me, Sara?" Hammond said with a wink as he turned his attention to Tigg. "Alright there, tubby, it's your turn."

"Are you going to catch me this time?" Tigg asked, remembering the last time Hammond told him to jump.

"Yeah, I suppose, if you're gonna be a whiny little girl about it, I'll catch you." Hammond said with a bit of a giggle, remembering the face plant himself.

Tigg looked up at the crucifix and quickly crossed himself before stepping off the edge into the hole. He closed his eyes and hoped that this time he would have a gentle landing. To his relief, Hammond caught him. Tigg looked up at Hammond as he winked back at him. Tigg got that sudden feeling in the pit of his stomach, the kind he always got right before Hammond played some ill-conceived joke on him. Before he could even finish his thought, Hammond dropped him squarely on his butt.

"Oops! My hands were sweaty, man, I couldn't hold on . . . Sorry." Hammond said with an evil-looking smile.

"I thought you said that you changed, man, but you're still the same jackass I've always known." Tigg grinned back, as he stood up and brushed himself off.

"You'd be surprised how much I really have changed. You'll see when we get out of here, bro."

Hammond turned and led the way down a long, winding tunnel. He didn't know where it ended, but he trusted the words of the priest. Even his vision was limited in the darkness of that tunnel, yet he moved with a speed and grace that he never knew he possessed. The others formed a sort of train behind him as he ran. Bailey held on to his shirt and Sara held Bailey's and so on with Tigg. Hammond could feel the end of the journey coming closer as he ran. With a sudden loud thud, his run ended with all of them running into him.

"Ouch! Didn't see that comin'".

Hammond reached into his pocket and pulled out his Zippo lighter. He struck the flint wheel several times before the flame flickered to life. Hammond was greeted by a large steel door with a small round window, about eye-level. The latch seemed to be more for keeping people on the outside from getting in rather than the other way around. Hammond decided it would be best to retreat, so he walked to the wall of the cave and grabbed one of the torches that had been mounted on it. When he lit the torch the full extent of the room appeared. The ceiling of the room was no more than seven feet high, but it was enormous in width and length.

Hammond lit the rest of the torches as he went to afford his friends the same luxury of sight that he enjoyed. Bailey stayed close behind Hammond and watched as the thing in his back moved under the Jacket. She was amazed that it didn't bother him anymore, because to her, it looked much larger than it ever had. Hammond felt her thought and pulled her up next to him and winked at her with his beautiful silver-toned eyes. There was something that he was not telling her, and she knew it, but she was still a little afraid to ask him what it was.

Tigg lingered back, pulling Sara up close to him. He held her tight as he got a sudden feeling of foreboding. He got the same cold feeling that he had when he had first encountered the darkness on that cold, dark night. It was as if he knew something was going to happen, but he was powerless to stop it. Tigg had taken the shotgun from Bailey when Hammond went into the church and he didn't like what he saw. There was only one bullet left in the gun and he didn't have the knapsack anymore. Things looked increasingly grim to Tigg as he took stock of what little they had.

"Sara, I think that our little journey here is at an end. I think that we are pretty well screwed, now. We don't have any more shells for the shotgun, nor do we have any food or water. We pretty much don't have anything and now we have to go back out there and that is like signing our death warrants. So, I guess all I want to know is, would you marry me? I mean, if we would have lived, that is . . ."

"Tigg, I will marry you, and we're not dead, yet. Even though he scares me, I still have faith that Hammond will get us out of this . . . I hope".

Sara's voice trailed off as a growl came echoing through the darkness. Only Hammond knew what it was, and it clearly frightened him. He threw Bailey back behind him and walked backward, leading them back to the steel door. Hammond grabbed the handle in a panic and forced the large door open. On the other side, Tigg realized that the door wasn't meant to keep anything in or out. It was nothing more than a large door with a handle on either side. This made Tigg feel a little better but in a sickening way. Even though they could open the door from the other side, Satanel could open it from this side.

Hammond forced the girls through the door where an old wooden elevator waited. It didn't look entirely safe, but they really didn't have much of a choice at this point. Hammond stood tall as the two women went through the door.

"Go Tigg, I got this. Get up to the outside world and get as far away from this place as humanly possible. Please take care of Bailey for me—man, she is the only thing that gave my life meaning."

"No way, man, I am not going to leave you. You have been the hero this whole time and I am not going to just walk away when things are at their worst."

"Alright, man, I understand. But you had better kiss your girlfriend goodbye."

Tigg stepped through the door and beckoned Sara to him, but before he could kiss her goodbye, he felt Hammond's hands on his back pushing him forcefully into the small elevator. Hammond slammed the door and ripped the crank off, jamming it shut. Tigg yelled but Hammond couldn't hear him through the thick door. Tigg took the shotgun that he was still holding and slammed it against the glass as Hammond started to walk away. The glass would not give and in desperation Tigg fired the last round through it, shattering the glass and barely missing Hammond. Hammond turned around and shot Tigg an evil glance.

"What are you trying to do, kill me?!" Hammond asked angrily. "You need to get the girls and yourself out of here before that thing gets here. I have seen it and there is no stopping it!"

"You're my brother, Hammond! I love you, and I'm not going to let you do this. If you are going to die then let me die with you, I don't want to be alone, man!" Tigg cried out with tears streaming in a thick flow down his dirty cheeks.

"You have Sara now, and you're a good man. You don't need me anymore. Just, please, save them, Tigg. I don't want to die for nothing. My life has been meaningless and I don't want my death to be meaningless, too."

"How could you say that? Your life meant a lot to me, you were my best friend and you were more, you were my brother!"

"Tigg, I have to ask you something and its important, so answer honestly . . . Do you like yourself?"

"Yeah, I guess so. What does that have to do with anything?"

"I don't. I hate myself. I hate myself for all the things that I have had to do in my life just to get by. I hate myself for not being able to save everyone. I hate myself for not being able to love Bailey with my whole heart because my heart is cold and dead."

"If that's true, then why are you willing to die to save us, huh? If you are such a horrible person then why are you giving up your life to save us?" Tigg was crying hard now, reaching his hand through the small hole just trying to touch his friend one last time.

"Because, my dearest friend, I have been looking for a reason to like myself, and now I have finally found one." Hammond said, reaching out and touching Tigg's outstretched hand.

"I love you, Tigger, you will always be my brother, and I hope I will live in your heart and memories forever. But please, smile when you think of me . . ." A sound echoed again as two of the thing's heads entered the far side of the room. "Goodbye, my friend." Hammond said, letting go of Tigg and turning to face his adversary.

"No, Hammond, No! Please, God, no, please . . ." Tigg sobbed as he watched his friend move toward the approaching beast.

Bailey ran to the little window when she realized what was happening. Bailey and Tigg both shared the view of Hammond walking away. Bailey's heart felt as though it was ripped from her body as she understood this was probably going to be the last time she would ever see Hammond alive. She turned to Tigg and cried into his shoulder with huge heaving sobs. She wanted desperately to yell to Hammond but she knew it would only distract him. She forced herself to take one last look at the man she knew she would miss desperately.

Hammond dropped the jacket that had been covering the large mass on his back. Bailey and Tigg both gasped in unison at what it revealed. Hammond stood with large silvery-white wings, the span of which was nearly twice his height. Tigg grabbed Bailey and forced her into the elevator. She fought him with every step. She didn't want to leave without trying to help Hammond. She knew that all she could do was hold the elevator and wait, and if that was all she could do, then she wasn't going to let anyone stand in her way.

"Look, I'm not going to leave and spend the rest of my life wondering if we had just waited a little longer if we could have saved him!" Bailey screamed through her tears.

"I understand." Tigg said gently as he sat down on the wooden elevator, feeling its cold touch on his sore back.

Bailey took her place at the window to watch the angel that would always be hers fight the angels that had fallen.

Chapter 34

NEPHLIM

T he beast sniffed cautiously as Hammond moved deftly around it. Before it even knew what it was facing, a wing streaked in from the shadows, removing three of its seven heads. Azazel screamed with its four remaining heads and reared back, falling onto its wings. Hammond bolted back across the cave to give himself more room to utilize his newfound powers.

His wings were movable in a way that Hammond could never have even dreamed. Along with the obvious ability of flight, he could move them like hands and they were as sharp as a scalpel at the ends. They had a span of about twelve feet and protruded from his shoulder blades. Hammond was a sight to behold. He wrapped his immense wings around himself defensively as he waited for the next phase of the demon's attack.

Azazel arose as Satanel approached. He cowered behind Satanel like a wounded dog as Satanel softly caressed one of his remaining heads. Satanel walked arrogantly towards Hammond, clapping his hands in a blatant show of superiority.

"Now this is an unexpected surprise, isn't it?" Satanel said, as he moved in closer. He still kept his distance. "Of coarse, you know that this is in no way going to change the fact that I am going to rip your spine out, don't you?"

"You might find that a little harder than you think, there, gramps." Hammond said indignantly.

Satanel raised his hand and all of the sudden the room changed. Hammond found himself back on the ancient stone bridge with Satanel. He turned to look behind him and still saw his friends watching through the window. Hammond now stood face to face with Satanel. The air was heavy with anticipation as he spread his wings to make ready for the fight. Satanel laughed arrogantly as a crown of flames atop his head ignited and a large pair of black bat-like wings spread from behind his back. The sound of screaming souls being tortured echoed eerily through the strange landscape as Hammond carefully approached his opponent.

"Alright, lets do this, old man!" Hammond said, shining Satanel on.

"Why the rush to die, my impetuous little friend?" Satanel asked as Hammond still moved forward.

"Enough talk. I am so sick of this!"

With that, Hammond shot forward, attacking his enemy. Satanel stepped quickly out of the way, leaving Hammond to fall flat. Hammond shook off the pain and slowly raised himself up when a glint of metal caught his eye. Could it be? Yes, it was! A sword! Satanel walked calmly toward Hammond assured of his own superiority. Hammond reached forward quickly, grabbing the sword from the body of a fallen angel and swung around with it trying to take out his enemy with one swift blow. With a flash of metal and the sound of grinding steal, Hammond was surprised to find Satanel deflecting the blow with a large flaming sword.

Hammond sat staring in awe as Satanel pulled his massive blade up to his shoulder. The flames did not even seem to affect him as he stood, beautiful and laughing. Satanel stepped back as a cloud of the darkness started to build in the sky above them. The darkness swirled and formed what appeared to be a whirlpool in the night sky. The black lightning swirled around inside of the vortex, as Hammond watched, gape-mouthed.

"You see you can't stop it. The end has already begun!" Satanel proclaimed, raising his arms to the sky.

Hammond refused to believe it was over, but he knew if he didn't stop Satanel soon, the end would come swiftly enough. He used his wings to lift himself up as he shot into the air. On the ground he was no match for Satanel, but he thought that maybe in the air he stood a better chance. Satanel looked at him curiously as he swooped down past him. Hammond's wing clipped the side of Satanel's face as he went, creating a long, clean cut. Satanel felt his face and looked in shock at the sight of his own blood—a sight that he had never before seen.

Rage filled him as he took flight after the teen that he had so under-estimated. For the first time since he had fallen he finally had an adversary that could pose a threat to him, and he didn't like it one bit. Hammond hovered above as Satanel flew toward him, thrusting the flaming blade right toward Hammond's heart. Much to his disappointment, Hammond was able to dodge the attack and cut him yet again, this time with the sword. It had been many thousand of years since Satanel had taken flight, but he still should have been able to take down someone so new to his power and strength.

Hammond hung suspended in the air with his wings flapping silently, waiting for the next attack. Satanel moved level to him as he slightly cradled his wounded arm. For just a moment Hammond thought he had gotten the best of the fight until he saw that oh-so-familiar grin on Satanel's face. Hammond held his ground as Satanel slowly sheathed his sword, and fear started to build in his mind as he wondered what the fallen angel had up his sleeve. Satanel raised his hand to the sky and out of the castle behind him came a series of the chains that had once dangled from the ceiling. The chains hooked into Hammond's flesh, dragging him down to the ground. He struggled against them, but they would not release him and the more he struggled, the more they tore into his already pained skin.

The ground grew closer and closer as Hammond flailed his wings madly in an attempt to free himself from their grasp. The ground came hard and fast as the wind was ripped from his lungs. He felt the pain as the hooks dug deep into the flesh of his chest and arms. His wings were pinned hard under him and there was little he could do to move. Satanel glided back down to him and stood for a moment, staring at his helpless pray.

"I told you this would end badly for you." Satanel said as he approached his fallen enemy. "I was apt to let you join me, but then you went and did this to my beautiful face." Satanel waived his hand across the wound as it healed to a scar. "It didn't have to end like this, you know . . . You could have just let it go. I would not have followed you. I am far too busy! You could have had a few good months with them." Satanel motioned offhandedly toward the window where Bailey and Tigg were still watching dumbfounded. "Now I am going to give you a little parting gift. Look deep into my eyes to see the future that awaits your friends when you fail!"

Hammond got that familiar swimming feeling as things once again dissolved around him. This time there was nothing friendly about it. He opened his eyes to the screams of Tigg as he took in the new surroundings. Tigg was laid out flat on a mid-evil stretching board as three of the half-human creatures stood around him and slowly pulled out his organs. With every pull Tigg howled in pain. The next sight was even worse. He watched as several demons, one by one, had their way with Bailey—screaming, pregnant, and chained to the wall next to his own dead body, now nailed up in a sick display with his wings broken and spread out. Sara's head was lying on the floor in front of him while her body was being sodomized.

"No . . ." Hammond whispered, building his hate. "I won't let you do this!"

As he yelled, the illusion faded from around him and he found himself once again face to face with Satanel's wide grin. Hammond had a sheer look of hate in his eyes as a smile began to spread slowly across his lips. Satanel was not sure what to make of it as Hammond started to laugh.

"Ahh, I see the madness has finally taken you." Satanel said smugly.

"No it's not that . . ." Hammond said with an evil grin as he started rubbing his feet together, as if he were trying to take of his boot. "You're just forgetting one thing, gramps."

"Oh yeah? And what is that, hmm?" Satanel asked, bemusedly.

"That your blood runs through my veins, and with that comes your treachery and ability to keep secrets!"

"Oh do tell, I can put off killing you for a moment, after all . . ."

Before he could finish his sentence, Satanel heard a loud click from Hammond's boot as Hammond brought it square into his chest. Satanel stood with his mouth open and blood dripping from it as he pulled back off of the knife that had come from Hammond's boot. Satanel stumbled back, trying to heal himself quickly, but the knife had made its way into his heart. Hammond used one last burst of strength to rip himself free from the chains, leaving bits of his flesh behind. The wound in Satanel's chest was slowly beginning to close, but it bought Hammond the valuable time he needed. He leapt up behind Satanel and buried his boot knife into his back as he grabbed onto his wings and ripped them from his body.

Satanel howled in pain as the crown of fire disappeared from atop his head. Hammond threw the wings off both sides of the bridge as he freed the boot knife from the back of his enemy. He then reached down and clicked the switch on the side of his boot, pushing the knife back in.

"You'd be amazed what you can get off of the Internet, these days." Hammond said with a laugh, as he started to walk away from Satanel. "Guess you should have paid more attention to what's gone on in the world over the years."

"You fool!" Satanel yelled out. "Do you have any idea what you have done?"

Hammond was tired of this game. His body hurt and all he wanted to do was go home, wherever that might be. "No, but I bet you're going to tell me, anyway . . ." he replied as he kept walking. Hammond waited to hear the reply, but instead, he turned to find Satanel rising to his feet. Hammond wasn't ready for another fight, but he steadied himself for the attack. He was surprised to see that instead of attacking, the cave opening that they had come in through materialized in front of Satanel, who limped away and disappeared into the darkness.

The ground moved below Hammond's feet as an earthquake shook everything around him. A cave-in sealed the opening where Satanel escaped. Fire shot up from the sides of the bridge as the dark void opened up. Two hands, each the size of a city block, reached up out of the cavernous opening. In the center, the face of the Devil himself appeared—a set of jagged teeth and a pair of enormous red eyes threatened. Fear held Hammond where he stood only for a moment before the earthquake shook him out of it. The bridge was collapsing underneath him as he took to the air.

The flames reached higher and higher as Hammond focused his efforts on reaching the door where his friends were screaming and beckoning him forward. Hammond felt a searing pain as the flames began to lick at his already tender flesh. He pushed forward as fast as he could, but the flames were already consuming him.

Bailey and Tigg watched as Hammond almost got close enough to touch the outstretched arm of Bailey, but the flames had fully engulfed him. They cried out to him in unison as his pained screams echoed through the little room. Bailey felt Hammond's finger tip as the fire reached up and seemed to pull him down, and watched helplessly as he disappeared into the flames. She continued screaming as the flames subsided, and the scene of the bridge and castle vanished, leaving only the dimly lit cave. The earth continued to shake as the weak roof of the cave gave way, spilling rocks down in front of the door.

"Bailey, we have to go—now!" Tigg yelled as the sound of the cave-in got louder and louder. "Bailey! He told me to keep you safe, and that's what I'm gonna do!"

Bailey wouldn't budge from her little window, forcing Tigg to grab her by the waist and force her onto the elevator with Sarah. Bailey beat on Tigg's chest as she tried to free herself and get back to the window. She knew in her heart that he couldn't possibly be gone—not after everything they had been through.

"Let go of me!" She yelled at Tigg, still trying to break free of his grasp while he and Sarah moved the elevator up. "He's not dead, he's not! Let me go!" she was crying hard, now. "He wouldn't leave you, and you know it! Now, let me go!"

This statement hurt Tigg deeply because he knew it was true, but he also knew that the only thing he could do for him now was to honor his last wishes.

"Bailey, he's gone. I'm sorry." Tears were streaming down his face, but he spoke evenly and firmly. "He gave his life for us, so let's not screw that up by dying now, ok?"

Bailey didn't want to accept it, but she found herself nodding in agreement as Sara pulled her close. She collapsed into Sara's arms as Tigg hoisted the old elevator up with all his might. "I will come back for you one day, my love." Bailey thought to herself as the spot of daylight grew in front of her.

Chapter 35

LAST GOODBYES

Tigg, Sara, and Bailey emerged from the darkness of the cave into the blinding light of the midday sun. The feeling of the warm sun and the sound of the singing birds was bittersweet. Tigg could hear the soft sound of a babbling creek nearby and he remembered what Hammond had said about the world and how he had never stopped to enjoy it. Heartbreak hit them all as one by one the effect of their loss sunk in. Hammond would never again get to hear the sound of a creek or the songs of the birds or feel the warmth of the sun on his skin. He gave his life so that they might live, and Tigg vowed to himself that he would live as much as he could. He would live for both of them.

"They'll be back, you know . . ." Sara said, more to herself than anyone else. "This is only the beginning, not the end."

"That may be true, but next time we'll be ready for them. We have to find those knights the journal talked about. We have to tell them what happened here, and we have to make sure it doesn't happen again."

"You guys talk like we are heroes or something." Bailey said, tears welling up in her eyes. "We didn't win—we just survived. I think that the only ones that can really be called heroes are the ones who are still down there."

Tigg looked down at his feet then he raised his head and held it high. He would never again look down at his feet in shame or despair. He would walk tall and strong like Hammond did. He turned and looked at the cave entrance and thought to himself, "I am a hero, my friend, and I hope one day I can prove that to you".

"Goodbye, my friend and brother, I hope that wherever you are now, you can hear me and know that I will never forget you or what you have done for us."

Tigg began to cry as he thought of his childhood friend that he would never see again. He thought of the time that they ate ice cream until they got sick watching Care Bears and how Hammond had always stuck up for him. He would never again hear a joke and look at his friend who would have that strange smile. He would never again just lay on the grass watching the clouds move and talk about girls and growing up. But most of all, he would never have the person who would tell him everything was ok, even when his own world was all messed up.

Bailey watched as Sara held Tigg. Her mind wandered to all the times that Hammond held her tight when hell itself was trying to take them. She imagined seeing him come home from work and holding her gently while she kissed him and asked how his day had gone. Now that would never happen. When Hammond died, he took her heart with him. Her mind just kept playing back that smile that he had on his face; it was like he was telling her for the last time that everything was going to be ok. Bailey looked up at the bright blue sky and wished with all her heart that Hammond could be there to share it with her.

They were getting ready to leave the mountainside when something floating in the air caught Bailey's eye. A white feather floated down to her like a sweet dove in a sea of blue. She held out her hand and the feather landed gently in her palm. Bailey smiled as she looked at the feather and saw what almost looked like 'I love you' streaked across it in a black plume. She closed her eyes and wished that she could see him just one more time. When she looked back up above, she saw a bright shooting star streak across the blue sky.

"And all the world will love you just as long as you are my shooting star . . ." Bailey whispered as she tucked the feather delicately into her pocket.

Tears flowed freely from Bailey's eyes as she followed the others down the long mountain trail. Something in her heart told her that she would see him again one day. He would be there when she needed him most, but for now, she had to face the world alone . . . like a stranger in a land she only thought she knew.

LaVergne, TN USA
05 May 2010
181683LV00002B/2/P